Advance Praise for *Altar to an Erupting Sun*

"This is a very provocative book, dangerous in the way it makes us think hard about what we might need to do to save Earth's biosphere, our only home, from a mass extinction event that is being caused not by all of us, but by some of us in positions of power. We have a wonderfully articulated rhetoric for arguments in words, but we don't have good rhetoric for actions in the world. What would work best? What would be morally justified in the fight for the Earth, our extended body? These are the questions that Collins explores here, and as we live these urgent questions through his characters they tug at our hearts and minds. **We need more books like this one.**
—KIM STANLEY ROBINSON**, author, *The Ministry for the Future*

"This novel is indeed a gift to our remembrance and inspiration for our future. Collins tells a story of a movement, or movements, which need to be told. I know these stories, love them, and have lived many of them with characters bigger than life, more courageous than any heroes of the past, and a commitment to Mother Earth."
—**WINONA LADUKE**, Honor the Earth, author of *All Our Relations: Native Struggles for Land and Life*

"**A fascinating look at movements and the people who make them up**, in the spirit of Kim Stanley Robinson's *Ministry for the Future*."
—**BILL MCKIBBEN**, co-founder, Third Act and 350.org, author of *The Flag, the Cross, and the Station Wagon*

"The future imagined in *Altar to An Erupting Sun* bursts with strategy and celebration, spirituality and sacrifice, ritual, and reverence. It is not magic or cataclysm or a zombie apocalypse. You'll weep because the writing is beautiful, the people feel real (and in most cases, they are thinly novelized versions of real people), and the vision is sound. This book has it all: a recipe for poppy tea, a short history of U.S. imperialism in the last 70 years, highlights of the nonviolent resistance that met it every step of the way, a compelling argument for green burials and funeral services for the living. You will fall in love with these characters, which will help you love your friends and yourself a little more. You will remember to revere this planet. You will mistrust the state a little more. You will feel called to make an altar to those you have lost. You will want more worship in your life (even just a little)."
—**FRIDA BERRIGAN**, activist and author of *It Runs in the Family: On Being Raised By Radicals and Growing Into Rebellious I*

"As one who has long admired Chuck Collins's superbly documented writing about inequality, I followed him into a fictional past and future with fascination and enjoyment. He is as bold and on-target in this book as in his others. The story may be fanciful, but the issues are the most serious we have ever faced."
—**ADAM HOCHSHILD**, author of *King Leopold's Ghost* and *American Midnight*

"A wonderful read! Collins has written an epic history of an era as seen through the eyes of complex and engaging characters. Having lived through that era myself, I can say he got it right—the tone, the energy, the milestones."
—**STARHAWK**, author of *The Fifth Sacred Thing, City of Refuge*, and *The Spiral Dance*

"Chuck Collins has inspired me my entire adult life, and this book is no different. We need stories like this, a great tale about brave people who push up against the powers that be and sometimes make them budge."
—**VICKI ROBIN**, author, *Your Money or Your Life*, and host of the podcast, "What Could Possibly Go Right?"

"*Altar* introduces us to Rae Kelliher, a richly drawn heroine who accompanies us through some of the most dynamic and creative social movements of the past half-century, including present-day efforts to avert climate catastrophe. Collins weaves a riveting near-future story about the power of organized people to build resilient communities and thrive in harmony with the earth. As a lifelong campaigner, his inside depiction of grassroots movements transcends stereotypical activist caricatures and reaffirms that people make history together. A welcome antidote to a future vision of unconnected individuals and apocalyptic wastelands. This novel reminds us of the human potential to face the future with humor, possibility, and imagination."
—**TOPE FOLARIN**, author of the award-winning novel, *A Particular Kind of Black Man*

"*Altar* offers a moving history lesson on several decades of social movements through the life of a character that is a lovable cross between an activist Forrest Gump and a modern-day Dietrich Bonhoeffer."
—**TIM DECHRISTOPHER**, climate activist, Bidder 70

"Collins' warm, affecting tale raises an important question, one well worth our pondering: Is there any measure or action that is too radical, too extreme if truly necessary to save the planet and its people? I love this book. Its characters will live with me now."
—**JAMES GUSTAVE "GUS" SPETH**, author of *They Knew: The US Federal Government's Fifty-Year Role in Causing the Climate Crisis*, former Dean, Yale School of the Environment

"Chuck Collins starts with the unthinkable and rewinds the clock to explore what leads people to extreme actions, and the consequences of those decisions. Along the way, he asks us to question what crimes are acceptable, and what actions are judged harshly—and by whom. *Altar To An Erupting Sun* is an intentionally provocative book. It will leave you with questions. It will provoke thought, and hopefully conversation. If you're lucky, you'll find yourself discussing what really matters at this critically important time in human history."
—**RIVERA SUN** author, *The Dandelion Insurrection*

"Literary fiction can be a tool for exploring distressing moral choices forced upon us by social or environmental circumstances. In the best instance, we get both good fiction and moral insight. That's certainly the case here: Chuck Collins tells a gripping story that bravely probes the questions: How far would you go to stop climate change? What might be the unanticipated results? And, must you try anyway?"
—**RICHARD HEINBERG** Senior Fellow, Post Carbon Institute, author of *Power: Limits and Prospects for Human Survival*

"I am a longtime fan and great admirer of Chuck Collins' work. And now a near-future novel that charts new territory in envisioning a relocalized, democratic, sustainable, and resilient future. Wow!"
–**FRANCES MOORE LAPPE,** author, *Diet for a Small Planet*, cofounder, Small Planet Institute

"As a person raised in an activist household, *Altar to Erupting Sun* brought back a flood of memories of the campaigns and political moments of my childhood. The story also brought into focus the life choices of my adulthood and their political context. This is contemporary fiction at its best, delving into the personal amidst the political while providing a radical yet realistic hope for the future."
—**DEDRICK ASANTE-MUHAMMAD,** author, activist, and Chief for Race, Wealth, and Community in the National Community Reinvestment Coalition

"In *Altar to an Erupting Sun*, Collins offers the reader an insider's view of five decades of social and political movements brought to life with real and complex characters and an exploration of the tools of self-awareness and solidarity that are the basis for an examined life. A compelling work of speculative fiction, imagining how resilience, resistance, and repression will develop in a world of climate change, economic collapse, and polarization."
—**KATHERINE POWER**, peace activist, author of a forthcoming memoir, *Surrender: A Journey From Guerrilla to Grandmother*

"In the plucky protagonist of Rae Kelliher, Chuck Collins shows us that meeting intractable greed and inequity in the world requires curiosity, courage, and community. A bildungsroman of conscientious care, *Altar to an Erupting Sun* lights a path toward a better world by showing us how to love beyond our immediate families to a broader community of kin."
—**KIMI EISELE**, author, *The Lightest Object in the Universe*

"A book for these turbulent times from an author who dares to explore the bigger questions. Amid so much despair and confusion, Chuck Collins can be relied upon as a prophet of truth who never fails to cut to the core. A voice of vision and integrity, courage and reason, he lights the way with his skillful writing and tireless advocacy. Collins also knows how to tell a good story. In *Altar to an Erupting Sun*, he brings us on a voyage of adventure, understanding, and discovery like no other."
—**RUAIRI MCKIERNAN,** author of *Irish Times* No. 1 Bestseller, *Hitching for Hope: A Journey Into the Heart and Soul of Ireland*

"Pressing with passion and energy, Collins takes readers into the heart of the beauty and contradictions of social movements. What does it mean to be an activist when the world is falling apart? And what is the activist's moral responsibility? These are vital questions that *Altar* helps us explore."
–**MAY BOVE,** Executive Director, 350.org

"Chuck Collins has been a consummate storyteller for a few decades. *Altar to an Erupting Sun*, his first work of fiction, is an excellent example of his prowess and it kept me fully engaged. Through Rae Kelliher's life as an environmental activist, Collins weaves historical facts of deliberate climate devastation both prescient and now unfortunately all-too-obvious. And as an early proponent of death-with-dignity, Rae's final life choice is one that I found disturbingly provocative: Is it acceptable to murder someone doing evil things? Perhaps the most interesting part of this book is that this haunting question is still very much with me, long after I finished Collins' story."
—**RENEE REINER,** Co-owner, Phoenix Books, Vermont

Altar
to an
Erupting Sun

Altar
to an
Erupting Sun

a novel

CHUCK COLLINS

GREEN WRITERS PRESS | *Brattleboro, Vermont*

Printed in the United States

10 9 8 7 6 5 4 3 2 1

Green Writers Press is a Vermont-based publisher whose mission is to spread a message of hope and renewal through the words and images we publish. Throughout we will adhere to our commitment to preserving and protecting the natural resources of the earth. To that end, a percentage of our proceeds will be donated to environmental and social-activist groups. Green Writers Press gratefully acknowledges support from individual donors, friends, and readers to help support the environment and our publishing initiative.

GReen
wriTers
press

Giving Voice to Writers & Artists Who Will Make the World a Better Place
Green Writers Press | Brattleboro, Vermont
www.greenwriterspress.com

ISBN: 979-8-9865324-6-2

COVER ART:
"Solar Amulet" from *Morning Altars* by Day Schildkret.
www.morningaltars.com

MAPS:
Casey Willliams. www.CaseyWilliamsART.com

A portion of proceeds from this book will support the Nelson Legacy Project.

The paper used in this publication is produced by mills committed
to responsible and sustainable forestry practices

The woman who fell from the sky was neither a murderer or a saint. She was rather ordinary, though beautiful in her walk, like one who has experienced freedom from earth's gravity.

—JOY HARJO

Today there are once more saints and villains. Instead of the uniform grayness of the rainy day, we have the black storm cloud and brilliant lightning flash. Outlines stand out with exaggerated sharpness. Shakespeare's characters walk among us. The villain and the saint emerge from primeval depths and by their appearances they tear open the infernal or the divine abyss from which they come and enable us to see for a moment into the mysteries of which we had never dreamed.

—DIETRICH BONHOEFFER

CONTENTS

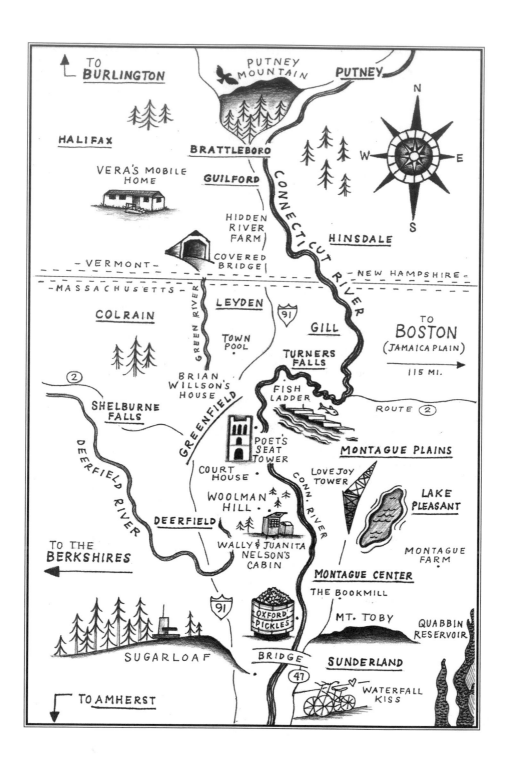

Prelude

Das ist das Ende—für mich der Beginn des Lebens.
(This is the end—for me the beginning of life.)

<small>DIETRICH BONHOEFFER, APRIL 9, 1945</small>

EASTER MORNING

(April 9, 2023)

Rae and Alix depart Guilford at dawn, driving south through the valley fog along the Connecticut River. The sun burns off the haze as they pass through Hartford. There is little traffic on a Sunday morning, especially Easter Sunday.

Alix drives her forest-green pickup truck, without its cap but with its bolted-in toolbox. Rae sits in the passenger seat, breathing in and exhaling, eyes fixed on the river and valley hillsides. Her straw-gray hair is woven into a long braid down her back. It is uncharacteristically quiet between them, which means that Alix can sense every defect in her rusty truck: the pings, grinds, and shakes.

They exit off the interstate onto an auto-only parkway. Alix sets the GPS on her phone for an address in Westchester County, still more than an hour south. The green leaves are emerging weeks ahead of southern Vermont as they pass under several stone arch bridges, 1930s Depression-era infrastructure that endures almost a century later.

A half hour from their destination, Alix pulls over at a tree-lined rest area. She leaves the engine running as she dashes behind a tree to pee. After squatting she stands up, shivers in the cool morning air, and looks up into the tree canopy for a moment. "Oh Lord," she says.

Returning to the truck, she pours another steaming mug of tea from her thermos and places it in her cupholder. She glances at Rae, but Rae doesn't return the gaze. She appears to be in a trance. Alix knows she is weak and tired and on painkillers. Alix eases back onto the parkway and keeps driving.

The wordless drive continues as Alix follows the GPS directions spoken with a female Irish accent, the narrator of her choice. She prefers phrases like "Turn into the car park" rather than "Turn into the parking lot." They exit the parkway and are now on a narrow, tree-lined road, entering a residential neighborhood with large houses and compounds. They pass several residences with metal electric gates and guard stations. A misty rain begins to fall.

They arrive at a compound surrounded by an eight-foot-tall red brick wall, the mansion set far back from the road. Alix silences the GPS after it says, "The destination is on your right." Rae pulls out her binoculars and looks up the driveway. They proceed a mile down the road, turn around, and slowly drive past the entrance again.

Rae appears to have scouted this out. She mutters something about a person that will be climbing into their SUV in thirty minutes to be driven to a church a few miles away.

There is a large clump of thick pine shrubs along the wall. She slows along a thickly tree-lined stretch.

Rae turns to Alix and finally meets her gaze. "Thanks, honey," she says, with a fierce green fire in her eyes. "I love you and everything about you."

Alix's eyes swell with tears. "You want me to just leave you here?"

"Sure as rain," says Rae.

Rae pops the passenger door and leans over the bed of Alix's truck, lifting the tool box lid and pulling out a small duffel bag. She half climbs back into the truck cab, kneeling on the seat, and grabs one last hug with Alix, smiling, shaking her head. Alix feels Rae's heartbeat and a slight quiver. She hands Alix a bundle of stamped envelopes.

"Mail these if I don't call," Rae says. "Now skedaddle!" she yells, slamming the door.

Alix tenses and then stomps on the gas pedal as a sob escapes from her mouth. She drives for several miles before realizing she is speeding, and she pumps her brakes to slow down. She pulls over at a forested roadside to reset her map app for Vermont, choosing a longer route back on blue highways.

Rae slips into the shrubbery and kneels over the duffle bag. She shimmies out of her blue raincoat and pulls a wired vest over her sweater. She hoists the raincoat back over the bulky vest and dons a droopy hat, letting her braid fall over her shoulder. She walks along the wall toward the secure gate and waits.

She reaches into her blouse and pulls out a necklace with her favorite amulet stone. Leaning against the wall, she closes her eyes and directs her mind to an image. She is a little girl, lying on a small grassy bank next to a pond. Toby is lying opposite to her, the tops of their heads touching. They are listening to frogs.

Her mind shifts. She is at the farm and it is winter. Wearing tall snow boots, she walks across the white expanse of the main fields after a fresh snowfall. Reggie is with her, and they embrace as they stop and look out over the fields. Their sheepdog, Hayduke, is hurtling through the snow toward them, leaping like a porpoise in the surf. Then her mind travels to another image, a circle of thirty people standing at the edge of the field, gathered around a willow-basket coffin. She is leading a funeral, wearing a white dress and a colorful stole.

Rae soundlessly weeps, feeling so many losses—Reggie, Alix, Toby, Hayduke, her community, her vision of her final years. *This feels right. I am at peace.* She presses her back against the brick wall and begins to sing quietly:

> *May nothing evil cross this door,*
> *and may ill fortune never pry about*
> *these windows; may the roar*
> *and rain go by.*

She hears a car coming down the drive. She opens her eyes, pulls Hayduke's blue dog leash from her pocket, and steps out into the road.

"Excuse me," she calls loudly, as a bulky Humvee slowly rolls through the open gate. "Have you seen my dog?" She waves the leash.

The window on the passenger side comes down. It is him. The Oil Baron. She recognizes him from hundreds of photographs. With a car full of people heading to Easter services. He smiles.

"What kind of dog?" he says, signaling the driver to pause with a raised left hand.

Rae leans toward the window, with one hand on the leash. The other hand pushes the button on the vest. There is a brilliant flash of light, the sun erupting on Earth.

SEVEN YEARS LATER

(May 5, 2030)

Reggie Donovan rolls over and notices the first traces of light coming in through the cabin skylight. It will be another two hours before the sun crests the eastern ridge and warms his favorite Adirondack chair on the porch. But this is the hour that his mind and body begin to wake up, the time when the May songbirds are most entertaining, and when he can get some work done without interruption.

Today will be different, however, with the marking of Rae's birthday and a memorial gathering in her honor. He has offered to tell Rae's story. Seven years after the bombing event.

He slides stiffly out of bed, touching his toes and slowly standing to his full five foot ten. Reggie puts on his wire-frame glasses, combs his head of gray hair and even grayer beard. *Strength and flexibility*, as Rae would remind him every morning. *Don't forget the flexibility*, she urged, inviting him into her morning stretching and yoga routine. Very little of this regime has remained with Reggie in Rae's absence, but he does touch his toes and reaches for the ceiling.

He hears a train whistle, which is rare as the railroad tracks beside the Connecticut River are three ridges away. The wind must be blowing to the west. The first birds start to chirp as he puts the kettle on his propane stove—enough water to fill his thermos of

Irish Breakfast tea. The blast of the stove temporarily masks all other sounds.

He pulls on thick woolen socks, his self-designated "dawn socks," and tugs on a woolen cap he got when he was organizing paper workers in Maine a few decades earlier. Jay, Maine. What a time that was, standing at the plant gates at 5:00 a.m. They had won that strike. International Paper backed down. Won the battle and lost the war.

Reggie laces on his boots, wraps on a pair of tickproof gaiters, pours some tea in his "walking cup," and steps out for his dawn ramble. He scans the Hidden River Farm. The main house is dark and there is only one light on in their little village, over at Katrina's cabin—Katrina, his fellow elder dawn-riser. She's probably writing a poem for the day, Reggie muses with affection.

In another hour, the village will awaken, distant sounds of babies stirring, children talking, chickens clucking. But now it is just Reggie and the morning birds. He turns toward the forest trail, checking his pocket for an empty cloth bag to collect fiddleheads, mushrooms, or anything else interesting he finds.

Reggie tells visitors he is a "late-in-life back-to-the-lander," having moved with Rae to Vermont in their late fifties. Twenty years ago, he couldn't tell kale from a collard, a parsnip from a pawpaw. Before that, he and Rae did everything they could to make their urban Boston neighborhood a just and healthy place. Neighborhood assemblies, worker solidarity actions, campaigning for progressive candidates, community gardens, forums and films, all while working their day jobs.

It was Rae who turned his political pink a deep shade of green— tempering the rough class politics that he had inherited growing up in Dorchester, a relatively tree-deficient neighborhood in Boston. Reggie thinks of his father, an ironworker at the Quincy shipyard near Boston, and his father's gruff impatience with middle-class tree-huggers. "They care more about birds than working people," was one of his refrains.

Rae lured Reggie into a study group, the climate discussions, the fight over the pipeline. He recalls standing behind Rae at a Boston Common rally where she was speaking, her long straight hair falling down her back, feeling his heart skip with affection after their decades together. *Ha*, he thinks, *now I'm the prince of the tree huggers*—Bernie meets Rachel Carson meets Winona LaDuke.

Reggie turns off the road and onto the old carriage path, as more daylight breaks through the forest canopy. He pauses and listens to a hermit thrush, usually a dusk singer, and another bird he doesn't recognize. "You hear them before you see them," Rae taught him. Broad Brook is high this morning, a few days after the last rain. The ferns are coming up. Reggie wades in and cuts a few fiddleheads from a lush little cluster, tucking them wet and dew-dropped into his bag.

What can he say today about Rae that he hadn't already said before? Each year that goes by validates everything she predicted. She was *prescient*—a channeler, a manifester. She could see things that other people didn't see. She said he had that power, too, if he wanted to tap into it.

He was going to lose her either way—either to the cancer that had metastasized throughout her body or her decision to go out with a violent bang. She could have ended her life here at Hidden River Farm, surrounded by loved ones. People could have sung songs to her, as she had done with so many others who had passed before.

She could have gone gently to the other side. But no, not Rae. She was fueled by love, music, dancing, and rage, an anger so slow-burn that it was chilling. Cold anger, as Reggie's old organizing friend Ernesto "Ernie" Cortes used to say, was what you looked for in a leader. The hot-anger types would flame out, act impulsively, turn off allies. The cold-anger types could strategize, build alliances, think long term, and persist.

Reggie was witness to Rae's practice of "nonattachment." But he suspected that Rae would not have enjoyed losing control over her body. It was Rae who convened the hospice and green burial ministry here at the Hidden River Farm. Many days he listened to her talk energetically about conscious dying, not letting the medical industry and the funeral profiteers get their talons into you. "We need to speak about death, face it, accept it as part of the great cycle." She loved to point out the various death practices from indigenous and other cultures from around the world. "We have so much to learn from these traditions."

Reggie turns off the main path, crosses the brook on a simple log bridge with a hand railing, and walks toward the trail that circles back up to the farm. He is now heading toward the sacred grove. In the winter, this is one of his favorite routes to snowshoe, following the animal tracks of rabbits, fishers, and the occasional bobcat.

Behind the farm is three hundred acres of forest conservation land—abutting another large stretch of woods and ponds stretching a couple miles to a beaver pond. To the south, you can walk through the woods all the way to Massachusetts except for one dirt-road crossing.

The woods are at the edge of a habitat corridor full of vernal pools, dens, wandering turkeys, active beaver ponds, and the occasional bear or bobcat. Rae believed that some of the bobcats had biological traces of ancient catamount, the Vermont puma that later interbred with escaped zoo animals and exotic pets. Reggie thinks of Isabella Stewart Gardner, the patrician walking her lions in the Boston Fens near her mansion. Those oligarchs couldn't just have a simple dog or cat.

Reggie thinks about how, every March, Rae enlisted him to join the salamander crossing teams that gathered along the roadways after the first warm spring rain. Wearing reflective vests and holding flashlights, they made sure that the frogs and salamanders, eager to attend wild spawning orgies in the vernal pools, made it across the road alive. Salamander protection required staying up to 11:00 p.m., several hours past "Quaker midnight" in Reggie's book. But nothing could deflate Rae more than holding a squished wood frog in her hand knowing she could have saved a life. So he happily joined the crossing guards.

Save a life, take a life. Rae's reverence for life was consistent until her final minutes. Then she took her own life and three others. Reggie takes stock of his inner compass. He can almost think about Rae's final days with only a slight ache, a welcome change from when it felt like a knife in his side.

Reggie's pants are covered with dew and various hitchhiking seeds as he pauses to look through the trees toward the farm. Even since yesterday's dawn walk, Reggie can see that leaf canopy is filling in further. *Life wants to happen*, as Rae would say. He heads down a deer path toward the woods and the bridge that will take him into the sacred grove.

The sacred grove and memorial area at the farm are home to over two hundred human remains. No concrete crypts, no carbon-burst cremations, nothing that can't quickly break down. "Wrap me in that wine-stained table cloth and lay me down three feet in the good soil," as Rae would say. "Make me one with the compost, fertilizer for the trees." In her case, of course, there wasn't much left to compost. Reggie smiles with the inkling of gallows humor that comes from a few years of distance. He did create a shroud from Rae's favorite table cloth at her private memorial service.

That was their last and biggest disagreement. Reggie argued that Rae's act of violence would become the story, that the US media and culture would latch onto the act and so Rae's message would be lost. The right-wingers would label it "terrorism" and use it to unleash repression toward climate-justice movement leaders. And he thought it might embolden the fossil fuel industry, distracting from the urgent organizing work of shutting down the oil and gas extractors.

I was both right and wrong, he thought as he came into an open field full of early milkweed, insects hatching, and birds circling overhead.

As Reggie predicted, the blowback was fierce. The fossil fuel industry pressed state lawmakers to criminalize any nonviolent protest against infrastructure, even peaceful nonviolent assemblies. One peaceful anti-pipeline encampment in Virginia was broken up and bulldozed by aggressive state officials. Movement leaders were locked up and tried under conspiracy laws. The industry had a martyr, and they attempted to taint any opposition as borderline terrorism.

Rae's detonation had led to copycat actions targeting fossil fuel executives and infrastructure around the world. When a group of six grandmothers calling themselves "Good Ancestors" immolated themselves in the lobby of ExxonMobil, the story broke through and touched millions. Those actions sparked intense debate about the urgency of climate action. They led to additional lawsuits and the creation of an international carbon-crimes tribunal, investigating when fossil fuel companies knew about the harms of emissions and their actions to fund denial and doubt. The carbon extractors further militarized their operations—and enlisted the military and intelligence forces around the world to protect their right to dig, extract, and burn. But it was hard to fight a decentralized army of terminally ill people acting independently.

Reggie saw things begin to shift in 2024, the beginning of a cascade of changes. The oil and gas industry rapidly lost legitimacy, thanks in part to investor lawsuits and mass divestment. Politicians and the media increased scrutiny of their plans to keep building carbon-extracting infrastructure despite their full knowledge that it would push the planet past a "liveable and sustainable future."

Rae had drawn attention to a handful of carbon barons, the prime decision-makers, whose short-term outlook cost the world so much. Now those oligarchs lived in fear in militarized fortresses, their children shuttling to gated schools in bulletproof Humvees. Rae had called them the "face of evil," a phrase she declined to use for any other living creature.

Reggie could never have imagined her legacy—how her story and her action would capture people's imagination. Seven years later, her words have been translated into dozens of languages and her photo sits on many altars around the world. Rae would have been moved by this, Reggie thinks. She was the great builder of private and community altars.

Reggie approaches the grove and burial ground at the south end of the farm. He slowly paces the circular path through field and forest. Laid out with benches and shrubs yet maintaining a wildness, the grove is what Rae used to call the underground community, where our bodies get plugged into the "wood-wide web" of mycelium networks and tree roots. The Hidden River Farm Sacred Grove is a popular spot, what some community residents have described as one of the "ministries" of the farm, with its focus on hospice care and giving birth to a new world.

The grove has commemorative stones with names carved in them. Reggie stops in front of the special stone he placed there for Rae (and a small one for Hayduke, their dog). Her birth date is carved into the rock, seventy-six years ago today.

Today, at the celebration of Rae's life, he will try to assemble the stories that formed her.

Reggie walks out of the grove and into the open field, stopping at a small bench overlooking his garden of poppies. He started growing them a few years before Rae learned she had cancer.

His friend Peter from Maine, another back-to-the-land labor organizer, had tucked a packet of poppy seeds into Reggie's pocket when they were sitting by a lake one day. "You don't want the state to control all the painkillers," Peter said, words that took on greater meaning in later years. Peter made poppy tea, a gentle pain reliever, for friends suffering from chronic pain.

Opium. There was a time in the late 1800s and early 1900s when Vermont was rife with opium addiction, even as other states regulated opium and its derivatives. The rural life, long winters, and an excessive political focus on liquor prohibition masked the gushing flow of opium into the state. Men and women of all classes had easy access to patent medicines from itinerant quacks as well as prescribed painkillers procured at their local apothecaries.

Reggie flashes back to finding a young man passed out from an overdose on a Brattleboro bridge, and feeling his powerlessness to help. Now he carries a Narcan canister in his day pack. A high number of memorial graves in the grove mark people whose lives were cut short by opioids.

When their friend Echo was dying, she loved the teas he made. And when Rae was in pain, he could brew her a cup from the poppies he had grown and crushed himself. He would take ten dried-out poppy heads, crack off the stems, and pour out the seeds. Then he'd run the empty heads through an old coffee grinder, pour hot water over the grounds, and strain the cup of tea. His attitude could be summarized as: "Fuck the state when it comes to painkillers."

Reggie sits on the bench, unscrewing the top of his mug and taking a sip of Irish breakfast tea. He misses Rae every day. He knows that a part of himself has not recovered. There was a deep and mercurial love and affection between them, a mutual devotion that was all the more spicy for their different temperaments and disagreements. They were committed to dancing, laughing, and staying sexually alive. They committed to a practice of looking into one another's eyes for several minutes every day

But he's come to enjoy his solitude and elder status at the Hidden River Farm. One of his perks is that he is not obliged to go to meetings. In arguing for this exemption, he pointed out that he had already spent the equivalent of three full years of his waking life in meetings. But secretly, he can no longer sit through discussions with twenty-three-year-olds who are convinced they already know everything there is to know.

Rae used to say that "their brains are still developing" and "one of the last maturation traits to emerge is doubt." She would smile at Reggie and joke, "Be patient, grasshopper." But there's a limit to the number of hours in your life you can spend listening to people tell you things you already know and have lived. His meeting reprieve means that he can putter about, keep his mouth shut, and contribute to the common good in his own way. Like growing poppies.

Reggie brushes burdock seeds off his pants and takes another sip of tea. Across the field, he hears the sounds of people talking, children asking questions, vehicles starting up. He slowly stands, stretches, and walks out of the grove and back to his cabin.

Reggie reflects that he has a deep well of patience for discord and difference. He most enjoys spending time with the refugees with disrupted lives from the American South and from overseas that the farm community has absorbed over the last decade. There are some youngsters he enjoys, like Alix and Rachel, who have not lost the ability to laugh at themselves or forgive human failures. They are the ones who show up on his porch, with a growler of hard cider, and ask him about Rae. "What was she like as a young woman? How does someone with a lifelong commitment to non-violence—with the elders she had—do what she did? What do you miss about her?"

ALIX RETURNS

(May 5, 2030)

The first thing Alix sees when she opens her eyes is the funky floral wallpaper at the main house. The antiquated design, reminiscent of a vintage greeting card, is probably a century old, and the paper has held up well.

It was in this room that Alix woke up seven years ago, on the Easter morning when she drove Rae to Westchester County. On that day, she rose in the dark after a fitful sleep. Nothing has been the same since.

Today, Alix has slept well past her normal waking time of 6:00 a.m. She can hear the stirring of people downstairs in the common house. She smells something savory and delicious wafting up from the kitchen. Outside, she hears a tractor starting up and a group of clucking chickens and bleating goats. Oh, how she missed these sights, sounds, and smells!

She arrived late last night after almost a month on the road visiting friends and sister communities in the Northeast Kingdom of Vermont and seeing firsthand many of the transitions that have been taking place in the region. She departed the truck-charging station near Island Pond at around 9:00 p.m. after a birthday celebration for her friend Val. She then arrived at the farm after midnight and quietly slipped into her old room.

She gets out of bed and settles into a large, comfortable chair overlooking the window, which has been cracked open to let in the morning coolness and the cacophony of birds.

Alix takes a deep breath and pulls out a small black journal. In prison, it was challenging to hold to daily meditation and to set intentions, what with the constant noise and periodic interruptions of outside authority. But these practices kept her alive, reminding her on a daily basis that while the state held her body, they did not possess her mind and soul.

Rae once told her about the life of Dietrich Bonhoeffer, the German theologian who was imprisoned and executed after his failed attempt to assassinate Adolph Hitler. Bonhoeffer wrote in his prison letters that it helped him keep his spirits up during his years of detention to think of prison as a monastery.

The daily assertion of her own self kept her centered and focused. As a result, she made lots of friends in prison, wrote poems, learned arc welding and other skills, and pushed successfully for minor reforms in her prison, such as prisoner-led education programs. She herself organized a meditation group and a study gathering of fellow inmates to read about the ecological and social transition of the nation and the world.

Released two months earlier, Alix spent the first month back at the farm, with periodic trips to visit family. For the last month she has been on tour, making the most of her own small bit of notoriety. She saw old friends but also met many new people who knew her story and nodded with recognition when she was introduced. The only people who didn't recognize her were the Amish people she met. Most people wanted to hear stories about Rae.

She reads the previous passage in her journal, written a week earlier. *I feel like Rip van Winkle, except I wasn't asleep, just locked away for six years. I'm seeing an accelerated culture shift. I know this isn't happening everywhere in the US but primarily in pockets of northern New England, the Great Lakes, and Pacific Northwest. Reggie described how states have splintered along political and cultural lines, with some becoming mini-theocracies and authoritarian states. But here in northern New England, the changes are most visible.*

Alix was impressed by the changes in the villages, especially in terms of race. New England communities that were traditionally composed of White ethnic groups were now being populated by Black, Indigenous, and people of color in farm communities, as well as climate refugees from the southern USA and other parts of the world forming their own enterprises. It was a mashing up of old New England Yankee culture with a global music backbeat.

She's excited to see people at Rae's seventy-sixth birthday party and commemoration. She knows she will see Jade, PJ, Rudy, Rachel, and many other old friends that she hasn't seen in a month. She feels a surge of energy that she hasn't felt in years, a rekindling of connections with people, plants, and animals. A group of children in the community, born while she was in prison, have discovered her playful nature and are constantly pursuing her to play games and read stories.

One intention for the coming days is to get some clarity about her future role at the farm. She has meetings tomorrow with the berry-patch team and hospice collective, groups that she had previously been part of. No one is pressuring her to immediately plug back into anything. And it being May, she can easily be deployed into one of the farm and garden projects for several months without formally rejoining a work team.

She looks forward to a walk and porch sit with Reggie, Rae's old partner. He vocally disagreed with Rae about her proposed actions. And he stood steadily by Alix and visited her in prison every two weeks, bringing her socks and books and treats.

Alix closes her journal, stands up slowly, and pulls on her favorite farm overalls. She looks in the mirror and smiles at what she sees. Her friend Val cut her hair a few days earlier and the new look is growing on Alix. She's just one year shy of forty; her brown hair now has a few streaks of gray.

She grabs her green travel mug and pads down the stairs in the front hallway and into the kitchen. She greets the three visitors standing in the kitchen. "Good morning, good morning," she says, shifting to take in everyone's faces. "I'm Alix. I got in late. Hope I didn't disturb anyone."

"Good morning," says a slight older person, smiling in recognition. "I'm Ty."

The others introduce themselves, and Alix asks them where they are visiting from. After several minutes of chitchat, Alix steps toward the electric kettle, grabs a scoop of chicory from a glass jar, and fills her mug. She bows and heads to the front porch, hoping to catch an Adirondack chair, some direct sun, and a few familiar faces.

As she steps on the porch, she hears her name called from the corner.

"Alix Leblanc!" It's PJ Starkweather, one of the farm elders and a treasured friend. "Hallelujah!"

"Sweetie!" trills Jade, also jumping up to give her a warm embrace. "Come pull up a chair."

Alix feels warmth flood her body from their attention and delight. PJ and Jade are among the founders of the Hidden River Farm. Alix met them all at a rather wild Halloween party at the farm, shortly after the founders bought the farm. They were all dressed as witches, with Rae donning a flowing red cape. They had all embraced Alix, inviting her to visit and eventually join the farm community.

Though Alix is a generation younger, she always felt respected by the original five founders, in part for her plant knowledge and farming skills. But, as they had told her, they also delighted in her goofy humor and generous spirit.

Alix is not tall, but she towers over both PJ and Jade, who are both just under five feet tall, with compact and strong bodies. But that's where their similarities end. Jade has jet-black hair, small wire-rim eyeglasses, and wide hips. Alix knows she was born into an upwardly mobile middle-class family from South Korea that exhorted her to go to the United States to get rich. Her brother had succeeded in this. But as Jade jokes, she greatly disappointed her family on that front. Brainy, quick-witted, and sometimes introverted and mistaken for aloof, Jade is a steady and reliable worker bee in the community.

PJ, with reddish gray hair and thin features right down to her narrow fingers, is from an old New England family, with a family tree going back to early settlers and Puritan clergy. But, as she explains, her family has been steadily sliding off the rails for generations. Her father was an architect, a first-generation Zen Buddhist, a master gardener, and an early builder of green eco-buildings. Alix loves the story of what happened when PJ was twenty: she swerved to avoid hitting a rabbit and totaled the family car, upon which her father told her that she had done the right thing. The Starkweathers might have been considered "old wealth"—except for their lack of money. PJ calls her family "unlanded WASPs." So different from Alix's economically precarious French Catholic heritage.

Alix scans about for Rachel, the person with whom she feels the strongest heart connection. Jade informs her that Rachel is working on ritual setup. Rachel wasn't an original founder of the farm, but she joined not long after Alix. Rachel and Alix are peers in age, temperament, and aspiration. Rachel was raised in a secular Jewish family from Portland, Maine, and ran away to a back-to-the-land community in way-up-north Aroostook County, land of long winters and potato farms. Rachel, with curly dark hair and a round face, is a fiddler, willow coffin weaver, and expert on medicinal herbs. She and Alix worked and played together, sometimes as lovers, in the first seven years of the farm.

Alix thinks of this group as the core of Hidden River Farm residents, those who rode out the 2020–22 Covid pandemic together, a community of a dozen at the time, with endless shifting protocols, flare-ups of anxiety, and social pods. While many in the wider society experienced the pandemic as traumatic, the farm community found it a mostly enjoyable test run for a disrupted future. Since no one went anywhere, they become one another's small and sometimes complete universe and university.

"How was the trip up north?" PJ asks. "Must have been nice to be on the open road after being locked up."

"Hell yeah." Alix settles into one of the porch chairs, forming a half circle with Jade and PJ where they can talk but also gaze out at the fields. She looks them each in the eye and takes a sip of chicory. "Though I think I'm finally having staying-put fantasies. I was worried I'd never want to stop wandering."

"Do what you gotta do," said Jade. "Just keep us as your home base." Alix appreciates how everyone assumed she would come back to the farm after her release from prison. They welcomed her to take her time figuring out her next move, to come and go as she pleased, to visit people, and to make use of the farm's electric vehicles whenever she needed one. After two months free from prison, Alix is beginning to feel the desire to settle down.

"It was cool to see small towns transitioning away from the fossil fuel economy to relocalized everything." Alix was captivated by the new local businesses and cultural institutions, including the gift exchanges, mutual aid networks, and cooperative marketplaces.

"All that fiesta and carnival," PJ says. "Rae would have loved it."

"For sure. I loved perusing the community bulletin boards with the colorful flyers for all the events and meetings." There were dances, concerts, author talks, meet-ups of every stripe. At a few of these she was pressed into speaking about Rae, or telling her own story. "And all the work on death and dying made me feel like our Hidden River farm work was rippling outwards."

Alix and Rae had created a program to train "death doulas," people who not only assist with the dying process, but the whole approach to dying long before death. Up north, Alix attended two gatherings for elders who were terminally ill and had proclaimed their "death dates" and were holding what Rachel called "living shivas."

"Alix, you should be proud of the work you and Rae did," says Jade. "You seeded a shift in the culture around death and dying."

In prison, Alix had missed the farm's fall rituals celebrating Day of the Dead. Rae encouraged the building of a large public altar along with personal private altars. Each year Jade brought photos to Alix in prison from the community altar. Last year there was a special section for Alix's friend Alice, who had died a few months earlier. On the altar were pictures of Alice and her daughters, bottles of her favorite wine, ceramics she had made (with copal and aromatic herbs burning in them), elaborate Alice-made quilts and weavings, and a triptych of childhood photos. It was painful for Alix not to be able to see Alice at the end of her life, so the pictures from the altar helped her grieve and feel connected. She had even maintained an altar in her prison cell.

"Can't help but think about Rae, all this talk of intentional dying," says Alix. They all nod, their thoughts going to Rae. Rae who led workshops at the farm about conscious dying. Rae who refused to go into the hospital and walked away from the million-dollar machines and the treatments that, she believed, would deplete her mind in her final months. Rae who loved Day of the Dead rituals, with her elaborate costumes and altars. In a way, Alix thought, Rae was organizing today's birthday commemoration at the farm, convening us from the other side, smiling and leading the songs.

Jade breaks the momentary silence. "Rae used to say that for those on the edge of death, it is reassuring to know that society will pause to remember them. She was probably speaking for herself." Her eyes wander to a bicyclist coming up the driveway past the towering ancient maple trees. "Here comes Rudy."

Alix looks down the hill. Bouncing up the driveway, partly propelled by an electric assist bicycle, is one of the other fearless founders, Rudy.

"Alix!" he shouts, flashing a toothy smile as he steers his bike onto the grass and up to the edge of the porch.

"Babbu!" Alix calls back, using her nickname for Rudy, which is itself already a nickname for Radra Ranganathan. She jumps off the porch to grab him affectionately. He has always found a way to make her laugh, even when she was in prison.

PJ pulls over a chair for Rudy, welcoming him into their semi-circle. "Tea?"

Rudy pulls a large water bottle from his bike bag, signaling that he is fine. He removes his bicycle helmet and the sun sparkles on his bald head, which he immediately covers with a cap.

"Babbu, have you been riding since dawn?" asks Alix. She admires his healthy glow.

"I did get an early start," says Rudy. "Oh, the things you see. I was coming down Stage Road, barreling downhill, and I came around a bend and a giant stag was standing in the road. I hit my brakes and for a moment we just stood eye to eye before he bounded off into the forest."

They all laugh at this image.

"You would be a scary thing to encounter at any time of day," ribs Alix.

"We were just starting to hear about Alix's trip up north," says Jade. "Come join us."

"Ah, continue," says Rudy, accepting the chair and turning it to face Alix.

The discussion continues on, a thoughtful banter. Alix feels a swelling of love come over her as she sits with these familiar family members. Oh, how she missed these discussions, the openhearted curiosity, and the warmth of these people.

In the first month after her release, Alix spent significant time with each of them one-to-one, taking walks, accepting help and offers of healing. Rachel accompanied her everywhere the first week as she adjusted to life outside the walls. Jade gave her massages and physical healing sessions. Rudy invited her to help with a few projects where they could talk and tell jokes. During the first month, PJ checked in with her almost every day with a motherly gaze. Alix was unable to hide anything she felt from PJ, and she found herself weeping or laughing in her presence.

They all expressed in various ways a deep appreciation for how Alix defended the community from attack and the injustice of being treated as a scapegoat for a crime that Rae had involved her in. There was a moment in 2023 when the farm residents thought they might lose everything to overzealous law enforcement.

But what became clear, even to federal authorities, was that Rae had been scrupulous in separating her action from the farm community. Only Reggie and Alix were vaguely aware of what the media called Rae's "suicide bombing mission." Alix had known no details. And in a written letter, Rae pointed out that Reggie had opposed her action and refused to cooperate. It was only Alix, a driver, who was charged with any crimes. How Rae got hold of the explosive devices was a secret that died with her, as she meticulously left no trace.

•

Not that things were easy in the year of blowback that followed. For months, federal investigators effectively opened a field office at the farm. They interrogated everyone multiple times. They crawled all over Reggie and Rae's cabin and other common spaces, searching for physical evidence. The residents of the farm, numbering about sixteen at the time, took small amusement watching FBI agents being chased by goats and getting their cars stuck in the mud. The feds attempted to construct a conspiracy where none existed and finally gave up. Alix was the only thing they had, a thirty-three-year-old farmer who had given a "violent terrorist" a three-hour, one-way drive on Easter morning.

After the bombing, the farm residents were in an emotional bind. Rae was one of their founders, and a guiding spirit. She was deeply loved and respected—and there would have been over-whelming grief with her death from cancer. But, in the end, she didn't die of cancer. In a community that was weaving a new culture around death and dying, the circumstance of Rae's horrific action made the process of grieving all the more complex. In addition, many felt Alix was wrongly imprisoned and believed that Rae was responsible for that.

Reggie and other community members decided against a public funeral, an event that might have drawn unwelcome attention to the farm, from both right-wing mobs and unstable elements celebrating a martyr. Instead, they had a number of small, private rituals and memorial circles behind closed doors. It was Reggie's idea, after a year, to celebrate Rae's birthday and have that be the focus of her legacy. And with Alix back for the first May observance she could attend, many who had moved away were making a special effort to return to the farm.

The morning passes with conversation and a lively game of corn hole, Alix demonstrating that prison life may have improved her beanbag-tossing skills. At midday, before the two o'clock gathering, people slip off to eat, nap, dress. Alix unpacks the truck, cleans it up, and takes a quick dunk in the brook. She has not seen Reggie, so she walks in the direction of his cabin to see if there are any signs of life.

Knowing Reggie, he may be in siesta mode. But she sees him sitting on his small porch, reading a book, and gives him a friendly bird call of a greeting. Even from fifty yards, she sees him sit up with a joyous grin.

"I thought you'd be snoozing, old man."

"Already did. I was up early, wandering about and thinking about this birthday memorial." He wraps Alix in a friendly embrace. "Having you here makes things really special."

"Aw, shucks." Alix plops down in Reggie's other sturdy Adirondack chair, glancing at the cracked-open book of Celtic blessings by John O'Donohue. "Cramming some inspiration?" She nods at the book.

"From the maestro."

Reggie asks about her travels. His attentiveness is riveting. During his visits to her in prison, Alix found herself weeping in his presence and even more after he left.

Reggie gets up for a moment and returns with a plate and several pieces of blueberry cornbread, offering a slice to Alix.

"Oh my God, I love this recipe." Alix reaches for one piece and devours it. "Rae's recipe, right?"

"Yep. With our own blueberries from the freezer. I like to think that bag of berries at the bottom of the freezer was picked by Rae."

"Ha! Probably." Alix reaches for a second piece. "I guess I'm hungry." She looks up and smiles at Reggie. "I tried to replicate this in prison, but it was too dry."

"If Rae were here, the berries would have been rotated in the freezer with dates written on them. That was the last bag in there with a Sharpie marking."

"Yup," Alix agrees.

For a few moments they both think of Rae and her scary-organized systems.

"I did bring you a treat." Alix reaches into a tote bag and pulls out a paper sack of strawberry hand pies. "I got these at this very cool Amish farm stand."

"Yum." Reggie unwraps one of the pies, what he grew up calling a Pop Tart. "Did you get a sense of the Amish presence in the Northeast Kingdom?"

"Oh, this is fascinating," says Alix. "Val told me there are now over a thousand families, maybe more." Alix had several long chats with Amish women at an Amish farm stand in Brownington where she bought baked goods. Their market stand was stocked with early-season vegetables, jars of homemade pickles, jams, wax candles, and, of course, fresh-baked hand pies. It appeared to be a magnet for both Amish families and Kingdom "English" neighbors, who stood in clusters talking or snacking at tables in the shade.

"Oh, let me describe this one scene." Alix lights up. "Val and I go to this campfire with all these Amish men and women talking with members of this Black women's farm collective. They're animated, talking about everything from soil fertility to natural childbirth. I'm, like, shaking my head at this scene that is not without its tension, but was full of possibilities."

Reggie's eyes light up with this report. "The Amish in Vermont are infinitely better positioned for the transition as a subculture than everyone else."

"The transition" is a common shorthand among the Hidden River Farm core. It has been their shared assumption that the climate disruption, along with the decline of cheap, easy-to-get fossil fuels—what the old timers called "peak oil"—would alter the way of life that prevailed from 1950 to 2020. "The next thirty years will not be like the last fifty years," Rae would say.

Alix knows Reggie is always at work on multiple projects, some things that no one else on the farm entirely comprehends. While many Hidden River Farm members are building the alternative economy, plant by plant, pine board by pine board, Reggie is still involved in fighting the destructive forces, the organized forces of greed.

Alix knows, for example, that Reggie is on a formal commission that meets by video conference, overseeing the nationalization and managed decline of the fossil fuel industry, ensuring that their carbon assets remain in the ground. On days when she is weeding carrots, he is arguing with European bureaucrats about carbon reserves and transition benefits for workers. But then he comes out and weeds around the carrots, too.

Alix and Reggie compare notes on the reflections they will be giving at the birthday memorial.

"We're expecting Toby," says Reggie, referring to Rae's older brother. "That will be a wild card. I haven't seen him since the month before Rae died."

"That will be interesting," Alix muses. She's only heard about Toby through Rae's commentaries. "I can't wait to hear your stories, how you weave all this together—all the journals, letters, and books."

"Yeah, and I'm counting on you to pull out the hook if I'm off course."

"I'll be there with a long stick." Alix smiles, knowing that Reggie will talk for a while but also that everyone will be eager to hear his reflections about Rae.

Alix returns to her seat on the porch of the main house, a prime location to greet arriving friends and guests. She watches the trickle of visitors arriving on foot, bicycle, ATV, horse-drawn wagon, and electric vehicle. A couple of the farm members set up a welcome table to greet visitors, steer them to parking, and point them toward the sacred grove.

Alix sees Enid, a close friend of Rae and one of the founders of the Farm. There are John and Rita, Melony and Renee, who have driven up from Eastern Massachusetts. There are visitors from neighboring farm communities—Meadow Bee, Wild Carrot, SUSU, and Ujima, a Black women's land collective.

More than one hundred and fifty people gather in the grove, some with temporary folding chairs and others sitting on blankets or standing. There is an ancient carved stump that serves as a podium for such gatherings. The farm is blessed with many fine singers. For this occasion, a group of residents who have formed an *a cappella* quartet, open with several of Rae's favorite songs, including one that she wrote herself.

After a song, Reggie stands at the stump with a single sheet of paper. Alix, sitting close by, can see his hand shake just a little.

"It is a blessing to have Alix back," he begins. "It brings the circle to a close. Without Alix here, previous memorial birthday celebrations have had a missing chair. I know I speak for everyone here, Alix, from the bottom of our hearts: Thank you.

"We are also honored to see Toby, Rae's big brother." People crane around to see him standing in the back. He smiles and waves. Alix turns to get a good look at Toby, whom she has never met or seen in person.

"Toby, I hope you might say a few words."

They nod to one another, and then Reggie continues. "Some of you have heard me talk about Rae, her life . . ."—here he pauses, trying to find the right word—". . . her dramatic exit.

"But with Alix back, and the passage of seven years, I have been thinking about Rae's life, about the experiences, people, and ideas that shaped her, right up until the final hours. Alix and I have been reading her journals and letters and the underlined passages in her favorite books."

Reggie looks at his paper. "Let me tell you the story of Rae, as best as I understand it today. Not every detail, but the parts that may have influenced her final hours. Settle in. Stay open if you can. I have a few stories to tell."

PART 1
FORMATION

The ultimate weakness of violence is that it is a descending spiral, begetting the very thing it seeks to destroy . . . Returning violence for violence multiplies violence, adding deeper darkness to a night already devoid of stars. Darkness cannot drive out darkness; only light can do that. Hate cannot drive out hate; only love can do that.

—Martin Luther King, Jr.

MONTAGUE FARM

(1973)

A giant rubberized conveyor belt with baby dill pickles hurtles along, rolling past a dozen workers wearing white hairnets. Rae Kelliher snatches up handfuls, four or five at a time, until she tops off her jars. The little cukes are fresh from the brine vat, where they looked like shiny sardines floating in elephant-size wooden bathtubs.

Standing in her spot beside the assembly line, Rae gazes up at a large factory clock on the far wall. In ten minutes, her shift will be over. She glances across the noisy room and spies Nina, working in a seated position at the capping station. At that moment, Nina looks up at her and they exchange smiles.

Rae is in her fourth week working at Oxford Pickles in South Deerfield, Massachusetts. In September, she dropped out of Amherst College after the first week of her sophomore year. She walked out of her humanities seminar after a painfully abstract discussion, something about sexual repression and dialectical inwardness in *Middlemarch*. Every fiber in her body said *No!* to sitting in classes that had little meaning for her.

She had to tell her parents, neither of whom had been to college, about her decision. And she reluctantly had to tell others, like Mrs. Douglas, the high school guidance counselor who had helped with her applications and financial aid forms.

She thinks of her brother Toby, who is two years older. They were fiercely close all their younger days. But then he became negative and embittered about her decision to go to college. Now he is equally sour about her dropping out of school. Their phone calls are mostly barbed exchanges.

"If they could see me now," Rae says out loud, words that are absorbed in the clattering din of the giant pickle shed, a room the size of a football field. Not even her assembly line neighbors, a couple of ancient Deerfield women who are among the year-round workforce, can hear her utterance. "I'm twenty years old, living at a hippy commune, and working at a pickle factory." Rae smiles at her good fortune.

Finally, after ten minutes that seem to last an hour, the buzzer goes off and the assembly lines roll to a stop. A rare silence fills the pickle shed as forty workers tidy up their work stations in anticipation of the second shift, which will arrive shortly. Rae walks to Nina, who loops her arm into hers as they waltz toward the locker area to collect their jackets, lunch pails, and bags.

"Hey honey, how ya doing?" asks Nina as they exit the plant door into a cool fall afternoon. Nina peels a hairnet off her curly brown hair. She has piercing dark eyes, long black eyelashes, and two silver dot earrings. At twenty-eight, she is one of the co-founders of Montague Farm, and one of several community members who work at the pickle factory. Three of the residents prefer the night shift. "They're always hiring," Nina told her a month earlier. "Most people don't last a week."

"I'm good." Rae pulls off her hairnet, shaking her long straw-colored hair out of captivity. "A lot of time for thinking."

"Ha," says Nina, her brown eyes twinkling in the afternoon sun. "Too much time. I try and write a poem every day, work the words around in my head. I like the capping station since I can keep a piece of paper and pen next to me."

"Wow." Rae is impressed and slightly envious. All she is doing is obsessing about her life. She opens the passenger door to Nina's dusty blue Chevy Nova. The acrid smell of baked brine escapes.

"Yeah, my car smells like a pickle jar." They both laugh. They each stash their pickle-plant attire in Nina's car to contain the workplace aromas. Since so many people at the farm work at

Oxford Pickles—or have worked there—there is a shared joke about the distinct *eau de brine parfum* or *fragrance de pickle*.

The farm sells a good percentage of its organic cucumbers to Oxford, filling dozens of white pails and burlap sacks that are shuttled to the factory and added to the massive storage vats. Oxford doesn't care if they are organic, as long as they're pretty. At pennies on the pound, however, the farm isn't getting rich.

Rae also works at their farm stand, where they post a colorful sign: *No Nukes, Yes Cukes.* This caused one out-of-state tourist to ask Rae, "When do you expect to have nukes back in stock?"

"Hopefully never," quipped Sam, a fellow farmer working alongside her that day. Sam has been active in opposing the siting of a nuclear power plant on the Montague Plains, a couple miles from the farm.

Nina drives south across the Sunderland Bridge over the steel-blue Connecticut River. The sun slowly heads toward the horizon, casting brilliant light along the east side of the river, accenting the brown, yellow, and red leaves that still remain on the trees at river's edge. They pass Morrison's Ice Cream, a favorite destination on summer evenings. Nina turns north on Route 47 and follows the river along the maple-lined streets toward Montague.

"So you're running for town meeting?" Rae asks Nina, picking up from their interrupted lunch conversation at an employee picnic table. Rae is curious. She has never considered that someone so young and female could run for office.

"Yes, on the Nuclear Opposition Party. Me and Sam are running for town meeting, and Sarah is running for selectboard." Sarah Saleh is a super-smart activist who can explain at length what is wrong with nuclear power. Rae has sat through a number of her talks and teach-in presentations. She is only six years older than Rae, but she seems infinitely more experienced and wiser. One thing Rae loves about Montague Farm are the strong and confident women and their sisterly regard for her.

The men aren't so bad either—generally fun and respectful. Once Rae deflected a few unwanted sexual advances, these same men shifted into thoughtful and sibling-like friends. She doesn't reject all the advances, however. She has a few crushes, not to be pursued for various reasons (like already-taken). She has a lovely occasional sleeping and sexual companion in Gary, though both know they are not destined for a real partnership.

Nina chats about her campaign as they turn onto the old Chestnut Hill road and arrive at what some locals still call Ripley Farm. She pulls her Nova into a parking area set apart from the houses. There are a few other battered and broken-down cars and trucks and a few "parts vehicles" that Tom, a mechanically inclined member of the community, uses to keep the other cars running. He prefers Volkswagen Rabbits, of which he has several in different colors and stages of dismemberment.

Learning the history of Montague Farm makes Rae feel even luckier to be there. The farm was founded in 1969 by leftist activists from New York and Boston in anticipation of a fascist crackdown in America. A few residents are activist journalists working with the Liberation News Service, a sort of left-wing Associated Press. After facing harassment, wiretaps, and office break-ins, they packed up the typewriters and printing presses from their New York office and brought them to Montague. A sister group bought a farm in Guilford, Vermont, just over the state line to the north.

Rae notices that some outsiders derisively label them a "hippie commune," but residents reject that identity. As she has learned, within the political left there are growing splinters between life-style hippies, political organizers, and militant revolutionaries. The farm is not your "get high, drop out" commune, as other back-to-the land experiments appear to be. Rae finds that the residents are serious-minded and interested in radical change, even "revolution," though clearly within a tradition of nonviolence. The armed-struggle factions seem to remain in urban areas or have gone underground.

Rae's housemates are writers, journalists, filmmakers, radio producers, natural healers, and a few people with farming skills and pickle-making prowess. One of the founders, Marshall Bloom, told Rae that the news service needed a rural location, "a place where people can begin to think clearly, a place to get all those city poisons out of their systems."

Dinner-table discussions are more about politics, the war in Vietnam, and feminist theory than about the depressed price of cucumbers. Rae quietly absorbs the conversation among more seasoned activists. And with the recent announcement of plans to build a nuclear power plant in the town, the residents of Montague Farm have become the nucleus of a resistance effort.

Nina and Rae go to their respective rooms at the farm. Rae is in an attic section of the house, a small room that she has decorated with pictures of friends and family as well as paintings and posters. Thanks to Rae's dousing, it smells like patchouli oil and sandalwood incense. She has one window that looks to the west with its purply sunsets over the Connecticut River Valley.

Rae met Sarah and Nina at a college teach-in on nuclear power at the end of her first year at Amherst College. She accepted their invitation to visit the farm at the end of her spring term. While everything about being in college registered *No* in her body, the visit to the farm was an overwhelming *Yes.* But she put aside her inner instincts in order to return home to Ohio for her summer job, waitressing at Patty's, a restaurant owned by a family friend, a job she had done since she got a work permit at age fourteen. Even she believed she would return to Amherst and finish college.

Rae spent the summer daydreaming about Montague Farm, the lush green of the valley, the shape of the hills and riverways, the intriguing people, and most important, the sense of purpose that these people shared. She felt a seed blossoming inside her as she thought about the farm residents. That summer, the Watergate hearings were broadcast "gavel to gavel," and during slow times at the restaurant, she and the other waitresses sat around watching the proceedings while filling salt and pepper shakers and rolling napkins. She longed to be watching with the group from Montague Farm who would no doubt have interesting things to say.

A few months earlier, after moving to the farm, Gary and Rae had a picnic on a blanket in the apple orchard where he coaxed Rae into telling her family history. She explained that her full name was

Ruth Anne Kelliher, the name recorded on her baptism certificate at St. Mary's Roman Catholic Church in Portsmouth, Ohio.

"Basically," she continued, "my whole world, until going to college, was our family house in the little town of Rosemount, Ohio, a few miles from a bigger town, Portsmouth, on the north bank of the Ohio river."

Seeing that she still had Gary's attention, she went on to describe her parents. Her mother, Dot, short for Dorothy, grew up in an even smaller town called Firewall, on the south side of the river in Kentucky. Both her parents have Irish and German heritage.

"We're more Appalachian than Southern." Rae explained to Gary that she resembles her mother—nearly six feet tall, straw-colored hair, same pert nose and crooked smile. "I'd come home from school and she'd be sitting at the kitchen table smoking a cigarette and reading a magazine. She was a super volunteer at our Catholic elementary school, organizing cake raffles and dressing up as a fortune teller at the annual church bazaar. I inherited my love of dress-up and costumes from my mother, who insisted on hand-sewing our Halloween costumes."

"My dad is named Maurice, known to friends and family as 'Mac.' He worked for a plumbing company out of Portsmouth, installing heating and air conditioning units. During my high school years, he started his own independent business. Toby apprenticed with him and got his trade license. Dad changed the name on his truck to Kelliher & Sons.

"It's a family joke," Rae explained, since he had two children and only one son. 'There's room for you in the family business,' he would say to me. My mom did the books and billing, so those three were in business together. I was the odd one out. We are economically precarious. My parents worry a lot about money."

Rae lit up describing her brother Toby. "He was loving and protective. He rescued me from all kinds of perilous situations, like getting locked in closets and barn rooms. Once I had climbed too high in a tree and froze up from fear. He climbed up next to me and gently coached me down. He encouraged my reading and my endless questions about how things worked. I was a bookish nature girl, returning from adventures in the woods with Toby carrying favorite rocks, bird feathers, and crowns of wildflowers woven together."

She thought silently about her teen years, her body growing tall and curvy, attracting a lot of attention at Notre Dame High school and at Patty's restaurant. But she found most of the boys, including sometimes her brother, to be foolish and immature. She formed a few friendships, mostly with cousins and teachers.

"I got a lot of encouragement at home and school to be the first person in my family to go to college. This created some tension with my brother."

"You don't have a Southern accent," Gary observed.

"Yeah, that's true. Wait until you meet my brother. He's pure Kentucky."

Rae's father drove her to college for her sophomore year, deliberately taking two days to explore a northern route across the Allegheny mountains and the New York thruway so they could stop along the way. Mac wanted to see Drake's Well in Oil City, where the first oil derrick spouted in 1859. She wanted to go to Seneca Falls to see where the 1848 conference on women's suffrage was held. They made both stops.

They talked about their family and a little about the state of the world. As a Nixon supporter, her dad was incensed by the Watergate process. The Kellihers had all sat together on a humid August night and watched Nixon's resignation speech on their black-and-white TV. "What a crying shame," her father said, watching the speech.

Mac couldn't relate to anything about the college experience, and Rae didn't share much. She knew that after he dropped her off, he would drive nonstop back to Ohio, not wanting to miss another day's work or spend money on a motel.

Throughout their trip, her dad was concerned, bordering on agitated, about how few things she was bringing to college. "That's all you have?"

Rae had brought one large camping backpack, a duffel bag of winter clothes, a milk crate of books and notebooks, a sleeping bag, and a Huffy bicycle ("made in Dayton, Ohio," as her father regularly pointed out). She had to reassure him that she was choosing simplicity, not broadcasting their poverty.

Her father's concern was no doubt a reaction to the previous year, when he and Rae's mother both drove her east for freshman year. Her parents watched in awe as wealthy Amherst College families pulled up in large station wagons—and in one case a moving van—and unloaded recliner chairs, lamps, fancy stereo systems, framed paintings, and trunks of who knows what.

Rae's freshman roommate, a preppy girl from a wealthy New York City suburb, had shown up with a four-season wardrobe, twenty stuffed animals, a makeup table with a mirror (and extra light bulbs), a miniature fridge, and bulk boxes of snacks. Rae's parents were uncharacteristically quiet upon meeting the girl's parents, who were dressed like they were going to a fancy restaurant and asked lots of probing questions about her hometown in Ohio and what her parents did for work. For weeks after her arrival, Rae's parents sent her care packages, things they could scarcely afford, including a desk lamp just like her roommate's and some of the same snacks. With each package, tears rushed to Rae's eyes at the thought of this indirect form of love and sacrifice coming from her parents.

While Rae's parents felt shame and embarrassment about the Amherst class divide, Rae initially felt confusion. But by the end of her first year, she felt disgust and amusement at the foibles of these affluent students who cared nothing about the world beyond their elite social circle.

On their second fall trip to college, Mac didn't linger. He took her for pizza in Amherst and kissed her goodbye, giving her a wrinkled hundred-dollar bill that he had probably been saving folded up in his wallet all summer. Rae felt momentarily bereft as she watched his truck pull away.

That night, she wrote in her journal: *Mac gone, motoring home through the night. Thinks I'm going to embarrass the family with my poverty. Went to see his historic oil well. Not much to talk about. He doesn't want to hear about Chile or Vietnam. His Nixon world turned upside down. What am I doing here? Feels like I parachuted into a country club of kids who have no idea what's going down. I wonder what's happening at Montague Farm?*

After one week of college, Rae had reached her limit. She found it unsettling to sit in beautiful wood-paneled classroom talking about *Middlemarch* while there was a war raging in Vietnam, a US-backed coup unfolding in Chile, and a new president threatening to pardon the former crook in the White House. She went to the Amherst College administration to tell them she was quitting. She asked if she could get a refund of her $150 student activity fee, which brought consternation from the dean.

"We'll just say you're taking a medical leave," said the dean. "You can always reenroll."

"Thanks," Rae said, imagining no scenario where that might happen.

Rae called Nina at the farm from the payphone at the end of her dorm hallway. Her head was spinning from her decision. She told Nina, in a quaking voice, that she had quit college and had nowhere to go. With no hesitation, Nina said, "You can come here. I'll be there in forty minutes to pick you up."

Back from the pickle factory, Rae surveys her room. Her worldly possessions perfectly fill her attic digs, her milk crate turned sideways as bookshelf, her sleeping bag on a single twin mattress. She slips on a pair of baggy overalls, pulls on her favorite pine-green woolen sweater, and heads down to the kitchen and common area.

Rae's housemates Gary, Peter, and Sarah are cooking up a feast of a dinner in the enormous farm kitchen with both a wood-fired stove and a gas range. Rae sets the large oblong table with room for fifteen. They are brimming with excited chatter. They have spent the day opening up a new office for what they are calling the Alternative Energy Coalition in Turners Falls, one of the five villages of Montague and the one that had the most commercial storefront space.

Peter, like many of the men at the farm, has long hair and wears antiquated vests that he collects from tag sales. He tells Rae that Northeast Utilities recently announced plans to build a twin nuclear reactor on the plains of Montague at the cost of $1.5 billion, the biggest of its kind ever proposed. As Sarah can recite by heart, the plant will also suck up twenty thousand gallons of water from the Connecticut River every day, and will be cooled with two six-hundred-foot-tall towers.

At a meeting of farm residents, shortly after Rae's arrival, they together affirmed their opposition to the plant. "Let's be a center for abolition," said Peter at the time. "Let's stop the plant in Montague and help support opposition efforts around the country."

Their timing is auspicious. The 1973 energy crisis has shocked US politicians into wanting to reduce dependence on foreign oil. The Nixon/Ford administration has proposed building more than two hundred nuclear power plants, along with more domestic coal mines, power plants, and oil refineries. Rae has studied the proposed map, released by the government, illustrated with dots for potential sites for a dozen new nuclear power plants in New England, including Montague, Massachusetts, and Seabrook, New Hampshire.

Sarah rings the dinner bell on the back porch, and a dozen people begin to trickle into the kitchen, grabbing seats, glasses of water, bottles of beer, and cloth napkins rolled up in a cubby holder with everyone's individual slots. Emmy comes in carrying four-year old Sequoyah, chattering away about bugs. Verandah, visiting from the Total Loss Farm community in Guilford, bounces an infant in her lap, and Michael shepherds two five-year-olds, Echo and Skye, to the table. The kids are so integrated with all the adults that it took Rae a week after her arrival to figure out who the biological parents are. One parent quipped that it is like living at a kibbutz where the children are everyone's responsibility.

"Vegetable stir-fry with tofu and brown rice," Peter announces while ceremonially placing a large black wok on the table and lifting off the lid, releasing steam fragrant with saffron and other spices.

"Chicken thighs," announces Gary, offering up his pan of chicken and homemade barbecue sauce. Gary winks at Rae, his large bushy eyebrows bouncing about.

"And fresh pickles," Sarah boasts. Rae glances at Nina, who sticks out her tongue with mock nausea.

They briefly hold hands around the table, in a silent blessing. When everyone's eyes open, Sequoyah chirps loudly, "Rubbadub-dub, thanks for the grub. Yeahhhhh God!" The others chuckle and cheer.

"I passed a new apartment building going up in Sunderland today," said Sam, biting down on a pickle. "The marketing sign says 'Total Electric Living.' They're probably banking on nuclear power being too cheap to meter."

"Crazeee," responds Peter. "I'll bet Northeast Utilities is going around to these developers and getting them to back the nuke."

"How's the office coming in Turners?" asks Nina, passing her plate to Peter for a big scoop from the stir-fry.

"Great," says Sarah. "We got the sign up over the window, moved in some furniture, and set up a couple desks. Tomorrow I have to hang around waiting for the phone company."

"I think we need to bring the lessons of the civil rights movement to this," says Sam. "We need to think like SNCC—the Student Nonviolent Coordinating Committee. How do we open up the non-violent action wing of the safe-energy movement?"

"Protests," says Peter. "You know, blocking construction."

"If they've got the bulldozers lined up, it's too late," says Sam, his passion level rising. "The problem is we have no recourse. The laws are rigged in favor of the industry."

"No recourse," Nina repeats. "We need to go outside normal channels."

"Outside the law," affirms Sam. "They aren't building that plant. Not over my body."

"Use your body to stop the machine, as Thoreau said," says Peter, paraphrasing a quote from an article he is writing.

Rae takes in this conversation as she pushes the stir-fry around her plate. She can't imagine wanting to be anywhere else.

One sunny, crisp Saturday in January, Rae and Sam are washing dishes after breakfast. Rae watches him from behind, his pony-tail falling down over his orange flannel shirt. He's tall and reedy, but Rae finds him attractive for his sly humor and playfulness with the kids at the farm. She is slightly flustered when he invites

her to go for a walk around the Montague Plains. Rae knows that
Sam has a girlfriend in Seattle who has visited for extended peri-
ods, so it isn't a flirtation. Or is it? She eagerly says yes.

They borrow Nina's car and drive over to Lake Pleasant, another
one of Montague's five villages and the smallest and most remote.
Rae has never been there.

They park near the frozen lake and begin walking on a snowy
circumference road. Sam asks Rae about her reasons for leaving
Amherst College. Rae explains about her deep feelings of "I gotta
get out of this place" while sitting in her classes at Amherst.

"It's good you did that," Sam assures her. "There's a lot of fucked
up things in the world that need our attention. College is not the
answer."

He also attended Amherst College. "At Amherst, one of one of
my classmates was David Eisenhower, the son of the president. One
the squarest dudes I'd ever met."

Sam tells her about growing up in Wilbraham, Massachusetts,
where at a young age he worked at a neighbor's orchard and learned
to love growing fruit. Rae feels a spark of attraction walking with
Sam.

They walk past a weathered building with a sign reading
"National Spiritual Alliance." They see no people. But there are a few
indications of humans living through the winter in buildings that
were built as summer cottages: plastic-wrapped doors and windows and old cars sitting next to shoveled walkways. Sam explains
that Lake Pleasant has been a destination since the 1870s as a camp
for "spiritualists."

"What's a spiritualist?" asks Rae.

"The spiritualists are interesting." Sam packs a small snowball
with his bare hands and throws it at a tree. "They believe the soul is
eternal, that life extends past these bodies we are in, that the spirit
lives on. They talk to the dead, do séances. Their leaders can channel
messages from the other side. There were a bunch of encampments
like this around New England."

They walk away from Lake Pleasant and toward the Montague
Plains, a large, open, sandy area with scrub pines and rolling fields.
A mid-January thaw has melted the snow. As they emerge from a

grove of trees, they see a giant tower rising five hundred feet, with blinking lights and weather instruments.

"That's the tower that Northeast Utilities put up to get weather data for their nuke project," Sam says, pointing upward. "Let's take a closer look."

They walk closer to the tower and peer straight up. Rae strains to look up at the full colossus of metal beams and thinks it looks like a space invader from *The War of the Worlds*. "Freaky."

Sam lights a cigarette and squats on his haunches at the base of the cables, studying their assembly.

"Look at these plains," says Sam, standing up and extending his arms. "It's a huge underground aquifer. It's like a filter for all this water that flows into the Connecticut River. A few years ago, the town was considering this as a dump site, so we could make money hosting Boston's garbage. But they decided against it because toxins would leach into the aquifer. So now they want to put a nuke here? Madness!"

Rae quietly gazes across the plains, with its sandy loam soil and scrubby pine trees. She tries to envision the giant underground waterway and feel its flowing vibration.

When they get back to the car, Sam lights another cigarette. "Hey Rae, can you keep a secret?"

"Sure," says Rae, her heart beating a little faster. She wonders if this might be a profession of affection.

"I think I'm gonna knock over that tower," Sam says. "As a way to draw attention to the nuke and the fact that we have no other way to stop it."

"Right on," smiles Rae, a tad disappointed. "Your secret is safe with me."

∾

One evening, after dinner, Rae gets a call on the farm telephone line from her brother Toby, calling long distance.

"Rae, what are you doing?" Toby says. She envisions him sitting in the family kitchen at the house in Rosemount, speaking into the handset that is attached with a long spiral cord to their one phone, mounted on the kitchen wall. When they were growing up, whoever washed dishes got to the privilege of talking on the phone after dinner. All their phone calls were public affairs.

"I'm working at a pickle factory," Rae says impishly. "You would like these pickles, Toby."

Toby doesn't see any humor in this. "You could work in a factory here in Portsmouth and live at home," he said. "What happened to the college education and the free ride you got?"

"It wasn't working for me." Rae hears a defensiveness in her own voice. "It was a waste of time. The world is going to hell. I just couldn't sit and discuss nineteenth-century literature, okay?"

"Well, you could study something useful. Like business or computers," says Toby. "Jesus—Mom and Dad are so worried."

Rae has had heart-to-heart conversations with both her parents. "Are you sure? They seem to understand," says Rae. "They haven't said anything to me."

"They aren't getting any younger," says Toby, a statement that Rae can't make sense of. Her parents are in their mid-fifties, but they're pretty robust and healthy. *Is Toby trying to make me feel guilty?*

"Amherst College is a bunch of rich kids, Toby," she said, repeating a put-down she's heard him say before.

"Yeah, Dad told me about taking you there," Toby replies. "Are you going to come home?"

"And work at Patty's?" says Rae.

"What's a matter with Patty's? You too good for us all now?" There's an uncharacteristic meanness in his voice. Rae thinks of the few times she injudiciously betrayed her feelings about the limits of their small Ohio town.

"No, Toby, that's not it. I like it here. I'm living with this great group of people at this farm in a town called Montague. You would love it here. It's like home. We've got a big river, the Connecticut, that reminds me of the Ohio. And lots of rolling hills. It doesn't cost me much. It's sort of a commune." She knows that's the wrong word the moment it comes out of her mouth.

"Commune?" mocked Toby. "Do you have a boyfriend?"

"A few . . ."

"'A few'?" Toby interjects, with a sneer in his voice.

"I mean not all at once," Rae sputters. "A few *possibilities* is what I mean. Nothing serious."

Why does she feel so under attack and defensive? She envisions Toby twirling his dirty blond hair with his finger. When she last saw him two months ago, he was growing a patchy beard and wearing a seed-company cap on his head. He was on track to be a "mini-Mac," a replica of their father.

After she hangs up, she walks outside and looks up at the stars, exhaling her tension. The truth is she does feel some guilt about leaving home. *I selfishly want my own life. My life path is different.*

Rae remembers a time years earlier. She is eight. Toby is only two years older, but seems to Rae much more worldly. He takes her to a secret place in the woods that he and his friends like to explore on the border of a state forest.

"I'm taking you to water wonderland," says Toby in her memory. "But you can't tell anyone about this place."

"Okay," says wide-eyed Rae, aware of the privilege of accompanying her big brother to this important place. She suspects that this is where he and his friend Robin escape to.

They walk down a forest path, passing a large copper beech tree, surrounded by saplings, and continue toward a ravine and swamp. The path winds slightly downhill and along the edge of spongy terrain, but then continues up a small rise and onto a drier plateau. Farther along, they come to the first of several truck-size boulders that form the perimeter of the magic area. The trail peters out into a deer path, and Toby stops next to two boulders that create a passage.

"This is the entrance," Toby says. "I'm not sure a girl has ever been here." This is said with more speculation than a tone of willful exclusion. He squeezes Rae's hand.

They slide between the two rocks and enter an old-growth grove of tall hardwood trees, protected from logging by the lack of roads and access through the rocks. They arrive at a small pond. There is a primitive raft that the boys have constructed, leaning against a tree.

But what catches Rae's eye is a small mossy peninsula that sticks out into the pond.

Toby leads her onto the peninsula, which is only about four feet wide, and kneels down at the end, looking into the water.

"If we sit here for a while, you'll see lots of things," Toby says quietly. "But we have to be quiet."

Rae sits down beside him as he touches the water.

"Here, the first thing we do is lie on our backs and look up at the sky and treetops," says Toby, initiating Rae into the practice that he has done dozens of times with his friends. They lie side by side on the moss, which is dew-dropped but not sopping wet. They both gaze up into the treetops, watching several squirrels bounce across the limbs. The noise of a woodpecker fills the air, and Toby points to the area where the noise came from. "Piliated," he says authoritatively.

A large bullfrog lets out a croak and there's a splashing noise from the pond. Rae turns her head and sees five turtles sunning on a log.

They lie quietly for half an hour, losing track of time. She feels safe here, far from home, with her big brother. And she has a glowing feeling inside from his trust and her initiation.

Toby gets up and starts hunting for mushrooms in the water wonderland. He finds a morel, and then another. He shows Rae how to study the leaf litter and let her eyes adjust until she spots her first mushroom. Soon she has eight, then nine, going into Toby's cap. He shows her the false morel, which is poisonous, placing them side by side and pointing out the differences.

They return to the house and Toby pulls out a stick of butter, cuts up the mushrooms, warms a pan, and fries them up. He places them, luscious and steamy, on a plate in the center of the kitchen table and they eat them with toothpicks.

Rae smacks her lips and says, "This is the most delicious thing I have ever tasted."

For years to come, in all seasons, they return to the water wonderland. "You can bring a book if you want," encourages Toby, and he even finds a waterproof bag to protect her books. This is the beginning of Rae's journal-writing practice, starting with a small black bound book. She always brings a novel, a history book, or a nature guide, along with her journal. In the spring, they listen for the first peepers and glimpses of frog spawn. They hunt mushrooms and catch and release turtles. They float on the raft, gazing at the pond bottom.

Rae spends a lot of time looking at the rocks exposed by the tiny stream and pond. Something about these rocks speaks to Rae with their enduring power. She writes: *What stories can they tell?* She collects a few that adorn her room. One rock has an extraordinary design on it, a sort of three-dimensional cell structure. Rae names it "the eye of god," and she places it on the windowsill next to her bed. A few years later, she renames it "the eye of the goddess" and writes: *A rock you can talk to.*

The water wonderland is the place where she and Toby's friend Robin exchange an innocent and awkward first kiss, lying nervously on the mossy outcropping. At thirteen, Robin is a gentle boy, and he is immediately embarrassed and apologetic for kissing a girl two years younger.

They all three become savvy mushroom hunters, able to identify a dozen varieties that they are comfortable harvesting and three poisonous ones to avoid. After rainstorms, the forest is full of bounty, especially as their eyes adjust. They gather chanterelles, puffballs, and hen-of-the-woods mushrooms, bringing them home to cook up.

Years later, as young teenagers, Rae, Robin, and Toby venture off to visit their secret haunt. Rae notices that the two boys wear almost identical jeans and work boots. They each carry air rifles that they use to shoot BBs at soda pop cans.

A half mile up the trail, they come across a freshly cut logging road in their path. Savagely hacked-down trees clutter the previously serene woodlands, with piles of slash and briars. A large area has been surveyed and staked out, with trees wrapped in red ribbon slated to be cut down for some kind of access road.

Rae watches Robin and Toby as they absorb the assault on their forest. Robin is visibly shaken. "Damn!" he yells. "Fuckers. Some developers are coming in here."

"How long until they come for the water wonderland?" says Toby, shaking his head in disgust. New subdivisions have been popping up around the town. Favorite patches of forest and open fields are being converted to cul-de-sacs at an alarming rate.

The boys each pull out matching hunting knives from their pockets and begin cutting the ribbons from the trees. Toby pulls up the survey stakes and makes a pile, igniting them with his yellow BIC lighter.

"Rae," he commands. "Grab those survey stakes." Rae follows the route of the stakes as they wind through the woods, pulling up each one and carrying a pile back to Toby. He adds them to his fire.

"We may not stop them," says Toby. "But we can slow them down."

"Hell, I'll be back the next time they stake this," says Robin. "They're not taking this forest down while I'm here."

In her journal, Rae writes: *Toby and Robin are defending the forest. I love them both.*

One night at Montague Farm, Rae is startled awake in her attic room.

"Hey Rae," someone whispers into her darkened room. "You awake?"

"Is that Sam?" Rae whispers in the almost pitch black. "What time is it?"

"Sorry to wake you," Sam whispers back. "It's about 1:00 a.m. Remember that thing I have to do? I wonder if you could give me a ride down the road."

"Sure." Rae switches on her light and looks for her clothes. Her sleepiness quickly gives way to a spark of intimacy in secretly helping Sam with his action. "I'll be down in a minute."

It is Presidents Day, a long weekend, so no pickle plant today. She can go back to sleep after giving Sam his ride. She dresses and finds Sam in the kitchen, standing by the woodstove, wearing sneakers. He has stuffed his feet into wool socks and plastic bags. She looks at his boyish grin, his calm demeanor.

"You don't have boots?" she asks. There are now several inches of fresh snow on the ground.

"No, but my birthday is coming up," Sam deadpans.

They walk out into the frigid February night and Rae starts up Nina's car, the pickle jar express. Sam sits in the passenger seat with a couple of large metal tools, one that looks like a crowbar, between his legs.

They drive three miles toward Turners Falls and Sam points her onto a side road. "You can drop me near where we went for a walk that day."

"Sam, are you gonna . . ."

"Don't ask, Rae," he says carefully. "I don't want you involved. And this ride never happened. It's our secret. If anyone asks, I walked here."

"Okay, Sam."

Rae pulls to the side of the road. She can see the tower lights flickering on the plain, maybe a half mile away. Her excitement turns to concern. It's a hulking tower. "You gonna be okay?"

"It's going to be a great day," he smiles, lighting a cigarette and pausing for a moment before opening the door. "I'm prepared in my head and heart. I even wrote up my statement."

"Right on," says Rae, turning in her seat to look at Sam. He leans back in his seat, his long hair tucked under a wool cap for warmth, his skinny, lanky body barely filling out the rest of his clothes. "It's a new moon, very dark."

"Yes, that's the idea."

"Should I wait? Or come look for you in a while?"

"Naw, I'll figure it out." Sam smiles and pops open the door of the Nova. "Get out of here and remember this never happened."

Rae turns the car around, listening to the crunch of snow. When she looks up, Sam has disappeared into the darkness. She returns to the farm, strips off her winter clothes and slips back into bed. But she lies awake, thinking. *What if it falls on him, or a cable snaps? Should I go check on him?* She falls into a fitfull sleep.

Within a day, all of Franklin County knows what Sam had done. He walked to the tower and, using his crowbar, loosened the turnbuckles holding the cables in place. It took him almost forty-five minutes to disconnect the first cable and it went zinging into the night. Every couple seconds the scene was illuminated by a flashing strobe light at the top of the tower, disrupting the darkness of a moonless night. After disconnecting the third cable, he watched the tower sway and buckle, collapsing on itself and making a noise that Sam described to his housemates as "the twang of a five-hundred-foot guitar string."

Sam then walked to the Turners Falls Road, flagged down a Montague police car, and asked for a ride to police headquarters. He turned himself in to the police, handing the sergeant his four-page typewritten statement explaining his action and the dangers of nuclear power.

Rae is incensed that the *Greenfield Recorder* published a scathing editorial on its front page. One columnist compared Sam to assassins Lee Harvey Oswald, Sirhan Sirhan, and John Wilkes Booth. In conservative Montague, with a population of roughly eight thousand residents, there is an initial rejection of Samuel Lovejoy and his "destruction of property."

Rae and several members of the farm drive to Greenfield for Sam's arraignment. She sits behind him in the courtroom, where he represents himself. He is charged with "willful and malicious destruction of property," a felony with a five-year prison sentence. He pleads "absolutely non-guilty" and says that he looks forward to a trial where he will present his defense. He is released on personal recognizance.

At the pickle factory, Rae and Nina find themselves in lunchtime arguments with fellow workers, defending Sam's tower action. Sam is right about one thing: his action gets attention. But Rae isn't always sure it's the right attention.

"People are very hung up about private property," Sam says at dinner one night in frustration.

Rae watches with excitement as the pace of life at the farm quickens. The phone rings off the hook, both at the farm and at the new Turners Falls office, with people offering to volunteer and get involved. Sam retreats to a shed with a pile of law books and a notepad, intent on acting as his own attorney. Rae occasionally brings him a sandwich and a cup of tea, and he is humbled and appreciative. Farm-community members help with press statements, support rallies, and community outreach to neighbors.

As the weather warms, Rae joins others in staffing information tables at the supermarket and food co-op, canvassing door to door, and organizing teach-ins around the Pioneer Valley. As Sam's trial approaches, she quits her job at the pickle factory to do full-time activism. She has saved a couple thousand dollars and knows she can always go back to pickles.

Sam is true to his word, never mentioning to anyone Rae's giving him a ride or her advance knowledge of his plan. Occasionally he winks at her when talking about his four-mile midnight walk to the tower. Rae feels an illicit pleasure in this secret. And only she knows that he probably wouldn't have made it in his plastic-bag-lined sneakers.

A trial date is set for the middle of September. Sam, Sarah, Peter, and a whole team work together to frame the arguments and line up expert and personal character witnesses for Sam. While Sam is intent on representing himself, he leans on local attorney Tom Lesser for guidance. Rae is not included in this circle and feels a pang of exclusion. But she also knows she has little experience to contribute.

On the first day of the trial, Rae and a dozen of Montague Farm residents fill the wooden benches at the Franklin County Courthouse. Rae looks around the room and nods to the dozens of people she knows.

The judge, Roger McNaughton, who looks to Rae like the cartoon character Elmer Fudd, presides over jury selection and the opening arguments. On the first full day of the trial, the entire jury and legal teams board buses and cars and drive to the scene of the crime on the Montague Plains. The tower has been rebuilt and is now protected by an eight-foot-high security fence, barbed wire, and alarm sensors. Rae joins the crowd as over one hundred people tour the scene.

Sam makes an impromptu speech, talking about the "mighty aquifer" below the ground they are standing on. The judge becomes visibly nervous, and one of the prosecuting attorneys formally objects to "Mr. Lovejoy's" soliloquy. The judge instructs the jurors to disregard Lovejoy's speech on the environmental significance of the Montague Plains.

Back in the courtroom, Rae figits in her seat as the prosecution begins its case tediously, calling on police officers and utility officials to review the rudimentary basics of the crime, facts that Sam is not contesting. Rae grows sleepy at one point, leaving the courtroom to get a cup of coffee and walk around the center of Greenfield. Finally, the prosecution rests its case and it is Sam's turn to present his defense.

Sam argues that he is motivated by a higher value of defense of community. Rae sits in his sightline and beams at him with affection, as if he is speaking to her alone. In the face of great harm and danger, Sam argues it was his civic duty to take action to stop the dangerous nuclear power plant from being built.

The defense calls an expert witness, Dr. John Gofman, a scientist, expert on nuclear power, and outspoken critic of the Atomic Energy Commission. Sam was greatly influenced by Gofman's book, *Poisoned Power*, the dog-eared copy of which is in Rae's purse.

Gofman begins his testimony reviewing the dangers of nuclear power and the lack of real oversight of those from outside the self-interested industry. Judge McNaughton, however, halts the testimony. He eventually rules that Gofman can testify, but not in front of the jury. *Unbelievable*, thinks Rae. *How is this possible?*

The jury is sent off to play pinochle in the jury room while Gofman offers blistering testimony on the Atomic Energy Commission's lax standards on radiation exposure, a "license to commit murder," in Gofman's words. The AEC, Gofman argues, is focused on helping power operators recover their investments, not on protecting the public. When he talks about the health dangers of plutonium, Rae cannot avoid squirming in her seat, feeling her body bombarded by dangerous radioactive rays. Why risk an accident, Gofman notes, when "we have so many safer ways to generate energy?"

The defense's next witness is historian Howard Zinn, who tells the court and jury that Sam is acting in the great tradition of Henry David Thoreau, Mahatma Gandhi, and others who engaged in civil disobedience in response to a higher calling. He even mentions the courageous witness of abolitionist Elijah P. Lovejoy, a distant cousin of Sam's, who was hanged by a pro-slavery mob in Illinois in 1837.

Rae is riveted by Zinn's testimony and his command of history. Many years later she reads Zinn's book, *The People's History of the United States*, and remembers the day she saw him in court. She would recount that Zinn's testimony sparked her lifelong interest in becoming a history nerd.

After these expert witnesses, Sam calls several character witnesses, including the librarian and constable from the neighboring town of Gill who talk about Sam's integrity, civic-mindedness, and generous character. Another neighbor testifies that he bought the busted-up tower for $250 and has built three windmills from the materials. By the end of this testimony, Rae believes it will be impossible for the jury to view Sam as someone with "malicious intent."

At the end, Sam takes the stand. Though he has served as his own attorney, his friend and attorney Tom Lesser poses six hours of questions. Sam accuses the Atomic Energy Commission of being a "kangaroo court . . . a panel that acts as promoter and regulator, judge, jury, and thief all rolled into one." In the end, he tells the jury, his action was inspired by four-year-old Sequoyah at the farm, who couldn't defend herself. He had to act.

After the testimony, Judge McNaughton convenes the court to dismiss the case on a technicality. Rae can't believe this is happening and feels deflated and then angry. Having studied the faces of the jurors during the trial, Rae believes they would have voted to acquit Sam, which would be a great victory for the anti-nuclear-power movement.

Sam begs the judge not to dismiss the case but allow his guilt or innocence to be determined by the jury and the "people of Franklin County." Rae sits in her pew and prays, *No. No. No.* But McNaughton calls in the jury and orders them to render a verdict of "Not Guilty."

Despite the disappointing end to the trial, there is a great celebration at the farm that night. To Rae's relief, Sam is, after all, innocent and free. He lifts a glass of bubbly and toasts his community and little Sequoyah, who has already been whisked off to bed. Rae gets a little tipsy and joins several of the other women dancing to disco on a boom box. She gives Sam a hug that lasts a bit too long for him and offers a messy kiss. As she lies in bed, her room spins slowly. She writes in her journal one sentence before drifting off: *I love Sam. Look at what one person can do.*

ACRES OF CLAMS

(1977)

"I walk the line, because you're mine," Rae sings to Nina.

"Is that a railroad song or a prison song?" asks Nina.

"Hmm. Prison, I think." Rae feels giddy from excitement and sleep deprivation. "Guess we should get our prison work song repertoire together."

Rae and her affinity group from Montague Farm, including Nina, Peter, and Sarah, cross onto the railroad tracks leading to the Seabrook Station nuclear power plant construction zone. She's wearing tan army boots and a large rain poncho over her green woolen sweater. Over her shoulders is her backpack with sleeping bag, army canteen, and extra woolen socks. While essentially prepared for a back-country camping trip, Rae and the others are ready to occupy the Seabrook site for as long as it takes.

It is May Day, 1977, and more than two thousand protesters are moving toward the site, probably the largest anti-nuclear civil disobedience in US history. The leaders of the New England–based coalition, called the Clamshell Alliance, have been inspired by the anti-nuclear movement in Germany, where more than twenty thousand protesters blocked a power plant in Wyhl. Some affinity groups are singing songs like "We Shall Not Be Moved" and "Acres of

Clams." Rae blinks her eyes at the sight of hundreds of people filing in ahead and behind her. There has been elaborate planning with groups entering the site from the north, south, and west, and from the water to the east.

It wasn't long after Sam Lovejoy toppled the tower in Montague that Northeast Utilities suspended their plans to build that power plant. But a few months later, Rae read that New Hampshire's utility, the Public Service Company, is planning to build a double nuclear-power plant on the New Hampshire coast, in the hamlet of Seabrook. Local seacoast residents opposed the plant, but as with many mega-energy projects, the plans were rammed through over local objections. The utility immediately began to clear the land for construction, and now the Clamshell Alliance intends to block further work on the site.

This time Rae is at the center of the action, learning new skills and finding her own purpose in the growing Clamshell Alliance movement. The "Clams" have an elaborate governing structure and consensus-based decision-making process. Each affinity group—usually eight to fifteen people—is like a small New England town meeting. They, in turn, are affiliated with a regional council, with Rae's Montague group linked to a Western Mass "cluster."

Within each affinity group are people prepared to be arrested and others who agree to support them. Every affinity group member has been through elaborate nonviolent direct-action training where they role-play conflict and arrest scenarios, review the principles of nonviolence, and mentally prepare for arrest.

Rae is impressed by the Clamshell Alliance nonviolent training collective, led by several people she finds to be charismatic, funny, and essential to the tone and success of actions. They are sage and skilled meeting facilitators, artful in weaving points together, and firm in limiting the expositions of the blabbermouths. Over the winter, she is invited to a weekend "training of trainers" where she builds a new set of friends and connections. In Western Mass, she co-leads a dozen trainings for Clamshell participants in anticipation of today. To her delight, Rae is now included in the strategy meetings and has become a central figure in the local activist in-group. And instead of sitting quietly in the back, Rae is now at the front of the room.

There is 100 percent alignment on today's action scenario: walk to the entrance of the plant, scale the fences if necessary, and occupy the construction site. Rae is impressed with how the Clamshell leaders have been transparent with the New Hampshire State Police, informing them of the plan so that there will be no surprises. The police, in turn, are equally prepared with several hundred troopers and a dozen school buses to transport the detainees.

Rae is exhilarated as she witnesses the painstaking plans come together. Two thousand protesters enter the site and set up a mini-village overnight. Rae learns that Howard Zinn is camped out just one row over from her, and she sets out to see him. She finds him standing by a tree wearing a blue rain poncho and a black cap and smoking a cigarette. She introduces herself as a housemate of Sam Lovejoy who attended his trial testimony.

"That was a great trial," says Zinn. "Too bad your judge wouldn't let the jury of his peers acquit him."

Rae is a bit starstruck and moved by the fact that the professor and scholar is camped out with a mostly younger crowd, willing to risk arrest for what he believes.

The next day, Rae is handcuffed, fingerprinted, and transported to the Somersworth Armory, one of five armories that the state has prepared to hold the protesters. She feels grounded through the whole process, even leading a few songs on the bus to the armory. New Hampshire governor Meldrim Thomson, a devotee of "the peaceful atom," is irate with the troublemakers and wants to punish them. Yet there is no single jail that can hold all of the 1,414 protesters who are arrested. At this point, no one anticipates that they will be confined to the armory for two weeks.

The guards march Rae and 250 other protesters into a large open room of army cots. She is pleased that they are allowed to bring their camping gear and belongings with them, including musical instruments, juggling balls, and craft projects.

The prisoners immediately set about self-organizing a programmed "village" of activities, making the most of their time in captivity. There are, of course, long meetings. But several groups form to coordinate concerts and workshops on various topics; a media committee is formed to talk to journalists, as well as another committee to formally liaison with the guards.

Rae joins the facilitators group, taking turns facilitating meetings. But she has a fair amount of free time to roam about talking to others, attend workshops, and even lie on her cot and read the autobiography of Emma Goldman, *Living My Life*. Rae feels more alive than she ever has, making new friends and finding people looking to her for leadership.

What they jokingly call the "Somersworth University" is full of daily lectures and workshops, the schedule written up on large butcher paper. Topics include civil rights history, beekeeping, nonviolent theory, juggling, and safe-energy policy. The evenings are filled with sing-alongs led by a surprising number of talented musicians who are among the detained.

In one corner of the armory, Rae is drawn to a buzz of conversation around one man who has embarked on a hunger strike. She has met Chuck Matthei before, a Clamshell leader who is well versed in direct action and movement history.

A crowd of fellow prisoners, guards, and state officials have gathered around Chuck, a twenty-nine-year-old who sits resolutely on his cot. Matthei has a long reddish beard and the beginning of a bald spot. For three days, he has refused to take in food. Rae stands close by and listens as a National Guard doctor presses him to end his hunger strike.

"I'll start eating again if you let my friends and me walk free," Chuck explains to the physician in a pleasant but firm voice. He means his 1,413 friends spread among the five armories.

"Well, we can't let you go," says the National Guard doctor. "You broke the law."

"The construction of this power plant would cause greater harm," Chuck responds. "My conscience requires that I put my body in the way of its construction."

"Listen, you need to eat," says the doctor. "You could get very sick, including brain damage."

"Sir, as a physician, have you studied the health risks of a nuclear accident?"

"Yes, of course."

"Is this an acceptable risk to you? A nuclear accident? Can't we adopt safer forms of energy? You understand that this entire project is being driven by guaranteed profits for the utility shareholders?"

The doctor doesn't respond but seems befuddled by this man who won't eat because of his convictions.

"Open the door and let us out of here—and I'll eat. You're in charge."

"I'm not in charge, believe me," says the doctor, revealing his own impatience with the state. The newspapers are full of criticism of Governor Thomson—especially for the cost of imprisoning all these harmless people. "I think it's silly . . . ," he starts to whisper, but he doesn't finish his sentence.

"If you don't agree, why do you still work for illegitimate authority?"

"Wait a second," says the doctor, exasperated. "We're talking about *your* health, not my conscience."

"We all have choices. Just tell the attorney general to let us out, and I'll start eating."

The doctor throws up his hands and walks away. Rae is intrigued to watch Chuck make this powerful witness, to hear someone essentially say, "*You may have my body, but I still have power.*" But she also feels slightly uneasy with his righteous tone.

She writes in her journal: *Who does he think he is—Mahatma Gandhi? Saint Chuck? Here he is solemnly dying on a cot, and the rest of the protesters are having a carnival around him.*

The exchanges between the doctor and Chuck continue for six more days. Each day the doctor seems to enjoy his conversations with the hunger striker a bit more. Rae walks by and sees him nodding, laughing, and lingering at the side of Chuck's cot. Finally, the guards pick Chuck up and deposit him on the sidewalk outside the armory. But instead of leaving, he remains there for two more days, fasting until everyone is released.

After two weeks, Governor Thomson capitulates, releasing the prisoners from the armories. At this point, many of the prisoners and guards have formed friendships. Rae has become friendly with a female guard named Theresa who works as a beautician when she's not doing National Guard duty. They organize a reunion and dance party for several months later, renting one of the armories.

The Clamshell Alliance expands quickly and Rae is busy coordinating meetings, leading nonviolent action trainings, and helping Sarah with her book, *Stop the Nukes*.

～

The summer and fall at Montague Farm are a blur of activity. There is plenty of work to do from dawn till midnight. Rae feels exhilarated and happy to be engaged.

Rae and a new resident, Adam, have a sweet romance around the edges of Rae's work at the pickle plant, direct action trainings, and helping out with the local and national anti-nuke work happening at the farm. She writes in her journal: *I love kissing Adam. He's very playful and not hung up on any trips. And I love being a trainer and running role-plays. I'm not feeling out of my element anymore.*

Around the Fourth of July, Rae gets a call from Toby. He wants to visit her in Montague and says he will drive out in a couple weeks at the end of July. Rae feels mixed about this, as she misses her brother but also doesn't want to suffer his judgments about the farm and her new life. For weeks, Rae feels anxious about his impending visit.

The night before he arrives, Rae has a dream about Toby. They are children, walking in the woods. Toby is holding her hand, finding mushrooms hidden in the leaves. Suddenly, they are in a rocky mountain range, somewhere in the West though Rae and Toby have never been to the West. They come to a magic passageway that leads to a cascade of water into a beautiful natural pool. She interprets her dream to mean she should connect with Toby through nature and water.

On the big day of his arrival, Rae hears Toby's pickup truck roll up to the farm at around three in the afternoon. He parks his truck with the "Kelliher & Sons Heating & Cooling / Portsmouth, Ohio" logo on the doors.

Gary calls out to her in the garden. "The Kelliher truck has arrived! Your brother!" Rae thinks that her brother's arrival will unmask her working-class roots with this mostly college-educated group.

"Hey, lil' sis," Toby says, offering a warm embrace. "I did get a little lost coming up from Springfield. Nice part of the country here." Toby has never been to New England, but he has traveled up north to Michigan and down south a few times.

"Yeah, I can't wait to show you around," she smiles, not wanting to betray her anxiety. She's wearing her favorite coveralls and green sweater. "Let's take the farm tour."

They walk the perimeter of the land, with Toby remarking on the old stone walls and the age of the barn. She introduces Toby to the farm residents and animals they encounter. "This is Vladimir, the rooster." She has made a list of things to do that she thinks Toby might like. So far, so good.

"Where did you sleep last night?" she asks. He has his usual dirty blond hair and hunting jacket, his beard a little more filled out than the last time she saw him.

"I slept in the truck. Somewhere in Pennsylvania."

"Well, maybe you'd like a swim before dinner?"

"Hell, yeah!"

Rae is heartened by Toby's boyish grin, his gameness for adventure. She grabs her swimming shorts and a couple of towels, and they drive down to one of her favorite ponds. They stand on a couple of big granite slabs and, as they did as kids, Toby counts to three and they jump together, making one big splash.

"Wow, cold!" shudders Toby.

"Spring-fed," laughs Rae. Colder than those Ohio farm ponds they grew up floating in.

There's a large group gathered around the dinner table at the farm, with Tom having made his standout vegetarian chili, a huge cast-iron pan of corn bread, and a salad of fresh greens from the garden.

"Welcome Toby!" says Nina, as she ladles out bowls of chili. "Great to meet some of Rae's family." There are murmurs of welcome.

As they start their dinner blessings, Rae turns to the children at the table. "Would you like to hear one of the blessings from the Kelliher family table?"

"Yes," shout the diners, including young Sequoyah.

Toby takes Rae's hand and they both recite a blessing that their mother liked to say.

Back of the loaf is the snowy flour
And back of the flour the mill
And back of the mill is the wheat and the shower
And the sun and the Father's will.

"I like the wheat and the shower," pipes in Sequoyah.

"You may not know that I gave Rae her name," Toby says, passing a bowl of shredded cheddar cheese as chili topping.

"Do tell," says Peter, slathering his corn bread with maple syrup. "We just thought her name was Rae."

"Well, I don't want to blow your cover, Sis," he says glancing at her.

"Too late," smiles Rae. She expects this family story from Toby.

"Her real name is Ruth Anne. Ruth Anne Kelliher. But my parents called her by her initials, 'R.A.,' since she also has an Aunt Ruth. And when I was a little kid, I didn't understand, so I just called her 'Rae' and she's never been called anything else since then."

"I am forever indebted," Rae acknowledges, as she likes her nickname. "Toby was a dreamboat of a big brother. He was protective when I was little, but he was also adventurous. He included me in some of his exploring."

She looks at Toby and around the table. "One time my parents wouldn't let me go out with friends to hang out at the lake. They said I had to wait until I was fourteen. Toby spoke up and said that they let him go to the lake when he was twelve and they were treating me differently 'cause I was a girl. My parents changed their mind. He was that kind of brother."

"That's great," said Nina, flashing an appreciative look at Toby. "I wish I had a big brother like you. So you're a feminist?"

The question hangs in the air. Rae can tell that Toby doesn't know how to respond. In her family, a feminist is someone who burns their bra, with pictures in *Life Magazine*. Rae feels her body warming and a full-blown blush coming on.

"I just didn't think it was right," says Toby cautiously, his eyes darting around the table.

"A true feminist," Nina says and everyone laughs.

"He also taught me how to drive," interjects Rae, artfully changing the topic. "Risked his life."

"So you're to blame," says Nina, winking at Toby. "I've got a few nicks in my Nova that are Rae's doing."

"Not true!" says Rae.

"You should take Toby up Mount Toby!" suggests Peter.

"Ha! That was one of my planned adventures," said Rae. "Not everyone has a beautiful mountain named after themself."

The conversation turns, as it often does, to the campaign against the nuclear power plants in New England.

"There's a plant being constructed near us in Ohio, the Zimmer plant," interjects Toby, after listening briefly. "A lot of good jobs. If it wasn't a two-hour drive, I'd consider it."

Rae knows that Toby says this to be provocative, but Sam is quick to defuse.

"They *are* good jobs. They pay better than anything else around here," Sam acknowledges. "But the technology isn't safe. There's no plan to manage the waste. So we need to find other good-paying jobs for skilled workers. Like solar energy or community hydro."

"Nukes make sense to me," counters Toby. "Sure, better than oil from the Middle East."

"You're right, we want to have energy independence," says Sarah. "How about harvesting the sun, the wind, the flow of the waters? We don't have to pay some huge centralized utility. For nukes, we have to import uranium from some pretty unstable places in the world."

Rae figures Toby has the wits to not tangle with the experts, but after dinner he lets out his feelings with her.

"Wow, you live with a bunch of hippie tree-huggers."

Rae hears his sarcastic judgment but responds with humor. "Well, we *are* tree-huggers. Heck, you taught me to hug trees. Remember?"

Toby is momentarily silenced. Rae wonders if is he is remembering their water wonderland and the trees marked for cutting. He changes the subject.

"And that guy Sam, how can you get a job with hair that long?"

"Helps to be an organic farmer and future lawyer," jokes Rae. "Oh, and 'that guy Sam' is the one who knocked down the tower I told you about."

"And has led you to a life of crime?" Toby says, referring to her arrest at Seabrook.

"Best thing I ever did."

"Nina is pretty cute," he offers, changing the subject.

Rae is relieved that after his long drive and short night, he falls asleep in her room. She slips off to share a bed with Adam.

The next day, a Sunday, they hike Mount Toby and jump in another pond that reminds them both of the water wonderland of their childhood. Rae insists on taking Toby out to dinner. Toby wants to see Amherst College. Rae only knows two places to eat down there that aren't too expensive: the pizza place her dad took her to and a Chinese restaurant that a lot of the Amherst students patronize.

Rae drives Toby by the pickle factory. And later they drive past a sign reading "Mount Toby Friends Meeting."

Toby perks up. "Wow, a whole hall where the friends of Toby can gather," he says.

"There are a lot of future friends of Toby here," said Rae. "You should move here, too."

"Ha, but seriously . . . ?"

"They're *Friends*—you know, Quakers," says Rae.

"Quakers?"

"You know, the religious Quakers, the quiet ones."

"No friends of Toby I know are quiet."

They both laugh.

Rae asks Toby about his life. He's apprenticing with their dad, still dating his high school girlfriend Monica, on and off. Currently on. Most days end with beers at Sullivan's. His best friend, Rob, moved to Michigan to work in an auto plant. He hunts with Mac and they've built a hunting cabin up north.

Rae and Toby walk around the Amherst College campus, which is almost empty in July. Rae hasn't been back since the day Nina picked her up.

"Rae, you're the smart one," says Toby, looking out at the playing fields. "You were going to get the college degree. Now you've squandered it. You're the one who got out."

"That's not how I feel. I'm getting a real education. And I love our hometown. I just wanted to see somewhere else." Rae feels confused by Toby's hot-and-cold emotions.

"Pickles and no-nukes," says Toby. "Don't get brainwashed by the tree-huggers. Don't be naïve."

"So, I'm the smart one, but I'm also naïve and brainwashed," says Rae. "Which is it?"

She is feeling testy. For most of her life, all she's known from Toby is kindness and a big-brotherly protectiveness. To hear the harshness of his words now rattles her. It feels like a complex bundle of resentments on his end.

They walk in silence to the Amherst Chinese restaurant. They both order hot-and-sour soup and several dishes to share.

"You could be making a lot more money than canning pickles," says Toby.

"I work at the pickle factory so I can cover my living expenses, even save a little money. But that's not my work. My work is . . . trying to stop these nukes. Protect the valley."

"Is that your plan?"

"Toby, I'm twenty, I don't have to have a perfect plan." She pauses. "I think it's great you're apprenticing with Dad. I never felt that was an option open to me. You know, Kelliher and Sons."

She can see Toby soften a bit. "Okay, well, see the world, but then come home. You can work with me and Dad. We'll bail you out of jail when you decide to block a nuke. Kellihers!"

Rae silently admits to herself that she won't be returning home anytime soon.

"You tell Mom and Dad that I'm doing just fine."

Rae is more than just fine. She loves her life at the farm and the passing of each season. She treasures her attic room and the web of friendships she has formed. Next to Rae's bed are a stack of books, including Howard Zinn's history of the Student Nonviolent Coordinating Committee, *The New Abolitionists*, and a biography of A. J. Muste, a Dutch Reform minister and pacifist who said, "There is no other way to Peace, Peace is the Way." In school, her history classes were tedious. But now she is inspired by the histories of social change movements.

Rae immerses herself in nonviolent theory and attends a two-week training program organized by the Movement for a New Society, a Quaker-inspired social change network in the neighborhood of West Philadelphia. There she meets George Lakey.

She writes in her journal: *There is a tall, handsome Quaker with a beautiful singing voice and an uncanny ability to play anything on the piano by ear. I think he's into men more than women. I love being part of this community of activists. I feel alive here, full of energy and ideas. The folks here don't know that I'm a young nobody in New England and they don't care. And they seem to appreciate my spoken contributions, facilitation skills, and singing voice.*

Lakey leads a number of workshops on social change theory that Rae soaks up, along with his book, *Strategy for a Living Revolution.* So much of what she reads are dissections of problems. But Lakey and the MNS people seem interested in strategy, tactics, and the practicalities of social change. There's also a strong commitment to feminist leadership and theory and what people years later would describe as queer culture, an open questioning and resistance to rigid gender roles. She meets one man, Robert, who wears a dress around the house.

Rae immerses herself in the whole package of the Movement for a New Society. About a hundred activists live in the West Philly neighborhood, not far from University of Pennsylvania campus. They have purchased and adapted roughly twenty low-cost brick row houses, scattered within a ten-block area. These three-story structures prove to be ideal homes for six or more unrelated adults and their families.

There is a training collective that convenes the experiential program that Rae is part of. There is also a food co-op, a local anti-nuclear action group, a day-care center, a publishing house, and ad hoc groups that come together around solving problems or designing books and training resources. By living communally, they are able to keep their living costs down. Like Rae, many residents work part-time jobs to earn what they call their "bread labor" and keep their remaining time free for activism.

One of the workshops Rae attends is led by a soft-spoken, bearded man named Bill Moyer. Rae finds his humility and laughter disarming and fixates on every word he says as he weaves together history and theory. Moyer has created a theory about the stages of social movements. The first stage he calls "movement preparation"; the middle stages are called "the trigger event" and "the takeoff," and the later stages are "policy victories" and "co-optation."

Using the anti-nuclear power movement as an example, Moyer explains that there have been many "trigger events" over the years. But if a movement is underdeveloped, if it hasn't done the movement preparation work of community education, training, presenting alternatives, and developing leaders, these trigger opportunities will pass by.

"In October 1966, the Enrico Fermi nuke outside Detroit had a partial meltdown," said Moyer. "That's the subject of that new Gil Scott Heron song that came out last year, 'We Almost Lost Detroit.' But there was no anti-nuke movement. The event passed by without any change in nuclear policy. Now today there are hundreds of nukes being proposed around the country, but there is also an opposition movement emerging. I think we're about to hit another takeoff moment, especially if there is some kind of trigger event, like an accident. But movements can provoke their own trigger events, too."

Rae studies Moyer's booklet and thinks about the stages of the anti-war movement, the civil rights movement, and even the women's movement to respond to domestic violence. Each of these movements went through stages corresponding with Moyer's theory. What Rae finds most interesting is the idea of "movement preparation," and all the work that must be done to lay the groundwork. It helps explain the importance of plugging away, even when it doesn't feel like any progress is being made.

•

A year has passed and Rae has watched the No Nukes movement mature into a powerful political force. By spring 1978, the Clamshell Alliance is preparing an action that they hope will change everything, a massive occupation at Seabrook scheduled for June 23. Rae has matured, too, confidently leading training sessions, attending regional meetings of the training collective, and earning her bread labor with periodic night shifts at the pickle factory.

While the demonstration a year earlier involved two thousand protesters, Rae and other organizers anticipate a crowd at least ten times bigger. Dozens of buses have already been booked to transport protesters to the biggest anti-nuke occupation in US history. Members of the Seacoast Chapter of the Clamshell Alliance express alarm that too many undisciplined protesters might invade the site and cause problems for locals.

Only days before the action, the coordinating council negotiates with the New Hampshire attorney general to shift the weekend from a mass civil disobedience to a large legal rally on the site of the plant. This greatly upsets the ranks of consensus-based affinity groups, who cry foul that a deal was cut.

Rae feels deeply disappointed that they will not be able to flex their nonviolent muscles. But she doesn't feel betrayed by the leadership, who were faced with the need to make an emergency decision. She understands the risks of a large action. And she and some of the other trainers are relieved by not having to juggle the logistics of thousands of people getting arrested. As she and Sarah pack up their car, they feel as if they are going to a music festival rather than off to combat.

Over ten thousand people "legally" occupy the site of the power plant. A huge stage is set up for speakers and musicians, including singers Jackson Browne and Pete Seeger, the poet Denise Levertov, energy expert Amory Lovins, comedian Dick Gregory, Dr. Helen Caldicott, and environmentalist Barry Commoner. Rae walks alone around the site, taking in the speakers and meetings. She is delighted to greet so many people whom she knows from her two years of organizing.

There are long, tense meetings around the edges of the legal occupation. A segment of the participants are furious at the coordinating committee's betrayal of the direct-action plan. A dissident group, "Clams for Democracy," announces that they will splinter off and undertake aggressive direct action. Some of them advocate for property destruction, including cutting the fences that surround the site and chaining themselves to construction equipment. But the overall feeling for participants is tremendous satisfaction. Ten thousand people have drawn attention to the dangers of nuclear power.

The protests are front-page news all over New England. Rae soaks it in and for weeks afterwards feels a glow of happiness. She writes in her journal: *YES! After the mass mobilization, there is a call to work locally. There is meaningful work to do every day. I'm helping Sarah finish her book about nukes. We are having an impact.*

"Hello, anyone home?" Rae is standing at the screen door of Wally and Juanita Nelson's cabin, a rustic wooden structure. She hears voices inside. Rae visits them regularly to help with harvests and hear their stories.

"Come on in," she hears, and she pushes the door open.

Rae and many neighbors believe that Juanita and Wally Nelson are local treasures, and among the few Black people in largely White and rural Franklin County. They are determined war-tax resisters, back-to-the-land subsistence farmers, and apostles of radical simplicity as the ultimate nonviolent witness.

Rae knows much of the Nelsons' story. Wally is a civil rights activist and an early leader in CORE, the Congress on Racial Equality. Many years later, Rae would enter the civil rights museum in Memphis, built out of the Loraine Hotel where the Reverend Martin Luther King Jr. was assassinated. In the entryway is a large photo of a racially integrated group of Freedom Riders boarding an interstate bus. Wally stands wearing a blazer and holding a small suitcase next to his White friend Ernest Bromley, who is tall and wearing a dark suit.

Juanita met Wally when he was in jail for refusing to fight in World War II. He had refused conscientious objector status as well. Juanita, a young journalist from Cleveland, went to interview him. Forty years later, they are still together, living off the land in Western Mass.

Rae has several Nelson quotes emblazoned in her memory. "If you want to stop poverty and oppression, take your boot off their back," Wally would say. "You need to understand how your cooperation with this economic system is part of the boot."

"If you abhor war, why do you cooperate with the government by paying for it?" Juanita would ask earnest peace activists with their anti-war placards. A central theme of the Nelson doctrine of nonviolence was to resist unjust systems through noncooperation.

Chuck Matthei is visiting and Rae reintroduces herself. She reminds him they met in the Somersworth Armory. Understandably, he doesn't remember. They all sit around the kitchen table, and Chuck regales Rae with the story of how the Nelsons took him in after he was kicked out of his family home at the age of eighteen for resisting the Vietnam-era draft.

"I always have a room at the Nelsons," said Chuck, beaming at his two elders. Rae is envious of Chuck's decade-long connection with Wally and Juanita. She is eager to know more and asks them questions about their history together. *What makes this guy tick?*

Wally describes Chuck's colorful history, explaining that "Chuck was shaped by the civil rights and anti-war movements." Wally says Chuck grew up in the Chicago suburbs and at age seventeen marched with Dr. King against housing segregation. At eighteen, he refused to register for the draft and chose to actively resist.

Wally is animated in the telling. "Chuck was arrested, and refused to cooperate when he was brought to Chicago for a trial in 1969. He went limp rather than walk into the courtroom." Wally demonstrates Chuck's posture by slumping over.

"He started on a hunger strike in his jail cell. Each time he was brought before the judge, he refused to stand. 'Your honor,' he would say to the judge. 'I respect you as another human being, but I don't recognize your authority to imprison me.'" Wally chuckles. "Back to jail he went, where he continued his hunger strike."

Juanita chimes in with her recollections. "The prison doctors tried to force-feed him with tubes and needles, leaving bruises on his arms. One day the judge had Chuck brought into his private chambers. There, the judge told him that he wasn't required to stand. The judge hoped they could just talk, off the record. They spoke for several hours, and the judge listened to Chuck's rationale for refusing both military service and conscientious objector status. This judge, who had sentenced other draft resisters to five-year prison terms, released Chuck that day." As at Seabrook, prison officials plopped him on the jailhouse steps, a free man.

"He was famous for his stubborn resistance," says Juanita, who then stands and pulls a book of poetry by Denise Levertov off her shelf. She reads aloud from a 1969 poem that includes a reference to Chuck.

> *Chuck Matthei*
> *travels the country*
> > *a harbinger*
> *(He's 20. His golden beard was pulled and clipped*
> *by a Wyoming sheriff, but no doubt has grown*
> > > *again*
> > *though he can't grow knocked-out teeth.*
> > *He wears sneakers even in winter,*
> > *to avoid animal-hide; etc.) . . .*
> *(And if his intransigence*
> *brings us another despair*
> *and we call it 'another form of aggression,'*
> *don't we confess*
> > *wishing he had a sense of humor—*
> *our own extremity?)*

Rae listens attentively as they all discuss Chuck's plan to relocate to the Greenfield area. He is helping settle an organization founded by Quakers and civil rights activists to encourage property and land reform through the creation of community land trusts for affordable housing. He describes an effort he is part of in Georgia working with civil rights leaders who have purchased five thousand

acres to create a massive community land trust for Black land ownership called "New Communities."

Chuck talks and waves his hands energetically about the need
for a Gandhian-style "constructive program," along with nonviolent direct action. "We need to build a community economics,
new forms of local ownership, and community control that protect
people from absentee owners and wealth extractors."

Rae appreciates this approach. She later writes in her journal: *It
is not enough to stop the bad. We need to be part of building the local alternatives to meet people's needs for land, housing, and jobs. Juanita, Wally
and Chuck say nonviolence is not just a tactic, but a principle for organizing
the economy.*

"Rae, sit with me," commands Echo, a five-year-old who loves to
climb on Rae. Rae has just padded down the stairs to the living room
at Montague Farm. It's a snowy Sunday morning in early March
and she's wearing her red flannel nightgown, fleece slippers, and a
sleeping cap for warmth. The second floor of the farmhouse is chilly
on cold nights. The living room, with a wide variety of couches and
easy chairs, is toasty warm from a crackling woodstove.

Tom, wearing a jaunty black beret, is baking blueberry corn
muffins in the kitchen. "Blueberries picked in July and frozen until
today!" he exclaims.

Several of Rae's housemates are spread out on the couches drinking coffee and tea and reading several Sunday newspapers. Nina
and a visitor, Ramona, lean over a tarot reading at a table next to
a window with a snowy panorama view of the backyard and fields.
Sequoyah and several of the children roll around with two kittens
on the carpeted floor.

"Read me a story Rae," insists Skye, waving a picture book,
Blueberries for Sal.

"Skye, Rae just woke up, don't be so demanding," says Mimi, her
mother. Mimi is submerged behind the Sunday comics and doesn't
look up.

"It's fine. I'll be right there, Skye." Rae loves being in demand with the kids. She pours a mug of tea and lifts the cover off a large skillet with home fries, onions, and eggs with scallions.

"Help yourself," said Tom as he pulls a pan of muffins from the oven.

Rae settles on the couch with her tea and cuddles with Skye. Two other toddlers wander over to compete for her lap. She loves these Sunday mornings in the winter, especially with these children.

"Remember how last winter we lost power?" says Sequoyah. Last year's blizzard is fresh in everyone's memories. For the farm residents, with their woodstoves and a shed full of firewood, the loss of power wasn't a stressful time at all, but rather festive. Rae recalls snowshoeing through the deep woods, breaking trail through two feet of fresh powder.

"Rae built snow forts with us, remember?" Sequoyah releases a black cat from her grasp and is ready to put her boots on.

"Maybe we can go skiing or sledding later," says Rae, opening the story book to its first page.

"Yay! Rae is going to take us sliding," shouts Echo, jumping up and down. She is assembling a small stack of books for Rae to read.

Rae begins to read the story, sitting on a plush couch. Soon all five children are perched around her. Three-year-old Mirabel touches Rae's face and strokes her hair as she reads.

"You're going to be a great mother, Rae," say Mimi, looking up from the newspaper. "The kids love you."

Rae is warmed by this thought. But she is in no hurry to begin parenthood. *First things, first*, she thinks. *Like, find a dependable co-parent partner.*

"Check out the piece in the *Boston Globe* about this new movie," says Peter from his couch perch. "It's about a nuke meltdown."

Sarah is already in the know. "It's a big Hollywood movie called *The China Syndrome*. It's about a nuke in California that has an accident after a string of cover-ups. It's got a great cast: Jane Fonda, Michael Douglas, and Jack Lemmon."

"Wow," says Nina. "We should leaflet people as they leave the movie."

After her muffins and breakfast, Rae takes all the kids sledding in the back field. Then she takes a hot bath in the clawfoot tub on the second floor and meets up with Adam to make love in the late afternoon. Lying alone in her bed, she writes: *A perfect day here at the farm. And now a purple sunset. I could happily live like this for the rest of my life.*

⁓

By late March, when *The China Syndrome* movie is released, Clamshell Alliance chapters across New England have created educational leaflets to distribute at screenings. Rae, Nina, and fellow activists sign up for shifts at movie theaters around the Pioneer Valley. Audiences exiting the theater are rattled and ready for more information.

"Don't let the China Syndrome happen at Seabrook," Rae says, as her leaflets are eagerly snapped up. She is wearing her "9-to-5" formal skirt and her hair is up in a bun.

One afternoon, Rae is home at the farm chopping vegetables for a stew. She and Nina are planning to head out around six in the evening to leaflet *The China Syndrome* screenings at a large cinema complex in Hadley that is mostly patronized by college students from Amherst and Northampton.

Sarah comes bounding into the kitchen, breathless. "There's been an accident, in Harrisburg, at the Three Mile Island nuke!"

Rae is startled, not knowing any details. She jumps up to flip on their fuzzy black-and-white television set and watches the breaking news bulletins. Sarah gets a call from a reporter and then another. She starts to write down talking points for a press release.

The scene in central Pennsylvania is bedlam. Around Harrisburg, pregnant women and children within five miles are urged to evacuate; then the advisory is expanded to twenty miles. In the confusion after the accident, tens of thousands of people jump in their cars to escape central Pennsylvania. An estimated 140,000 people flee in panic, attempting to outrun the threat of radiation exposure. All over the East Coast, highways are jammed with cars full of people and pets, especially around New York City. *This is it*, Rae thinks. *The accident, the panic, the radiation exposure. Will it reach Montague?*

There is a knock at the door and Rae answers. It is a reporter who has come to take a staged photograph of the farm group bundling leaflets together. The photo appears in the *Hampshire Gazette* the next day along with the story about the accident. Their photo runs next to a picture of President Carter wearing booties and touring the plant to reassure an anxious nation.

Nina and Rae revamp the leaflet with a new headline: "Nuclear Accident in Pennsylvania." They crank out several hundred copies on the farm's mimeograph machine and jump in the picklemobile to drive to Hadley. At the theater, there is a long line of people snaking through the parking lot toward the entrance to see *The China Syndrome*. The theater has doubled the number of evening screenings from four to eight. Nina and Rae walk up and down the line, leafleting and talking to people. Rae feels exhilarated by the gratitude that people express for the information.

Rae and Nina buy tickets and slip into one of the last showings of the day to watch the film a second time. At one point in the film, Jane Fonda, who plays a television reporter exposing the dangers of the California power plant, is told that a meltdown "could render an area the size of the state of Pennsylvania permanently uninhabitable." The audience gasps at the line.

On the way out, one guy complains to Rae that the accident was "probably staged to boost movie ticket sales."

"I don't think so, sir," Rae replies politely. Later she writes: *The guy must be getting his news from the* National Enquirer. *Where do people make this shit up? I occasionally meet these people living in a parallel universe.*

Four days later, Nina and Rae unlock the doors at the First Congregational Church in Montague Center where they hold their regular Clamshell Alliance meetings. Ten new people are waiting when they arrive. Instead of the usual group of twenty, more than one hundred people cram into the meeting. Rae feels a takeoff sensation, the satisfaction of being in the right place at the right time. Sign-up clipboards and petitions are passed around. Mimeographed action alerts are passed out. "Call Congressman Silvio Conte," Nina says. "Tell him no nukes in New England."

"No nukes anywhere," says a young woman nursing her baby under a shawl.

The protests are huge. Thousands march in Harrisburg, Pennsylvania, within a week of the accident. In May, more than a hundred thousand people march in Washington, DC, against nuclear power. Adam and Rae travel on a rented bus to the protest, and Peter and Sarah speak at the rally. On the return trip, somewhere on the New Jersey Turnpike, Adam falls asleep on her shoulder. Rae, wide awake on the darkened and quiet bus, writes in her journal: *Wow. So cool to be part of this no-nukes fight. This is people power.*

At a dinner after their return, Rae jokes with her Montague Farm group. "I thought the *China Syndrome* movie was our trigger event. But the accident at Three Mile Island was a transformational event. Good thing we were prepared."

In the following months, Rae watches in delight as the nuclear industry faces unprecedented scrutiny. Many plants, including Seabrook, were in the permitting and construction pipeline prior to the accident. Some go on to be completed. But plans for thirty-nine plants are scrapped.

It will be many years later that Rae looks back to realize no new power plants were licensed over the three decades after Three Mile Island.

BRIAN WILLSON'S WAR

(1984)

Rae is awakened by a shout from across the darkened room. As she gets her bearings, she realizes the shout is from across her bed.

"Brian," she says calmly. "Brian!" She reaches over and finds his warm body, soaked with sweat, writhing next to her. "It's Rae. I'm right here."

In his transition to waking, he pulls the bedsheets off her.

"Brian, it's okay. It's a nightmare. It's a bad dream." She leans over to flip on a bedside lamp in a still unfamiliar bedroom. Brian Willson has been her boyfriend for only two months, and she's only spent the night a few times.

The light on, Brian bolts upright in bed. They are both naked and uncovered, Brian's hair matted with sweat.

"Oh God," he says, rubbing his eyes and shaking his head. "I'm sorry."

"It's okay, honey," she says, touching his face. She turns on her side, putting one of her legs over his midsection and wrapping him in her arms.

"Yuck," he exclaims. "Just a nightmare. Getting shot at." He rolls to face her. "I'm sorry to wake you," he says tenderly.

She looks into his eyes as he traces his finger down her smooth and bare skin and down her hip line.

Rae knows better than to ask about his nightmare. Brian carries demons from his years in Vietnam and his rough-and-tumble childhood. She will wait until morning.

"I can help you fall asleep," Rae says, kissing him softly and caressing his hips. She guides him onto his back and slides gently on top of him, moving across his sweaty skin and invoking a moan of pleasure.

"That's better," whispers Rae.

In the morning Rae finds herself wrapped in a sheet that smells like Brian, alone in bed. The aroma of bacon and coffee waft from the kitchen. She looks around, taking in Brian's bachelor apartment with its mismatched furniture, pile of laundry, and blank white bedroom walls. Slipping on one of his flannel button-down shirts, Rae goes in search of the cook.

Brian is sitting at the kitchen table, fully dressed, wearing a St. Louis Cardinals cap on top of unruly hair. He is intently reading the newspaper. She notices he is wearing boots.

"Hello, beautiful," he says, looking up, setting the paper on the table. Rae wraps her arms around his back and gives him a warm smooch on the cheek.

"Coffee?" Brian offers.

"Sure, but I got it." She walks to the counter, looking out the window at a blue-sky morning on a tree-lined street in Greenfield. She pours a mug and eases into the chair across from Brian.

"Do you have to work today?" Brian asks, leaning back in his chair.

"No, I'm not going to work on Saturdays anymore." Rae has shifted her schedule to have more Saturday mornings like this one. "Maybe we can take our ramble around town?"

"I'd love that. Go by the farmers market?"

"Sounds like a plan." Rae nods toward Brian's newspaper. "What's the news?"

"Fucking Reagan," Brian says. "Fucking Contras."

"The Contras are in the news?" Rae is well versed on the news, especially about Nicaragua. She recently attended a briefing by a member of their local solidarity committee, which had just returned from a fact-finding mission to Nicaragua.

"Counter-insurgency," Brian explains. "Backed and trained by the US to undermine the Sandinistas—with secret training bases in Honduras. That's how these things work."

"Didn't Congress cut off US aid to the Contras?"

"Yeah, that's the official position. No CIA money. But trust me, babe, there are a hundred other ways a warmongering president can subvert the will of Congress."

Brian stands up to insert two slices of wheat bread in his toaster. He turns up the heat on the bacon and stirs some already-chopped onions and peppers into the sizzling cast-iron pan on his stove. Rae admires his lanky body and tight jeans when he turns his back to her.

"It's a familiar pattern, unfortunately," Brian says, stirring some eggs into the pan. "Guatemala 1954, Iran 1954, Congo 1961. Dominican Republic, 1965. Chile 1973. It's a shameful story."

Rae knows a lot of this history, but not in the encyclopedic way that Brian does.

Brian scoops the cooked eggs onto two ceramic plates, popping the toast and bacon on, and serves Rae restaurant-style. He sets another platter down with salt, pepper, salsa, jam, and a butter dish.

"Yum," says Rae. "I like this café . . . a lot."

"Our challenge is to make this matter," says Brian, sitting down and placing his St. Louis Cardinals cap reverently on the table, not wanting to risk impoliteness by eating with a hat on.

"For most people, these countries might as well be on another planet. The gap between their daily lives and the reality of a Nicaragua or an El Salvador is huge. And my neighbors . . ." He pauses and points to the houses next door. "They don't understand that the US has so much power to shape other people's lives. They just know that Greenfield Tap & Die is closing."

In the two months that Rae has been consorting with Brian, this has been his steady refrain. *How do we reach people? How do we build a movement similar to the one that contributed to the end of the war? And,* when he's tired and impatient, his questions are more like, *"How the hell can we get people to care about something happening so far away?"*

Brian devours the breakfast, beckoning Rae to add condiments and try the bacon.

After breakfast, Brian clears the dishes away and insists on washing up. Rae wanders into his living room, taking a closer look at several enlarged photographs. Unlike his bedroom, there are few sections of his living room walls that lack bookcases or framed posters. One photo is of Brian in Vietnam.

Rae is more than a decade younger than Brian, so her experience of the war is entirely different. She was eleven in 1966 when he shipped out to Vietnam. When she was fifteen, she wore four POW/MIA bracelets like bangles on her wrists. Each of them had the name of a missing soldier, their serial number, and the date they disappeared.

Rae reflects on the fact that Brian's current job, at the Veterans Resource Center, is a perfect platform for him to do nonstop organizing among veterans. He is chair of the local Veterans for Peace chapter, a legacy from his leadership of the Vietnam Veterans Against the War in the 1970s.

Rae has looked at the photos on Brian's walls on previous occasions. But now she gets Brian to talk about each one. One color photo is of a youthful Brian, in military uniform, leaning against a green 1965 Corvette Sting Ray convertible. "That's what I looked like before going to Nam," Brian narrates. "See the brash, insolent, and ignorant look, fully absorbed in the myths of American exceptionalism, patriotic mumbo jumbo, and anti-communist tropes."

"Whoa," Rae objects. "That's a pretty harsh assessment of your younger self. We all grew up in very different times."

"That's for sure. A steady diet of 'I Like Ike' and 'Praise God and Country.' Mister Born-on-the-Fourth-of-July."

As Rae knows, Brian was in fact born on the fourth of July.

"So, who's this?" she asks, pointing to the next picture, a black-and-white war-correspondent photo. Brian explains that the photo was taken three years later—a war-weary Brian in the Vietnam Delta, his face darkened, hair a tangled mess, with sleepless eyes.

"Now, there's a man whose entire worldview has been shattered by reality, the rapid dissolution of one's founding myths about country, history, masculinity." Brian laughs and points to his younger self. "He's questioning the whole American Way of Life, the holy grail. And he's also been shot at a few times in the dark, which can definitely upset your sleep."

"Like last night," Rae says, putting her hand on Brian's back.

"I don't remember much. I can't remember the nightmare. But usually I'm being chased by some creature."

Rae stays quiet. She touches his shoulder and squeezes it gently. *I'll learn more if I stick around*, she thinks.

She gazes at an enlarged photo of a clean-cut White man, not Brian, wearing a suit jacket and tie.

"Who's this?" Rae asks.

"That's Norman Morrison, a Quaker peace activist from Baltimore. I think about him every day."

"Why?"

"When I was drafted in October 1965, I was all gung-ho. I had no idea what I was talking about." Brian shakes his head and takes the picture of Morrison off the wall and holds it in both hands.

"Norman made a different choice. In November 1965 he went to the Pentagon. Standing just below the office of Robert McNamara, the secretary of defense, he doused himself in kerosene and set himself on fire, taking his own life. I heard about Norman Morrison immolating himself and thought, *What crazy guy would do such a thing?*"

"Holy . . . ," says Rae.

"He did it as an act of protest, in tribute to the innocent women and children in Vietnam. I remember reading about it in the paper. It stuck in my mind, the whole time I was in Nam. Later, I came to think it was true act of courage and resistance. It helped turn the tide of public opinion against the Vietnam War."

"I heard about the Vietnamese monks who had set themselves on fire," Rae recalls.

"Yes, there was one Buddhist monk, Quang Duc, who set himself on fire in Saigon in 1963 in protest of the corrupt Diem regime. In the months that followed, several more monks burned themselves to death. It shook everyone, including President Kennedy."

"When Norman Morrison died, he was thirty-one," Brian says, then pauses. "A few years later, I was evaluating the impact of an area that US troops had bombed, a village in South Vietnam that was supposedly sympathetic to the Viet Cong. But all the bodies we encountered were women, children, and old people. Not a living soul around, just some recently extinguished fires and a few chickens."

Brian has been talking without looking at Rae, but now he meets her eyes. "I went into one of the huts—and there was this altar you would often see in Vietnamese homes. Picture it: this village is empty, abandoned, all the people have fled or are dead. But here is this altar and there are little candles still burning on it, with small photos and drawings. And right in the middle is a picture of Norman Morrison."

"Wow," Rae says. "That's freaky."

"Okay, here's another detail. Morrison brought his infant daughter with him. Her name was Emily. She wasn't a year old. And he held her and then released her, handing her off to a bystander, just before he ignites into flames shooting twelve feet high. Her mother comes and gets Emily that night, and she doesn't have a scratch on her."

"Did he change his mind, about igniting her too?"

"No one believes that was ever his intent. Later, he was on a Vietnamese postage stamp. And one of Vietnam's most famous poets, To Huu, wrote a poem, "Emily, Child." Brian closes his eyes, drawing on this memory. Then he recites:

Emily, come with me
Later you'll grow up you'll know the streets, no longer feel lost
Where are we going, dad?
To the banks of the Potomac
To see what, Dad?
Nothing, my child, there's just the Pentagon
Oh my child, your round eyes
Oh my child, your locks so golden
Don't ask your father so many questions, dear!
I'll carry you out, this evening you're going home with your mother.

Rae's eyes widen as she looks at a transfigured Brian, bent and stricken, his eyes closed. This is a part of him she's never seen. Memorizing poems.

"Okay, here's another thing," says Brian, opening his eyes and fixing her with an intense gaze. "We went to the same high school, Chautauqua High School in upstate New York. I actually knew who he was. Norman was seven years older than me, but he was the first Eagle Scout I'd ever met. I looked up to him."

"Wow," said Rae, feeling goose bumps.

"After I got back from Nam, I visited Norman's mother near Chautauqua. I just showed up on her doorstep. She could have reasonably shut the door in my face, but she invited me in. It was, like, fifteen years after Norman took his life. I told her about the people in Vietnam who revered her son. I told her about a Vietnamese man singing me a song, 'Ode to Norman Morrison.' And the postage stamp issued in his honor in North Vietnam. I just sobbed at her kitchen table. She was really kind to me, a complete stranger."

Brian's eyes have welled with tears as he looks at Rae. "When I look at this picture, I hear Norman speaking to me: *Hey, Willson, what are you willing to sacrifice to stop the harms you know are happening?*"

⸺

"First we work, then we talk," says Juanita Nelson, pulling on her floppy straw hat and picking up a bushel basket. It is four in the afternoon on a sunny July day. The heat of the day has passed, and there is a gentle breeze blowing up Woolman Hill along the Connecticut River Valley.

From the Nelsons' farm on top of Traprock Ridge, Rae can see the Montague Plains and the spot where Sam Lovejoy toppled the tower almost ten years earlier. Rae thinks back to her first exhilarating days at Montague Farm, days of learning, activism, romance, and drama. She recently turned thirty. Her body is fuller and her hair longer than the twiggy teenager who showed up at the farm in 1973. She still lives there but spends more time staying with Brian. Her job, working at a women's shelter, also centers her in Greenfield.

She recently wrote in her journal: *Turning 30. Being with Brian is different than the younger men like Adam. He is a man who has been to war. His body and mind have been imprinted with this experience. Brian says I should talk to Juanita about Nicaragua and how to build a nonviolent movement to stop the US government from invading.*

She follows Juanita through the field, carrying her own bushel basket and garden shears. She has spent many hours in these fields, helping the Nelsons fight back the persistent encroachment of weeds and bring in the harvest. Today is no different, except that Rae has questions on her mind for Juanita, ruminations about nonviolent strategy. But first we work, as Juanita says. A barter for her insights.

Two hours later, they have harvested most of the items they will load into the Nelsons' rusted yellow pickup truck and drive to the Saturday farmers market. The July bounty includes carrots, cauliflower, fennel, beets, beans, scallions, kale, and a bevy of salad greens. The air is starting to cool and the light is shifting, though there are still three remaining hours of daylight.

They amble over to the Nelson cabin, filling a large wooden bucket of water from the wellhead and entering the cabin. On a sprawling wooden table is a simple wildflower arrangement in a ceramic vase, a barter from a local potter. Juanita puts on the kettle to make two cups of chicory tea and pulls out a plate of carrots and a hunk of cheddar cheese. Rae sits at the table and, without being asked, begins to shell a basket of peas and beans that are sitting on the table.

Rae has been part of many discussions with Juanita, both in groups and one-to-one. Many people trying to figure out their lives look to Juanita and Wally Nelson as elders, as secular pastors. There is a sturdy group of a couple dozen war-tax resisters in Franklin County, disciples of the Nelsons. Half of them, like the Nelsons, earn below a taxable income, barter what they can, and aspire not to own much, at least in their own name. Other tax resisters in their group provocatively file their tax returns, refuse to pay, and have had their cars and other assets seized.

In anticipation of talking to Juanita, Rae has written in her journal: *I'm not interested in talking about war-tax resistance. That is not my personal path. I want to ask Nita about tactical nonviolence. Yes, we should all live radically more simply so our government doesn't have to send armies around the world to defend the resource supply chain so the US, with 5 percent of the world's population, can continue to consume over 30 percent of the planet's resources. I know the whole rap and agree with it. But how do we to stop an invasion?*

She updates Juanita about the local community-organizing effort to prevent the United States from intervening in Nicaragua in order to reverse the revolution. As recently as October 1983, the US invaded the tiny Caribbean island of Grenada to eliminate a leftist government that was charting an independent course. When the US military encountered resistance from the Grenadian army, they amassed seven thousand US troops to overwhelm an island with a population of 96,000 people at the time.

Brian said Grenada was a fun military exercise for imperial USA, but he believed the real purpose was to send a message to the Nicaraguan Sandinistas: "Look what we can do."

"How do we use nonviolent tactics to stop an invasion of Nicaragua?" Rae asks, with a growing sense of dread. "It won't do much good to protest *after* a mass invasion. Once the troops are on the ground, it's too late for domestic resistance. Everyone rallies around the flag. How do we prevent an invasion?"

"Well, I don't know much," Juanita begins, as she often did. "But we need to demonstrate to the US government that millions of people are watching. And that if they invade, there will be a stiff resistance."

"But you need to be very public—if there's to be a deterrence, right?

"Yes, you need a public nonviolent response, massing to act," says Juanita. "You need a disciplined, trained *satyagraha* peace force." Juanita is referring to the Gandhian disciples who were trained to respond nonviolently when being provoked, like the Salt Marchers who were clubbed.

"You need people ready to use their bodies to stop the machine, as Thoreau said," observes Rae.

"Yes," said Juanita, glancing toward her bookshelf. "I believe the exact quote is 'Let your life be a counter-friction to stop the machine.'"

She stands up, plucks a copy from her bookshelf of Thoreau's *On Civil Disobedience*, and flips through its well-worn pages. Rae remembers her pulling down the poem about Chuck Matthei on an earlier visit.

"Here it is. '. . . Let your life be a counter-friction.' And next: 'What I have to do is to see, at any rate, that I do not lend myself to the wrong which I condemn.'"

Rae recognizes that "let your life" and "do not lend myself to the wrong which I condemn" are part of Juanita's total nonviolent lifestyle approach.

"Well, how do we be a counter-friction to the state?" Rae asks.

"I guess you need a show of power," Juanita muses. "What is the nonviolent equivalent of a parade of tanks?"

Rae looks out of the screened window and thinks, *What would that look like?*

"Hey Rae, look at this issue of *Sojourners*." Brian hands her a copy of a magazine. They are sitting together on one of their treasured Saturday mornings, drinking coffee at Brian's kitchen table. "Check out this Pledge of Resistance."

Rae had seen an earlier article, by Jim Wallis and Jim Rice, the editors of *Sojourners*, describing a covenant, a "Promise of Resistance," where they called on Christians to physically resist and obstruct a US invasion of Nicaragua. One tactic they proposed was for Christians to occupy congressional offices in the event of an invasion, and refuse to leave until troops are withdrawn.

Rae and Reggie have several friends, including Karen Brandow, who have joined a new effort called Witness for Peace, where US nationals physically travel into areas where the Contras have been attacking civilians. Their mission is to accompany Nicaraguans facing war. But this new effort is focused on the witness that people can do in the United States.

The Pledge of Resistance is designed to build a nonviolent response to invasion, but to publicize it well in advance—sort of what Rae has been musing about, something preemptive. According to the article, the seven regional Witness for Peace chapters are serving as organizing hubs for people willing to take the pledge.

"Wow," Rae says as she scans the magazine, pleased with the news. "This is what I was talking to Juanita about."

"Great movement minds think alike." Brian smiles.

Rae picks up the phone and calls Karen at Witness for Peace. Karen has recently returned from Nicaragua and has thrown herself into organizing new volunteers. They talk for half an hour about Karen's trip and the new pledge of resistance. Rae offers to help organize the nonviolent direct-action trainers, as she did with the Clamshell Alliance.

"Let's go for a walk before it gets too hot," she says to Brian after she hangs up. Brian quickly agrees and laces up his trusted walking boots and dons his St. Louis Cardinals cap.

They walk out the door into the warmth of an August morning. Their Saturday walking route meanders around Greenfield's downtown, with a stop at the farmers market, past the old mills, and up to the ridge to a tower called Poet's Seat.

They walk past Green River Café, where Rae sometimes fills in as a waitress and sometimes as a cook.

"Best darn home fries in Franklin County," Brian says. All the café tables outside are filled with happy weekend brunch patrons.

They arrive at the farmers market, a cluster of fifteen produce and craft stands at the green in the center of town. Brian gives a big bear hug to Wally Nelson, who is staffing the Nelsons' market booth out of the back of their yellow pickup truck.

Like Rae, Brian has spent many hours talking with the Nelsons about everything from war, veteran's issues, usury, tax resistance, and nonviolence, to recipes. They are one of the reasons that Brian moved to the Greenfield area.

"Look at you two," says Wally, who is always elated when he sees new couples forming. He wraps his arms around both of them. "Take good care of one another in these times."

"We're trying," says Brian, winking at Rae. Rae smiles but wonders if people think she's too young to be with Brian.

"I can imagine he's a bit of a handful," says Wally knowingly to Rae.

"That's for sure," Rae laughs. "The man hardly sleeps." It's true, and sometimes a sore subject that Brian seems driven to work seventy hours a week. Rae safeguards these Saturday-morning walks.

Juanita appears next to Wally, a small brown bag in her hands. She smiles at Rae and Brian. "Look, Wally—your favorite muffin. I bartered with Clea over there."

"Hmm, yum, Clea's muffins," Wally says, tapping his tummy.

It is a well-known fact that Juanita has banned bananas from the Nelson household. "Talk about a food that is soaked in blood," she says publicly, referring to the feudal plantation conditions in which many bananas are grown. But when Wally stops by Brian's house to do a load of wash in Brian's machine, he accepts Brian's gift of a banana while sitting at the kitchen table. "Oh lord, this is a divine fruit," he would say, slowly peeling the banana like it is a sacred talisman and savoring each bite. "Don't tell 'Nita."

"Well, Rae's gonna organize the pledge of resistance," Brian says. "Get thousands of people to form a mass nonviolent army to discourage a direct US invasion."

"Like your *satyagraha* peace force, Juanita," Rae offers.

Other friends and neighbors gather around the Nelson produce table, listening in on the conversation. Rae appreciates that, for a little rural county in Western Massachusetts, there is a high level of awareness about the Nicaragua situation and a desire to do something about it.

"Well, sign us up for the peace force," Juanita says in the midst of selling a bar of her homemade lavender soap to a customer.

Brian and Rae say farewell and keep walking, down to the old industrial section of Greenfield, where several mill buildings are still operating.

"Sounds like you're fired up about the pledge," said Brian, reaching out for Rae's hand.

Rae is pleased that Brian is so tuned in to her urgency. "I've been thinking about starting something like this," she says, "so it's great to see it spark. And also great that it started with *Sojourners* and faith-based groups. But I think we can make it broader."

"Maybe this is something we can work on together," says Brian. "I can organize veterans to take the Pledge of Resistance."

They walk through a more affluent neighborhood and slowly climb the ridgeline to the lookout tower, Poet's Seat. At one point, the trail ducks into the woods and they're surrounded by hardwoods and a shady canopy of leaves.

Under the cover of the woods, they stop by a large oak tree to hug and kiss.

Rae touches the bark on the tree. "Look at the canopy of this oak, how wide it is in the middle of the woods. You can tell that about a century ago this was in an open area." She's been reading up on the forensic signs of old New England, where the land was once 80 percent cleared, mostly for sheep.

Brian laughs. "Sheep fever." They walk farther and cross the road to the trail leading to the tower.

"Sheep fever indeed," Rae laughs. "Oil, wool, cotton . . . make the world go around."

They climb the stone tower at Poet's Seat and look to the west over the town of Greenfield and toward the western hills of the Berkshires.

"You know what our national religion is?" Brian asks. "It's not Christianity or a supreme being. It's consumerism, materialism."

"Yeah, I've been thinking about how to live more simply, how to drive less." Rae sheds her sweater and wraps it around her waist.

"Me too," says Brian. "Food from the valley here. Less flying. As Juanita says, look to uproot the seeds of violence in your own way of living. Don't lend yourself to the wrong you condemn."

They stand quietly looking west from the tower. White billowy clouds rise on the horizon. Rae is not sure what more to say.

Rae throws herself into organizing the pledge. By the end of 1984, pledge organizers have collected tens of thousands of pledges, with half the people promising to commit civil disobedience if there is a US invasion. Rae gives talks and trainings on the campuses of community colleges and the Five Colleges to the south. She even returns to Amherst College, which seems to complete a full circle after her not being on the campus for over a decade, except for her brief visit with Toby.

All this organizing may be having an impact, as there is no direct invasion. But the Reagan Administration imposes additional economic embargoes on Nicaragua and then presses Congress to approve millions in aid to the Contras. While the threat of direct military invasion still looms, the leaders of the pledge pivot to protesting the embargo and aid to the mercenary Contras. There are massive demonstrations and acts of civil disobedience across the country, with over ten thousand demonstrators, two thousand of whom are arrested.

In Franklin County, a group of twenty people, including Rae, Brian, and Wally Nelson, occupy the local IRS office and are arrested. They go to trial and put forward a necessity defense, like the one advanced by Sam Lovejoy a decade earlier. And like Sam's case, after months of preparation, including a substantial legal brief, their case is thrown out on a technicality after jury selection. But Rae appreciates the process of writing her own statement, even if she doesn't get to present it in court.

By September 1985, over eighty thousand people have signed the pledge to resist the US war and oppose military aid to the Contras. Rae writes in her journal: *I feel like this work is making a difference in stopping an invasion. So many people pledging to put their bodies on the line. Central America still feels unreal to me. I think it's time for a visit. I need to see things for myself.*

PART 2
ACCOMPANIMENT

A country that exports repression will one day unleash that repression against its own people. A nation that wages war against the poor in Nicaragua will ignore the needs of its own poor. A country which in the name of 'democracy' fights wars against self-determination of other peoples cannot remain a democracy. I have felt for a long time that the people of the United States will one day be the most repressed people in the world.

—Father Miguel D'Escoto,
Maryknoll priest, Nicaraguan
Minister for Foreign Affairs, 1979-1990

SEÑORITA ONION

(1985)

Rae is dozing as the Greyhound bus rolls into Texas and crosses a wide open plain. After two and half days on a cross-country bus, she feels woozy from interrupted sleep. It seems like a month since her going-away party at the farm and Nina dropping her at the Springfield bus station. In fact, it was only three days earlier.

She has been saving money for a year. Her plan is to attend language school in Mexico for a month, work on a three-week harvest brigade in Nicaragua, and then volunteer at a refugee camp in El Salvador for a couple of months. Departing in October and returning in April will also allow her to miss the New England winter, which she has never done before and seems exotic.

After an intense year of organizing the Pledge of Resistance and a decade of reading about these places, Rae feels a need to improve on her rudimentary Spanish and see things for herself. Some of her friends have embarked upon multiple-year stints of working for service projects in the region. Rae knows that her work is in the United States, in the belly of the beast, working to change US policy. But a little more direct experience in the region will be important.

Her relationship with Brian has wound down. On the bus, she writes in her journal: *He is a sweet soul, but not my soulmate. I learned so much being with him, about the militarism and the trauma that some veterans hold. It is hard to be partners with someone so driven, who has few moments of lightness or desire to dance. In the last year, I've seen more of his shadow side. Wally Nelson is right, "Brian is a handful." I know people think I'm serious, but I know I have a playful and celebratory spirit.*

Rae feels like she and Brian parted ways on loving terms. They encountered one another frequently both in activist circles and around the neighborhood. Brian will also be traveling in Nicaragua and maybe she will run into him.

She signed up for a language school in Cuernavaca, Mexico, to begin at the end of October. But three weeks before her departure, a devastating earthquake, registering 8.1 magnitude, struck Mexico City. A few weeks later, she called down to the language school to make sure they were still in business, which they were. A friend from the Mount Toby Friends Meeting has told her that there are earthquake-relief volunteers working out of Casa de Los Amigos, a guesthouse run by Quakers in Mexico City. She has signed up to do three weeks of volunteering, staying at the Casa, before starting language school.

On the bus, she writes: *I feel excitement, anxiety, and a shadow of loneliness about to descend on me. Especially after years of living in close community, it will be wild to not know a soul.*

The Greyhound bus drops her at four in the afternoon in the border town of Brownsville, Texas, at a bus station that looks like a 1950s A&W drive-in. Her plan is to find a cheap hotel, take a bath, and get some shut-eye. In the morning, she will walk across the border bridge to Matamoros, Mexico, to catch a bus to Mexico City.

She steps off the bus, and the heat, bright sunlight, and dust blast her senses. She feels stiff, sticky, and definitely not in New England anymore. She is overdressed for the hot weather. But she is not about to put her backpack down and start disrobing on the street corner, so she presses forward, perspiring under her layers.

She pulls her hat down and puts on her tinted sunglasses. She's as ready as can be for the unwanted attention drawn to a single young woman traveling alone. She already moved her seat on the bus several times to avoid creepy guys and have two seats to herself. She smiles at her fake wedding ring, her favorite heavy hiking boots, and her deliberately dull clothing to disguise her curves.

Rae walks down the main street of Brownsville Station, rows of tiny stores hawking jewelry, cowboy boots, and Mexican food. There is a side street with a row of hotels and motels, most with a shabbiness that shocks her. Even on a tight budget, Rae has been advised that it is worth spending the extra $10 to find secure and clean lodging. One hotel has a nice courtyard with trees and a functioning fountain, and it looks cleaner than the others.

She checks in, and when she shuts the door to her room and bolts it, she feels an enormous relief flow through her. Tears come to her eyes, and she mouths the words, "Far from home." She sheds her clothes, shaking out the dust in one corner, then hanging them on lamps and chairs to air out. The bathtub shower is disappointing in both water pressure and cleanliness, but she stands under the luke-warm trickle and lathers herself full of soap and shampoo. She brushes out her long hair and stands naked under a rotating ceiling fan, peeking out the single window into the courtyard at the shadows and silhouettes of people walking about.

Rae has packed light, so every article of clothing has a certain functionality and meaning to her. She slips on a long T-shirt that slides over her butt and could pass for a short skirt in a dark room. She considers this her "sexy sleepwear" with a design of chickens on it. Exhausted, she lies down and falls into a fitful sleep, stirred by loud Spanish voices in the courtyard, a screeching parrot, and trucks and deliveries rattling at the front gate.

She awakens in the dark and looks at her wristwatch. It is only 8:00 p.m. She is awake, and worse, famished. *Argh*, she thinks, *I should have gotten food before falling asleep. Should I go out, in the dark, in this funky border town? Is it safe? And should I leave my passport and everything here in the room?* She lies there obsessing over this and decides to stay put. She pulls out her dwindling food bag. There is a squished, three-day-old peanut butter and jelly sandwich, a sturdy Cortland apple holding its shine, and a well-picked-over bag of nuts and raisins that she bought at the food co-op. They taste delicious.

As she dozes off, she is surprised by a longing. *I wish my big brother were here*, she thinks to herself. *Toby would be good company. He would have gone out and gotten me some food.* But in her last phone call with Toby, he criticized the foolishness of her trip and her being brainwashed by propaganda in her sympathies for the Nicaraguan revolution. She feels even more alone.

In the morning, wearing cooler clothing, she sets out to cross the border bridge to Matamoros, Mexico. She had envisioned that the Rio Grande would be a substantial river, but after a drought it is a disappointing, muddy rivulet on this October morning. She crosses the bridge and steps onto Mexican soil. A Mexican official looks at her passport, stamps it, and waves her through the pedestrian line. "Bienvenidos," he says.

The bus to Mexico City zigzags down through the interior of Mexico, passing through small towns and arid plains. She has never been to Mexico, never been outside the US except for a trip to the Canadian side of Niagara Falls that she took with her parents when she was thirteen. Rae is glued to her window seat, taking in every detail of the passing landscape and people's faces. Bakeries, older women with aprons, churches and chapels with colorful flags, little roadside *tiendas*, aimless dogs, small fenced-in farms, old men with *sombreros*, and endless car-mechanic shops with signs offering *vulcanización*. She looks up the word in her dictionary, which offers "tire repair." (She later learns that *vulcanicación* is the process of retreading a tire by burning a new tread onto the old, something almost unknown in the US but common among resourceful Mexicans.)

The approach to the colossus of Mexico City begins two hours before arriving at the destination bus terminal. Slowed by extreme traffic jams, complete with endless honking, the bus lurches past sprawling *colonias* of improvised, half-built concrete houses, with pieces of rebar pointing heavenward, and precarious mounds of post-earthquake debris.

Rae's head has been filled with written and verbal warnings about Mexico City, with its reputation for abductions, bandits, pickpockets, and chaos. She disembarks the bus, her passport and money belt wrapped around her belly, a small daypack on her chest, and her tightly packed knapsack strapped on her back. She has had hours to study her map and has traced out a walking route to Casa de Los Amigos. On the way, she sees many buildings damaged by the earthquake and huge piles of refuse; now scarcely a month since the earthquake, she sees the word for that, *terremoto*, everywhere. The streets are crowded with people walking, hawking, and sitting on street corners, some protesting with hand-painted banners and sheets.

She arrives at the Casa de Los Amigos, a four-story building undamaged by the earthquake. She has read that the building once belonged to the Mexican painter and muralist José Clemente Orozco. She is buzzed in and greeted by a Mexican woman named Reina, who she guesses is about her age. Reina speaks little English but explains that Casa volunteers are helping with a large outdoor soup kitchen located outside a collapsed apartment building, about a twenty-minute walk from the Casa. Rae signals that she is ready to volunteer, and Reina tells her to report at 8:00 am, drawing a route on a faded xerox copy of a map of this district of Mexico City.

Rae gives Reina her passport and a package of American Express traveler's checks to put in the Casa's safe, and then she walks up the shiny wooden stairs to the women's bunkroom. She drops her backpack on the floor next to an open bed with a sigh of liberation, like a burro shedding its saddle. With any luck, she won't pick it up again for three weeks, when she travels to language school in Cuernavaca. She switches into another set of clothes, grabs her considerably lighter daypack, and sets out to walk to the city's *zócalo*, the main plaza.

While there is evidence everywhere of a devastating *terremoto*— rubble, fenced-off buildings, and people sleeping outdoors—there is a festive air to the plaza. Children run and shoot balloons into the air and an Aztec shaman performs cleansings with a conch shell. A few dozen feet from a magician staging tricks, a group of dancers perform for street change. Food vendors, many of them children, wind between the clusters of people, selling gum and snacks. What in New England would be considered a summer sunshine bathes the whole plaza, though the late-afternoon shadows of the surrounding buildings and churches begin to creep across the park.

Rae finds a café with outdoor seating and sits facing the remaining sun and the plaza. She orders a *limonada* without ice and pulls out her journal, opening to a blank page and looking up, pen poised over paper. The *limonada* arrives in a tall soda fountain glass with a straw and she takes a first sip, the cold tart liquid hitting the back of her mouth like an electric shock. "Wow," she says aloud, wiping her chin and almost draining the entire glass with another slurp. "*Qué rico*," she says to the puzzled waiter, who smiles at her with two silver teeth. Next she orders a hot chocolate and looks over the menu for something savory.

She soon discovers that a *gringa* sitting at an outdoor table on the *zócalo* is fair game for every passing merchant and needy person asking for money. A steady stream of people approach her, including women selling bark paintings, handsome men in cowboy hats selling wood carvings, children selling knickknacks or simply asking for change. One girl brings her blind brother over, both holding out their hands. She tries to look each person in the eye and say, "*Lo siento*," or about art work, "*Es bonito, pero no, gracias*." It is heartbreaking to hear the price for an art work continue to come down, as the hourly rate for these artisans falls into the centavos. "*No, gracias*," she says with uncertainty.

In her journal, she writes: *To them, I represent great wealth. Of course, they should ask.*

After eating an enchilada slathered in cheese, Rae walks back to the Casa and climbs into her sleeping bag for a sense of security. She sleeps a deep and uninterrupted sleep.

She rises a little after dawn for her day of volunteering at the soup kitchen. She hard-boils and eats a couple eggs, pulls on her boots, and ventures off through the morning streets. She hears a brass band playing nearby and passes a formation of police officers parading in a courtyard. Through the traffic chaos and the litter, Rae is struck by the beauty of bougainvillea flowers thrusting out from metal gates, and jacaranda trees with their purple fall blossoms.

The earthquake has left many buildings untouched, while others are pancaked or cracked beyond repair. Passing one decimated building, Rae sees a framed painting of a sailing ship, still hanging on a second-floor interior wall, slightly askew. On another block there is a car completely flattened by fallen debris.

Even in a bustling city, the side streets are quiet and tranquil on this weekday morning. An occasional street sweeper pushes a straw broom, or someone walks out of their gate on the way to work. In the more affluent neighborhoods, the streets are lined with walled courtyards. Occasionally Rae peeks past an open gate or a crack in a wall into someone's private paradise, with lush grass, flowering trees, and occasional fountains and swimming pools.

Rae arrives at a crowded plaza full of tarps strung up by webs of rope to light poles. She spies a sprawling outdoor kitchen under one set of blue tarps, slightly barricaded by boxes of supplies. A small cookfire and a number of large *comales*—cookstoves—for tortillas are fired up on one side. In the background is a hulking eight-story apartment building, badly damaged and listing to its side like a battleship ready to sink. Next to the soup kitchen is an expansive city of tarps, cardboard, plywood shacks, and tents full of people. As she gets closer, she can hear children crying and adults arguing, and she smells the pungent blend of excrement, truck exhaust, urine, woodsmoke, burnt food, and garbage.

She approaches the kitchen area, telling a youthful soldier with a rifle that she is a volunteer. There is a large woman in a floral apron who seems to be in charge of a dozen workers standing at stations performing different cooking tasks. Rae introduces herself and explains in broken Spanish that she is a volunteer from the Casa de los Amigos.

The woman, who introduces herself as Dolores, looks her up and down and asks something unintelligible in rapid-fire Spanish. Rae shrugs and pantomimes a cutting motion. Dolores lights up with a grin and utters, "*Cebollas!*" She leads Rae to an open table with several wooden and plastic cutting boards, large plastic tubs, several large knives (one looking like a small machete), and a dozen enormous bags of bulbous white onions.

"*Cebollas,*" Delores says, pointing at the onions. "*Está bien?*" She pulls out an onion, slices it open, slips off the peel in one motion, and chops it quickly, placing the cut pieces in a plastic tub.

"*Sí,*" says Rae, figuring she'd do a shift of onion chopping. She certainly has no skills in the tortilla department, so she won't be gathered around the *comal* stoves with the other women.

She pulls her first onion out of the bag, whacks into it with the dull knife, and begins chopping away. Ten minutes later, her eyes are so teared up she can barely see.

"Reya," she hears, as Dolores appears by her side, holding out a pair of industrial goggles.

"*Gracias.*" Rae puts on the foggy goggles and feels instant relief.

And so begins several weeks of volunteer work, roughly ten hours a day of chopping onions, mountains and mountains of onions. Occasionally, one of the cooks walks over and grabs one of the tubs of onions to add to a large soup pot for beans or stew. She may exchange a few words with them, but otherwise she works in silence. There are other international volunteers, including two young white women from the Netherlands. She knows they speak English, but they are unfriendly and don't have anything to do with Rae, presumably because she is an American.

From Rae's onion-chopping station, she can watch the mass of human experience in the plaza. Many of the people living under tarps, she learns, are former residents of the precarious apartment building. Some have lost family members, along with all their belongings, and have nowhere to go. And a few are clearly traumatized, along with their children, sitting with their heads in their hands or shouting out in rage at invisible demons. Others flash toothy smiles at her, or dance to *campo* music blaring from tiny cassette players.

After each of her onion-cutting shifts, Rae wanders the city. The smell of onions is so pervasive, in her clothes and skin, that she cannot get the smell off. If Nina were here, she would tell her that she loves pickle brine even more. Every evening, she scrubs and scours her skin until it is raw. Juanita's lavender soap doesn't make a dent, and Rae buys some strong detergent. The fragrance of onion is so intense that strangers on the bus, in a church, or bunkmates at the Casa all politely sidle away from her. She douses herself in patchouli oil, which, blended with the onions, gives her an entirely unique odor.

After work, she returns to one of two favorite cafes where she can order flavorful foods and exchange a few words with familiar waiters. With her small knapsack at her side, she writes letters home on blue onionskin airmail ("Par Avion") envelopes, scribbles in her journal, or reads newspapers with her pocket Spanish dictionary in hand.

One newspaper, *La Jornada*, is vigorous in its attacks on government corruption and incompetence in the aftermath of the earthquake. The newspaper is full of reporting on corrupt building inspectors accepting bribes and failing to enforce earthquake-resistant construction standards. On the other hand, there are heroic stories of people helping one another, forming food committees, health clinics, and soup kitchens like hers to operate in the vacuum of government inaction.

She learns about the valiant *topos*, the "moles," a volunteer brigade that in the weeks after the *terremoto* dug and rescued people from the rubble of the estimated thirty thousand broken buildings, sometimes digging solely with spoons. When working on a site, if they heard a person's cries beneath the rubble they would hold up their arms in a signal for quiet.

She sees protesters in the street and learns about the plight of the *costareras*, the seamstress workers in various sweatshops. In the days after the earthquake, the factory owners brought earthmoving machinery to rescue their equipment while ignoring the pleas of their workers, still alive and buried under rubble.

In her journal, Rae writes: *Two weeks ago, I was at home, harvesting vegetables, riding my bicycle along the river, sitting with people I love. Now I am alone, unable to communicate, with no friends. I was starting to come out of my shell in Montague, and now I'm back deep inside. I'm completely overwhelmed by the suffering I see and the smell of onions. I've never traveled anywhere in the global south, never really faced poverty outside the US, and here I am, dizzy, like a deep-sea diver who has surfaced too quickly into this new world.*

Occasionally someone at the soup kitchen or the Casa speaks to her, but she has no idea what they are saying. Days go by when she doesn't talk to anyone outside of a few rudimentary words of greeting. She calls home once to talk to her mother, but it seems to cause more worry for her parents than if she'd sent another blue airmail letter.

It is a time of solitude and sometimes painful isolation in a city of fourteen million. She knows that in a short time she will travel to Cuernavaca, where there will be other students, people who speak

English, and her home stay with a family. She marks her time by chopping, walking, writing, and thinking.

There is one old church where Rae likes to sit in the back pews whether there is a Mass in progress or not. It is here that she begins to reconnect with her meditation and prayer practice. She is surrounded by people praying and sitting in the church as a place of peace. Each visit, she lights a votive candle and puts a peso in the metal box, sometimes making a wish or sending a message. During one church visit, she copies these words from a book by Dorothy Day into her journal: *"What good can one person do? What is the sense of our small effort? They cannot see that we must lay one brick at a time, take one step at a time; we can be responsible only for the one action of the present moment. But we can beg for an increase of love in our hearts that will vitalize and transform all our individual actions, and know that God will take them and multiply them, as Jesus multiplied the loaves and fishes. . . . A pebble cast into a pond causes ripples that spread in all directions. Each one of our thoughts, words, and deeds is like that. No one has a right to sit down and feel hopeless. There is too much work to do."*

In her final days at the soup kitchen, she starts to relax and joke with some of the regular workers. She gets a nickname, *Señorita Cebolla*—Miss Onion. On her last day, they present her with a ceremonial onion of her own. On the bus to Cuernavaca, Rae estimates that in three weeks she has cut up three thousand onions.

DYING FOR THE LITTLE THINGS

(1986)

Two months have passed since Rae's lonely days of cutting onions in Mexico City. After language school she traveled with
new Canadian friends to Oaxaca for Christmas. After New Year's,
she met up at the Mexico City airport with a friendship delegation
of US citizens setting out for a month in Nicaragua to assist with
the cotton harvest.

Rae's group of eighty-five volunteers is one of the first harvest
brigades from the United States. Most are part of church-based
groups that engage in community education, demonstrations, and
lobbying—a citizen's movement to change foreign policy. A national
network has formed to organize the brigades, drawing volunteers
from all over the US and Canada, including many involved in the
Pledge of Resistance.

Rae's delegation of cotton pickers lands in the capital city of
Managua and boards buses to Chinandega, the provincial capital
of a northwestern department. From there, they stand in crowded
trucks for a three-hour ride to the coastal village of Apascali.

On the truck ride, Rae stands next to a guy named Reggie
Donovan, a labor organizer from Boston. They are the same height,

and Rae feels a spark of attraction, a sensation that has been dormant for a couple months. The spark increases as they bump skin to skin on the bouncy truck ride. He knows all about Montague Farm and asks about Sarah and Peter.

"That's a heavenly part of the world," Reggie says, referring to Montague. "I like to bicycle that loop around Sunderland and Montague."

"Oh, that's a great ride," says Rae, excited after almost three months of traveling to meet someone who knows her corner of the world. "Nice and flat!" They talk for several hours over the grind of the truck gears, both looking out over the unfamiliar Nicaraguan landscape. Rae realizes that she hasn't laughed with someone for months, and Reggie has a lightness and humor that is part of his attraction.

The trucks arrive in Apascali after dark, and brigade members unpack into ancient wooden barracks where generations of cotton harvesters have previously bunked. Each building contains a dozen small rooms with three-level bunk beds. Lit by flickering bare lightbulbs, their sleeping quarters are layered in dust, a dust that they will eat and breathe for the next three weeks. Upon arriving, Rae and the others are exhausted, happy to be motionless at last and eager to unroll their sleeping bags. Rae takes note that Reggie is bunking in the next room over.

She lies in her dusty bunk thinking about how unusual this delegation is. Many of the participants, like herself, have learned how the Cold War mentality of the Reagan administration does not permit any openness or nuanced view toward the Nicaraguan Revolution. In 1979, a popular revolution expelled the corrupt US-backed dictator, Anastasio Somoza. Instead of seeing a restless nation aspiring to self-determination and wanting to forge its own diplomatic and trade relationship with the United States, the Reaganites see only Communist expansion, another Cuba. Instead of helping the new country on a path to independence, the US government trains and funds mercenaries, the Contras, to attack Nicaragua's borders.

The harvest brigade's presence is both practical and political. Nicaragua needs additional labor to harvest its cash crops of coffee and cotton. More important, in the last few months the Reagan administration has been threatening to invade Nicaragua with US troops, inspiring people like Rae to organize the pledge. The presence of hundreds of *norteamericano* allies and witnesses in the cities and fields may discourage a full-out invasion. Once Rae and her fellow *brigadistas* return home, they intend to fan out and show their slideshows in church halls and libraries across the land, spreading awareness and lobbying for legislation to ban military aid to the Contras.

The next morning, Rae and her compatriots emerge squinting into a bracing sun to greet their Nicaraguan hosts. Apascali is centered around a plantation farm, with several large equipment sheds and stacks of suspicious metal fertilizer drums, a sort of Nicaraguan "Love Canal" toxic waste depot. A small creek flows through the village. Upstream are dozens of small wooden shacks, surrounded by clotheslines and tethered cows and sheep. A five-minute walk west, Rae is able to look out over the Pacific Ocean from a bluff. North to the horizon are miles and miles of cotton fields.

Rae waves to the inquiring children that cautiously peer at the gringos. The Nicaraguan adults follow, no doubt also curious and stunned by the sheer amount of stuff the visitors have brought. By breakfast, dozens of cameras are clicking, capturing the domestic scenes in the compound—chickens, pigs, and dusty smiling children. The US delegation, it appears to Rae, is prepared for anything short of a direct bomb attack by US warplanes. They have more Gore-Tex, Vibram, and Velcro than an L. L. Bean store—and enough electronic gadgets to stock a Radio Shack store. Rae is embarrassed by this excess.

Around the village there are soldiers from the Nicaraguan army. Twenty teenage men and women in dark green military uniforms carry antiquated rifles with hand-woven straps. They have their own marching drills in the morning, but mostly they work alongside the pickers in the fields with a cotton sack in one hand and a rifle slung over the opposite shoulder.

When Rae was in high school, she trained as a paramedic and volunteered on an ambulance, so she joins the brigade's two nurses and one doctor to establish a clinic to care for the ailing among the *norteamerico* brigade. By the fourth day, there are a dozen sick gringos who need to be woken up every several hours and rehydrated with sterilized water.

The US visitors have brought duffel bags of medical supplies to donate. Forty-three years of rule by the Somoza dictatorship have devastated the country's infrastructure and health capacity. Only eighteen months earlier, a health clinic opened in Apascali for the first time. The Nicaraguan health worker, who splits her time between six rural villages, gives the US health team her blessing to offer medical services to Nicaraguans out of her one-room clinic. Soon, fifteen to thirty locals appear at their door each day.

At Apascali, the medical team mostly deals with infections, worms, and dehydration. Dr. Jim, from West Virginia, handles stitches and anything more serious. Their satchels bulge with Band-Aids, stethoscopes, and antibiotics, but essentials like anti-diarrhea medicine are soon in short supply.

When Rae worked as an ambulance paramedic, she mostly transported people between hospitals and nursing homes. But her limited experience doing wilderness and sports medicine is actually more useful here, far from fancy medical equipment. Her most useful tool is an English-language edition of *Donde No Hay Doctor* (translated as *Where There Is No Doctor*), with its helpful illustrations.

The baby that Rae holds in her arms is skin and bones. His mouth is opening, but no sound comes out.

"*¿Cómo se llama?*" Rae asks the mother. "What is his name?" She has just placed her bundled boy into Rae's arms.

"Hector," she says, looking Rae fearfully in the eye. She is a short woman with jet-black hair and two round silver earrings. She wears a purple shawl and dusty blue flip-flops. "Hector Donaldo Muñoz Ramirez."

"Hector," Rae repeats. "*Tu tienes un nombre tan grande para un bebito.* You have such a big name for a small boy." Rae observes that he is shriveled like a raisin. He can't be more than three months old.

"How old is he?" she asks in Spanish. After a month of classes in Cuernavaca and another month traveling around Mexico, Rae can now carry on a basic conversation.

"Six months."

Oh my God, she thinks. *This baby is in trouble.* She looks at her watch and rocks Hector gently in her arms. She has no idea where Dr. Jim is.

"*El doctor va a regresar pronto.* The doctor is returning soon," she assures the mother. *Really soon*, she hopes.

Baby Hector has fallen asleep in Rae's arms. He is severely dehydrated, and she feels that treating him is beyond her skills.

"Doctor," begs Hector's mother. "Help him."

"*No soy médica*—I am not a doctor," Rae explains. "Just a paramedic." This appears to be meaningless to the mother. Rae takes out a stethoscope, listens to Hector's heart, and takes his infant pulse, which is racing like hummingbird wings. Hector's limp and quiet body is in distress.

Rae feels a maternal ache flow through her body, a desire to nurse and nurture this small baby—or one of her own. She has had similar feelings at Montague Farm, with the small children crawling over her to cuddle and read stories. But this sensation is stronger, a tremor made stronger by the baby Hector's hunger and need.

"Is he drinking? When was the last time he nursed?" Rae asks.

"Formula," says his mother, lifting a tin canister from her woven shoulder bag. "But he is not drinking much and has diarrhea."

Rae feels a flash of anger toward the multinational companies that aggressively market infant formula to mothers around the world, claiming that it is better for babies than breastfeeding and more modern. Even her own mother gave up nursing her and her brother in favor of the modernity promised by powder formula.

Rae remembers how, in the 1970s, the Nestlé company marketed their infant formula in developing countries using salespeople dressed as nurses. Yet in much of the developing world, the water supply is too contaminated to be mixed with formula for infants to drink. Breastfeeding is obviously free, healthier, and much safer. An international boycott of Nestlé forced them to end their deceptive marketing. Now she holds Hector, a real victim of this unethical practice.

Nicaragua's new health ministry is actively promoting breast-feeding for both its healthy nutrients and maternal bonding. On the highway outside Managua, Rae snapped a photograph of a large billboard with a nursing mom and the slogan, "*La leche de la mamá es lo mejor*" (that is, "Mother's milk is best"). But rural areas still have few health promoters and pro-breastfeeding educa-tion. Hector's mother probably spends half her income on infant formula.

"Let's fix up something for Hector," Rae says, handing him back to his mother and peeling the plastic off a sterile bottle. She mixes up some infant formula with treated water and pediatric anti-diarrhea medicine.

"*Donde está el sacerdote?*" Hector's mother asks softly. "Where is the priest?"

"*¿El padre?*" Rae looks at her concerned face and milky black eyes. "He is around. But we're going to help Hector. We're going to help him."

"*Padre,*" the mother whispers. *Oh no,* Rae thinks. *She wants the priest to do last rites.*

"I'll get him," Rae assures her. "But first, let's get Hector to drink something."

The residents of Apascali are jubilant that a Roman Catholic priest, Father Gerry McGorian, is part of the brigade. He is quickly pressed into pastoral duties and relieved of some of his cotton-picking responsibilities. No priest has visited Apascali in more than a year. Many new babies need to be baptized, and weddings consecrated. Gerry is known to all, even the gringos, as "*Padre*"— the most popular man in town. He spends his evenings lying on his bunk bed with a flashlight, crudely translating sacraments and blessings into Spanish with a phrase book. "*In the name of the Father . . . En el nombre del Padre . . .*"

Rae laughs as Reggie teases him. "Padre, how come you didn't bring your sacrament flash cards in Spanish?" Reggie and Gerry appear to have bonded over a number of things, including their Boston Irish heritage and affinity for the Red Sox.

On his second day in the village, Gerry humbly tried to explain to a gathering of Nicaraguans that he was "embarrassed by his poor Spanish." In his Anglo-Southie Spanish accent, he actually said, "*Soy embarasada por mi Española pobre*"—which, to the Nicaraguans, roughly translated as "I am pregnant by my poor Spaniard." The Nicaraguans broke into wide grins and covered their mouths to muffle their giggles. When Rae whispered to Gerry what he had actually said, he laughed the loudest of all. "Well, better to massacre the language than the people—as our government is doing."

By day, Gerry, as Padre, performs a nonstop series of baptisms, retroactive marriages, and blessings for children, sick people, animals, houses, and crops. When Rae is not in the cotton fields or at the clinic, she helps Gerry keep track of these sacraments in a special book that he will later deliver to diocesan headquarters in Managua.

Rae is aware that Hector's mother fears that a priest might be more useful than she. "What is your name?" Rae asks her.

"María," she says.

Fortunately, Dr. Jim strides up at that moment. Rae points to Hector—and with her eyes lets him know the gravity of the situation.

The second-most-popular man in town, Dr. Jim is not getting much rest. And while Padre has a priestly collar, Dr. Jim wears a long brown ponytail, torn jeans, and a West Virginia State T-shirt.

He holds Hector like an experienced doctor and father, lifting up the baby's closed eyelids, checking his pulse and breathing. Rae tells him she was making up a bottle with medicine. "Yep," he concurs, passing the baby back to Rae, a vote of confidence. "Go for it." He shifts his attention to several other patients lined up at the clinic, including a man with an infected six inch machete gash on his leg—a common farm worker injury.

Rae shakes the bottle with sterile water. Hector wakes up and turns his head away, refusing to drink. Rae locates an eyedropper and puts a drop of milk on his lips. Slowly he opens his mouth, and his tiny cheeks start to move. Rae is reminded of a time when, as a little girl, she found a baby grackle bird and her mother mixed up an eyedropper for her to nurse the bird.

"Come, sit," Rae says, steering María to their only chair in the shade of a jacaranda tree. "This might take a while."

María sits for an hour, feeding Hector with the eyedropper. Rae prepares a gallon jug of sterile water and medicine for her to take home.

Rae feels useful at the clinic, but her contribution in the cotton fields is questionable. The Nicaraguans amiably rib the US volunteers about their pathetic cotton picking. At weigh-in time each day, experienced pickers turn in sacks weighing between 150 and 200 pounds. Small children surpass Rae in the fields with sacks of more than 50 pounds. "Hey, gringa," one boy giggles, "why so slow?" Rae's daily labors top out at 35 to 40 pounds of white fluff.

Rae complains to Padre Gerry that she doesn't think the gringos are earning their keep as farm workers. They are sitting on the dusty wooden steps of their bunkhouse in the heat of the day, when everyone rests from picking. The sacrament machine is taking a break and mopping his broad forehead with a white handkerchief.

"Half our crew has Somoza's Revenge," Rae says, referring to the diarrhea plaguing the gringos that keeps them from the fields. "And we're such lousy pickers. Maybe we should have stayed in New England and sent them our plane-fare money—or five doctors instead."

Gerry looks at Rae, his eyes wide with surprise. "It's not about our contribution to the harvest," he says. He is among the pokiest of the pickers. "It's about bearing witness, our *accompaniment*."

Accompaniment. This is the first of many times Rae hears this concept in her Central American travels.

Gerry explains the biblical imperative to "stand with the poor" and "accompany the poor as Jesus did." "We are not doing *their* work for them," he explains. "We are, however, laboring beside them. This is not an act of charity, because it is as much *for us* as it is for them. We are *accompanying* the people of Nicaragua in their struggle for liberation. And we are mostly white bodies making ourselves vulnerable to US war."

Gerry loosens his priestly collar. His fair Irish skin is pink and flushed. Though Rae likes him a lot, he initially reminded her of priests she knew who were enamored with the timbre of their own voices. But here in Nicaragua, something quite different is sparking in Padre. A few nights earlier, he said offhandedly to Reggie and Rae, "Now I remember why I went to seminary twenty-two years ago."

"We have to go back to the United States and bear witness," Gerry says. "We need to 'speak truth to power,' as the Quakers say. We must do our job to change US policy. That is different work, critical work. But here, our job is to *accompany*. We want these Nicaraguans to know that our government doesn't speak for all of us. We are citizen diplomats—forging friendships while our governments are at war."

Gerry turns and looks at Rae sitting on the bunkhouse step as if he were getting a good fix on her face for the first time. "The other reason for being here is *for us*. It is to *transform us*. Lord knows, we're the ones who need to change." He gives Rae a pastoral wink and gazes back out at the village square. "God, what I wouldn't give for a cold beer."

One blazing day the volunteers do earn their rice and beans. A siren wails and a muffled voice is broadcast over the loudspeaker with an urgent call to help extinguish a fire in the cotton fields. Almost everyone who is healthy picks up a shovel, a machete, or a hoe, and they quickly form teams with Nicaraguan leaders, jogging in formation toward the rising smoke.

Rae and Reggie join a team of ten that whacks down row after row of precious cotton plants to create a five-yard-wide firebreak to contain the blaze. As the flames approach, Rae's eyes smart from the smoke and she pulls a bandanna over her mouth. The cotton leaves crackle, and the pods explode with a popping noise.

Their leader is a Nicaraguan soldier with a rifle that would be in a Civil War museum at home. He shouts and signals for everyone to move back. They stumble and watch in horror as the flames leap across their firebreak, propelled by a sudden gust of furnace-hot wind.

The leader is unfazed. He whistles and leads them in a military jog to another spot a hundred yards downwind. They begin slashing another firebreak, this time ten yards wide. But before the fire reaches their new line, the wind dies down, depriving the fire of oxygen. They move back toward the dwindling flames and scoop dirt onto them. An hour later, after sunset, Rae and Reggie join others in patrolling the smoldering fields, burying any remaining embers flickering in the dark.

During their final week, both Rae and Reggie help to dig two bomb shelters for the village. Teams of Nicaraguan and gringo workers take shifts during the day, working until their hands are blistered. There are running jokes about the absurdity of US volunteers helping their humble Apascali friends construct shelters to protect them from US bombs. "Should we get Padre to bless the bomb shelter?" quips one Nicaraguan.

"*¿Por qué no?*" Rae responds. Why not? "He's blessing everything else in town."

"He'll pray that the bombs miss their targets and fall in the sea," said Reggie, hoisting a large shovel of dirt.

Despite the enormous divide in culture, language, and wealth, Rae is struck by how the US volunteers form friendships with Nicaraguans over these three weeks. After each day in the cotton fields, Rae and Reggie walk with two Nicaraguans in their late teens, Camillo and Carmen, to the ocean to watch the sunset. In their limited common language, they tell stories and joke with one another. Carmen wants to be a doctor so she can do what Dr. Jim is doing at their clinic. Camillo wants to study agriculture and improve the farms in Apascali. They all pledge to become pen pals, and Rae promises to visit if she returns to Nicaragua.

On one of their final walks, they see the lights of the US warships patrolling the coastline, reminding them that their two countries are at war. Two years earlier, US Navy Seals under the direction of the CIA mined the Port of Corinto, sixty miles to the south, damaging ships and burning millions of gallons of oil.

"There are Ronald Reagan's warships," Carmen observes. Rae appreciates how the Nicaraguans consistently make a distinction between US citizens and their government. *Padre is right*, she thinks. *Being here is important, even if we are lousy cotton pickers.*

"They are listening to our conversation with their radar," jokes Camillo. "Don't reveal any secrets about our cotton harvest."

"Yeah, like how half of it burned up." Reggie adds. They all laugh, and Rae studies Reggie's face, the lightness in his step, his gestures, his mischievous smile.

Walking back, they cross paths with María carrying Baby Hector. He is crying powerfully. María smiles broadly and shows him off under her *rebosa* shawl. He looks a few pounds heavier.

"Nice work, doctor," Reggie says, gently intertwining his arm with Rae as they walk on.

Rae smiles, happy to feel his affection. "I keep thinking of that Jackson Browne song: *People die for the little things. A little corn, a little beans.*"

By flashlight, Rae writes in her journal: *I'm sweet on this guy Reggie. He is kind, a good listener, and unattached. He's got a sense of humor and playful vibe. He is serious-minded about the problems of the world but doesn't sink into the gloom. I haven't felt such a strong attraction for anyone since the early months with Brian. Maybe I've just been traveling and sleeping by myself for too long? Ha! But I don't think so. We have a lot of things in common. He's working-class, Irish, political, intellectual. For Pete's sake, his father is an ironworker and his mother has an Irish knickknack store!*

On their last night in Apascali, Camillo organizes a farewell party. The Nicaraguans set a large, bald tractor tire on fire, like a wood bonfire but more toxic. A cow is slaughtered and roasted. Musical instruments come out, and Rae and Reggie join the group, spinning and dancing the night away.

Rae says farewell to her friends in the brigade, who are returning to the US. She is heading north to El Salvador to visit friends and volunteer in a refugee camp, catching a bus instead of riding with the others.

As Reggie is about to board the truck back to Managua, they exchange a long embrace.

"I would really like to see you when you get back," Reggie says, digging his hands into his pockets. Rae sees a flash of vulnerability, maybe even loss, as Reggie appears to push through a bit of shyness. She likes him even more in this moment.

"I'd like that," says Rae. "I'll write you from El Salvador and let you know my return plans."

As the *norteamericanos* board the trucks, their Nicaraguan hosts press small gifts into their hands—flowers dipped in wax, candies, tiny weavings from cotton husks, lemons, pieces of colored fabric. There are tears of farewell. Padre Gerry and Dr. Jim are smothered with garlands.

A few minutes later, Rae boards an old school bus heading in a different direction. She is surprised by the tears that overtake her. Something about the Apascali generosity and kindness has scrambled her understanding of her place in the world. *Our countries are at war*, Rae thinks, *yet these Nicaraguans are accompanying us home.*

THE ALTAR AND THE PASSPORT

(1986)

"If you don't want to wake up with a rat turd in your mouth I recommend sleeping on your side, with your mouth closed." Ruthie Ganzer is orienting Rae to her new accommodations at the Betania refugee camp in Zaragoza, El Salvador, fifteen miles south of the capital, San Salvador.

"The good news is, this room is entirely reinforced with chicken wire so the rats can't barge in," Ruthie says with a bemused grin. Her fair, round cheeks are pink from the Salvadoran sun; a long, blond braid points down the center of her back. She appears to relish the wide-eyed reaction she is getting from Rae.

"But that doesn't stop the rats from trying," she continues. "At night you'll hear them crawling and scratching overhead." She points her flashlight up toward a chicken-wire ceiling beneath the wooden roof. "They're trying to get into the kitchen storage area next door."

Rae has been well oriented to the regional perils of scorpions, poisonous spiders, and unfamiliar snakes. She has gotten into the habit of shaking her boots out before putting them on. But she hadn't thought much about rats.

Four army cots are placed around the perimeter of the room, leaving only enough room for one person to stand in the center.

Ruthie explains that the camp workers take turns in the morning getting up and dressing. She meets Rod and Jennifer, a couple from Seattle, who are the two other full-time international volunteers in the camp.

"I hope you're not modest," she adds drolly. She is younger than Rae, maybe twenty-eight, but seems mature after several years working in the Betania camp. She lives in this ten-foot-by-ten-foot room with two or three other volunteers for weeks at a time. Only an embroidered pillow that Ruthie bought at a Salvadoran craft market distinguishes her cot.

"And *ta-dah!*" Ruthie says with fanfare. "This is the bathroom." She pulls back a blanket hanging in one corner to reveal a bucket with a plastic Tupperware-style lid. "We take turns emptying it into the latrine. I'll show you where."

Rae immediately takes a shine to Ruthie, her friendly direct gaze, and matter-of-fact way of describing rats, latrines, and military abductions. She is tall, solid, and lean—the leanness, Rae soon learns, being an occupational hazard of life in the camp. She and Rae quickly figure out that they share Midwestern roots and German and Irish heritage.

Rae's job at the camp is straightforward. She is part of a rotating team of four White North American church workers who, by their presence at Betania, discourage the Salvadoran military from entering the camp.

International law forbids any national military from entering designated refugee camps. But that doesn't stop Salvadoran soldiers from periodically showing up in the middle of the night to conscript young men involuntarily—or to "disappear" someone they suspect of being an anti-government rebel.

The Archdiocese of San Salvador believes that, because the United States writes the big checks and trains the Salvadoran military, US observers could help relief workers stand up to the military. In 1980, the Salvadoran army murdered four US Roman Catholic sisters, and the US temporarily cut off aid to the Salvadoran government. "We are human tripwires," deadpans Ruthie. "They trip over us; they lose their helicopters."

In her journal, Rae reflects: *Getting my US passport at the Greenfield,*

Massachusetts, post office took only half an hour, a bureaucratic task to check off my list before traveling, along with a hepatitis shot, water purification tablets, and a supply of onionskin-thin airmail envelopes. It didn't occur to me then how that slim passport would be deployed as a giant shield to protect the very lives of people I hadn't yet met.

Standing on a slight rise and surrounded by tall, leafy green trees, Betania is a sprawling, low-rise city of what look like hastily constructed woodsheds and shacks. It is one of several large internal refugee camps filled with Salvadoran citizens fleeing conflict zones in other regions of the country. Many of the residents come from San Vicente and Morazán departments, zones of heavy fighting between guerrillas and the Salvadoran Army.

What started in the late 1970s as an electoral battle between political factions devolved by 1981 into an armed conflict. After so many pro-democracy and reform activists were murdered and abducted by government and right-wing death squads, the left felt they had no choice but to take up arms to defend themselves, forming the Farabundo Martí Liberation Front, or FMLN. They contested the military, which was backed by hardcore, right-wing politicians, and an oligarchy of fourteen families. As in Nicaragua, the United States sided with El Salvador's oligarchs and authoritarian right in a global battle against Communism and its perceived cousins.

The Salvadoran military's strategy is to drain the deep well of civilian support in rural areas for the guerrillas by torching villages and forcing people to move into camps like Betania. Many Betania refugees witnessed their homes burned to the ground by the military. Some have lost everything and have nowhere to go. Despite the displacement—or perhaps because of it—the whispered sympathy among Betania residents is for *los muchachos*, as the guerrilla fighters are known.

Built by religious organizations to accommodate two thousand people, Betania now bulges with more than four thousand inhabitants. Extended families of as many as fifteen share a wooden-shack room the same size as the room that Ruthie and Rae share with two others. New arrivals sleep beneath tarps or under the stars.

Small cook fires around the camp contribute to a languid haze by mid-afternoon. For a town packed with so many people, Betania is strangely quiet. There are no honking cars, smoke-belching buses, or haggling market vendors. Only the murmur of human voices, crying children, and a few transistor radios cut through the subdued silence.

On Rae's first night, she is awakened by a scratching noise. She clicks on her flashlight and shines it at the ceiling. Two large brown rats crawl six feet above her head, looking for a hole. Her three roommates sleep soundly, heads turned sideways, mouths closed.

Her down sleeping bag is too hot, and she squirms and turns, wondering why she has put herself here. *I could be anywhere*, she thinks. She could be back in Greenfield swimming in the Green River, or eating the delicious cornbread that her housemate Tom makes in a large cast-iron pan, or sniffing the savory smells coming from the pot on her kitchen stove. Comforting images come to her—the snow falling in Montague, the social gatherings around the dinner table, folk dances at the Guiding Star Grange Hall. She drifts into a shallow sleep.

At 4:30 a.m. she is awakened again, this time by the *slap-slap-slap* sound of chattering women making tortillas for several thousand refugees.

After the sun rises at about 6:00 a.m., Rae takes her turn getting dressed and using the bucket bathroom. The cool, clear morning air is a welcome relief after the stuffy room and her smothering sleeping bag. She is thankful to have brought her favorite flannel shirt.

"*Buenos días,*" chirp the cooks. They have already hand-produced many mountains of tortillas. About a dozen women stand in a circle around a large, flat, metal cookstove in Betania's open-air kitchen. Four women knead huge piles of *masa* cornmeal. Others flip hot tortillas with their bare fingers on the round *comal* stove.

"*Buenos días,*" Rae replies unsteadily, taking in their warm smiles and grins. They each wear light-blue or green button-down polyester sweaters over cotton dresses and floral aprons.

Several children are already kicking a deflated soccer ball outside the kitchen. Other children have looped sections of a broken garden hose over several metal pipes and constructed a swing set.

Rae walks down to the river, where people are bathing and washing clothes. She scrubs her face and dunks her head, enjoying a moment of submersion in the cool water of the sandy-bottomed creek. It is not the flowing, clear Green River, but it feels great.

Ruthie joins Rae at the stream with two plates of beans and tortillas to share. She sits down on a log, crosses her long legs, and closes her eyes to offer a silent blessing before she eats. Ruthie is connected to a Lutheran volunteer corps and tells Rae her reasons for being in El Salvador are "two parts biblical call and one part botched romance."

"We eat the same food as everyone else," she counsels, waving her rolled tortilla in the air. "But its barely enough calories. Some of us pack in granola bars and other food." Somehow Ruthie has mastered the art of looking clean and put-together while living in a refugee camp. Rae feels a little ragged, with her bedraggled long hair dripping down her flannel shirt.

"I personally look forward to egg day," Ruthie smiles, nibbling a tortilla.

Noticing her upright posture, Rae straightens up. "Egg day?" Rae asks.

"Yes, everyone gets an egg on egg day."

"One egg?"

"There are four thousand people here."

"Right."

Soon Rae also anticipates "egg day" and the food shipments sent by Italian humanitarian aid organizations that include large packets of *pasta e fagioli* soup . . . just add water! But Ruthie is right. It isn't enough. At thirty, Rae is fit and, in her own estimation, healthily chubby. But after ten days, she bores two new notches in her belt to keep her pants up. "My hips are disappearing," Rae jokes, "thanks to the 'Betania diet.'"

Similar to Apascali Nicaragua, the main job of the volunteers at Betania is to be present as observers and always carry their precious passports. But sustaining four thousand people in such makeshift conditions requires a lot of work, and everyone who is able is expected to pitch in—with food preparation, caring for children and elders, sweeping, medical care, religious services. Still, cut off from her life and usual responsibilities at home, Rae has a bit of time to read, write in her journal, hang out, talk, and make new friends. She writes a long letter to Reggie in Boston, describing the Betania camp.

On her third day, Ruthie introduces Rae to a midwife named Chepa who, Ruthie reverently explains, has delivered half the babies in San Vicente department, the part of El Salvador where many of the residents of Betania originally resided.

"In Betania," Ruthie says appreciatively, "anywhere from one to four babies are born each day, so her services are in high demand. She's amazing."

Chepa greets Rae warmly as she strolls purposely through the camp. Like most women here, she is about four and a half feet tall, sturdy and dark-skinned. Like the kitchen workers, she wears an apron over a floral dress and dime-store flip-flops on her bony, weathered feet. Her long, jet-black hair has a few streaks of gray.

"There are many babies today," Chepa explains in Spanish, pointing to the clinic. "The doctors need my help."

Rae and Ruthie walk with her to the clinic while Chepa asks Rae about her mother, father, and siblings—a customary Central American way of starting a conversation.

"They're all fine," Rae assures her.

Three days a week, European doctors and nurses from the international aid organization Médecins Sans Frontières—Doctors without Borders—come to the health clinic. They drive up from the capitol, San Salvador, in Land Rovers and care for long lines of patients. The other four days of the week, the traditional midwives and healers are on call.

Rae notices how the international health workers are very respectful of Chepa and the other Betania midwives. They are eager to learn from these women who have delivered hundreds, maybe thousands of babies, without high-tech medical tools. Whenever the European docs encounter complications during child deliveries, they urgently call for Chepa. When Chepa starts scrubbing her hands and walking briskly toward the clinic, the locals nod knowingly: another breech birth at Betania.

•

One day Chepa invites Rae to visit her family cubicle to see her altar. Amidst the chaos and bustle of life in the camp, Chepa has created a sacred space on a shelf in the corner of a single room shared by six. On her altar are several burning candles, devotional statues, and a dozen photographs. Rae recognizes Archbishop Oscar Romero. With few flowers anywhere near the camp, she has placed freshly fallen tree blossoms and leaves around her altar; their fragrances blend with the smell of ash and other herbs. She points to the voter identification card of a young man. "This is my son, Ramón," she says in Spanish. "He was assassinated by the army."

"Oh God, I'm so sorry," Rae responds, squinting at the postage stamp-size photo.

"That is my husband, Raúl," Chepa says, pointing to a blurry photo of a man holding a machete. "He was also killed in the conflict." With her voice steady and tears clouding her eyes, she introduces Rae to her universe of loved ones, many of whom have died and suffered in the war. "*Mi altar es mi fuente . . .*" she says, letting the sentence hang in the air. "My altar is my source . . ."

Rae understands her meaning. This altar is where Chepa can grieve. But it is also the source of her spirit to live and to accompany mothers bringing children into the world. She has endured massive loss—her loved ones, her home. Yet Rae feels how Chepa pulls toward life.

Almost as if someone scripted it, two military helicopters buzz over Betania at that moment. Chepa leans in her doorway, points up, and smiles. "Ronald Reagan's helicopters," she teases wickedly. "*Sus dólares.*" In other words, "Your tax dollars at work."

"Yep," Rae agrees sheepishly.

"Did you know that Archbishop Romero wrote to your former president Jimmy Carter? He said, '*If you are Christian, stop sending weapons that are killing my people.*'" Chepa fixes her dark eyes on Rae to gauge her reaction.

"Yes," Rae says. But she had only recently learned this fact from reading a book about Bishop Romero. President Carter ignored the request and continued supplying military aid. Rae wonders how these rural peasants know so much more about our country than we do. *With all our news outlets,* Rae wonders, *why do we know so little about the world?*

Every other week, Rae rotates out of the camp for two nights, and other volunteers take her place. On one of these breaks, Rae visits a friend, Rebecca whom she knows from Western Massachusetts and who now works at a Lutheran orphanage in San Salvador. Rebecca gives her a tour of the orphanage where she meets dozens of huggable children. From there, they take a bus to a hilltop called Los Planes, where dozens of food stands sell the local delicacy, pupusas, a tasty masa tortilla stuffed with beans, cheese, and pork.

Rebecca and Rae order a stack of *pupusas* and a bag of *curtido*, a spicy cabbage coleslaw that is the perfect complementary condiment. They sit on a wobbly picnic table on a bluff and look out over the sprawling city of mostly low-rise houses and shacks. Rae can make out the cathedral in the late-afternoon smog as well as a few of the taller buildings in the city center.

"Does working with all those children inspire you toward motherhood?" asks Rae.

"Yes, for sure," Rebecca answers without a pause, putting another spoonful of *curtido* on her paper plate. "It also makes me think more about adoption. All these children looking for homes."

Their conversation is punctuated by a local pop song, *"Me Gustan las Pupusas"*—"I Like Pupusas"—blaring from a tinny radio speaker near their table.

"How about you?" Rebecca asks Rae.

"I feel the stirring. So many sweet, loving children, hungry for affection. Both here and in the US."

After dinner, they walk along a summit road and Rebecca points to the cliffs infamous for being where Salvadoran death squads dump the bodies of their victims.

"As long as the bodies don't have US passports in their pockets, no one will know," Rebecca says plainly. "It won't be news in *el Norte*."

On another afternoon off, Ruthie and Rae catch a bus, overloaded on top with boxes, bags, and bundles, headed to San Salvador to meet up with friends and to boost their calories. The bus is full of campesinos, men from the countryside wearing white straw hats, and women wearing reboso shawls holding loads of vegetables, fruits, and scrawny chickens to sell at the city market. They steal glances at Ruthie and Rae, two tall, Germanic apparitions standing in the aisle.

It is the heat of the day and the bus is stiflingly hot. Rae's stomach lurches as the bus rocks and heaves forward along the curving highway, grinding its gears. A loud radio blasts Salvadoran country music, clashing scores of trumpets and trombones. The front of the bus is decorated with a curious juxtaposition of signs, icons, and sayings—the Virgin Mary next to sexy pinups of supermodels alongside religious quotations ("Jesus is my savior") and irreverent sayings. Rae's favorite is "Better Dead than Late." She is relieved when their bus reaches the central plaza and they can walk.

Through Ruthie and the well-networked community of international aid workers in El Salvador, volunteers like Rae are periodically invited to discussions with Jesuit priests who teach at the Central America University, one of whom is Ignacio Ellacuria. That night, Rae and Ruthie join several Jesuits for dinner at a neighborhood restaurant. In addition to Father Ignacio is Father Segundo Montes, a sociologist who studies the refugee situation. Another is Father Joaquín López y López, a shy and bookish man who occasionally says Mass at Betania.

In El Salvador, it is difficult for those working in refugee camps to decode the news and rumors and know what is really going on. These two priests are a reliable fount of updates and analysis about the war and the refugee camps.

As their food is served, the restaurant plunges into complete darkness. Immediately, waiters bring candles and adorn the table. Sticking their heads out the door, they see that the entire neighborhood has lost power.

"The power is out, either because of our inept government utility," observes Father Segundo, "or because the guerrillas have blown up a transformer. Either way, the guerrillas will be blamed."

Their young group of international volunteers is never more than one degree of separation away from people who knew the martyred Archbishop Oscar Romero and can recount stories about him. While living at Bethania, Rae works with several Maryknoll sisters who previously lived with Ita Ford and Maura Clark, two of the nuns who were murdered by death squads in 1980.

A custodian at the cathedral sells Rae a cassette tape of Monsignor Romero's sermons. The Betania team listens to them while lying on their cots in the dark. In the sermon he gave days before his assassination in 1980, he directly addresses members of the Salvadoran military:

> Brothers, you came from our own people. You are killing your own brothers. Any human order to kill must be subordinate to the law of God, which says, 'Thou shalt not kill.' No soldier is obliged to obey an order contrary to the law of God. No one has to obey an immoral law. It is high time you obeyed your consciences rather than sinful orders. The Church cannot remain silent before such an abomination. . . . In the name of God, in the name of this suffering people whose cry rises to heaven more loudly each day, I implore you, I beg you, I order you: stop the repression.

Rae listens to this sermon over and over. She writes the words in English and Spanish in her journal. Hearing the pleading and anger in Romero's voice building at the end—"*I implore you, I beg you, I order you*"—Rae feels her body overtaken with shivers.

Romero, as one worker at the cathedral whispered, was the first bishop to be assassinated at the altar in eight centuries. Rae wonders if the previous one was Archbishop Thomas Becket, depicted in T. S. Eliot's *Murder in the Cathedral*, one of her Amherst College course selections.

Life feels intense and precious here. The simple dinners, social gatherings, birthday parties, and anniversary observances are infused with the concentrated joy and gratitude rooted in lives that have known deep loss and sorrow. Rae feels grateful to be accompanying these people, sleepless nights and all.

One night the volunteers are awakened from their Betania cots by the unmistakable sound and vibration of a helicopter hovering over the camp. Several people bang on the wall to inform the *internacionalistas* that army trucks are at the entrance of the camp. It is time to do their job. All four pop up at once, colliding in the center of the room.

The thumping of the US-made Huey helicopter vibrates the ground, its shifting searchlight a frightening tentacle of light scouring the shacks. Rae suspects that for the residents of Betania, the sound of a helicopter rekindles the trauma of death and displacement. People sleeping outside run for shelter to escape the rhythmic chopping sound overhead. Rae is filled with an adrenaline-fueled rage at the helicopter and the Salvadoran army, a nervy and probably foolish emotion.

The four gringo church workers rush to the front gate with their cameras and passports. Ruthie, the most experienced and fluent in Spanish, does the talking.

"You are not permitted to be here," she yells in Spanish to the Salvadoran colonel, above the din of the helicopter. The colonel puzzles at the *gringa* wearing blue jeans hastily pulled up over a billowing pink nightshirt.

"*Somos de los estados unidos!* We are from the United States!" she shouts. They all flash their blue passports. "No army in the camp."

Rae realizes that she doesn't have any film in her camera. But she is able to make the camera flash. Her heart races as she pretends to take pictures of this absurd scene: four gringos in their pajamas facing off twenty soldiers wielding rifles.

After gruff exchanges and walkie-talkie consultations with superiors, the colonel waves to his unit and climbs back into the front cab of a transport lorry. The helicopter rises and turns away. No conscriptions or abductions tonight.

Long after the army leaves, adrenaline continues to surge through their bodies. They stand around replaying the scene. "Those US passports," Ruthie wisecracks. "They work 95 percent of the time. The other 5 percent—well, we don't hear from them."

As the four walk back to their cubicle, Rae observes how this is a strange international version of pulling privileged rank: "Do you know who *we* are?"

Ruthie brightens up. "It's more like: 'Do you know who my uncle is? Uncle Sam!'"

Rae has been thinking about the irony of their mission in Betania: to flaunt their global privilege in the service of human rights. Their common US citizenship trumps the power of the Salvadoran military, at least on one night. Their passports and white skin are their calling cards (and they know that it would have been far riskier for darker-skinned Americans).

Back in the bunk room, the four volunteers lie awake in the darkness on their cots. Ruthie pulls out her small cassette player and pops in a homemade cassette. She whispers, "I've got a bit of contraband here. New album brought in by my Canadian friends. Since we can't sleep."

The sound is all treble but it is the voice of Bruce Cockburn, a popular singer-songwriter and guitarist from Toronto. The first verse:

Here comes the helicopter — second time today
Everybody scatters and hopes it goes away
How many kids they've murdered only God can say
If I had a rocket launcher . . . I'd make somebody pay . . .

They lie quietly after the song.

After a long pause, Ruthie murmurs "I heard that song was inspired by what Cockburn saw in a refugee camp on the Mexico–Guatemala border."

Rae is moved by the song. "I understand that rage and also the powerlessness." She's not sure she would play that song for some of her Quaker friends. But being nonviolent doesn't mean denying a human fantasy of revenge. "Maybe there's a way to nonviolently lasso a helicopter, disable it without killing anyone."

The others chuckle at the image and slowly drift to sleep.

Rae lies awake feeling the rage rise and fall in her body. *Using my body as a human shield*, she thinks, *is inadequate*. She wants to fully understand her responsibility to look in her own life for the "seeds of war," as the eighteenth-century Quaker John Woolman put it. She recalls Brian telling her what their friend Juanita Nelson says: "Look to uproot the seeds of violence in your own way of living."

Rae writes in her journal: *My government is providing the money, weapons, and training to a repressive government. These are my "tax dollars at work," as Chepa observed. Isn't my government acting to protect my privileged interests? Won't I go home and benefit from the Salvadoran government's violent opposition to trade unions and land reform policies— resulting in cheap imported food and clothing? My standard of living and way of life are implicated in all of this—it's a global economic system. I don't have to do much to keep winning the global lottery. It is rigged in my favor.*

During Rae's two months in El Salvador, she begins to feel more viscerally each decision in her life, especially around consumption of things, food, and energy, and how she benefits from this international system of advantage. She begins a journal entry with a quote from Monsignor Oscar Romero: *"Aspire not to have more, but to be more." Each decision I make requires a certain mindfulness. I don't feel burdened by it. It is like a spiritual practice where I try and often fail each day. What I do know is, I HAVE TO DO MORE and consume less. What will I do in the US, where, as Brian says, consumption is the national religion?*

Most days, Rae is filled with gratitude for the life she has back in New England. She has a job to return to and abundant food and loved ones at home. Rae gently handles her blue US passport, thinking about all the privilege and power that goes with it. More important, Rae now has an inner knowledge that no matter how hard things might get, she can always build an altar with the photos she can salvage—and draw strength from it.

After six months in Central America, Rae returns to Franklin County feeling a jumble of contradictory emotions. She has daily flashbacks to the soup kitchen in Mexico City, the rural village of Apascali, and the refugee camp at Bethania. She writes to Carmen and Camillo in Nicaragua and Ruthie in El Salvador. When she closes her eyes, she sees the views from the bus windows as she passes through the countryside.

A few days after arriving back in Massachusetts, Rae walks into a supermarket and bursts into tears. She is overwhelmed by the abundance and variety, choice and color—bright packages, succulent kiwis from New Zealand, eighteen brands of mouthwash, products for every whim. She flashes back to the scantily stocked neighborhood groceries in Mexico and "Egg Day" at the Betania refugee camp.

She writes: *We are so wealthy as a people compared with the places I have been. How many miles would someone from Apascali be willing to walk to get the small tube of antibiotic ointment in my grocery cart?*

Rae feels her heart physically enlarging to include the people she has met—and she feels accountable to them—as she attempts to chart her path back in the US. She talks to others who have traveled and worked for an extended time in Central America about the shared disorientation they felt upon their reentry from seeing the complexities and contradictions of American life—the abundance of our supermarkets and the resources of our health care system in contrast to the suffering caused by US foreign policy. She also sees the growing gap between the rich and everyone else in the United States, which adds another layer to the picture.

Since her return, Rae has experienced a number of restless nights of lying awake, feeling the anger and rage pulsing through her body. One day she sees Eliot Abrams, a Reagan foreign policy official, on television droning on about "Communist influence" in Nicaragua. She tastes the bile rising in her mouth, the desire to strike out and punch Eliot Abrams through the television set. Her fury is directed toward these men, the architects of a foreign policy that punishes innocent people.

She resumes work at the women's shelter where she worked before her trip. Now she considers "accompaniment" to be part of her work. To prepare, she culls her best photos and creates a forty-minute slideshow.

At her first presentation, before a group of parishioners at Holy Trinity Church in Greenfield, she breaks down in tears as she describes all the aid projects funded by other countries. "Traveling in Nicaragua and El Salvador, you encounter health clinics funded by the Dutch, staffed by French doctors, playgrounds built by Spaniards and Italian food donations. If you want to see the impact of US aid, you have to visit a cemetery or see people's altars. It makes me ashamed to be an American."

She offers her program to more church groups and anyone willing to listen, giving over thirty presentations in the following year. With her citizen solidarity group, she lobbies Congress to cut off aid to the Contras. Their efforts make a difference in Massachusetts, where their congressional delegation takes the lead in instigating a more positive foreign policy in the region.

The Reagan administration defies Congress by illegally selling weapons to Iran and then channeling funds to secret bank accounts to support the Contras.

By 1987, the Reagan administration is embroiled in the "Iran–Contra" scandal, and funds for their covert war against Nicaragua dry up.

Two weeks after her return, Reggie comes to visit the farm for the weekend. Rae can't recall a time when she has been more excited to see a potential companion. They take their bicycles out along the Montague plain and sit by the Connecticut River. They visit the Montague Bookmill, a bookstore with the motto: "Books You Don't Need in a Place You Can't Find." Rae describes her rocky reentry to life in the USA, and Reggie knows exactly how she feels. She takes Reggie's sunglasses off and kisses him on the lips.

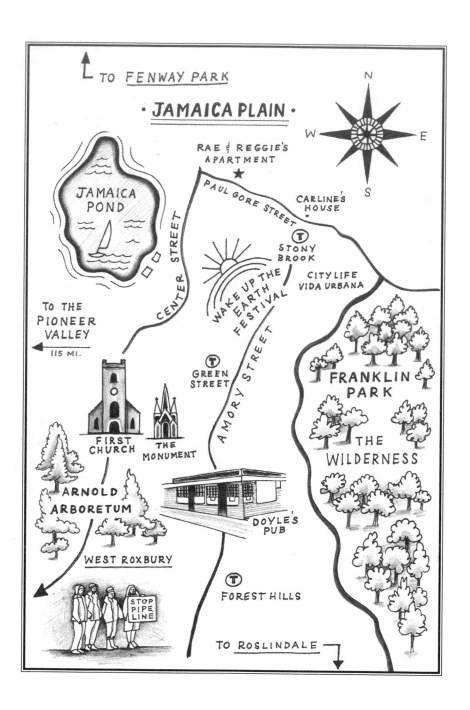

PART 3
RESISTANCE

We are not to simply bandage the wounds of victims beneath the wheels of injustice, we are to drive a spoke into the wheel itself.

—DIETRICH BONHOEFFER

WAKE UP

(1987)

Reggie unlocks his bicycle from the rack near the Boston Common and contemplates his ride home. In the mornings, when he is focused on the day's work ahead, he often bikes the most direct route down the bike path on top of the Orange Line subway. But in the afternoon, especially on a beautiful day like this, he likes to ride up the Esplanade and along the Muddy River back to Jamaica Plain.

This is a Muddy River day. Carpe diem. Enjoy the late summer. Rae is at First Church, doing a training for the Pledge of Resistance. She'll be busy until 8:00 p.m., but maybe he can stop by and catch a glimpse of the action. Reggie's softball team, the Loan Sharks, isn't playing tonight.

Reggie starts peddling down the common and across the Arthur Fiedler bridge toward the Esplanade, past the Boston Pops bandshell, and up the paved bike trail along the Charles River. The first faint whisper of fall is in the air, this first day of September.

Today is the one-year anniversary of Reggie and Rae moving into their apartment. Maybe he'll take Rae out for dinner after her training.

After meeting her in Nicaragua in January 1986, Reggie eagerly awaited Rae's return to Western Mass. He received several airmail letters from Rae describing her travels in El Salvador. With each communication, his infatuation with her grew. After her April return, Reggie went to visit her in Montague, his heart beating in anticipation. And after four months of sweet and passionate visits in Montague and Jamaica Plain, Reggie lured Rae to come live with him in Boston. Rae willingly made the move, making him promise frequent outings to Western Mass.

Rae. Reggie shakes his head. His happy bachelor life has been totally upended by this force of nature that he has fallen in love with.

Reggie pulls his bike over at a bench, pausing to watch the sun ripple off the Charles. There are rowing sculls cruising by, crewed by students from area colleges with their boathouses upstream. Across the river is MIT and its domed building and dormitory towers. He crosses another bridge over Memorial Drive, turns away from the river, and weaves his way past Fenway Park.

Reggie knows that the Red Sox are on the road, so the stadium and surrounding neighborhood will be quiet. On other evenings, he might stop in at one of the sports bars near the stadium, have a cold beer, and watch on TV while the game is played inside the park. He loves the current team, with Mike Greenwell, Ellis Burks, Dwight "Dewey" Evans, Wade Boggs, Jim Rice. Unfortunately, it's already clear that the Red Sox won't be playing in the postseason. The "curse of the Bambino"—the fateful 1920 Red Sox trade of Babe Ruth to the Yankees—has kept them out of contention for another year. A local joke is: What is the difference between the Red Sox and the Yankees? Answer: October baseball.

One thing Reggie appreciates about Rae is that she's not allergic to sports, like some of the feminist women he knows. She actually takes pleasure in going to the ballpark, closely watching the game, and jumping up and down. And she doesn't mind having the ballgame on the radio in the background on a summer night. She grew up running bases with her brother and dad—playing a game they called "pickle"—and rooting for Johnny Bench and the Cincinnati Reds. But she has quickly adapted to the American League Red Sox.

Reggie admires how Rae arrived in Boston and leaped into local activism with both feet, emotionally on fire after her six months in Central America. She joined two active solidarity groups and plugged back in as a trainer with the Pledge of Resistance movement. She's formed a cadre of women friends and staked out a plot in a community garden, making even more friends around the neighborhood. During her first May living in the neighborhood, she organized a bunch of women to march in costume and drums in the annual Wake Up the Earth festival.

Another thing about Rae: She says she won't get married until her gay and lesbian friends can also legally get married. "If the state won't recognize their love and bond, then I'm not going to sign up," she disclosed early on. Reggie is fine with that position. He's in no hurry himself, and it relieves the pressure that he's felt in other relationships, though he does feel some pressure from his family to settle down, especially his mother.

"You need to be a role model for your siblings," Reggie's mother would inveigh. "You're stacking up and living in sin." (He later repeats her malapropism for "shacking up" with delight.)

His mother, Brigid Maeve Sullivan—"Missy" to her siblings—is one of nine children from a large Dorchester Irish Catholic family. Ostensibly destined for a religious order, she met Reggie's father, the youthful Conor, at a dance at St. Mark's Church and embarked instead on marriage and family.

She raised Reggie and his six younger siblings while Conor worked at the Quincy shipyard. Conor drank until last call every night at the Eire Pub and tottered home, a highly functioning alcoholic who didn't miss a day's work until he dropped dead of a heart attack at the age of sixty-one—"God rest his soul." Reggie was thirty then, two years before meeting Rae.

Missy never spoke an ill word about her husband, tolerating his temper and gruff parenting. Only when he physically threatened the boys did she intervene to challenge him. She provided the unconditional love and acceptance of her brood, all but one of whom remain living within ten miles of the small family house in the Adam's Village section of Dorchester.

Months after Conor's sudden death, the ever-resourceful Missy opened a small gift shop with the death benefits from Conor's Ironworkers Union contract, a fact she never let her children forget. "Your father's union meant we weren't destitute."

She named her shop the "Irish Cottage" and chose a storefront in a strip mall off Route 3A in Hingham, just down the road from the shipyard in what some locals called the "Irish Riviera." Missy's shop was chock-full of Irish kitsch, including tri-color flags, "Guinness Makes You Strong" dish towels, hand-knitted Aran Island wool sweaters, shamrock pillows, and crocheted samplers with "May the Road Rise Up"–type sayings. A permanent soundtrack of fiddle music and revolutionary Clancy Brothers songs greeted her customers, members of the Irish diaspora for whom the Irish Cottage might be the closest they ever got in this lifetime to the Emerald Isle. Those who do get to Ireland for a two-week bus tour stop by the shop to regale Missy with stories of how lovely everything was. (She herself never made the trip until many decades later, with Reggie and Rae.)

Reggie inherited his mother's peacemaker qualities and the conflict avoidance that is a survival instinct among so many children of alcoholics.

"My mom is all worked up because we're stacked up," he would report to Rae. But the reality was that Rae and Missy were charmed by one another. And Missy loved Rae's Irish wit, altar-building practices, and devotion to her son. She was permanently smitten with Rae after Rae made a large altar on All Saints Day in tribute to Conor, complete with fuzzy Polaroid pictures, small Irish flags, a Saint Brigid's cross, and a glass of Bushmills whiskey.

Reggie could see that Rae loved his family, felt at home at their events, and enjoyed the laughter and banter. It didn't matter to Rae that his siblings were religiously devoted to upward mobility and focused on bigger houses, new cars, private schools for their kids, and consumption *maximus*. As she does with everything, Rae dove in and made friends with his sisters. She shows up at holiday or birthday parties with handmade gifts and cards while everyone else brings store-bought items.

Reggie warned Rae that living in Boston would be accompanied by endless social obligations. In a large Irish family, the social calendar is almost entirely filled out by birthday parties, wakes, funerals, weddings, christenings, special masses, anniversary parties, and other command performances. Rae initially insisted on attending most of these events until she realized that there would be no time for anything else and she was seeing Missy's parish priest more than her closest friends. But Reggie and Rae have always heeded Missy's one commandment not to miss any funerals, often rushing back from Western Mass or the beach or wherever and changing clothes in their car. This happens so regularly that they've taken to keeping a decent set of "funeral clothes" and dress shoes in the car.

Reggie rolls up to the First Church and parks his bike at the gate next to a dozen other bicycles. The back door of the church is open and he can hear a buzz coming from the main parish hall. But above it all, he hears Rae's voice, speaking authoritatively. He tiptoes in and sees an overflowing crowd, with roughly sixty people in chairs and more seated on the floor or standing. At the front of the room is Rae, standing and leaning forward. Her co-trainer, Cathy, is sitting next to her on the stage with a large flipchart on an easel. Rae is wearing a purple jumpsuit and white T-shirt, with her long hair tied back.

"Okay, I've got two more people on the stack with questions, then we're going to move on." Rae points at one person and then the other. Rae is one of the few people Reggie has ever witnessed who can corral a bunch of over-talkative activists into order. She spies Reggie across the room and flashes him a quick smile.

A participant in the training asks a question about the pledge. "What if we have concerns about the Sandinistas, about their treatment of indigenous people? Is our action an implied endorsement?"

Rae leans forward. "Good question. Understandable question. Look, our witness, the Pledge of Resistance, is focused on the behavior of the US government. We're saying: It is not okay to invade another country. We don't have to endorse everything the current Nicaraguan government does. But we believe that Nicaragua should be able to develop and evolve without the threat of an invasion hanging over their heads, and without the economic embargo. We are US citizens. Our job is to resist the illegal and immoral actions of our own government."

The discussion continues until Rae invites another question, this one about the history of nonviolent action. Reggie watches Rae, her attentiveness and light touch. She steers the question to Cathy though she could ably respond herself.

The meeting winds down and people stand in clusters talking to one another. A group of a dozen gathers around Rae, asking her questions. Reggie stands and starts to fold chairs, knowing that the sooner the room is tidied up, the sooner Rae will be able to leave. He sees his friend Jack also helping with the chairs and picking up cups and paper plates. They exchange a brotherly hug and greeting.

Finally, the room is almost empty except for a few stragglers talking to Rae. Reggie packs up her easel, markers, masking tape, and her little tool box, tucking them into the church office where Cathy and Rae are allowed to store their training materials.

Rae, finally liberated, skips over to give him a huge embrace. "My lover," she says, a little too loudly for Reggie's comfort, but he's getting used to being embarrassed by Rae's public displays of affection.

"Hey, you know what today is?" Reggie asks.

"September first?" Rae guesses.

"Our one-year anniversary of living together," Reggie says triumphantly.

"Wow," says Rae, smiling. "It's only been a year? Seems like a lifetime."

"Can I take you out to dinner? How about Galway House?"

"Oh, that's a nice thought," said Rae. "But I made you your favorite stew. Let's go home and save our nickels."

"Okay!" says Reggie.

They walk out together. Reggie walks his bicycle and Rae keeps pace alongside him.

"Mind if we stop by the garden plot, for a short watering?" she asks.

"No problem." Reggie has not seen the garden in a couple weeks.

Rae smiles at Reggie as they cross Centre Street in Jamaica Plain and wander up Greenough, a quiet street that immediately leaves the traffic and commercial buzz behind.

"Riley and Tucker barked pretty much all day," says Rae, referring to two dogs, one that lives downstairs from them and the other next door.

Reggie laughs. He and Rae have an ongoing shared rant about the dogs in the neighborhood. They are surrounded by dogs—in the apartments upstairs and downstairs in their triple-decker, and in houses on both sides of them. It's Rae's strident view that people should not have dogs in the city, that it's narcissistic and cruel.

Rae is particularly critical of two young women who have a dog but are almost never home. They work all day and hit the clubs all night, barely touching down to sleep, let alone take care of their poor animal.

Reggie and Rae arrive at the garden and Rae turns the spigot, aiming the hose, covered with her thumb, toward her garden plot. There are staked tomatoes, rows of hearty greens, and a small circle of herbs. Rae simulates a gentle rain on the plot.

"And then there's the dog poop!" Rae continues describing the little bags that pile up in the refuse bin, attracting flies. And bags left on porch steps, to be collected later (then forgotten). And these are the so-called responsible owners, the ones who pick up after their dogs. There's plenty of rogue dog poop in the parks, on the sidewalks, and on any open spot around Stonybrook.

Reggie is quite familiar with this rant, but encourages Rae to vent. Ever since her trip to Central America, Rae smolders about the amount of money Americans spend on pets and their fancy food, their health care procedures. "For the cost of one doggy procedure, you could support a health clinic in Apascali," she says, shaking her head.

As strongly as they both feel about this, they're careful to keep these harsh judgments to themselves. Neither of them grew up with dogs, so they know they don't have the full picture. And they are surrounded by pet lovers and people for whom their relationships with their animals are vitally important.

They resume walking toward home.

"If I lived in the country, I could see having a dog or a bunch of barn cats," says Reggie, in a conciliatory way. "But here, in the city, I think it's cruel to the creature. They want to run and sniff and consort with other dogs."

The next morning, Reggie picks up the *Boston Globe* and the *New York Times* off their front porch. An alarming headline grabs his attention. "Protester Run Over by Train at Naval Depot." Activist Brian Willson? Isn't that Rae's old boyfriend? He finds Rae curled up in a corner of their bedroom.

"You heard?" Reggie asks, approaching her gingerly.

She looks up, tears in her eyes. "Yeah, I heard it on the radio a few minutes ago," she says, shaking her head.

"Here's the newspaper coverage," Reggie says, embracing her gently. "I'm so sorry." He has never seen Rae look so depleted and pale.

"It's weird," says Rae. "But I'm not surprised. This is what Brian has been preparing for."

Rae stretches out and looks at Reggie. "It's like he'd been disciplining himself for this. His obsession with Norman Morrison, with the monks who set themselves on fire. He had some wicked case of death wish or survivor's guilt."

"Who's Norman Morrison?" asks Reggie.

She tells him the story that Brian told her about Norman Morrison's self-immolation.

"He died?"

"Yeah. I didn't know about him until I met Brian. He had a picture of him on his wall. They went to the same high school in upstate New York. They were both Boy Scouts. Oh, and he told me the story of being in some remote village hamlet and entering an empty hut and there was a family altar, and on the altar was a photo of Norman Morrison."

Rae stands up unsteadily and Reggie reaches out to offer his hand. They walk downstairs and read the newspaper articles at the kitchen table.

"One observer says the train picked up speed instead of slowing down," Reggie says, turning the newspaper page. "The reporter says Brian was trying to get off the tracks. Lost his legs but also got a serious head injury, so he's not out of the woods."

"Jesus," says Rae. "I hope he makes it."

Rae tells Reggie what she has known about Brian since she saw him last, more than a year ago, when he moved away from Greenfield. Brian and a group of veterans did a hunger strike on the steps of the US Capitol, persisting for more than thirty days with only water to protest US aid to the Contras. While they were fasting, the Nicaraguans shot down an aircraft that was dropping weapons to Contras at positions inside Nicaragua. The only survivor was a US mercenary named Eugene Hasenfus, also a Vietnam vet, who was captured and confessed to his mission. The whole Iran–Contra arms connection scandal started to unfold.

"Brian actually met with Hasenfus in a Nicaraguan prison," Rae says. "Hasenfus told him, veteran to veteran, about the whole Contra arms-supply operation, how the weapons traveled to El Salvador by ship from the Concord Naval Weapons Station in California. Then they would drop them to the Contras by plane. That's what got Brian focused on blocking trains at Concord."

"Reggie," Rae says, looking at him through her tears. "I'd like to go out there. I'd like to see Brian and support his new wife, Holley, and join in the protests."

"Of course," Reggie says, thinking about his schedule. "I might be able to join you." Reggie suspects, however, this is a trip for Rae to take on her own.

Later that day there is a vigil for Brian at Boston Common, called by a local peace group. Rae and Reggie go downtown and see a number of friends. Their friend Randy Kehler is there, wearing a St. Louis Cardinals baseball cap.

Three days later, Rae is on an early-morning direct flight to Oakland with plans to stay at her friend Charlotte's house, visit Brian, and attend the protests. Charlotte picks her up at the airport and they drive directly to the Concord Naval Weapons Station for what promises to be a massive protest, with thousands outraged over Brian's maiming.

"Brian is at the John Muir hospital in Concord," Charlotte reports, her auburn hair blowing in the breeze from the open window of her cherry-red VW Beetle. She is chewing gum and talking nonstop.

"There's no question that Holley saved his life," she says, merging on to the expressway toward Walnut Creek. "She's a midwife and she had an IV in the trunk of her car. Cool as a cucumber, she immediately stopped the bleeding from his legs and stabilized him. The freaking navy ambulance comes, checks his vital signs, and then leaves, telling Holley that Brian isn't on naval property. They could have taken him to the hospital—but no! They have to wait another five minutes for the county ambulance to show up. Unbelievable!"

"What do you know about Brian's condition?" asks Rae. She's fearful that she might never see him alive again.

"Hasn't woken up yet. But he's stable. He had to have brain surgery for his head injury." They pull onto the road leading to the weapons depot and see hundreds of parked cars lining the roadway. "Guess we better park where we can."

Thousands of people converge on the scene of the crime, the train tracks crossing a public right-of-way. A stage is set up and Rae hears the thundering voices of speakers and cheering coming from the site. One speaker says that nine thousand people have come together at the very spot where Brian was run over.

Rae feels goose bumps ripple down her back. She hears a familiar singing voice booming from the rally stage and recognizes Joan Baez raising an anthem. Over the next hour she hears the Reverend Jesse Jackson, Daniel Ellsberg, and many others.

Standing and gazing at the rail yard, Rae feels her swelling rage toward the US military and their attempt to murder Brian. A group of protesters have begun to rip up the train tracks. Someone hands Rae a crowbar and she joins them, prying at a piece of the rail. With hundreds of people working, they pull up the wooden railroad ties and make piles of metal track, a sort of monument to resistance.

"No trains coming through here today," Rae says, impressed by their handy work.

She spies Duncan Murphy, one of Brian's closest veteran comrades, who was sitting next to Brian as the train raced toward them. He barely escaped being crushed himself. A few years earlier, Duncan had visited Brian in Greenfield and they came to the Green River Café so that Brian could introduce him to Rae. During World War II, Duncan was with Allied troops when they liberated the Bergen-Belsen concentration camp in Germany.

"Duncan," she says, in the swelling crowd. "It's Rae, Brian's old girlfriend from Greenfield." Duncan smiles and gives her a friendly embrace.

"Wow, it's great you came out. Brian will be happy to see you when he wakes up."

Rae is ready to sit on the tracks and block the trains, but since the tracks are ripped up that isn't an option. A large group prepares to block the gates to the naval station, but Rae feels her energy plummet after five sleepless nights.

"Let's go see Brian if we can," she says to Charlotte, who quickly agrees.

They drive toward the John Muir Concord Medical Center, stopping at a garden center so Rae can buy Brian a plant for his room.

The hospital receptionist tells Rae that they are trying to adjust to the Brian effect. Visitors, letters, packages, and phone calls—mostly supportive, but some threatening—are pouring into the medical center. Rae sends a message up to Holley, who proposes they meet at the intensive care waiting area.

Rae and Charlotte ride the elevator up to Brian's floor and are met by Holley as the door opens. Rae feels Holley's body shaking as she gives her a big hug, and Holley warmly thanks her for coming from Boston. "Brian is still unconscious, but he's stable and improving." She looks pale and exhausted.

Holley and Rae have met in person only once before, but they've talked a few times long distance, often with Brian on the line. "Yup, he's a handful," Holley joked one time, and they both laughed.

Accompanying Holley is a tall, handsome man in his fifties, David Hartsough, who Charlotte informs her is a prominent peace activist. "While Holley was stopping the bleed-out, David was guarding Brian's brain," Charlotte says, by way of introduction.

"I've always liked Brian's brain," said David, with a toothy grin.

"Anything we can do for you?" Rae asks Holley, presenting her with a blooming purple orchid she has picked out.

"I'm hanging in there," Holley said. "David just arrived, so I can go home and take a shower. It will be great to have you here when Brian wakes up. It will be helpful for him to see a longtime friend, in case he's lost some short-term memory."

They peek through a window at Brian hooked up to machines. Rae is shocked by how pale and whithered he looks on the hospital bed, surrounded by wires and monitors. *This is a body I know intimately*, she thinks to herself.

A few days later, Rae gets a call from Holley that Brian has regained consciousness. As Holley anticipated, he had no memory of what happened. Holley tells Rae that she had to break the news to him that he'd lost both his legs, as he was experiencing phantom pain and still believed he had his feet.

Rae heads straight to the hospital. Brian is happy to see her when she walks in, but he is also slightly confused. "What are you doing here?" he says, looking from Rae to Holley to the window.

Rae is choked up and initially unable to speak.

"Rae came from Boston, Brian," says Holley, maybe more loudly than necessary.

Rae's eyes fill with tears as she leans over to give him a gentle hug. "Oh, Brian," she sobs. "I'm so happy you're alive."

"Am I in jail?" Brian asks—not for the first time, according to Holley. He is reassured to see the plants and flowers. Holley gives him the medical report. His skull was fractured. He had a hole in his head the size of a lemon that they had to close up. In total, he has nineteen major injuries, including broken ribs, a damaged kidney, and a broken shoulder.

Rae comes to the hospital every day to sit with Brian for a couple hours. They talk quietly about people in Western Massachusetts. Brian asks about Wally and Juanita. The rest of the time she joins the encampment at the Naval Station. There are several large tents with banners saying "Stop the Bombing War: US out of El Salvador" and "BRIAN WILLSON, WE SHALL OVERCOME, Nonviolently." She quickly makes friends with a group of Bay Area activists, kindred spirits in the Pledge of Resistance from the Left Coast.

During her first week away, she calls Reggie every other day and they talk about what's going on. Since Rae is between jobs, she has an open-ended opportunity to be part of the West Coast protests.

"Ripping up train tracks, eh?" Reggie jokes after reading about the protests on Rae's first day. "Isn't that destruction of property?"

Reggie has sat through Rae's Pledge of Resistance trainings and heard her review the codes of conduct, including prohibitions on property destruction.

Rae laughs. *"Touché.* You had to be there. Nine thousand people were pissed. The navy tried to kill our friend. We made a nice sculpture of wooden rail ties and metal rails."

She has a brief call with her brother Toby, who is unpleasant and judgmental about Brian Willson. "What a fool. What was he expecting? You sit on a train track."

She doesn't even bother to explain. Toby seems distracted.

After two weeks, the railroad tracks at the Concord Naval Weapons Station are rebuilt. But the daily protests continue and every train that passes is stopped by protesters, who are arrested and hauled away. Rae and her new affinity group block the tracks and get arrested and booked. Rae is shocked at how rough the police are with some of the protesters, one cop even breaking David Hartsough's arm. The next time she sees David, his arm is in a cast.

One day she arrives at the hospital and finds Brian sitting up in his hospital bed, wearing a large white bandage on his head. "Brain surgery," he says, pointing to his head. "Holley hopes it will fix a lot of things." He smiles and holds up a package of autographs and mementos from the St. Louis Cardinals.

"Listen to this, Rae," Brian beams, reading from a card. "For being such a great Cardinal fan over the years." There is an autographed copy of Stan Musial's autobiography, Brian's childhood hero. Another package is from the San Francisco Giants baseball team, with a note, "Good luck to you. . . You are a very courageous man."

"You're in the big leagues now, Brian." Rae is pleased and relieved to see Brian's spunk reemerge.

Brian fixes his gaze on Rae and points to her. "This woman is a powerhouse," he says to Holley.

"Are you married?" Holley asks her.

"Got my sweetie, this great guy Reggie. You would love him. Labor organizer."

"I'd like to meet him," Brian says. "Come back and visit. Holley and I have plans for a big garden. And the doctor says I'm gonna have legs I can get around on."

Rae learns from Holley the unfolding story of what happened on September 1. The train operators say they were instructed not to stop, out of worry the train would be boarded by terrorists. An analysis of the film footage shows the train moving at 16 miles per hour when it slams into Brian, three times faster than navy yard rules allow.

Rae is part of the caravan as Brian leaves the hospital. Four weeks after arriving at the John Muir hospital in an ambulance, Brian shuffles out the front door, with help from a walker and Holley. They drive straight to the train tracks, where he is exhilarated by the sight of the encampment and the banners. Hundreds of people are gathered. As Brian opens the car door, a roar rises up in the crowd. Tears stream down Rae's face, and she is not alone.

Brian gingerly moves to the train tracks, using his walker and new prosthetic legs, accompanied on each side by Holley and her son, Gabriel. Rae and three dozen war veterans walk behind him. He stands at the place where he was run over and looks across the fence to the Navy Station.

"Not in our name," yells Brian with a sonorous bass voice. "These weapons are not moving in our name. The violence in Nicaragua and El Salvador is not in our name. Over my dead body!" There is a roar of approval.

Rae looks at Brian. He seems transformed. A deep, peaceful glow surrounds him. His spirit seems lighter, like a cloud has lifted. *Maybe that's what happens when you get a second life? Or been released from the ghost of Norman Morrison?* She decides that it's time to go home to Boston and Reggie.

For the next 875 days, no train passes this spot without protesters blocking the way. Over two thousand people are arrested in the blockades.

MARTYRS

(1989)

Rae steps out of the shower, wraps her long hair in a towel turban, and walks naked into the bedroom. Reggie watches with delight, commenting that she is as sexy as the day he met her. And now she has a barely discernable rounding of her mid-section.

"Ah, you're a beauty," Reggie purrs. Rae pirouettes in front of him before tucking into a bathrobe. She bends over and rubs noses with him. After almost a year and a half of not using birth control, Rae is pregnant.

They are both tingling with excitement. Rae writes in her journal: *I'm feeling part of the great cosmic flow of expectant motherhood. Everywhere I go, I feel this bond with other pregnant woman and parents swaddling infants. I know having a child is consuming, but I already feel my heart expanding for the job.*

At almost nine weeks, they have only told a handful of people and are waiting to tell extended family. Rae, ever attuned to her body, believes she knows the moment of conception, a warm night in August, camping by a river in Jamaica, Vermont. Her breasts have become tender and slightly larger. She's had a few nauseous mornings, but she quickly passed through that stage. Now she feels like taking a long nap every day.

147

A week earlier, after making love, Rae had a little bit of blood spotting. Alarmed, she called her doctor who said it was probably normal. At age thirty-five, she's considered a "geriatric pregnancy," and higher risk.

"Okay, Mister Dad, time for our walk." Rae insists on a rigorous morning walk, pushing up against Reggie's sedentary impulse to spend the morning reading newspapers, drinking coffee, and chit-chatting with Rae and housemates. It is Friday and he is planning to go in to work a little late.

"You parading in your bathrobe?" he asks with an amused grin.

"No. Watch this." Within two minutes, Rae has thrown on jeans, the kind with the expandable waist line, borrowed from a friend, and a body-fitting turtleneck sweater. "Let's go, pokey-man."

They walk past their Day of the Dead altar in an alcove of their living room. Rae has assembled one every November since her days traveling in Mexico and Central America. Along with pictures of loved ones, she has collected pine cones, red maple leaves, and acorns that sit next to candles. The altar includes marigolds that she grew in the side yard.

Five minutes later they cross busy Washington Street on their way to Franklin Park. A bus rolls by, and Rae turns her head and covers her mouth from the belching exhaust.

"Though infinitely adaptable, I'm still not entirely a city girl," Rae complains. "This street is so noisy!"

She can see that Reggie, accustomed to the city sounds, actively listens to her and tries to understand what Rae is talking about despite the jackhammers, beeping trucks backing up, people yelling, cars honking, a dumpster being emptied. But soon they are on a quiet side street, and the noises of the busy boulevard are muffled. They cross into Franklin Park, with tall trees in their fall browns and yellows.

Rae picks up on an earlier unfinished thread of conversation. "Hey, how do you envision our lives, you know, after the baby?"

"I'm happy being a homebody, not traveling so much," says Reggie. "I think it will simplify things, in a way." Reggie's work at the union has put him on the road traveling around New England a couple days a month.

"It's hard to live simply here in the city," says Rae, thinking about Wally and Juanita Nelson and their cabin on Woolman Hill. "It's hard to remember that most of the world doesn't consume as much as we do."

It will be several years before people start talking about ideas like ecological or carbon footprint. But Rae has an intuitive sense, from her time in Central America, that people in the northern hemisphere consume more than their fair share of the Earth's bounty. She has become incensed about food and energy waste, avoids buying things in plastic, and is focused on making things that will last a long time. Rae assembles an amazing collection of woven baskets, tote bags, and glass jars for transport and storage of household items.

"I don't know, people in rural areas drive a lot, burn a lot of gasoline," observes Reggie. "Here, we're hardly in our car at all." Their car, an old Volvo wagon, can sit for a week without being used.

"So much of our food comes from far away," Rae complains. "It feels like a vulnerability. One disruption, and the grocery store shelves are empty."

"Lenin said every society is three hot meals away from chaos," Reggie adds.

"Yeah, well, we have about three days' food supply in this city of seven hundred thousand people. Lord Cameron said that civilization is only nine meals away from anarchy."

"That's probably more accurate," says Reggie. "So do you want to hoard food?"

"I already do," Rae laughs. "But having a few weeks' supply of lentils and oats isn't exactly preparing for the end times."

They both laugh.

"I'm afraid my garden would only feed us for a week," she continues. "It will be a long hungry winter."

"I know you're only one meal away from severe crabbiness," Reggie teases. He can tell when Rae's blood sugar is dropping. There's a reediness in her voice, a warning signal to stop what they're doing and find calories. Rae's pregnancy has only enlarged this danger zone.

Rae laughs loudly. "Yeah, unlike you. You're like a boa constrictor eating a giant meal and then lying about for a day. Then you go two days without eating."

"Yeah, but I'm always hunting."

Rae's mind wanders to her worries about raising a child in the city. "Where will the kid play?" she wonders out loud.

Over the previous weekend, she and Reggie visited friends in Western Massachusetts who formed one of the first cohousing communities in the region. The cohousing idea, explained one of their hosts, is an import from Denmark. The communities are characterized by private living spaces, typically smaller, and a large common house, with a large kitchen, a dining room, gathering places, extra guest rooms, and play zones for children.

Rae loved that all the cars in this community of twenty households are parked off the side, away from the dwelling units. There are wagons for residents to haul groceries, and roads if a house needs a big delivery. But otherwise, children run right outside their door to a neighbor's house or the common house.

Rae burst into tears when she saw the arrangement, a visceral response to the sense of safety she felt there. "I just worry about kids and cars, and that's not a problem here." Later she observes, "This is exactly the kind of place to raise children—safe, lots of adults keeping an eye out, no cars and trucks zooming by, less pollution."

Reggie sees things differently, as a city kid raised in Dorchester. "You adjust."

As they walk, Rae reflects back on the visit to the cohousing community. "I think cohousing is more aligned with our nature than atomized, single-family homes or communal living where you share everything. Most conflict I've had in group living comes from a shared kitchen and bathroom. If I don't have to share those spaces, I'm a much happier camper."

"That's because you're an alpha girl in the kitchen, and not everyone has your strong opinions about appropriate sponge usage," Reggie jokes.

"You could live a year without dusting anything," Rae teases back. "You are oblivious to dust."

"What dust?" Reggie is sheepish.

"You don't see it because I dusted while you weren't looking. And your mother Missy is a prodigious duster." Rae has noticed, with only slight annoyance, how Reggie seems oblivious to some household work.

"Oh, I'm in trouble now. You're saying I've lived my whole life in a dust-free environment, thanks to the invisible labor of the women in my life?" He suspects he'll be getting his own feather-duster for Christmas.

Since her visit to Western Mass, Rae has carried a tiny heartache, a longing for a little stronger connection with wild lands and places and food growing. She attributes this in part to her pregnancy, the desire to create a better nest for their child. She's been thinking a lot about her memories of the children at Montague Farm, many of them young adults now, and the freedom they had to play outdoors. They were almost feral, running wild, in a kibbutz-like community. She also thinks about the parents of children in Nicaragua and the refugee camp, and her feeling of being connected to parents everywhere.

Walking in Franklin Park is not a substitute for nature, though Frederick Law Olmstead designated a section of the park as "Wilderness." The area is quiet and tree-lined and includes a picnic area that is so abandoned that the picnic tables have been overtaken by moss. Less wild than neglected—that's how Rae experiences it.

"We agree that we shouldn't have a dog in the city," Reggie observes. "Maybe the same applies to children." They have talked about relocating or building a cabin in the woods, and they are starting to save money. Reggie has his steady job at the union, with health insurance. Rae has a part-time job at a women's shelter in addition to some organizational development consulting, and her volunteering duties with Pledge of Resistance. Money, city-versus-country, and now a baby on the way—plenty to wrestle with.

Things are slowing down with Rae's Nicaragua work, with Reagan gone and the Iran–Contra scandal drawing scrutiny to Reagan's illegal war. The immediate threat of US invasion has passed, though US influence in the region has kept Boston area activists on alert. They worry that US interference will disrupt the Nicaraguan election called for the next year.

Rae occasionally sees photos of Brian Willson in newspapers and newsletters; apparently he is now an international luminary. In one picture, he is shaking hands with Nicaraguan president Daniel Ortega and standing next to singer Kris Kristofferson. In another picture, he is dancing with disabled veterans at a hospital in Nicaragua. Brian dancing! She jokes with Reggie: "If the man had danced with me, we might still be together."

In another photo, Brian is on a hunger strike at the US Capitol with Daniel Ellsberg and actor Ed Asner, whom Rae always liked in her teenage years when he played Lou Grant on the *Mary Tyler Moore Show*. Rae hasn't talked to Brian in more than a year.

Reggie and Rae wind their way through the neighborhood, passing Doyle's Cafe, a pub where they often meet friends after work. Doyle's is where Reggie's softball team adjourns after their games. A November breeze kicks in as they turn onto their street, passing fenced yards full of fallen leaves and windblown bits of rubbish.

As they return to their home, Reggie notices the blinking light on the answering machine and presses the button. It's Karen, Rae's friend from Witness for Peace, sounding distraught. *"Assassination, Ooo-Kah? Look at the newspaper. Call Back."*

"Rae," Reggie calls to Rae, who has walked into the kitchen and is standing in front of an open refrigerator door. "Rae, sounds like bad news."

He picks up the unread newspapers from by the door and sees the headline: "Jesuits . . . El Salvador . . . Massacre."

He hands the article to Rae, who reads while her face turns an ashen hue. Six Jesuit priests have been murdered at the university in San Salvador. She reads their names—Ignacio Martín-Baró, Segundo Montes, Ignacio Ellacuría—and flashes to the gentle, scholarly men she sat with at dinner with Ruthie back in El Salvador. They have been killed by the Salvadoran military. In order to eliminate witnesses, the assassins also killed the Jesuit's cook, Elba Julia Ramos, and her teenage daughter, Celina.

Rae folds over on the floor, engulfed by sobs. "Those men. . . They were so good. They were a threat to no one. . . . Fucking Reagan and Bush." She can barely speak.

Reggie kneels beside her, remembering Rae's description of meeting the Jesuits when she was working at the refugee camp.

Rae retreats to her bed, and Reggie calls work to say he won't be coming in. He hears sobs and furious cries coming from their bedroom as he reads the full account. Later, he peeks into the room and sees that Rae appears to be asleep.

The following morning, Rae appears at their bedside, looking wrecked and otherworldly. Her face and hair are twisted up.

"I lost the baby," she whispers.

Reggie looks dumbfounded.

"I had a miscarriage," she says again. "Just now. We lost . . ."

Rae makes two additions to their altar. One is a small illustration of a baby angel that she feels drawn to. She has cut it out and mounted it on a small stand.

The other is a picture of Ignacio Ellecuría, one of the Jesuits murdered on the previous day. She remembers sitting in the restaurant with him as the power went off. She handwrites a quote from Father Ignacio, from a commencement address he gave in California. He quotes Archbishop Romero: "Something would be terribly wrong in our Church if no priest lay next to so many of his assassinated brothers and sisters." Father Ignacio went on, "If the University had not suffered, we would not have performed our duty. In a world where injustice reigns, the university that fights for justice must necessarily be persecuted."

Altars for loss. This she learned from her travels in Central America. She gathers flowers and candles and tends to her altar several times a day. The loss of her child and the murder of the Jesuits become intertwined anniversaries.

Rae feels depleted. She writes in her journal: *Maybe I'm not supposed to have my own child in this world where injustice reigns. Maybe my work is for all children. Maybe my work is different.* She decides to keep this thought entirely to herself, even from Reggie for the moment.

She remembers baby Hector in the Nicaraguan village of Apascali and all the other children she met in her travels. She thinks of the toxins in the food, air, water, and the impact on her body, on all bodies. She writes in her journal: *Who is responsible? Who made this happen? The chemical companies? Eliot Abrams? Ronald Reagan? I feel them trying to manipulate my body and soul. Where do I channel this fury?*

SCHOOL OF ASSASSINS

(1990–99)

R ae stands next to Father Roy Bourgeois, a Maryknoll priest with a fluid Cajun accent and a fearless disposition. It is the one-year anniversary of her miscarriage and the murders of the six Jesuit priests along with their housekeeper and her daughter.

A small group of protesters have gathered at the gates of Fort Benning in Georgia, home to the School of the Americas, a training program attended largely by Latin American military commanders.

As Rae has learned, Bourgeois is a Vietnam veteran who was transformed by working at a Vietnamese orphanage. Later, as a young priest, he worked with impoverished communities in Bolivia and had been a witness to war in El Salvador and Nicaragua. He's already spent more years serving jail time protesting the Contra war than the combined sentences of all the Iran–Contra criminals in the United States, including two members of the Reagan administration, Oliver North and Eliot Abrams, for their various offenses.

"This is the school of the assassins," Father Roy yells through a megaphone. "This is where the murderers of our friends and countless others are trained, with US dollars and US bullets."

"Ignacio Martín-Baró!" he calls out.

"¡*Presente!*" the group answers responsively. I am here. They are with us.

"Ignacio Ellecuría!" Rae calls out, holding his photograph in her hands.

"*¡Presente!*"

"Ita Ford," says Father Roy, holding a cross with her name. Rae learned that Roy and Ita became friends in 1972 at the Maryknoll language school in Cochabamba, Bolivia.

"*¡Presente!*"

"Elba Julia Ramos!" Rae reads.

"*¡Presente!*"

They follow the litany. Other participants call out names.

"Ramón and Raúl," shouts Rae. She thinks of Chepa's altar in the refugee camp in El Salvador, the small photographs of her murdered husband and son.

"Archbishop Oscar Romero!" an older woman calls.

"*¡Presente!*"

It is Romero who inspired Father Roy with the words, "We who have a voice must speak for the voiceless."

The story Rae knows is that in 1983, Father Roy, with two others, entered Fort Benning dressed as military officers. They climbed a tree outside a military barracks that housed Salvadoran military officers in training. With a large Sony boom box and four speakers, Father Roy blasted the voice of Monsignor Romero and his final homily, the one that got him murdered. "*In the name of God, in the name of this suffering people whose cry rises to heaven more loudly each day, I implore you, I beg you, I order you: stop the repression.*"

Rae loves the story and recalls her own days in El Salvador, lying on her cot at the Bethania refugee camp, listening to the same words. Rae knows that Father Roy was arrested and served eighteen months in a federal prison. But he is back. In the years since 1983, he has researched the School of the Americas, based at Fort Benning, and its shady history.

Rae and Reggie read to one another the new revelations about the unseemly role of graduates from the School of the Americas. One SOA graduate, General Manuel Contreras, a member of the Chilean dictator Augusto Pinochet's secret police, is found to have masterminded an assassination in the streets of Washington, DC. This "murder on embassy row," a car bombing by a Chilean hit squad, took the lives of former Chilean foreign minister Orlando Letelier and Ronni Karpen Moffitt, a twenty-five-year old activist, both working at the Institute for Policy Studies. Rae adds their names to the litany.

"Orlando Letelier!"

"*¡Presente!*"

"Ronni Moffitt!"

"*¡Presente!*"

At the end of the litany, a group of a dozen protesters walk in quiet prayer to the entrance of the base. Each of the participants steps toward the gate house, hurling a ziplock bag with a pint of their own blood. Two guards stand at attention in the gate house as the building is drenched in fresh red blood.

Blood. Earlier that afternoon, as the nurse drew her blood for the protest, Rae couldn't help but think of her own miscarriage and the blood of the innocents shed by the soldiers at the School of the Americas. She wrote in her journal: *Only I know the multiple meanings for me of this blood . . . of my lost child, of the Jesuit priests, of the children whose lives were cut short by these torturers. This is my witness, against the helicopters, the kidnappers and the killers who have terrorized my friends in Central America. This is my scream, my howling keening self in action.*

At the second big protest, in November 1991, Rae returns with two hundred protesters. She becomes one of the trainers and leaders of what is called School of the America's Watch, or SOA Watch. November 16 becomes an important anniversary day, with protests each year marking the anniversary of the murder of the Jesuits. It is also the day, in Rae's heart, when she honors the loss of their baby.

The following year, the group of protesters grows as people learn about US culpability for training soldiers linked to atrocities all over Latin America. Rae reads a recent exposé in *Newsweek* linking graduates of the SOA to grotesque acts of military terror in Guatemala, El Salvador, and Honduras.

Rae arrives a week early to help with the preparations. She bunks on a church pew and spends two days training hundreds of people in preparation for civil disobedience. One evening, she and a few of the other SOA Watch leaders have dinner with Father Roy at a local catfish joint.

"Well, sometime you all have to come visit my part of Louisiana," Roy says. "No offense to the fine food here in Southwest Georgia, but my mother will spoil you with her crawfish étouffée, seafood gumbo, and shrimp Creole, along with her special red beans and rice."

"Sounds delicious," one of the volunteers replies.

"Now Rae, you need to be our point person with Congressman Joe Moakley," says Father Roy. Moakley, the dean of the Massachusetts congressional delegation, is chairing an investigation into the murder of the Jesuits in El Salvador. He and Massachusetts representative Joe Kennedy are the sponsors of legislation pending in Congress to shut down the School of the Americas.

Two days later, when they march toward Fort Benning, there are two thousand people carrying white crosses and signs. They recite the litany, each name answered with "¡Presente!" Then the protesters walk onto the base, with six hundred crossing the line and risking arrest.

Back in Boston, Rae dresses up in her business skirt and meets with Moakley's aide, Jim McGovern, who accompanied the congressman on all of the fact-finding missions to El Salvador. She immediately feels at ease as she enters McGovern's Boston office and finds him wrestling with a printer jam, a small smudge of black ink on his cheek.

"It's such a glamorous job," says McGovern. He ushers her to a chair. Rae thanks him for his and his boss's help and leadership. She knows that they were both deeply touched by the murder of the Jesuits and have become effective voices for closing what they describe as the "national embarrassment" of the School of Americas. Rae calls it the "national monstrosity."

"Heck, prior to going to El Salvador," McGovern says, "our foreign policy experience consisted in driving over to East Boston for an Italian sub." He smiles. "Tell us how we can help."

•

She immediately and intuitively trusts McGovern. She meets with him every couple months to strategize on legislation and share research. She describes him to Reggie as "the embodiment of decency."

Moakley's proposals to shut down the SOA fall short of the votes required in Congress. But the issue is now actively being debated. Defenders of the SOA argue that human rights abuses are caused by a "few bad apples" and that ten of the graduates of the SOA became presidents of their countries. But SOA Watch points out that all ten took power through coups and nondemocratic means.

Each November, Rae returns to Georgia. She appreciates the dinnertime discussions with Father Roy and the leaders, and their analysis of the role that the SOA plays in Latin America and US interests.

"The purpose of US policy in Latin America can be summarized in two words," says Father Roy at an orientation session that Rae is facilitating for new participants. "Control and exploitation.

"The US wants to control the economies, militaries, and governments of Latin America. We benefit from protecting and preserving a socioeconomic system that keeps power, land, and wealth concentrated in the hands of a small elite. And we exploit the resources and cheap labor. Anyone who advocates for change in this system, who speaks out against poverty and oppression, is considered subversive. And SOA teaches these militaries how to eliminate these so-called subversives."

In 1998, Reggie joins Rae and two friends and they drive down to Georgia from Boston. This year, more than seven thousand protesters descend on Columbus, Georgia, home of Fort Benning. Actor Martin Sheen co-leads the procession. He and more than two thousand protesters cross the line into the military base and are arrested.

The following year, more than ten thousand protesters show up. Rae helps train the five hundred peacekeepers so that the march maintains its respectful, religious, and nonviolent spirit. Bruce Cockburn performs at a large outdoor concert before the march.

Rae calls Reggie with the good news. The US Army has announced that they are closing the School of Americas, effective December 2000. But she later realizes this is a cosmetic public relations spin. The army creates a new institution, the Western Hemisphere Institute for Security Cooperation, a rebranding of the SOA in the same buildings at Fort Benning. Joe Moakley describes it to Rae as "perfume on a toxic dump," since it is still provides combat and counterinsurgency training.

The protests continue, even two months after the September 11 attack on the World Trade Center in New York City. Thousands of people march with crosses. Fort Benning constructs an eight-foot-tall fence topped with barbed wire to block the protesters. The fence becomes a memorial, with hundreds of crosses attached, with the names of victims of torture and murder from all over Latin America.

"Kind of a giant altar," Rae tells Reggie on the phone.

On the way home from most of her road trips to Fort Benning in Georgia, Rae detours to Ohio to visit her parents and Toby. The mid-November anniversary actions coincide nicely with Thanksgiving visits to the Midwest. And a couple of times Reggie flies out to join her for Thanksgiving, and they drive back to Boston together.

Rae looks forward to these return visits to Ohio as a way to recharge after the intensity of the SOA actions. She takes long walks, reads, naps, and helps her mom with cooking and craft projects. It is familiar and reassuring to hide out in her childhood bedroom. The only unpleasantness is Toby. He has become more like her father, more mini-Mac, but with a sharp and confrontational edge.

Her parents seem more fragile, and Dot whispers confidentially that Mac has certain unspecified ailments that he doesn't want to discuss. Dot tries to assert her Thanksgiving peacemaker role, with her "no politics at the dinner table" rule. But it's hard, given that Rae has just returned from intense protests at Fort Benning and Toby is borderline belligerent with his evolving right-wing views.

"He's become mentally unhinged," whispers Reggie in Rae's old bedroom. "Hijacked by Fox News."

"Well, he thinks we've been brainwashed, too," replies Rae. She tries to see things from Toby's vantage.

Rae notices that Reggie wisely steers clear of arguments with Toby, preferring to help Dot in the kitchen or watch Ohio State Buckeyes football with Mac. He tells her at bedtime how he enjoys his visits to Ohio and soaking up tidbits of Rae's childhood and the groundedness of the Kelliher's working-class lives. They are not trying to change the world, like their daughter, but to live another day with integrity.

In the months after the September 11 attack, Rae feels like Toby is taunting her with new resentments. "I can't believe you're protesting against the US military at this moment," he yells, minutes after Rae's arrival, as they stand in the yard. "Giving aid and comfort to the enemy. Are you going to carry pictures of Saddam around like Ho Chi Minh?"

"You know that Saddam had no role in 9/11, right?" Rae has no idea where the Ho Chi Minh stuff comes from. Must be some weird image he picked up from somewhere. They take their arguments out into the woods as Reggie unpacks the car and greets her parents.

"Yeah, he did. Who funded Bin Laden and Al Queda?" says Toby, brushing his hair back and angling his cap.

"Who funded them? Saudi Arabia. Major US ally!" Rae feels her temper being stoked, hearing this from her own brother.

"No way. Saddam has weapons of mass destruction."

"Hey, if you believe that, I've got a bridge to sell you in Kentucky."

"He's going to attack Israel," says Toby.

Rae wonders when Toby started to pay attention to this stuff. "Toby, do you understand the concept of blowback in US foreign policy?" she says assertively. "The US goes around the world siding with tyrants. The US funded the mujahadeen in the 1980s to fight the Russians in Afghanistan. Then we get distracted and pull out, and the mujahadeen and Taliban fester and grow."

"These people hate our way of life," said Toby. "Especially Saddam."

If Toby can raise his voice, so can I, thinks Rae. "Toby, they don't hate the US. But they sure as hell don't like US military bases in their region."

Her volume and fierceness startles Toby.

"Oh," she goes on, "and the US sided with Saddam Hussein in the war with Iran over the last decade, sent him weapons. He was a US ally." Rae has come to believe that history and facts are irrelevant to these discussions, but she tries anyway.

Toby is unpersuaded. "When you protest at a US military base, you are siding with the enemy."

"Toby, I'm trying to prevent the next blowback, the next 9/11." She exhales. "At Fort Benning, the US Army is training the triggermen assassins and terrorists of Latin America, the people who are repressing their own people. Don't think that people will forget that."

On some visits, she tries to shift the energy and get Toby out to the woods to look for mushrooms with her. But more often he makes outlandish accusations and then peels off in his truck for Sullivan's, his favorite bar. Rae has drawn out from him that he and Monica have permanently broken up and that she is engaged to marry someone else. And he has lost touch with Robin, his best friend from childhood, who has a family outside Detroit.

Rae writes: *I feel like I've lost Toby. Who stole my brother? Who hijacked his brain? Is it Fox? Or the Rush Limbaugh he listens to as he drives his truck from job to job? We still talk and argue, which I guess is a form of connection.*

During most of these visits, she lies in her childhood room on her narrow twin bed, gazing at the rocks on her windowsill, the view of her teenage years. Her collection of rocks remains where she left it, dusty and dulled. She always pulls down the "Eye of the Goddess" stone, rinses it off, and replaces it on the sill. She considers bringing it back to Boston, but each time decides it should remain here to keep an eye on things. She does take two polished Petoskey stones off her windowsill, souvenirs from a family camping trip to Michigan. They have an unusual web-like cell structure. She brings them home to Jamaica Plain.

Each time Rae departs Ohio, she feels a pang for being so far from her family. And also grateful for Reggie, his big extended family, and her life in New England.

WE SHALL NOT BE MOVED

(1997)

Jamaica Plain in the 1990s is a lively neighborhood and Reggie and Rae are happily installed in its cultural and political life.

They look for a slightly larger apartment, calling landlords and touring the neighborhood. There are still pockets of affordable places and a few old-school owners who keep their rents low. These are the apartments with pull-string light switches in the middle of a room and shag carpeting from the swinging 1970s.

Rae and Reggie rent a top-floor apartment in a classic Boston triple-decker on a busy cut-through street called Paul Gore. Their landlord, an old-time townie named Rena McCarthy, keeps their rent low in exchange for their shoveling and putting out and bringing in the trash bins. Rena doesn't own a car and walks to Mass every Sunday to Our Lady of Lourdes, down by the Haffenreffer Brewery. The ornate church was built with the patronage of James Michael Curley, the infamous "rascal king" mayor of Boston in the 1930s and 1940s.

Abutting a large community garden plot, Rae keeps a couple of raised beds for kitchen herbs and several productive tomato plants. At the bottom of the hill is the Stonybrook Orange Line T station, a subway that rolls downtown in one direction and out to the Arnold

164

Arboretum at the other end. On top of the subway line is Southwest Corridor Park, a prize from a 1970s community-organizing effort that successfully stopped the construction of a planned highway that would have ripped the neighborhood apart, funneling cars from the suburbs into downtown. Instead, there are skateboard parks, tennis courts, a bike path to downtown, and large fields for impromptu Frisbee throws and soccer matches.

Rae loves the annual rhythm of seasons and events. She volunteers to help produce festivals and fundraisers. Each May, a community arts organization called Spontaneous Celebrations organizes a parade and festival called Wake Up the Earth. The festival, founded in 1979, is a celebration of the stopping of the highway. Each year, at one of the concert stages, local residents tell the story of the successful opposition.

Rae joins the organizing committee for the festival. More people march in the Wake Up the Earth parade than watch it as spectators. There are kids on decorated bikes, a variety of marching bands, baton twirlers, and school and civic groups. Rae loves to march in the parade with the brass band she has joined. But after arriving at the finish, she runs back up to watch the other marchers process into the park. The festival runs all afternoon, with four performance stages, bountiful food booths, and information tables for every possible cause, civic group, and cult in the area.

Rae becomes friends with Femka, the founder of Spontaneous Celebrations. Femke tells her the story of recently walking on the Southwest Corridor and seeing a man spraying chemicals on the grass. Femka, an immigrant from the Netherlands, asked him what he was doing. "Killing the dandelions," he replied.

"What is the chemical?" she asks. She writes down the name and goes to the library to look it up. "Why is the city spraying toxic chemicals on the grass where the children play?" she complained to Laura, the librarian at the Connelly Branch.

Together, Femka and Rae launch a petition urging the city to stop the spraying. At an after-school program, hosted by Spontaneous Celebrations, the children create huge towering dandelions out of cardboard, colorful paper, and broomsticks. Rae wears a bright yellow pantsuit with a dandelion head crafted out of cardboard and paint. Later that week, they march into the City Council chamber, garnering additional publicity. They win a ban on the use of pesticides in the park.

The next Wake Up the Earth parade is led by a marching section of children with enormous dandelions. And at one stage, Rae organizes a group of children to present Femka with a bundle of dandelions, picked from the park. "This is the most beautiful bouquet of flowers I've ever been given," says Femka in gratitude.

Rae and Reggie walk everywhere: down the Muddy River to Fenway Park to watch the Red Sox; through residential streets to the Arnold Arboretum; to the shores of Jamaica Pond for a lap or two walking on the perimeter path; and the scenic route over Peter's Hill to Roslindale to visit friends who live there. They walk to the Arborway Video store, which often has one-dollar video rentals on Tuesday nights.

For the two of them, the "walking life," as Reggie calls it, is one of the important ways they stay connected with one another. They talk things out, sometimes argue, and keep one another apprised of their inner thoughts. It's also a way they stay connected to the life of the neighborhood and get some exercise.

On Sunday mornings, they often walk to the Unitarian Universalist church in the center of the village. The minister, a friendly man named Terry Burke, welcomes them on any terms. Many in the congregation were born into other faith traditions, and Terry navigates a wide liturgical territory between mystical and rational, prayerful and brainy, science and spirituality. Rae is drawn to the music and joins the choir, enjoying the fellowship of the singers.

The ancient church sanctuary has colorful stained-glass windows on its south side. One window has the family name "Green," and Rev. Terry tells them that Emily Green Balch sat in these pews and was later awarded the Nobel Peace Prize for founding Women's Strike for Peace, a pacifist group that opposed US entry into the First World War. There are frequent forums and events at the church that bring people together.

"I kinda liked going to church when I was a little girl," Rae says, kicking a pebble on one of their walking adventures.

"I was a reluctant altar boy," says Reggie. "That's why I'm drawn to you. You smell like incense."

"Sandalwood? Oh man, good thing you didn't know me in my Montague Farm days. I bathed in patchouli."

"I totally associate that smell with the hippie girls."

"That was me. That *is* me, I guess." Rae feels compassion for her younger self as well as joy for the day-to-day levity of their life together.

After a year of attending First Church, Reggie and Rae sign a century-old membership book, formally joining as members of the congregation.

Together, Reggie and Rae like to check out the local joints. On their Franklin Park walk they pass Doyle's Cafe, a pub that is a haven for local politicos. And Green Street Station, which is a punk-rock music venue. Not far from their house is Brendan Behan Pub, a dimly lit establishment that pulls a good pint of Guinness.

One weekend, they attend the grand opening of Bella Luna, a new pizza parlor a few blocks from their house. The four owners are community activists who started the restaurant with the modest hope that at least their own children would never go hungry.

Their decision to locate Bella Luna in the Hyde Square section of Jamaica Plain is to lift up the neighborhood with a new business, employ local people, and press the city to sweep up the syringes in the adjoining parking lot. Bella Luna is an instant success, and within a year they expand to a neighboring storefront with a defunct bowling alley in the basement. Reggie likes the Menino pizza, named for the city's current mayor, with its combination of pepperoni, sausage, and peppers. Rae looks forward to the Wednesday night karaoke where she tries her hand at being a crooning lounge singer.

Rae's sense of neighborhood well-being is disrupted one day by news that they might have to move. Their landlord, Rena, is taken to a nursing home after a bad fall on her stairs. Her nephew comes by with a real estate agent, explaining that they will be putting the property on the market. There are few affordable places for Rae and Reggie to move to.

Rae joins a local group fighting evictions, City Life / Vida Urbana. On Tuesday evenings they have a legal clinic and meeting to help tenants. At the first session that Rae attends, Maria, one of the organizers, explains that when someone gets an eviction notice and doesn't do anything, they will likely lose their home. But if they join with others to organize and fight the eviction, their chance of staying put greatly increases.

New tenants facing eviction are invited to the front of the room to tell the group about their situation. There are about forty people on Rae's first night. The first to step forward is an older Haitian woman named Carline Desire whom Rae recognizes from the neighborhood. Carline explains that she has paid rent for decades, but the absentee owner of her two-family house failed to pay the mortgage. Now the building is being foreclosed on by Advent Mortgage, an Atlanta-based company that refuses to communicate with her. She holds up the unfolded paper with tears in her eyes. "I have lived here for thirty years," she weeps. "I have raised my family here. I have paid my rent. And now I'm about to lose my home. I have prayed for help and God led me here." Listening to her story, Rae is touched, and she feels a flash of anger at a system that would put a dignified woman like Carline at risk.

The organizer, Maria, stands next to her. "Carline, do you want to fight for your home?"

Carline ponders the question, appearing to Rae to search inside for some untapped reservoir of strength. "Yes," she mouths.

"Carline, we can't hear you," says Maria gently. "Do you want to fight for your home?"

This time there is no hesitation. "*Yes!*" Carline yells, removing her thick glasses to wipe away tears.

"Then here, Carline, take this sword." Maria hands her a large dragon-slayer of a plastic sword. "Carline, do you want these people to help you?"

"Yes," she says, looking at everyone in the room over her reading glasses. "I need your help," she says, whispering again.

Maria turns to the group. "Will you stand with Carline? Will you pledge to fight with Carline to keep her home?"

Rae stands up and raises her arms.

"*Yes!*" shouts everyone in the room. Several of the group step forward, a form of secular altar call, and stand beside Carline. Rae joins the group at the front of the room. Maria hands one of them an enormous shield made of *papier-mâché*. "We will stand with you!" she says.

"We will stand with you, Carline," the group yells responsively.

Rae feels herself growing attached to this group. She returns each week to the organizing meeting, both to weigh her own options and to honor her pledge to stand with some of the other tenants. Each week there are new people facing eviction who are brought into the group with the sword-and-shield ritual. And there are updates from the negotiations with banks, landlords, and the city of Boston. Rae sits next to Carline, striking up side conversations and becoming friends with her.

Carline invites Rae for a visit and they sit on her porch, surveying her section of the neighborhood. All the neighbors know Carline and stop by to see how she's doing. One neighbor brings her a box of doughnuts.

"I can't eat these," she says. "I'll take them to church."

Carline points out all the people and animals and offers small tidbits of harmless gossip about everyone. "That cat is named Birdy because she's always hunting the little songbirds. I yell at her." Carline laughs heartily. "That lady there, Mrs. Donahue, grumpy old Irish lady. She got all these sons with trucks that come by to help her. Always double-parking like they own the street. Two of them in and out of jail."

Rae hopes to live in a place long enough to know everyone's business, like Carline.

A few weeks later, Carline gets another eviction notice, this time with a specific date and time. The foreclosing mortgage company wants the property empty, probably so they can resell it at a maximum price. They are not negotiating. Carline continues to pay her monthly rent, putting it into an escrow account.

"Should I begin to pack?" says Carline at another one of their porch-sit coffee dates. "I don't want them putting my furniture out on the street."

"We need to ask Maria," says Rae.

At the next meeting, they discuss Carline's eviction date, set for the following week.

"You're not going anywhere," says Maria, with a firm grip on Carline's shoulder. Rae is impressed with her certainty. "We are going to stop the eviction. And hopefully they will negotiate before that. They don't know yet how serious you are about staying."

The days pass and all the communications with the mortgage company falter. The day of the eviction arrives. Rae walks over to Carline's house and finds more than sixty people standing in the street with signs, "We Shall Not Be Moved," "No Eviction Zone," "Keep Families in Their Homes." "Advent Mortgage: Carline Lives Here."

Maria stands next to Carline on her porch with a large megaphone.

"Thank you for coming today," says Carline, visibly moved. "Thank you for standing with me."

Rae sees many of the neighbors she has met on Carline's porch in attendance.

Maria organizes the ten volunteers who have agreed to risk arrest to block the front porch. Rae has not joined this group, but is intrigued to witness the process.

At 10:00 a.m., the constable drives up, parks, and walks toward the porch. The crowd parts to create a path for him, but they chant, "We Shall Not Be Moved." A large moving van turns onto the street, but when the driver sees the crowd blocking its path, he turns around and leaves. Everyone cheers.

Maria talks to the constable, explaining the situation, that the foreclosing mortgage company has not negotiated in good faith with Carline to keep her in the house. The constable returns to his car, talking on his mobile phone, and then he drives away. Again, the assembled crowd cheers and dances in the street. *This is the power of organized people*, thinks Rae.

"Today we stopped the eviction," says Maria in the megaphone.

"We will not permit Carline to be evicted. If they come back, we will come back!"

After the crowd disperses, Rae asks Maria, "Is that how it usually works?"

"Usually our threat of a blockade brings the finance people to the table long before this happens," she says, pointing to the crowd. "But sometimes they have to see that we're serious. And, to be honest, sometimes we can't stop an eviction. But we can raise holy hell."

Two days later, they learn that Advent Capital is negotiating with Carline—and that the city of Boston is getting involved to help Carline buy her home.

Rae goes to another eviction blockade where the owner is a faceless shell company incorporated in Delaware, with no apparent individual to negotiate with. Forty people surround the house, but the police wade in and arrest the protesters. At the last minute, Rae and the state representative from the neighborhood, Liz Malia, join the protesters and are swiftly handcuffed and put in a police van.

"I guess I'll be late for work," says Liz Malia, keeping up a friendly banter with the police. Her work in this case is going to the State House. "I wasn't planning to do this, but I couldn't stand watching this woman lose her home."

"Same with me," says Rae, enjoying the company of a dozen veteran protesters who start singing "We Shall Not Be Moved."

Two hours later, they walk out of the District 5 police station with citations and a court date.

"My first arrest in Boston," Rae tells Reggie at dinner, describing her spontaneous joining in with their representative, Liz Malia.

Reggie smiles. "Sort of like losing your virginity."

"Much better," Rae retorts as she stirs her bowl of soup. "I know, I'm a White girl doing civil disobedience, not a Black man minding my own business."

"True. But your multiple arrest record might prevent you from getting appointed a judge or whatever."

"Hmm. Maybe I should have finished college instead of becoming a one-woman crime wave."

Reggie and Rae don't have to fight their eviction. Instead, they approach the downstairs neighbors, Juan and Lydia Rodriguez, a Latino couple with two young children, about buying the triple-decker together.

They all scratch together a down payment and get a mortgage from Countrywide Mortgage, a company that doesn't seem terribly concerned about paperwork or documentation of income. They buy the building for $185,000, a price that seems otherworldly and a stretch for both households. They fix up the rental unit, Rena McCarthy's old apartment, and rent it for well below the going rate in Jamaica Plain. The two couples are reluctant landlords, but as Juan observes, "I'd rather rent from us than a lot of these slumlords."

In winter the heavy storms come and go, reflecting Boston's northern clime and proximity to the warming impact of the ocean. There is a chronic shortage of parking on Paul Gore Street and in their neighborhood generally. Big winter storms bring out the worst instincts in some neighbors, who put out parking "space savers" such as busted chairs, parking cones, and other strange objects to claim their spot, sometimes for the entire winter. Rae rants about the ugly notes and acts of vandalism when people park in someone's "saved" spot. Reggie is more sympathetic to the idea that if you spend three hours shoveling out a parking spot, you do have a claim on it, at least for a couple of days.

On April Fool's Day there is a two-foot blizzard that brings the city to a grinding halt. Reggie and Rae cross-country-ski down Paul Gore and along the corridor park, encountering friends and neighbors along the way.

"A blizzard in the city is the best," exclaims Rae, kicking back on a park bench with her skis on, soaking in a beam of winter sunshine. "Everyone stops. Kids get a snow day. No one can get to work. You talk to the neighbor you pass by every day."

They shovel the walkway up to their front door. But they leave their car buried in snow, with no urgent need for it. It gets plowed in to the point where there is a six-foot wall of ice and snow boxing it in.

"If this was January, I might dig out," said Reggie. "But April? I'm banking on a thaw."

"Once again, the lazy option becomes your principled choice," Rae chuckles, and she begins to make a pile of snowballs. "Looks like the City is taking the same approach."

"The less energy I expend on shoveling, the more I have for love-making and housework."

"Okay, excellent point. Leave that shovel in the hallway, buster. You've got work to do indoors."

Reggie is right. Four days later he pops the car out of the spot, as the snow has melted into messy mud puddles. A week later, almost every trace of winter has evaporated, leaving behind scattered bits of litter and a few hardcore sooty ice deposits.

Ten days after the storm, Reggie and Rae walk to Fenway Park for opening day. It is a sunny spring afternoon with the temperature in the mid-sixties. Nomar Garciaparra leads off for the Red Sox, hitting a double. A week later, they walk down to watch the Boston Marathon pass by, the sleek front-runners escorted by Boston police on motorcycles.

I love Boston, Rae writes in her journal. *And I love my neighborhood. There is a sweetness to the rhythm of our daily and weekly lives. I'm only working twenty hours a week, which means I have the slack to do other stuff. I feel a sense of belonging to a place, and that is grounding. I miss the woods of Western Mass. But if I'm going to be in the city, this is where I want to be.*

PART 4
TRANSITION

Come with me! We'll make a ritual of our love, an explosion of each and every moment.

Giocanda Belli

PASSAGES

(2006)

Rae's parents die within three months of one another, both at the age of seventy. First Mac, who refuses medical treatment for congestive heart failure and slowly declines over a year. Rae visits several times, taking him out for breakfast at Patty's, which he enjoys, the final time in a wheelchair. Mac was never one for doctors and hospitals, and he dies at home with Rae, Dot, a hospice worker, and a visiting priest from St. Mary's.

The night before he dies, he is alone with Rae. His breathing is labored and he mostly dozes, but at one point he looks at her clearly, noticing that Dot is not in the room.

"Is it okay if I go now?" he asks.

"Sure Pop," Rae replies. "You can let go. I love you."

"Thanks Rae," he says relieved. "I'm so proud of you."

Rae is pretty certain that this is the first time she has ever heard him say these words.

The next morning, he takes his last breath. Toby flashes in and out of the scene, dropping acerbic comments and political put-downs like small grenades. He is clearly having a hard time with Mac's passing and is emotionally untethered.

•

A few months later, Rae is surprised to get a call from Toby that Dot passed in the night.

"She just said she was tired," Toby says. He still lives at home. "When I woke up in the morning before her, I knew there was something wrong."

Neither of them anticipated losing Dot, who seemed like she might live into her nineties at her steady pace.

"We're orphans now," said Toby.

"Yeah, orphans in our fifties," said Rae in a lighthearted way. Toby is fifty-four and Rae is fifty-two. But she knows that the loss is huge for Toby, who has lived his entire life with his parents and will remain living in the family home, now without their daily presence. She can only imagine how disorienting that must feel.

Their parents leave them the house without a mortgage and about $11,000 in savings, with nothing else to their names. There is a truck and some tools that naturally flow to Toby. Rae tells him the house is all his, signing over her ownership interest. "I got one already," she tells him.

Toby continues to be unpleasant to be around. She gets the sense that when he's not working, he watches TV or drinks too much at Sullivan's. Rae doesn't share with him about most of the things happening in her life—the work against evictions, the organizing in the neighborhood, and her growing interest in climate change. Anything she says is a prompt for a Fox News talking point from her brother.

"Hey Saint Rae," Toby taunts her. "Are you ready to surrender the USA to China?"

"Toby, what in heaven's name are you talking about?"

Only as she departs, after their mother's funeral, does he say anything personal.

"Take care Rae," he says to her, welling up with tears. "You're all the family I've got now."

It is true. Toby looks to Rae like he is now alone and seemingly destined to remain that way.

Reggie notices that Rae has a proclivity toward binge-learning. He finds this both endearing and maddening, as living with any-one with periodic obsessions might be. She gets fixated on a topic and plunges in, reading articles, talking to people, devouring books, watching documentaries. Most amusing, she adopts char-acters, ways of speaking, and a dramatic flair for whatever she is immersed in.

Rae listens to audiobooks from the library on a little Sony Walkman while doing chores or driving. While the topics vary wildly—history of places, practical skills, historical people, new developments in science—the process of immersion is the same. Reggie tries to keep up with what is on the curiosity docket by peek-ing at Rae's stack of books or tracking her sudden interest in going to an exhibit, watching a documentary, or interviewing a particu-lar acquaintance. The clues may be subtle, such as, "Would you be interested in watching this documentary about the threats to bees and pollinators?"

Reggie notices that Rae's initial curiosity spark is often ignited by a popular movie, a news event, or a historical novel. "I never knew you were such a history nerd," Reggie observes.

"Did I ever tell you about meeting Howard Zinn at the Clamshell protest?" Rae is holding a book, *King Leopold's Ghost*, about the Belgian monarch who plundered the Congo.

A news report of a 1998 car bombing in the northern Irish town of Omagh leads to an intensive self-taught course in Irish history, with a focus on "the Troubles." Reggie climbs on board for that one, resulting in an "Irish film festival" of video rentals and, later, red-envelope Netflix DVDs including Reggie's favorites, *The Wind that Shakes the Barley* and *In the Name of the Father*.

Reggie also joins Rae for her intensive-study course on Oscar Romero, especially during her early work to close the School for Americas. She reads biographies and sermons, and Reggie joins her for screenings of several documentaries and the dramatic film *Romero*, staring Raúl Juliá as the archbishop.

"Listen to this quote," says Rae. "*There are many things that can only be seen through eyes that have cried.*"

A novel, *Cutting for Stone*, about a doctor in Ethiopia, leads to Rae's immersion course in Ethiopian history, geography, and culture. As part of her research, she enlists Reggie to go to the local Blue Nile restaurant for Ethiopian food, where she asks the owner about his emigration story.

On a camping trip, Reggie spies Rae reading a biography of the psychologist Franz Fanon, who believed that violence against colonial oppressors could be a psychologically liberating for subjects of imperial denomination. She then reads Fanon's book *The Wretched of the Earth* and watches the dramatic film about the Algerian revolution, *The Battle of Algiers*, as part of a journey of country-by-country study about independence struggles. In a similar vein, Rae travels the world from her living room, doing her deep-dive study on countries that she feels she needs greater knowledge of: Turkey, Pakistan, Afghanistan, Iraq, Iran, and nations all over the African continent.

Rae's lifelong interest in Emma Goldman is revived when she reads a book about Goldman's relationship with Alexander Berkman, the Russian anarchist called Sasha by his friends. Berkman spent fourteen years in prison for his failed attempt to assassinate the Pittsburgh industrialist Henry Clay Frick. Rae is intrigued by their relationship and jokes with Reggie that they are Emma and Sasha. If Reggie is angry at someone, she says, in a bad imitation of a Russian accent, "Sasha, don't be upset. Don't go trying to shoot him." Or "Sasha, what are you plotting now?"

One day Reggie notices Rae toting around a dry-looking book of theology, *The Cost of Discipleship*, by the German theologian Dietrich Bonhoeffer. Rae has read a fictionalized version of Bonhoeffer's life called *Saints and Villains*. This primed her for reading a straightforward biography as well as histories about the rise of Nazism and English translations of Bonhoeffer's writings.

She lures Reggie to the local art house cinema, the Coolidge Corner Theater, for a screening of *Bonhoeffer*, a documentary directed by Martin Doblmeier.

"We can get a slice and a beer at Upper Crust after the movie."

Rae twitches with urgency, a signal that Reggie well understands to mean he should say "yes" to whatever is being asked of him.

"You think you can manipulate me with food?" Reggie is only vaguely interested in seeing a documentary about an obscure theologian, though he knows that Bonhoeffer is considered a martyr of some kind. They sit in the smallest screening room at the Coolidge with two other viewers, each sitting alone. Rae has her small black journal and a pen, just in case she wants to jot a note.

"Doesn't Bill Gates have a theater like this in his house?" Reggie is already halfway through a large bucket of popcorn and the previews are still running.

"A private screening room?" Rae laughs, trying to grab a few handfuls of popcorn before it all disappears. "Probably."

Rae appears riveted by the documentary, which includes several scenes of Hitler speeches and interviews in German with subtitles. She reaches for Reggie's hand as she hears the story of Bonhoeffer's resistance to Nazism, culminating in his joining a clandestine plot to assassinate Hitler. After more than two years in prison, he is executed on April 9, 1945, at the Flossenbürg concentration camp.

They adjourn to the Upper Crust, a pizza parlor with the Red Sox game on and a limited selection of beer on tap.

"Okay, I didn't know that the German church just entirely caved in to Nazism, including an oath of allegiance to Hitler." Reggie sits with his back to the TV screen, so he's not distracted by the Red Sox game. "Why the deep-dive on Bonhoeffer?"

Rae ponders this question as her stomach gurgles. Her eyes widen. "I'm just curious about how a Christian pacificist joined an assassination plot. Bonhoeffer was, you know, Mr. *Thou Shalt Not Kill*. He wanted to travel to India and study with Mahatma Gandhi. They corresponded, but he was never able to go because of the changes in Germany."

She bites into a slice of mushroom pizza and wipes her mouth with a napkin. "He lost his older brother in the First World War. He was close to a French pacificist, Jean Lassure."

"I love this thin crust," says Reggie.

"I like *your* thin crust." Rae is rummaging around in her bag.

"Better than a thin skin, I guess." Reggie turns around to check the Red Sox game score.

Rae pulls out her black journal notebook and reads out loud. "I like this quote: *We are not to simply bandage the wounds of victims beneath the wheels of injustice, we are to drive a spoke into the wheel itself.* It reminds me of Thoreau's *Be friction against the machine.*"

She waves an unfinished slice in the air. "Oh, and how about that interview with the old German student who was meeting with Bonhoeffer before he went to the US. He says, 'Out of the blue, Dietrich asks the group, Would you grant absolution to the murderer of a tyrant?'"

Rae later muses in her journal: *Is violence ever justified? If you can stop a Hitler, it probably is. If you can prevent the madman from pushing the button or rolling a grenade into a school, the violence prevents an infinitely greater harm.*

Rae pursues her study deep dives in any setting. She could be sitting on a park bench, riding a city bus, or installing herself in a coffee shop with a book, a black journal, a favorite pen—and later a laptop. But usually she sits at her favorite desk surrounded by rocks, carvings, photographs, and quotes.

Reggie and Rae participate in a festive day at Boston City Hall. Their friends and neighbors Hilary and Julie Goodridge are lead plaintiffs in a lawsuit against the Commonwealth for the right to marry. In a historic ruling, they win. They are the first same-sex couple to get married in Massachusetts—anywhere in the United States, in fact.

On a sunny morning in May, the first official day of gay marriage, Mayor Thomas Menino escorts Julie, Hillary, and their eleven-year-old daughter, Annie, from City Hall. Menino, raised in a traditional Catholic family, is criticized by the Archdiocese of Boston for his role in the wedding.

"We have a lot of serious problems in Boston," His Honor the mayor responds to his critics. "People loving one another and wanting to get married is not one of them."

Reggie and Rae gather at City Hall Plaza for the celebrations. They see lots of couples they know lined up to get their marriage licenses. Reggie waves to several childhood friends from Dorchester, couples who have lived together for decades and can finally marry. People are dressed up and dancing in the line. It's a milestone day in the life of the city, and everyone knows it.

On the subway home, Reggie wraps his arms around Rae. "You know, the only obstacle to your marrying me has now evaporated. Your gay and lesbian friends can now tie the knot, and so can we."

"Okay, I think I'm ready." Rae wiggles out of Reggie's embrace so she can look him in the eyes. "And Missy will be pleased we're not stacked up living in sin."

"Another good reason."

"Heck, most of our friends already assume we're married. My only sadness is that Dot and Mac aren't around to witness the blessed event."

At each stop on the subway, newlyweds get off to cheers and waves.

"How about a City Hall wedding and a potluck at the church?" suggests Rae. She's not excited about organizing a big social production, or the expense. They're trying to save money to buy land in Vermont.

"That sounds good. Though we have about a dozen gay and lesbian wedding parties on the calendar to get through first."

"Maybe in a year," Rae says with a sigh, feeling slightly deflated.

"Let's elope," says Reggie, only half joking. "That way we don't have to feed a hundred and fifty of my closest Donovan relations at a wedding. We can have a potluck picnic celebration at Carson Beach."

They agree to do the simple City Hall wedding without the full package. "Be good to get you on my health insurance policy," observes Reggie.

"Maybe I'll invite Toby, my orphan brother, to be a witness."

"Yeah, maybe connect him to a happy family event." They once talked about asking Toby to be a godparent to their child, before the miscarriage, with the same intention. Thanks to Reggie's siblings, he and Rae are godparents to four nieces and nephews, and they take their job seriously by taking their godchildren on special outings and picking out books for them.

Rae writes in her journal. *I'm going to get married to Reggie a month after my 52nd birthday. I've got my soulmate and we can now have a contract with the state to sue one another if things don't work out. Call me a sentimental gal.*

A day later, Rae appears before Reggie as he arrives home and takes his shoes off in the front foyer.

"I don't want Toby to come for our civil ceremony," she says curtly. "He just said some nasty homophobic shit about gay marriage to me on the phone."

"Yuck," said Reggie shaking his head. "What is his problem?"

"Some days I scarcely recognize him. And other times, I feel like it's a superficial jacket he slips on. Underneath he's the same lovable Toby. We just have to get him to shed the jacket."

They go to City Hall and apply for a wedding license, standing in line at a window next to where people pay overdue parking tickets.

"So efficient!" says Reggie. "We can get married and renew our resident parking sticker on the same visit."

"I can't tell what excites you more," Rae jokes as she presses her pen firmly onto the paper. "I'm thrilled to marry you."

They fill out the forms and pay fifty dollars. The process of getting the license takes a couple weeks, but they schedule their fifteen-minute slot at the City Clerk's office.

On the big day, they show up with Jade and PJ, two lesbian friends who each just got married to their partners. Rae wears a frilly, old-fashioned wedding gown that she borrowed from a friend. Reggie wears a colorful vest and one of Rae's top hats. They sit in the waiting area with several other soon-to-be-hitched couples.

The city clerk who officiates the ceremony, a woman named Maureen, takes her job quite seriously. She wears a colorful stole and holds an elegant leatherbound booklet with the words of each pronouncement printed in a large font. Rae and Reggie give her the original vows they have written. Maureen quickly reads them to herself and is delighted. "These are beautiful," she affirms.

Maureen tells them that the previous couple who came in just before them decided to postpone their marriage because the bride didn't want to take her male husband's last name.

"They hadn't talked it through before they showed up," says the rosy-cheeked clerk. "Can you imagine?"

"We've been together for eighteen years," says Reggie. "No surprises here."

After a pause, Maureen says, "Are you ready?" as if they are about to board a spaceship. She stands up in order to bring formality to the ritual in her small, carpeted clerk's office. PJ and Jade stand beside them. Maureen reads introductory words with a sincerity that moves everyone present. Reggie and Rae repeat their vows with her prompting. Each of them gives to the other one of the smoothened Petoskey stones that Rae has held since childhood and recently brought back from her childhood home in Ohio. She closes with a secular prayer about the power of marriage that has all four of them brimming with tears. "Now by the power vested in me, I pronounce you married to one another. Congratulations, Reggie and Rae. You may now kiss."

After their smooch, everyone exchanges handshakes and hugs. Maureen bids them farewell to take a five-minute break before her next nuptials. The wedding party stops to take photographs in the lobby, which has a wall mural that says "Married in Boston" under a rainbow of flowers. A soon-to-be-married bride, sitting in the adjoining waiting room, bounces over to snap their pictures.

They walk across City Hall Plaza to an Irish pub that Reggie likes named Kinsale. They order up pints of Guinness and seltzer and lunch.

On the subway back to Jamaica Plain, Rae is a little teary-eyed.

"What's a matter, my bride?" asks Reggie, wrapping an arm around her. Orange Line riders look up to smile at the subway bride.

"Oh I'm very happy," she says. "I was just feeling sad that I didn't invite Toby. I wish he was here."

"Hmmm."

"He doesn't have anyone. He would have risen to the occasion."

"That's hard. Let's call him and tell him we want him to give a toast at our beach party."

"Whenever that is," Rae says sadly. "It was a missed opportunity to include him. My mistake."

MUTUAL AID

(2008)

"I think this is the spot," says Reggie, looking at a paper roadmap. "Pull into that turnoff there." He points to a rutted pullover on the dirt road.

Rae stops the car, turns the engine off, grabs her red wool hat from the seat, and slams the car door. They start walking on a squishy, two-track dirt road, heading up a gentle rise through a hardwood forest.

"I like this time of year," says Reggie. "Before the leaves fill in you can really get a feeling for the shape of the hillsides. And where the streams are."

The logging road follows a small creek, frigid water cascading through a course of mossy rocks. A half mile up, the grassy road banks to the right and enters a grove of taller hemlocks, finally emerging into a clearing at the ridgeline.

"Wow. Look at that," Rae says, pointing to an opening in the woods. Looking east, they see surrounding ridgelines and a distant view of Mount Monadnock.

"Nice clearing," said Reggie. "Not too big. The sellers must have known this would appeal to the flatlanders looking at land."

"Well, it's working on this flatlander," said Rae, impressed with the expansive feeling. "A garden in the woods." They walk to the ridgetop, wading through a thicket of blackberry brambles and hardwood trees.

"A couple of good potential spots for a cabin," said Reggie, pointing along the ridgeline.

"I'd like to see it in the dark, just to see how dark it gets here," said Rae. "What about a pond site?" They stumble and wade through another thicket and find another tributary of the creek and a slightly swampy spring, surrounded by tall hardwood trees.

"This has promise." Reggie's boots sink into the mud.

Over the next month, Reggie and Rae look at a dozen other parcels of land before returning to this ridgeline, known as Owl's Head, with its woodsy approach and ridgetop view. One clear moonless night, they hike up with headlamps and perch on a rock on the ridgetop. They see no lights from the summit. The Milky Way forms a blurry river through the sky. This is the place, they think.

They make an offer and buy the land, thirty acres including some wetlands. Over the next year, they hire a local excavator to expand the logging road into a workable driveway, clear a site for a cabin, and dig a test hole for a pond. They visit several times over the summer, pitching a tent and camping on the land, picking blackberries and listening to the snorts and stomps of local deer that pass by their tent in the darkness. One night they hear a band of coyotes howling and yipping close by, probably attacking a deer or some other unfortunate creature.

"We're not in Jamaica Plain or Kansas anymore," Rae says in her half-sleep.

They order a pre-cut kit for a twenty-foot by thirty-foot cabin. It arrives on a large 18-wheeler truck that grinds its way up their gravel driveway access road and deposits a large pile of pre-measured and -cut timbers at the cabin site. With help from two carpenter friends and the short-term use of a logging truck with a loading crane, they assemble the roof timbers and frame in the cabin.

The cabin is "off the grid," with no running water, electricity, or heat, other than a woodstove. But they build an outhouse, get a small solar unit and battery, and construct a small kitchen and sink with an outflow pipe for gray water. They order a big cookstove from Ohio Amish country that comes on a freight truck and requires a group of four to pick it up, transport it into the cabin, and shimmy it into position.

As winter approaches, the cabin is almost finished and they light the first inaugural fire in the cookstove. Within an hour, the cabin is so toasty that they strip down to T-shirts.

"This is warmer than our house at home," says Reggie. "We can do naked yoga."

"And check out how quickly this cookstove oven works." Rae pulls a fully cooked sweet potato out of the oven. "It's quicker than a microwave."

Before the snow falls, they drive up with loads of scrounged furniture and boxes of books to install in the built-in bookcases. All these books are a form of insulation, Reggie observes. Rae points out that this is a thin justification for his book hoarding. They bring bulk supplies and stock provisions for the winter and beyond.

"Finally, our bug-out location is complete," says Rae. Lately she has begun to refer to herself as a "communitarian prepper" and "a survivalist without a gun." She makes long lists of things to look for at thrift shops: tools, quilts, mud boots, candles, saw blades.

"This is my retirement fund," Reggie jokes. "Cabin off the grid, water sovereignty, all the wood we need for heat. I'm cashing out my IRAs and buying tools." His favorite mail-order store becomes Lehman's, sort of an Amish Home Depot in Ohio that is chock-full of practical items for off-the-grid living. Slowly they accumulate a variety of saws, shovels, cast-iron cookware, and water capture and purification kits.

Rae posts a poem written by Juanita Nelson on the outhouse wall. A stanza from "Outhouse Blues" reads,

Well, I went out to the country to live the simple life,
Get away from all that concrete and avoid some of that strife,

Get off the backs of poor folks, stop supporting Uncle Sam
In all that stuff he's puttin' down, like bombing Vietnam
Oh, but it ain't easy, 'specially on a chilly night
When I beat it to the outhouse with my trusty dim flashlight —
The seat is absolutely frigid, not a BTU of heat . . .
That's when I think the simple life is not for us elite.

Rae takes a picture of the cabin and texts it to Toby. "Our piece of heaven," she writes. She knows Toby will appreciate what they've done. A couple years earlier, before her dad died, he and Toby built a small hunting cabin near the forest where Rae and Toby had played as kids.

"Can't wait to visit," replies Toby. With their parents gone, Toby and Rae have been in more frequent contact. Rae still holds a tinge of sadness that she didn't invite Toby to their City Hall wedding. Toby is living in the family house, still unable to remain in a relationship longer than a year. So Rae remains his mainstay family connection, outside of a few cousins.

"No Fox News up here," she texts back. "Actually, no news of any kind! Lots of fireflies."

"Sounds divine," Toby replies, ignoring the Fox News dig. "Keep those pictures coming."

As the weather warms, Reggie and Rae spend more and more time at the cabin in Vermont, often with friends along. Jade and PJ are regular visitors, along with Jade's new bride, Sandra, and PJ's partner, Wendy.

Rudy and his partner Elliot also visit to pitch in on projects and help explore the area. Rudy, whose real name is Radra Ranganath, grew up in South India. He is one of the pioneers of Boston's effort to build food forests, community gardens, and edible landscapes. He is well known for leading parades of school children into gardening projects and pestering city officials to turn over vacant land for food production.

Work on the pond is completed, with help from a local guy with an excavator and pond expertise. In hot weather Reggie often declares a "three-dip day" and takes regular plunges to stay cool.

"Reggie had a vision of this pond," explains Rae to Jade. Rae was initially indifferent to Reggie's idea for a pond but is now a convert to its blessings. "Before the first cabin nail was hammered, Reggie had a fantasy that he would rise in the morning, bow to the east, saunter in his birthday suit to the pond, and jump in. A man with a vision is a dangerous thing."

"It's what Rae would call the power of manifestation," Reggie jokes. "Envision it and it will happen."

"I exercise that power every morning," Rae tells the group. "I lie in bed envisioning a cup of tea and Reggie brings it to me."

"I'm not sure that's manifestation, just excellent training," says Jade, shaking her jet-black hair.

"Like a dog that brings your slippers," adds PJ.

They build a small, fenced-in garden, construct an herb spiral, and plant a collection of fruit trees including plum trees, heritage apple trees, and a peach tree by the outhouse. Rae digs up a thicket and plants low- and highbush blueberries. These plants have mediocre success, as Rae and Reggie are not around enough to tend to them.

The social gatherings are more successful. Rae and Reggie love hosting friends at the cabin and build a small screened-in guest cabin in the woods. In the spring, a couple of juvenile foxes pay them a visit, seemingly unafraid of humans. The kits jump about snapping up grasshoppers and hunting voles. At dusk, the little brown bats swoop about the cabin and the pond. Later in the evening the fireflies come out, reminding Rae of her southern Ohio childhood with Toby chasing what they called "lightning bugs."

Reggie's various upwardly mobile family members visit but they don't stay overnight. They think that a cabin without plumbing and electricity is self-inflicted barbarism. Reggie's sister Maggie teases her brother: "The Donovans have toiled hard over two generations to move from one-toilet Irish to two-toilet. Now you've regressed to no-toilet Irish."

"I'm getting in touch with my authentic roots," Reggie teases back. "You think that thatched-roof Irish cottage that Mom reveres had a flush toilet? Oh no, Maggie. They'd say those big lace-curtain houses on the South Shore are a *holy show*."

Maggie shudders. "Now don't you go be making a *holy show* of yourself, with all those spiders in the privy."

"I have a pact with the spiders not to show themselves when I'm in there," adds Rae helpfully.

"Heaven help us." Maggie genuflects in mock horror.

Back in Boston, Reggie begins a new job working for an organization called the Labor Network for Sustainability, engaging unions around climate change and protecting workers in extractive industries as coal plants are closed down. Rae continues her work doing organizational-development consulting. Both Reggie and Rae spend their nonfiction book hours reading up on climate change and the energy transition. With gas almost $4 a gallon—and growing signs of drought, wild fire, and hurricanes—they sense that the next couple decades will not be like the last forty years.

They realize together that climate change is not some problem for future generations, but something that will touch their lives. Reggie finds a quote he likes for Rae from the entomologist E. O. Wilson: "It is important to always keep in mind that Nature Bats Last."

"And as we know from when Big Papi is batting, it ain't over until the last out," adds Rae. This season, the local Red Sox favorite, David "Big Papi" Ortiz, seems to have a penchant for game-winning hits with two outs in the bottom of the ninth inning.

"Gaia is a fearsome hitter in a clutch," Reggie adds.

On Labor Day weekend, a whole crowd comes to the visit the cabin and attend the Guilford Fair, an annual old-timey carnival that includes an oxen pull and a fireman's muster—a series of competitive relays and drills pitting local volunteer fire departments against one another.

Rudy and his partner Elliot, Jade and her partner Sandra, and Toni all bunk into the cabin, while Enid brings her tent and camps in the field. This tight little group is spending more and more time together. Toni is a tall Black woman with dark glasses who has worked for a decade as a community organizer on housing issues. Enid is a short White woman who teaches in a day-care center and built a super-insulated house in Jamaica Plain. They build a big bonfire and sample Elliot's mead made from his own honeybees, housed on his rooftop in East Boston.

"Gas at four bucks a gallon, housing prices through the roof, George W. Bush on the war path," said Rudy. "What, me worry?"

"When does the bubble burst?" asks Reggie.

"What time is it?" jokes Jade, looking at her watch. "I'd say any minute."

"I've sold all my stock holdings and bought several hundred bags of pistachios," says Elliot. "I think they will become the next currency."

"Elliot had only $200 of stock," says Rudy. "So consider that along with his sage investment advice."

"Hey, at least it looks like Obama's gonna be president," says Jade.

"Do you see a pattern here?" Enid quips. "Republicans crash the economy and send the Black guy to fix it."

"Hey, Barack, can you come clean up this mess?" jokes Toni, cleaning her glasses. "I say give this dumpster fire to Sarah Palin."

Rae enjoys the banter as she weaves small St. Brigid crosses out of reeds and rushes. She gives her best work to Reggie's mother, Missy, to sell at the Irish Cottage store. The others she sprinkles around among their friends.

Two weeks later, Rae is back in Boston and glued to the radio, listening to the news. The Wall Street firm of Lehman Brothers has collapsed. President Bush's treasury secretary, Hank Paulsen, formerly of Goldman Sachs, begs Speaker of the House Nancy Pelosi on bended knee to pass his $700-billion, blank-check bailout bill.

The next day, Rae reads the headline in the *New York Times*: "Day of Chaos Grips Washington; Fate of Bailout Plan Unresolved." "If money isn't loosened up," President Bush warns congressional leaders at a White House meeting, "this sucker could go down." On September 29, after the first vote on the bailout plan goes down to defeat, the stock market plummets.

In her journal, Rae writes: *This could be the collapse we've been waiting for. Good thing I've got my prepper supplies in the basement. Another reason to prepare for both the short-term and long-term emergency. I don't feel scared. Bring it on. I know I can't say that out loud.*

At church on the Sunday after the market decline, Rev. Terry convenes a coffee hour discussion about how people are doing with the economy in meltdown. More than forty people linger, with several sharing their fears about job losses and economic depression.

"My retirement plan just evaporated," says an older congregant named Earl. "Looks like my timeline has just changed. Back to work I go."

"My boss told me to expect layoffs," says Edith, who works at a senior center. "I have no savings, no reserves. I pay my rent month to month."

Heidi, a teacher in a day-care center, confesses she has no health insurance and is postponing health care.

Over the next several weeks Edith and several other members of the congregation are laid off from their jobs. Enid and Rae create a "mutual aid" support group for members of the congregation to talk about their economic situations and help one another. People from outside the church hear about it and ask to join.

As winter approaches, a few people in the church are evicted from their apartments or get foreclosure notices on their homes. Other members of the congregation help people move or offer housing. One woman, Stella, organizes a "rent party," and a group of musicians from the church perform and attract dozens of people to come by. She raises enough money for two months of rent and is thrilled to keep the wolf from her door.

Rae's work with City Life fighting evictions becomes more pressing. There are multiple eviction blockades each month, as tenants bear the brunt of speculation in the housing market. Reggie laughs when he sees how Countrywide Financial repackaged their mortgage and thousands of others into complex financial assets that are sliced and diced and sold to investors. Several years of reckless lending practices emerge before their eyes.

Over the fall and into the winter, Enid and Rae facilitate these mutual aid groups, even getting a small grant to propagate the idea. They create a resource guide for other congregations to form mutual aid groups, or what one participant calls "resilience circles."

In the face of fear and scarcity, they design an activity to focus on the abundance within a community. First, they ask participants to identify five things they have to offer, in terms of skills, items, or tools—and five things they need. They create a ritual offering of "gifts and needs," with each person sharing both.

A woman in her late fifties named Gretchen says she joined the congregation in the spring after her husband, Larry, died suddenly from a heart attack. "I felt I needed to be around people and not be isolated." But she says that she really hasn't gotten to know people at the church yet. In her offering of "gifts and needs," she reveals that she badly needs help with all the things that Larry used to do: clean gutters, put up storm windows, even change lightbulbs when a ladder is required. "I'm embarrassed by my fear of ladders and lack of skills," she confesses.

"I don't have a lot to offer," Gretchen says quietly. "But I still have Larry's pickup truck. I keep paying the insurance on it, thinking maybe it might be useful to someone. But it just sits in our driveway."

Her words hang in the air.

Then one participant, Darryl, says, "You have a pickup truck?"

Andrea has the same thought: "You have a truck that people can borrow?"

"Yeah," says Gretchen. "It's just sitting there. In my driveway."

There is laughter around the room. Over the next month, Gretchen basks in the wealth of community. Neighbors come and do yard work, rake leaves, put up storm windows, and bring Gretchen pots of soup, staying to chat. In exchange, Larry's old truck is deployed to help people and pick up shipments for the church food pantry. The truck becomes part of a web of new friends and mutual aid. Gretchen is thrilled.

This is just one example of the immediate bartering matches made, underscoring the real wealth and resourcefulness of the group. Yvonne needs help with yardwork because of her arthritis. Melanie needs childcare. Paul is capable of yardwork but needs help budgeting. Yvonne takes care of Melanie's kids. Paul helps Yvonne with her yardwork. Yvonne helps Paul with his budgeting and tracking expenses.

Their resilience circle continues to meet weekly. "The reality is, our mutual aid muscles are badly out of shape," observes Rae. "We really don't know how to ask for help from one another. We don't know how to say no when we can't help. Instead, we just stay disconnected."

At home, she thinks about the whole process. "A lot of low-income and working-class people I know don't have trouble asking for help," she reflects to Reggie. "They need one another to survive. But when people become more middle-class, they buy into the myth of economic independence. They would rather suffer silently than ask for help."

Her friend Darrell, who is a member of Morning Star Baptist, a historically Black church on Blue Hill Avenue, tells her that his church has had a mutual aid ministry for a hundred years.

"The White, middle-class churches have divorced material aid from spiritual fulfilment," Rae complains to Reggie.

The resilience circles take off, with their own website and online toolbox. It flows from their experience starting and facilitating multiple groups. Rae, Enid, and a few others write up stories from the field and create a facilitator's guide. Deepening mutual aid practice is one of the key activities. Within a couple of months, there are over three hundred resilience circles around the United States reporting on their experience.

Enid steers Rae to more and more resources about climate change, peak oil, and the ecological challenges ahead.

"These resilience circles are helping people survive right now, this economic meltdown," Rae observes. "But they will be even more essential for the 'long emergency,' the need for community and individual resilience."

They add more and more articles and discussion activities.

"We should really form our own study group," Rae suggests to Enid. "This is the stuff I want to understand."

Rae writes in her journal: *Building this kind of face-to-face resilience will be critical as we face climate disruption and economic collapse. I want to be at the center of figuring this out. And I feel alive.*

TRANSITION BOOK CLUB

(2014)

Rae looks forward to hosting the book club each month, now entering its fifth year. She whips up some cranberry-orange scones, puts on the kettle, and arranges seven chairs in the living room.

How unusual it is to have a group of people, with different life experiences, come together to talk about real ideas, books, and those books' implications for their lives?

As she complains frequently to Reggie, most social encounters in their lives are endless small talk. Rae can play along with what she calls the "vapid banter." But what she hungers for are the discussions they have in the book club. Reggie can now repeat verbatim one of her unimpeded rants about social conversations among their peers and extended family, and how this shifts over time.

"When we were in our twenties," she begins, holding up three fingers, "90 percent of social conversation focused on three topics: relationships, work, and housing, usually the search for an affordable apartment. Ninety percent! Only 10 percent left over for the state of the world, spirituality, politics, and what the hell are we gonna do when the shit hits the fan!"

"Okay, that's a little harsh," says Reggie, though not entirely in disagreement.

Rae notices he usually stays quiet during peak banter, occasionally chiming in with a question or observation so as not to be mistaken for a complete misanthrope.

"And this," he adds, "is our sort of White middle-class subculture. I don't think this applies to everyone."

"In our thirties, it's relationships (sometimes marriage), real estate, and movies," she continues. "In our forties, its children, real estate, and vacation highlights. In our fifties, the topics are children, home improvements, and vacation highlights. When we hit our sixties, it's our bodies and health, retirement fantasies, and the activities of adult children."

"I like hearing about people's vacations anytime," says Reggie. "What about food? Seems like people talk a lot about food."

"Yeah, I guess that's the topic that cuts across all decades," Rae concedes. "And if you haven't seen people in a month, you basically just play catch-up on all these same things. You never get below the surface."

"Not everyone wants an encounter session when they get together," Reggie suggests. He has told Rae that she can repel people with her intensity.

"Yeah, I know. But all the superficial blather? Boring."

The book club is different. Seven people who are committed to meeting every month and reading a work of fiction or nonfiction to inform their thinking about the future.

They call themselves the "Transition Book Club," convening around the themes of ecological climate change, social disruption, and how to build a livable future. They read things that their friends and families won't understand or might think is far-fetched. Indeed, many of their conversations center around the fact that they don't know how to talk to friends and loved ones about the challenges ahead.

The book club was started by Rae, Reggie, Jade, Toni, and Enid, and two years later Rudy and PJ join. A couple of them work together or are part of political groups. And everyone but PJ is able to take a bus together to New York City for a massive Climate March in early

September, with an estimated 400,000 marchers, the biggest event of its kind ever. Reggie calls it their "book club field trip."

Their fiction choices range from Ursula K. LeGuin, Octavia Butler, Margaret Atwood, Starhawk, and other science fiction loaded with insights about future utopias and dystopias. A sampling of the nonfiction titles include: Rebecca Solnit, *Paradise Built in Hell*; Paul Gilding, *The Great Disruption*; Julian Cribbs, *The Coming Famine*; Dmitry Orlov, *The Five Stages of Collapse*; Richard Heinberg, *The End of Growth*, Elizabeth Kolbert, *The Sixth Extinction*, and Naomi Klein, *This Changes Everything*.

Rae enjoys the nonfiction and fiction writings of John Michael Greer, "the Grand Archdruid of the Ancient Order of Druids in America," including *The Long Descent: The User's Guide to the End of the Industrial Age* and *The Wealth of Nature: Economics as if Survival Mattered*. Lately, they've been drawn to books that also include some practical skills and insights, including: Toby Hemenway, *Gaia's Garden: A Guide to Permaculture*; Sharon Astyk, *Making Home: Adapting Our Homes and Our Lives to Settle in Place*; and Ben Falk, *The Resilient Farm and Homestead*.

Rae pulls the scones from the oven and flicks off a few burned tips to otherwise fragrant and perfect babies. There's a knock at the door and Rudy enters, holding his book, a little bag of store-bought pastries, and a plastic yogurt container of berries.

"Welcome Rudy," Rae says, offering a one-armed hug as she balances a plate of scones. "How are you?"

"Good! I just came from the garden and picked these raspberries." Rudy hands Rae the cup. "Berries still coming from those ever-bearing plants."

Seconds later, Jade and PJ walk in the door, finishing a conversation and greeting Rudy and Rae. Reggie emerges from his back office and a buzz of conversation begins.

Toni arrives breathless, having walked quickly from the subway. Enid follows a minute later, wearing a long cranberry frock that gets rousing compliments.

Everyone grabs tea or coffee and a plate with snacks. A few minutes later, they are seated in a circle. Rae calls the gathering to order with a moment of silence. Then they begin a round of what can sometimes be longish personal check-ins. They talk about what is going well and what is hard—and how they are making sense of what they are reading.

"I'm feeling like I'm in the wrong line of work," says Toni, daughter of a preacher. She works as an organizer at the local community-development corporation.

"I'm thinking about the pipeline project announced in West Roxbury. I'd like to talk to you all about that," said Rudy.

"Let's save some time at the end of the meeting for that," said Rae.

The book they discuss today is about the 1930s dust bowl, a history by Tim Egan called *The Worst Hard Time: The Untold Story of Those Who Survived the Great Depression.* It's a follow-on to the book club's previous month's discussion of *The Grapes of Wrath*, by John Steinbeck.

"I found this one of the most oddly useful books we've read," said Enid. "*Grapes of Wrath* was about the climate refugees, the people who left the degraded dust bowl region. This was about the people who stayed put and tried to survive the hard times."

"Yes, practical tips like how to corral and club hundreds of rabbits to make rabbit stew for the winter months," said PJ, referring to a passage of the book describing large community hunting parties to catch meat for survival. "You have year after year of crop failure, but you can at least preserve a lot of rabbit meat."

"Next book club meeting, I'm making my special rabbit stew," jokes Reggie.

Rae waits for a pause. "What was most revealing to me was the fact that even when it was clear that the dust bowl was a human-created ecological disaster, there was a solid group of . . . let's call them 'dust bowl deniers,' people who believed that the dust storms were acts of God, the result of sinful behavior. Or others whose boosterism and focus on positive thinking kept them from really facing the situation."

Rudy picks up from that comment. "Yeah, and there were the promoters, the hucksters, the people who really made money by opening up the territory, selling land in the plains to Easterners with promises of rain and bounty. They kept the promotions and land sales rolling."

"So what I'm hearing," says Jade, "is we shouldn't even try to convince a segment of society that climate change exists. There's just gonna be a hardcore 30 percent of the population that is anti-science, impervious to change."

"The unreachables," says PJ. "They won't be persuaded. Or they maintain religious or magical thinking about the future."

"I mean the dust literally blew all the way to Washington DC," said Jade. "It engulfed the US Capitol in a dark cloud until they passed the mitigation legislation."

"Talk about Gaia sending a message to the humans," adds Toni. "It's like Oklahoma getting earthquakes from fracking. Hello, deniers! We're going to knock your dinner plates off your shelves until you pay attention."

The conversation is like a dance between experienced partners who know when to push off one another. They clearly enjoy one another's company, even with periodic disagreements.

"We're close to the end of our time," says Rae after the allotted two hours have passed. "I want to make sure we hear from Rudy about this pipeline thing." She is weaving one of her St. Brigid's crosses out of reeds while Enid knits a sweater.

"Yes, thanks Rae," says Rudy. "I went to a meeting last night in West Roxbury about this new gas pipeline project." He sits bolt upright, holding a tea cup and looking at his notepad. "There were two hundred people there, almost all opposed to the pipeline. This company Spectra Energy wants to build a spur off the Algonquin gas pipeline coming up the East Coast. By the way, this is gas from the fracking fields of Pennsylvania. Spectra plans to construct a five-mile spur through a densely residential area to bring gas right into West Roxbury, to a terminus across the street from an active blasting quarry."

"What could possibly go wrong?" jokes Jade.

Rudy smiles and shakes his head. "Some of the neighbors of the quarry said they have cracks in their house foundations from the blasting explosions. But that's where this pipeline will end, at a metering station literally across the street from the quarry."

"How come we haven't heard about this?" asked Reggie.

"Almost nobody knew about it until a couple weeks ago, when Spectra called for an open house on September 2, the night before

school started. Still a bunch of people turned out to express concern. Last night most of the politicians were there—city councilors,
state senators, representatives of the congressional delegation."

"Isn't this mostly NIMBY stuff?" said Jade. "They wouldn't care if
it was in Black and Brown Mattapan. This is White Westie!"

"Maybe. A lot of the concerns were about health and safety,"
reflects Rudy. "And the pipeline—what they call the West Roxbury
Lateral—is pretty high-pressure, like 750 pounds per square inch
in the pipe. Most gas coming into our houses is at about 10 pounds
per square inch."

He pauses and everyone takes in this information.

"Turns out Spectra already has preliminary approval from
FERC."

"From what?" asks Enid.

"FERC—the Federal Energy Regulatory Commission. It's the big
federal agency involved here," says Rudy. "They seem to have all the
power when it comes to approving pipelines, including the power
to take land."

"You know, we might want to form an affinity group," suggests
Rae. "Any of us from the book club plus another half dozen people.
Really think about how to 'up the ante' in terms of tactics—you
know, prepare the community for direct action."

"Makes sense to me," says Jade. "We should invite Nathan and
Michael from the local 350.org chapter. Maybe a few more people
from West Roxbury."

"You can see where this is heading," says PJ. "But maybe we
should organize some teach-ins to educate the community. Most
people still have no idea where the pipeline is going."

"We should paint a red line along the route," said Jade. "Like a
Freedom Trail . . ."

"Yeah, who else should we ask?" asked Rae.

The following week, Rae and Reggie attend another big meeting
about the pipeline and listen to the local West Roxbury leaders
pleading with Mayor Marty Walsh and their politicians to do something. Dozens of residents stand up to ask questions and express
alarm about the dangers of a high-pressure pipeline next to an

active blasting quarry. Two people speak about the folly of building new fossil fuel infrastructure in the face of climate change. The mayor listens and pledges that the City will take action to protect the neighborhood.

The winter encroaches and Boston is walloped by several massive snowstorms. Reggie shovels a path to their front door, which has four-foot drifts on both sides. As spring approaches, Rae prepares for the campaign against the pipeline, reading up on the process of approval and talking with others about a direct-action campaign.

FERC YOU

(2015)

Rae is in Washington, DC, for a work conference that coincides with a monthly FERC hearing. It is a sunny late April morning as she walks from the William Penn Quaker guesthouse on Capitol Hill toward Union Station. The cherry blossoms are still blooming. From Union Station, Rae walks down a busy side street to a government building with its name emblazoned in large letters: Federal Energy Regulatory Commission. She feels invigorated by the warm air, the cherry blossoms, and the purpose of her mission.

Rae has studied up about FERC, with its five appointed commissioners. While she could watch the hearing online, she wants to experience the process firsthand. Plus, Boston city councilor Matt O'Malley, her district councilor, asked her to do a little reconnaissance in order to understand the process. At some point, the West Roxbury Lateral Pipeline will come up for another final approval vote before the FERC board, and Matt wonders if they are impervious to influence.

Rae stands in a security line to enter the building, along with a dozen others attending the hearing. Men in well-tailored suits with briefcases; women wearing elegant dresses or pantsuits, also holding briefcases and folios. Rae presumes that these are mostly industry lobbyists. Rae is more casually dressed in slacks, dress sandals, and a linen shirt, with a small satchel.

As she passes through security and shows her identification, she is told to wait to the side.

After a couple of minutes, a guard appears, a White woman with a military bearing. "Follow me," she says, personally escorting Rae up a set of stairs to a balcony and to the entrance of a side room with a large video monitor.

"You can watch from this overflow room," says the guard, pointing into the room.

"Why? Why can't I go into the main hearing room?"

"This is where you can watch the hearing," the guard says blankly.

"How come those other people aren't being taken here?" Rae notices a few other people being escorted to the room, the more casually dressed people. "Is this because I'm a not a lobbyist wearing a suit?"

Rae defiantly stands outside the room, the guard impatiently gesturing for her to enter the room. "Who decided this? I want to talk to who decided." Rae feels her fuse has been lit.

The guard exhales with an exhausted sound and picks up her radio, muttering something unintelligible. "Please wait in here," she says, pointing again to the room. Rae lingers inside the doorway.

Rae pulls out her cell phone and calls her contact in Representative Stephen Lynch's office, a labor movement friend of Reggie's. Representative Lynch is a former ironworker from South Boston, a more traditional lunch-bucket Democrat who doesn't always vote the right way on things Rae cares about. But on the pipeline, he has been a genuinely good ally, insisting on stronger public safety provisions for the project.

"Donny," she says, "I'm over here at FERC headquarters, trying to attend a hearing. But they've shunted me off to some overflow room. They won't let me sit in the main hearing room. They won't tell me why."

Donnie says he will call immediately. Just as Rae hangs up, a suited man enters the room and introduces himself as head of security.

"Why can't I go in?" Rae asks.

"We're expecting protesters and disruption. And your name is on a list."

"I'm not here to protest. I'm here to watch the hearing. And I'm here on behalf of my community and Boston city councilor Matt O'Malley."

"I'm sorry, you can watch from here—or we will have to ask you to leave."

Rae sighs. "What list am I on? I could have watched this from home. I came all the way from Boston."

The chief of security stands impatiently.

"Do you have a card?" Rae asks.

He hands her his business card, and she sits down in the room with the other outcasts. As the hearing begins, Rae can see the commissioners on the television monitor. She calls Donnie back.

"I talked to the head of security. He says I'm on a list." She gives Donnie the contact info for the head of security and hangs up. Her inner fury is starting to smolder.

She perches on a chair and watches the hearing. There is Cheryl Flores, the commissioner who lives in nearby Wellesley. She's the former head of the local gas company—and she's the Democratic appointee.

Suddenly there is a bit of disruption in the hearing room. A woman, indistinguishable from the lobbyists, stands up and shouts at the commissioners. "You just rubberstamped this project!" she yells.

Another lobbyist-dressed man holds up a fabric banner that must have been rolled up in his briefcase. "Stop the Delaware pipeline," it reads.

Several of the other exiled observers in the overflow room start to cheer. The other remote observers look puzzled as to what is going on. Rae is elated but doesn't say anything.

In the hearing room, security guards fly into action, wading into the auditorium seats to wrestle with these protesters and grab their arms, leading them roughly from the room. They continue to shout as they are taken out into the hallway.

Moments later, two security guards burst into the overflow room. "Okay, everyone out. You have to leave."

Rae and several others among the non-protesters are stunned and puzzled. "We can't sit in the overflow room?" one man asks, clearly as befuddled as Rae.

"Everyone out, now!" shouts the guard. One protester jumps up and runs to the front of the room, holding onto the screen and refusing to leave. Several other guards enter the room and tackle the protester.

A tall male guard rushes Rae directly, roughly grabbing her arm. "You must leave now!" he shouts through gritted teeth.

Rae, sensing danger, stands up and walks cooperatively toward the doorway. But the guard grabs her harder, pushing her arm up behind her back.

"Hey, that's not necessary, I've leaving!" Rae shouts.

The guard ignores her, roughly handling her down the stairs, several times lifting her arm behind her back to inflict pain.

"Hey!" she shouts. "You're out of line! That hurts!" For a moment she thinks, Holy shit, they're going to arrest me. She wonders if she'll be thrown into some police wagon or holding tank. But as the guard approaches the door, he slightly lets up on the pressure and shoves her out onto the sidewalk.

Several of the ejected protesters are there already, including the well-dressed lobbyist look-alikes.

Rae pulls out her phone again and calls Donny at Representative Lynch's office. "You won't believe this, but I've just been forcibly ejected from the building. I was just sitting in the overflow room. I was even roughed up by some guard. And I'm just here to sit in on a public hearing."

She can hear the disgust in Donny's reaction.

She hangs up and looks at the two guards standing at the door. "This is a little too Big Brother for me," she says. "Do you always rough up citizens who come to attend public hearings?"

They appear sheepish and shake their heads. A few minutes pass and Rae isn't sure what to do.

"Miz Kelliher?"

She looks up and the head of security is standing next to her.

"I apologize that there has been a mistake," he says. "You are welcome to come back in and attend the hearing."

Rae eyes him suspiciously. "What list am I on?"

"There has been a mistake," he repeats. "I apologize."

Rae follows him, skipping the security line. Passing the guard, she taps the head of security on the shoulder. "Sir, that is the guard who forcibly wrenched my arm. Where should I send my medical bill?"

The chief of security continues to lead her to the hearing room. He escorts her through the door, past the other guards, and to an aisle seat. He seems transformed into a kindly church usher leading her to her personal pew at St. Marys, her childhood church.

The hearing continues for another half hour, a series of unintelligible motions and votes. The voices of the protesters and dissenters have been silenced. As the hearing adjourns, the church-usher head of security appears again at her side to escort her back to the curb.

Rae has written her phone and email on a note card that she hands to the chief. "I'd like to know what list I am on," she says again. "Let me know, or I'll have my congressional delegation look into it."

Later, Rae takes the slow Amtrak train back to Boston, passing large oil refineries and the back alleys of New Jersey cities. She enjoys the view out the window and the longer transition time between Washington and home. She writes in her journal: *We are up against formidable power, this energy industry. They have wired everything in their favor, including FERC. Now I've personally experienced a taste of the big 'FERC YOU,' the authoritarian fist of US energy policy. The paltry power of our opposition is pathetic in comparison. But we will give them a holy fight.*

PIPELINE

(2015)

"So let me get this straight," Rae asks the group, including Nathan, who is an expert on FERC. "If a private gas company, Spectra Energy, wants to take Boston's streets by eminent domain to build a pipeline, is there anything that the citizens of Boston can do to protect themselves?"

Rae has been anticipating this meeting, which she is hosting in her living room. Her interest in FERC and its considerable powers are piqued by her eviction from the hearing in Washington, DC.

All the members of the book club—Reggie, Jade, PJ, Toni, Rudy, and Enid—are present. They are joined by six others, including Rev. Anne, the minister of the Unitarian Universalist church in West Roxbury, and Nathan Phillips, a professor at Boston University.

Rae continues, looking at Nathan. "Or if private Texas corporation Kinder Morgan wants to build a pipeline across the northern tier of Massachusetts, can they condemn private land, including the Mount Grace Land Conservancy, and take my land?"

"They can take a right-of-way," said Nathan. "The federal legislation essentially delegates public power to private corporations. There are a few leverage points to push back. Health and safety have some state and local oversight. That's why it makes sense to engage the Boston Health Commission and the Commonwealth as well."

"But with West Roxbury this is a done deal, right? It's all over except for the actual construction?" asks Rudy. His question hangs in the air.

"How could I live sixty years in America and never know about FERC?" says Toni. "It's obviously another example of a federal agency captured by the industry that they are supposed to regulate. Foxes guarding the henhouse."

"It has a reputation as a rubber-stamp agency," confirms Nathan. "They rarely meet a gas pipeline project they don't love. They've only rejected, like, two out of four hundred proposed projects over the last couple of decades. And they're a revolving door—the commissioners and senior staff all come out of the gas and oil industry—and some of them go back to work at these companies when they leave FERC."

"Yet that FERC guy I was talking to said, 'Hey, if you don't like what FERC is doing, then talk to Congress, since they write the laws,'" says Enid.

"But I looked at who is on the FERC oversight committees," says Rae. "It's all senators from fracking states—Oklahoma, North Dakota, Utah. The United States of Extraction. The foxes also sit on the congressional oversight committee." Rae thinks back to Sam Lovejoy and the Nuclear Regulatory Commission and its weak oversight of the nuclear industry.

"So don't look to FERC to save the day," says Toni. "The process is entirely tipped in favor of the industry. That's what we're seeing here in West Roxbury. The deal had been sealed before we even heard about it."

"Talk about a rigged game!" exclaims Rudy. "I don't think we should let it be built without a fight. Our group could help build a direct-action resistance to the pipeline. Start with teach-ins and educational events on the risks. Keep working every political channel. And if all else fails, try to block construction."

"What I don't understand is, there is no increased demand for gas in Boston or New England," says Reggie. "Our demand is actually going down. And with renewables going on-line, that will continue to decline. How can FERC approve pipeline infrastructure for projects with no demand?"

"All right, who here is taking longer showers?" jokes Rudy.

"I haven't showered in months." Rae waves her hand in innocence.

"Yeah, that's cause she's taking one-hour baths," says Reggie. "She has the ability to turn the faucet with her foot to add hot water. That has spiked demand across the grid."

"Well, think of us as pawns in a three-dimensional global chess game," says Nathan. "The US gas industry is trying to get all this gas to export terminals. The big geopolitical game is to compete with Russia and GazProm for the European market."

Rae is intrigued by this chess image and this entire conversation. Slowly she is getting the detailed picture, in her mind, of a rigged process.

Nathan points out that earlier in the month, Spectra announced the next phase of the Algonquin project—the construction of a ten-mile pipeline they call the Atlantic Bridge. "This is about export, getting gas to Canada and LNG export terminals to Europe."

Rae has been doing a deep-learning dive about fracking and the gas market. "Our politics haven't caught up to the fact that the US went from an importer of fossil fuels to an exporter again in a millisecond."

"They need to say it's about Boston gas demand to justify getting us local customers to pay the infrastructure bill," adds Nathan. "But the driver here is export markets, getting as much of this gas as possible to export terminals. And it's a race. These people are in a hurry because they know the market is volatile."

"Is there more the mayor or the city can do?" Michael asks.

The group asks Nathan more questions and bats around tactical ideas.

"Jade, I think we should implement your idea, painting a red line along the pipeline route," says Rae, having already urged Reggie to be part of the guerrilla line painters.

"I think it's a great idea," says Enid. "I know where we can borrow those line-sprayer wheely-things."

"Yeah, dress up like road construction workers with hard hats and reflective vests and paint the route," says Rudy, encouraged by the spirit.

"I'm in a custody battle over my kids right now," says Enid. "So I probably have to be careful about getting arrested. But I'll help in any way I can."

"Paint the line, but then turn yourself in to the police," Rae says, thinking of Sam Lovejoy knocking over the tower and then presenting himself to the Montague police. "Maximum publicity value."

They hatch a scheme and borrow rolling spray guns, reflective vests, and road crew swag. At the crack of dawn on a weekday morning, Reggie, Jade, and Rudy start painting the route of the pipeline, each starting at different sections. Michael and Rae follow up in a car, spray-painting stencils around the quarry that say "Stop Spectra."

After the job is completed, the entire crew of nine—including drivers, lookouts, and spray-painters—meet for breakfast at the West Rox Diner.

"You should see the lines that Rudy painted," teases Jade. "They look like a wobbly red snake." She takes a large bite of her veggie omelette. "Rudy, you're fired from the road crew!"

"Look at your shoes," Rudy retorts. "Did you leave any paint on the road?"

After breakfast, the three public line painters turn themselves in at the police station at the rotary in West Roxbury center. The puzzled detectives take down their statements with a fair amount of curiosity and a faintly detectable sense of sympathy. It's not every day that graffiti vandals proudly turn themselves into law enforcement. They are not arrested, but weeks later are summoned before the local magistrate, who drops the charges.

The publicity, however, is tremendous. Photos of the three line-painters, striking a Paul Revere pose in tri-corner hats, appear in several of the local community newspapers, one with the headline, "Spectra is Coming!"

Over the following weeks, Rae testifies at a hearing of the Boston City Council, which then votes unanimously to urge the city of Boston not to issue permits until the public safety matters are addressed. But Spectra and FERC roll over the process.

The City files a lawsuit to stop Spectra, and they countersue the City. Rae sits in the back of the federal courtroom. In silent slow motion, her fist pummels the cushion on the bench. The final door appears to be shutting on the legal remedies to stop the pipeline. She feels as if the blood flow to part of her body has been cut off, and there is a new heaviness in her extremities.

She already had a meeting with several organizers and has begun to plan a series of trainings in nonviolent direct action. She and her friend Cathy from the 1980s Pledge of Resistance days pull their band of trainers back together and start updating their materials and workshop designs. She creates a new chart titled, "We Have Exhausted All Legal Remedies," with a list of all the ways that neighborhood residents have attempted to legally stop the pipeline.

Meanwhile, the affinity group organizes a huge march and rally, with over three hundred people marching to the blasting quarry and the site of the pipeline terminus. Six city councilors line up to speak in opposition to the pipeline. Two days later, construction on the pipeline begins in West Roxbury.

The following Monday, Reggie, Rev. Anne, and another minister, Rev. Martha, who walks with a cane, step into the middle of the construction site, blocking a giant backhoe. The workers shut down the equipment and wait for the police. Several police officers appear, urging the three protesters to move. After a half hour of consultations with superior officers, the police reluctantly give the three of them a final warning before placing them in handcuffs and leading them to two transport vehicles.

Over the next month more than one hundred and twenty people are arrested in direct blockades of the construction site. After a group of college students is arrested, one of the local West Roxbury residents, a retired teacher named Bill, says he will risk arrest. "If these kids, with their whole lives ahead of them, are willing to be arrested for my neighborhood, I should do the same."

Construction stops in mid-November for the winter, giving protesters, police, and construction workers a bit of welcome respite. But this allows the protesters to organize, recruit, and train hundreds more potential resisters. Rae and Cathy do roughly one new training a week, adding to the ranks of future Henry David Thoreaus.

Rae also consults with friends in Western Massachusetts, some of whom she has known since Montague Farm days. They are working to stop another pipeline, the Northeast Direct sponsored by Kinder Morgan. Unlike the situation in West Roxbury, the towns in Western Mass were alerted to the pipeline project at an earlier stage of the process, enabling them to get organized sooner. At FERC's public meeting in Greenfield, over five hundred opponents attend.

Rae drives back and forth to Montague, sharing the lessons from West Roxbury and working with a group of trainers preparing for direct action. But the Western Mass groups still have more legal avenues for stopping the pipeline before construction begins.

Rae stays with her old pickle factory friend, Nina, who invites some of the old gang to visit when Rae is in town. Peter has moved to Ohio, Sarah lives in France, and Gary has died, but several of the original "no nukes" family have stayed local.

In mid-April, after meetings in Greenfield, she drives up to spend the night at the cabin in Guilford, arriving at dusk as a flock of wild turkeys crosses her path. She motors up the muddy but passable driveway and parks next to the cabin, hauling in a three-gallon water container.

As she pops open the door, she inhales the smell of cabin wood and herbs that she hung up to dry in the fall. She is rarely alone here. She stands for a moment on the porch in the twilight, bundled in a blanket. A barred owl hoots, not far away, and a truck grinds its gears on Stage Road, the sound carrying up the hill. But it is dark as dark can be, with cloud cover and no moon.

She lights a small fire in the woodstove to take the chill off and for the entertainment of watching the flames dance about. She writes in her journal: *I love it here in Vermont and the coming of Spring. The brightness of the stars. We have so much to lose with catastrophic climate change. We have everything we need here, but we keep consuming more. As Gandhi says, there is enough for everyone's need but not greed. I'm going to give this pipeline fight everything I've got.*

She's asleep by 9:30 and wakes with the sun.

•

At each training, Rae repeats what is at stake. "We are the first generation to fully understand the existential dangers of cata-strophic climate change. And we are the last generation that will be able to do anything to avert it."

Throughout the spring and summer, there is a wave of daily vigils and direct actions in West Roxbury. A retired teacher named Mary Boyle stands out every morning, rain or shine, a one-woman vigil at the site of the granite quarry and pipeline terminus.

An affinity group from Western Mass comes for a day to be arrested in West Roxbury and meet with Rae's team. The proposed pipeline in Western Mass would cross lots of private land holdings, including the towns that organized against the 1974 nuclear power plant forty-two years earlier.

The West Roxbury construction crew, mostly workers from out-of-state construction companies, make steady progress along the pipeline route. Once or twice a week, a group of protesters block the site and are arrested. Rae and Reggie get to know many of the workers by name. They explain that they are not against them having high-paying jobs—and that there is ample work in building a clean-energy economy. Reggie brings along some union workers from Boston building trades to talk to the pipeline workers about jobs in green-energy sector.

A spirited group of a dozen clergy, joined by a group of over one hundred religious supporters, assemble at the site and lie down in the trenches. The *Boston Globe*, which has remained largely silent about the pipeline resistance efforts, finally publishes a picture of the Reverend John Gibbons, a Unitarian minister in traditional par-son's garb, standing at the trench.

A group of "mothers out front" coordinate a march of three hundred to the site with dozens of mothers risking arrest. The construction crew decides not to work that day rather than face the wrath of the organized mothers.

One impatient affinity group lock themselves to equipment with bicycle locks around their necks. This escalation of tactics slows downs construction for two hours as police and fire fighters are dispatched to carefully cut the locks off the protester's necks. Tactics escalate on both sides; one day the police arrive before the protesters to block access to the construction site.

Rae attends most of the protests, helping brief the participants and follow up after arrests to make sure no one disappears in the jail holding system. But she also sees that the pipeline is proceeding, that their effort to use their bodies as friction against the machine is only generating a few sparks and not much heat.

"We knew going into this that we would probably lose," says Reggie, at a meeting of the original book club and affinity group. "But our job is to develop people, prepare leaders, and maybe stop the next pipeline."

"I know, but I hate losing," Rae says.

She writes in her journal: *I always thought it was likely we would not stop construction. But I'm still heartsick and disappointed. I thought we would get thousands of people out to be arrested, not just a few hundred. Where the hell are all the people who say they care about climate change? Are they worried about being inconvenienced? I thought newspapers like the* Boston Globe *would cover our actions, but they've done nothing to truly investigate the cozy capture of our energy policy. We can't get any real reporting about the real drivers and risks of this pipeline. It's all "he said, she said" bullshit. Or worse, total news blackout. Are we just shitty at our press work? Hell, the* Globe *probably sells a lot of advertising to these gas companies. And Mayor Walsh has not put any political capital out there. Pathetic. At least Western Mass has a shot at stopping this. And Reggie is getting sick of my rants about this. He looks at me like I'm the loony lady now.*

One morning, Cathy calls Rae to tell her the good news that Kinder Morgan has canceled the Western Mass pipeline, citing inadequate demand. She reads aloud from the news account. Western Massachusetts attorney Tom Lesser, whom Rae remembers as counsel to Sam Lovejoy in 1974, actively represents landowners opposed to the pipeline. He tells a reporter at the *Greenfield Recorder*, "This is a great victory for the people. It's a true testament to what ordinary people who band together can accomplish. Kinder Morgan would probably never acknowledge that what also halted the project was universal opposition throughout the Commonwealth."

Cathy complains to Rae. "We don't have any increased demand here in Boston either, but they were able to jam it through. I think

Kinder Morgan got a glimpse of the strong opposition they were going to encounter, watching our resistance effort."

"I'd like to think so," says Rae. "I'd like to believe our resistance played some role." She feels tears come to her eyes. *Maybe we accomplished something.*

On her sixty-second birthday, Rae is arrested blocking the pipeline. She misses a lobster dinner, organized by some of the Donovan cousins, that she didn't want to go to anyway.

By Fall 2016, the pipeline construction in West Roxbury is complete. Local politicians and activists continue to press FERC and Spectra on safety matters, but nothing slows the process. On January 9, 2017, gas begins to the flow through the pipeline to the depot at the quarry.

Rae writes: *We didn't do enough. I didn't do enough.*

At 4:15 p.m. on September 13, 2018, dozens of houses in Lawrence and Andover, Massachusetts, erupt into flames, several with explosive shocks.

Rae listens to the news accounts as she cooks chili in her kitchen. One reporter calls in live from Lawrence, describing how firefighters are responding to explosions and fires at more than forty homes, with eighty fires erupting across the Merrimack Valley.

The mayor of Lawrence calls on residents to evacuate the city while Merrimack College evacuates all its students and buildings. Thousands of people take to the road, causing panicked gridlock around the region. An eighteen-year-old man is instantly killed after a house explodes and a chimney collapses onto his parked car, where he is sitting with friends.

Gas and power are shut off to more than eight thousand residents. First responders rush from Boston and New Hampshire to help staff emergency shelters and clinics. Massachusetts governor Charlie Baker declares a state of emergency.

Rae reads in the first news accounts that the fires were caused by Columbia Gas company accidentally over-pressurizing their gas mains. The explosions were caused by gas flowing at half the rate of the West Roxbury lateral line.

She calls Cathy to commiserate. "If this had happened three years ago, the West Roxbury pipeline would never have been built. This was the trigger event we were missing."

At around 9:00 p.m., Rae's mobile phone buzzes. She sees that it is Toby. She almost doesn't answer.

"Gas explosion," are the first words out of Toby's mouth. "Un-fucking believable. R.A., you were right."

Rae is momentarily stunned by her brother's admission, but she remains on alert.

"Yeah, twenty months late for our effort," she laments. "Toby, where are you?" It sounds like he's in a noisy space.

"I'm at Sullivans," he says, referring to his favorite bar in Portsmouth, Ohio. "Watching the news on TV and thinking of you."

He pauses, and she can hear the chatter in the background. "You were right, Rae." She hears an unusual tenderness in his voice, probably the Bud Light talking.

"Thanks Toby," says Rae, cautiously waiting for a jab. But it doesn't come.

"I love you, Sis," Toby says. "You take care there. Don't give up."

"Thanks, Toby. I love you too." Rae waits a long moment to hang up.

Part 5
DISCIPLESHIP

If the people don't look after the dead they won't look after the living.

—Omar Torrijos

BACK TO THE LAND

(2016)

After eight years of visitors to their off-the-grid cabin, a group of Reggie and Rae's friends express interest in a shared rural tochold in Vermont. Fifteen friends gather for a potluck at their apartment in Jamaica Plain to talk about different visions for rural land ownership.

Enid moves first, purchasing a home in Dummerston, Vermont, about twenty minutes from the cabin. She plants fruit trees in her fields. Within six months, Enid has sold her Jamaica Plain apartment and became a full-time Vermonter.

Toni declares she is staying in the city. But Jade, Rudy, PJ, and their partners urge Reggie and Rae to be on the lookout for a property they could all buy together in order to form an ecovillage. An ecovillage, in their minds, is like rural cohousing with low-energy-consuming units. Like Rae's friends who live in Amherst cohousing, their vision is for individual homes, modest in size, with a shared common house, including a large kitchen for community meals.

"The shared kitchen and bathroom are the downfall of US community living," says Rae at one discussion. "At least for those of us raised in single-family homes."

Reggie has heard this a few hundred times before.

"I grew up with a communal well," says Rudy, who grew up in rural India. "And a communal privy."

"Reggie was raised one-toilet Irish, as his sisters are quick to remind us," says Rae, grinning at Reggie. "I know it's a First World problem."

Sometime in early 2016, they get word through the grapevine than an old historic farm is about to come on the market. Many times Rae and Reggie have driven by the Hidden River Farm, set back from the road under some towering maple trees.

Keeping the group intentionally small, four households chip in to buy the historic farm, relying on PJ's inheritance to avoid having to get a bank loan. "We tapped the Bank of PJ," Jade jokes. "She always said her family had no wealth, but then some distant relative died. Typical WASP story. Money in nooks and crannies."

The farm has an enormous white barn, an 1804 farmhouse that could use some insulation, and several ancient maple trees lining the driveway. It sits on fifteen acres in the town center, a little village with not more than two dozen residents. But it is home to four important buildings: the town's free library; a historic Grange hall being converted to a community center; the Guilford Historical Society; and a beautiful church structure that once served as the Universalist meeting hall.

Over the last two hundred years, the farm has had many incarnations. For most of its existence, it was a dairy farm. An antiquated milking parlor remains in the barn. At several stages it was a hotel and inn, with room numbers fixed on each of the doors, including five unheated rooms on the second level of the barn.

Its most unique history was as a spa resort, a destination for the "water cure," an 1860s trend imported from Germany. City dwellers left their polluted cities, took a train to Brattleboro, rode in a carriage to Hidden River Farm, and spent days at the spa and bottling plant up the Broad Brook. The dark-green-tinted bottles with raised letters, *Guilford Hidden Springs Water*, are stashed around the house, some converted to bedside lamps.

"The visitors drank the clean water, walked in the lush forest, and, not surprisingly, felt better," Rae often says, describing the water cure.

"The house has a positive vibration," said Jade, after several weeks sleeping there. "It has an energy of healing and happy people."

"I don't think anyone was murdered here," adds PJ hopefully. "You know, no suffering, wandering ghosts."

There's an 1870s publication that the Hidden Springs promoters put together to trumpet the medicinal benefits of the waters. The local historical society reprinted the 1860 booklet of testimonials, *"Hidden Spring Water: Its History and the Wonderful Cures, Performed by the Use of the Water. Testimony of Physicians and Invalids."* The booklet catalogs a variety of healing claims. It describes the springs as "Nature's Great Remedy" for dyspepsia (indigestion), erysipelas (cellulitis), costiveness (constipation), scrofula (tuberculosis of the neck), dysentery, dropsy (edema), eczema, chronic diarrhea, catarrah (mucus), and consumption (tuberculosis), along with other ailments.

The members of the farm community enjoy reading aloud from the testimonials—a source of great amusement.

"A young lady cured of scald-head," reads PJ from the booklet. "Constiveness Remedied!"

"Here's an important one. Dr. Stevens finds the waters help with 'female weakness.'" PJ holds up the booklet and reads in a regal voice: *"Young women would come to the neighborhood who were pale, puny, nerveless, their general health badly affected, and they would soon recover their strength, bloom, and elasticity."*

"PJ, you showed up pale and puny and I've noticed you have more bloom and elasticity," says Rudy. "Though you are still puny."

PJ stands and puts Rudy in an affectionate headlock embrace.

"Listen to this one, from S. W. Bailey, Esq., the well-known Dealer in Watches from Boston: *'Gentlemen—I wish to inform you that six bottles of Hidden Spring Water have cured me completely of the complaint called piles. I earnestly recommend it to all afflicted with the same. I used it internally and externally."*

"What are piles?" asks Rae

"Hemorrhoids," replies Jade. "Internal and external."

"Thanks for that. I do think this place could be a cure for consumption," beams Rae, proudly making a pun on the old term for tuberculosis. "Come visit, drink the water, get connected to nature, and you're not going want to buy as much stuff."

"No trips to Costco?" PJ frowns.

Jade takes a permaculture design class and learns about landscape planning, plants, and holistic practices. She meets a large group of young farmers and foodies who take an interest in the Hidden River Farm project.

"The first step is to have a few parties," suggests Rae at one of their meetings.

"Yes, play dates with others to see who surfaces," agrees Jade.

They rough out a master farm plan that includes each household building a modest home, each around eight hundred square feet. The main farmhouse is retrofitted to be more energy-efficient and serve as the temporary communal household as each of the individual houses is built. The long-term plan is that the farmhouse will be a common house, with accommodations for visitors and even a few short-term rentals in the old and new cabins.

They plan out the fields, with lots of help from neighbors and experienced gardeners and farmers. For generations, a local dairy farm family has hayed the fields. The plan includes several zones for fruit and nut trees, berries and shrubs, and pollinator meadows, as well as an area for greenhouses and annual vegetables.

At a fall work party to plant garlic, Jade invites twenty friends from the local permaculture network. A diverse group, in both age and race, descend on the farm for a work weekend and informal music jam. The farm residents cook up a feast, setting up a self-serve lunch on the porch.

One of the volunteers is a young woman named Alix Leblanc, who works at a gardening project across the river in New Hampshire. She and Rae form an instant bond, spending a lot of the weekend working together and talking.

Alix is brimming with both curiosity and insight. She tells Rae about her long-term hope to have her own small, three-acre farm where she can practice intensive gardening and create a perennial food forest.

"Do you mind telling me how old you are?" Rae asks her at one point, volunteering her own age. "I'm sixty-two."

"I'm thirty-six," replies Alix. "A wee lass."

"So, you were born in . . . 1980? What month?"

"Yeah, in June."

A Taurus? Rae silently registers the coincidence. Alix was born in the month and year that her miscarried child would have been born. Her interest in Alix is further piqued, and she wordlessly resolves to make a friend.

Dinner is a grand affair on the lawn of the farm, with six large tables set up end to end with tablecloths and late-season flowers. The buffet feast table includes fresh, local grilled sausages, peppers, and vegan hot dogs. There are several large salads, with fresh greens and veggies, a large pot of vegetarian chili, and assorted side dishes.

A few of the neighbors drop by for the dinner and music. After a good day of outdoor work, spirits are high among the visitors.

Reggie lights a large bonfire in the firepit, and musical instruments come out as the sparks shoot up to the stars. There are reels and ballads and a few sing-along songs. Children roast marshmallows and curl up in their parents' arms.

Rae and Alix sit to the side, each sipping a glass of wine and exchanging family histories.

Rae learns that Alix Leblanc was born in Manchester, New Hampshire, the youngest of four children in a French Canadian family. When she was five, they moved to the smaller town of Henniker, where her mother, Richelle, was an elementary school teacher. Her father, Paul, worked as an accountant at a small college in town. He was a joker. "Every day was April Fools' Day with my father. Toads on the breakfast table. Santa Claus leaving messages on the answering machine."

She went to college at Plymouth State, studying ecology. One cool professor was very active in the transition town movement and engaged a cadre of students to help design a plan for the city of Plymouth to transition away from fossil fuels. Their community resilience plan included strengthening the local food system, and Alix started several community gardens that are still flourishing. She confesses to Rae that she felt lost after college until she found her small community of local food and resilience activists around Keene.

Her oldest sister, Rebecca, married at age twenty and has three children. Alix takes her auntie responsibilities seriously, traveling an hour back to Henniker at least one day a week to care for her two nieces and her nephew. Her other sister, Julie, is pregnant with her first child. "I'm not sure I want to be a mother," says Alix, a comment that Rae lets stand, saving the topic for another day.

"Is your real name Alix?" Rae asks instead.

"Marie-Angelique." Alix laughs.

Rae sticks out her hand. "Meet Ruth Ann, that's my name."

They bond over the fact that they both have antiquated flip phones without cameras or texting capabilities. "I wouldn't mind going completely analog," says Alix.

They turn to the topic of love. Alix asks about Rae's relationship with Reggie and describes her recent breakup with a handsome man named Bobby who smoked a lot of weed and had no books in his apartment. "I'm no brainiac myself, but I *am* interested in ideas, history, and reading." Alix pauses, then asks, "Are people into weed or drugs here?"

"Not me, I'm high on life." Rae laughs. "Same with Reggie, who likes an occasional glass of whiskey. Now Jade and Sandra over there, they do an occasional microdose of something. But it's not a big part of life here."

"I'm sort of tired of the weed scene." Alix smiles. "Except horticulturally. I've grown some hemp. Fascinating plant."

"You'll like this crowd," Rae says, pointing around the farm. She looks at the gathered collection of outcast book readers and eco-radicals who think that ideas matter and have consequences. "A bunch of us have had a book club for six years, meeting every month. In fact, it was the book club that got us here. We wanted to prepare for whatever comes next. Food, land, water, energy, community—learning skills like how to preserve food, increase soil fertility, live without a lot of external energy."

"Right. Learning the things our grandparents knew." Alix thinks of her French Canadian grandmother, who knew a lot about animal husbandry—raising pigs, sheep, and chickens.

"Yeah, but also bring some of our modern notions of gender

equality, group process, healing from trauma," says Rae. "We're committed to a process of learning ancestral wisdom as well as unlearning the bad habits and attitudes."

Alix falls asleep in one of the guest rooms in the barn. She wakes up not long after sunrise. The morning sun is still on the other side of the ridge, but it is already a warmish and cloudless fall morning. Alix walks the land and fields, soaking her boots in the morning dew, listening to the birds.

She lets the restless chickens out of their coop and watches them as they retreat under a patch of bushes, alerted to some aerial threat by an early warning system of cawing crows. Alix looks up and sees a dozen hawks, circling high in the thermals, possibly with a chicken supper in mind.

Rae rises not much later, bringing Alix a mug of hot tea. They perch on chairs at the end of the meadow as the sun creeps over the ridge, quickly warming them to the point where they start shedding layers. Alix explains she has to depart in an hour for auntie duty.

"Are you guys . . . like, preppers?" Alix sips her tea.

"I guess so. I like to think we are 'prep-steaders.' You know, building resilience with tools, skills, land, plants—instead of guns and bunkers."

"I like that," says Alix, looking around the farm.

"Like Rudy and Elliot, they're big urban farmers, built a whole community garden network. And Jade, she grew up in South Korea. She's the queen of fermentation and knows a lot about medicinal plants. And PJ, she has these old Yankee sensibilities, and her dad built super-insulated houses. So, she's got a lot of carpentry skills. Sandra is really into trees and mushrooms. She's, like, the forest sprite. She's got some First Nation heritage."

"And you?"

"I'm good at dress-up parties."

They both laugh and look out at the meadow.

"Do people get along?" asks Alix.

"Ah, you know. Nothing's perfect." Rae thinks about how she and Sandra have little tiffs and avoid one another for days. "But the core of us have known each other for more than ten years. Book group. Affinity group fighting the pipeline. Lots of weekends camping at the cabin. You learn a lot about people when you camp with them. And there are a few of our friends who are not here, who dropped out along the way or weren't encouraged."

"This is kind of a magic place," says Alix.

"Glad you noticed," says Rae. "Come visit again soon."

At the end of the weekend, the seven founders of the Hidden River Farm gather. They are Rudy and his partner Elliot, Jade and her partner Sandra, PJ, and Reggie and Rae. They discuss the people who came.

"I propose we invite Alix to a chat about living here," offers Rae. "She's got all kinds of food-growing skills, and she's funny."

"We need to be super careful about who we invite into the process," observes Jade. "A lot of these community-building efforts falter because of toxic people."

"Yeah, beware of the psychic vampires," echoes Jade's partner, Sandra.

"I've been noticing Rudy is growing fangs," Rae jokes.

"And his cooking can be toxic," says PJ, piling on.

"I would like to be prince of the ecovillage," said Rudy. "And have everyone obey my decrees. That's not toxic, is it?"

"A benevolent dictator might be preferable to some of these New Age tyrants," adds Reggie.

"I'm the most oppressed person here, so I'm the king," says Jade. "Or queen?"

"I'm sorry, but Koreans lose out to South Asians," says Rudy. "We are closer to the equator and more oppressed. So I am king."

"But you are a man so you lose points," says PJ.

"I'm a gay Indian man, so I get back a few points," Rudy counters.

"PJ, aren't you 100 percent WASP?" says Sandra, who herself is a proud mash-up of First Nation Cherokee, Southern Black, and Irish immigrant.

"Yes, White Anglo Sexy Protestant," says PJ without a whiff of defensiveness. "Don't I get any points for that?"

"Sexy rates high," chirps Jade.

"It's clear that anyone initiated to this club better be able to laugh at themselves," says Reggie.

"That's for sure," says Rae.

"I had a long talk with Cyndy about living here," says Jade. "As a Black woman, she's wary about living in a community that isn't majority Black."

"That's understandable," says PJ.

"Remember, I had that talk with Chuck Turner about where five hundred Black people could relocate outside Boston, to build an economically self-sufficient community," says Reggie. "Like New Communities in Georgia, a Black landbase. And there's a movement of BIPOC folks in the county, buying their own land."

Rae thinks back to Chuck Matthei and the early community land trust movement.

"You know community is hard work," Rae says. "Marriage is hard work, and that's just two people." She smiles at Reggie. "And we're similar in terms of race, class, and culture. It's a tall order to create a genuinely multiracial liberated space, not without a lot of healing and work."

Sandra chimes in. "And what Cyndy is talking about is creating a Black space, a Black community in a rural area, parallel to what we're doing. But without a bunch of White people running their stuff and triggering everyone's trauma."

"There's so much White superiority and contorted guilt running around, twisting up organizations and communities," says PJ.

"I don't have any White guilt," says Rudy, with a mischievous grin. "Maybe the answer is a bunch of separate, you know, autonomous but affiliated communities."

"What are you talking about, Rudy?" says Sandra.

"Well, some of you get hung up on the fact that we're mostly a White group. But living in community is different than being next-door neighbors." Rudy looks around. "It's a deeper commitment and it's hard work, regardless of who's in the group."

Sandra waves her hand. "So are you saying that as long as we are not exclusionary, you think it's fine that lots of subgroups form communities?"

"Yeah, we can support that process, share what we know, help pool capital, learn from others."

Rudy has been in his own share of long discussions about decentering Whiteness.

"We should be very intentional about how we grow this community," says Jade. "We have a good thing going here. I'm more interested in younger people, people with some energy and skills. We're not getting any younger here."

"Like Alix," Rae beams.

In the coming months, Alix and Jade's thirty-year-old nephew, Eric, are invited to join the community, dropping the median age considerably.

The first winter is challenging. Nine people crowd into the main farmhouse with a kitchen that is a little small. Tensions periodically flare up around food, cleanliness, and how hot to run the heat and woodstove. Jade is never warm enough while PJ walks around in a T-shirt, complaining of the stuffiness and heat. The internet is slow, especially when a few people are streaming a movie or on a Skype call, adding to the strain.

Not everyone lives full-time at the farm, so there are many comings and goings. Several snowstorms are followed by freezing rain, covering local roads and pathways with slick ice and rendering walking a bit treacherous. Cabin fever sets in.

As Town Meeting Day and March thaw arrive, everyone is thrilled by the plans that are unfolding. Alix organizes a group to tap the maple trees and collect sap. She organizes periodic parties to get others to keep her company around an outdoor evaporator fire as they boil down the sap.

They host a town-wide Easter Egg Hunt, and sixty children and their families attend. Rae wears her forest sprite costume, and the Broad Brook beaver makes an appearance—Reggie dressed in a large costume that looks more like Yogi Bear than a beaver. The children are thrilled by the beaver, though Reggie has to constantly reintroduce himself. "I'm not a bear, I'm a beaver! See my big paddle tail."

During the summer, the Hidden River Farm community builds six modest super-insulated homes. Each has electricity, a composting toilet, a propane cookstove, and seventy-five-gallon water storage tank. For faster internet and a hot shower or bath, residents walk thirty to fifty yards to the main house. But this is a small inconvenience to save tens of thousands of dollars on each dwelling. Two units are set aside as guesthouses, a source of hospitality income.

"They're like large cozy motor homes," one urban visitor compliments.

A set of pathways and unpaved delivery roads weave around the cabins. Along the paths, they plant fruit trees and other edible landscape shrubs, along with a large bank of pollinator plants. Each house has a small kitchen garden.

They retrofit the old hotel rooms in the barn into seasonal bedrooms and mini-studios. Alix and Eric live in the main house as they consider their own living arrangements. They plunge into the agricultural planning, with Alix coordinating several workdays of friends and community members, and they prepare the next year's gardens and greenhouses.

One project is the planting of a large berry patch on land closest to the road. The vision is to create a pick-your-own business with the popular market berries—strawberries, raspberries, blueberries—along with some specialties like elderberry for health tonics, gojis, currants, and a few exotic experiments. In the berry grove, they carve out a small picnic and gathering spot for the wider community.

A subset of the farm community takes responsibility for the various animals. Rudy and Elliot enlarge the chicken coop and expand the flock to include two dozen Buff Orpingtons, Rhode Island Reds, and Bard Rocks. The farm quickly becomes an exporter of eggs.

Four barn cats are captured and fixed at the local Humane Society to reduce the large number of feral cats in the neighborhood. They spend their days hunting mice in the barn and their nights sleeping in the common house. The community is offered sheep and goats, but they wisely decline until there are more people who want to husband these animals.

Rae and Reggie move full-time into their cabin, with Rae placing various rocks, planters, natural sculptures, and chimes around their house. Each cabin home has a small porch, and Reggie parks his two favorite Adirondack chairs in a sunny corner. They sell their condo in Boston, helping to retire some credit card debt and pay for the cabin construction.

"Can we get a dog now?" says Rae, pointing to a notice at the general store about a dog looking for a home. Reggie silently remembers Rae's rants about dogs in the city. They adopt a well-trained English sheepdog that quickly adopts them as well. Rae names him Hayduke and they become constant walking companions in the woods. Hayduke lives as a dog should, in an outside world. He fits in well as guardian of the chickens, barn cats, and humans.

The community establishes a routine of two large common dinners a week, with residents signing up to cook and clean at the main farm house. These are lively affairs, celebrations of the life they are building together. As the season progresses, the table is more and more filled with food they have grown.

Rae has urged her friend Becca, a skilled calligrapher, to write the words to a blessing song, written by Louis Untermeyer, that hangs in the communal dining hall. Rae leads the singing grace before many meals, a form of protection for the community.

May nothing evil cross this door,
and may ill fortune never pry about
these windows; may the roar
and rain go by.
By faith made strong, the rafters will
withstand the battering of the storm.
This hearth, though all the world grow chill,
will keep you warm.
Peace shall walk softly through these rooms,
touching our lips with holy wine,
till every casual corner blooms
into a shrine.
With laughter drown the raucous shout,
and, though these sheltering walls are thin,
may they be strong to keep hate out
and hold love in.

At the center of their life together are several working groups, subsets of residents committed to collaborating in specific areas. Jade reminds them: our mission is both joyful living and also figuring out how to foster as many paying livelihoods at the farm as possible.

The farm forms a hospitality committee to run the two B-and-B room rentals in the farmhouse. They also host visitors at a Hipcamp site for traveling vans and campers, and rent two guesthouses. PJ and Sandra take the lead in cooking for and hosting guests. The revenue is split between the people doing the work and the farm for building use.

Another committee focuses on farm products. They build a small farm stand with eggs, maple syrup, black garlic, salad greens, berries, vegetables, and other farm products. Jade grows a patch of cannabis and creates a collection of tinctures for private sale. Reggie, Elliot, Jade, and Rae still have "off farm" jobs, but within two years seven of the nine residents are earning a significant livelihood from enterprises connected to the farm.

The Hidden River Farm group is unified in their vision of bringing a renewed vibrancy to Guilford Center. They quickly agree to host the community Halloween party and the Easter Egg Hunt on the lawn of the farm becomes an annual event. Rae convenes the celebrations and events group to plan internal parties and public events.

On Thursday evenings, as the weather warms, they establish a regular happy hour with local beer, cider, and distilled products. On any given Thursday, anywhere from ten to thirty residents and neighbors gather on the lawn or porch for drinks, cornhole, impromptu music, and dancing.

Reggie organizes periodic salons and conversations with friends passing through with a story to tell or a book to sell. Over several months, he builds up a list of three hundred invitees. Winter events are moved to inside the grange hall community center.

The farm community is constantly discussing ideas for new cottage industries and livelihoods. Rae, Alix, and Elliot go to a workshop on green burials, where they learn about Vermont's rules around dying with dignity and simple burial. They propose to the farm community that they create a business that hosts funerals and burials, and establishes a memorial grove at one end of the farm.

"The carbon embedded in the traditional funeral process is ridiculous," Alix reports from the training. "Your typical funeral home is selling coffins made of imported tropical woods, adding lacquers and varnishes made from fossil fuels. They release toxins when burned. Embalming fluids leave formaldehyde behind."

"You don't need concrete burial crypts or coffins. No cremation, which is incredibly energy-intensive," reports Elliot on the state law. "You can be buried in a fabric shroud three and a half feet down."

"The worms crawl in and the worms crawl out," interjects PJ.

"Exactly," said Elliot. "The whole process is super affordable."

"Or people can compost their remains in a tree-planting pod," adds Alix.

"What do you charge to plant a tree in the memorial grove?" asks Rudy. "And can I get a refund if I don't decompose quickly?"

"We could host memorial services and rituals," Rae suggests. She and Alix talk about their interest in hospice work, but beyond that, a sort of counseling service coming to be known as "death doulas." "We can coach people around conscious death and dying, help them push back against the medical establishment's bias toward prolonging life regardless of cost and patient dignity. We can help people be more intentional about how they want to live their final years and months."

"And we can create a culture of celebrating life and being less fearful of death," adds Alix.

Rae, Alix and Elliot spread the word informally among people they know and join a local hospice training program to build ties to local people who are committed to death with dignity. They meet with local alternative health practitioners, letting them know about plans for the memorial grove and their death doula practice.

They identify a section of the field and adjoining forest that would be well-suited for a memorial grove and gathering space for rituals and funeral services. They designate a natural clearing in the woods and construct several stone and wooden benches in a semicircle. They buy a large canvas tent, used primarily in the past for weddings, and create a sheltered gathering place in the meadow adjacent to the grove. Reggie rigs up an outdoor sound system so the faint of voice can be heard.

"You know what your plan is missing?" says Reggie, butting into a meeting of the death-with-dignity committee underway on the porch of the common house.

"Pallbearers? Are you volunteering?" asks Alix.

"You need a keener." Reggie steps into the sunlight on the porch.

"A keener? What's that?" Elliot turns his body to face Reggie.

"You know, a professional griever." Reggie looks at the group to see if it's okay for him to interrupt the meeting. "I had this Aunt Maura. Her job was to sit in the corner at the wake and moan and howl. We Irish, with our emotional reticence, give that British stiff upper lip a fat lip. But when the keener starts wailing, the flood-gates open."

"Wait, how does this work?" Elliot is puzzled.

"Okay, let's say we're having a wake in the back room of McGann's funeral home in Dorchester." Reggie has gone full raconteur. "Maura shows up and in a full Irish whisper that everyone can hear, says, '*Who is the deceased? Tommy, eh?*' Someone gives her a pint of Guinness, the first part of her compensation, and she perches on a stool off to the side and sips quietly for a while. Then she puts her pint down, puts her hands over her face, and starts a wailing like a banshee . . . *Oh Tommy! O Tommy! God oh God, not Tommy.* She starts keening—that's where the word *keener* comes from—a high pitched wail that stirs your heart. Now, Aunt Maura was a pro. She could do real tears. Sometimes she'd collapse on the floor, wailing away."

For this part of the story, Reggie falls to his knees. "*Tommy, Tommy, you were a good man, Tommy!* Next thing you know everyone else, even the tough Irish lads, are crying 'Tommy, no, Tommy!' Now Maura's got her white hanky out and she's dabbin' her eye. *Tommy, he was a good man.*" Reggie smiles, getting to his feet. "It's very cathartic for everyone."

"We definitely need a keener," said Alix. She's laughing so hard she's about to fall out of her chair. "And I think it's Reggie."

"For a pint, he'd do it," said Rae.

"It probably wouldn't work so well if Tommy's still alive sitting there for his living shiva," said Elliot. "Tommy be'd like, 'Who's the guy crying in the corner? Never seen him before in my life.'"

An article appears in the local newspaper about their new enterprise, which they've named "Passing Celebrations." A number of people who are facing debilitating and terminal illnesses reach out to them. Everyone in the farm community is involved when they host the first funeral at the grove, bringing fresh-cut flowers and a chorus of several songs to the event.

Rae, Alix, and Elliot formalize their counseling business, traveling Windham County and meeting individuals facing decisions about extreme medical intervention at the end of life. They form connections with a couple doctors who are sympatico to their mission and are skilled in palliative care and willing to do physician-assisted deaths. Together, they help more and more people chart their own final months and days.

Alix and Rae meet with an older woman named Vera, who lives alone in a mobile home on a dirt road nearby in Halifax, on land next to her youngest son. They visit her every couple days and delight in her stories of growing up on a farm in Guilford and walking to one of the fourteen one-room schoolhouses in the town.

Vera tells them she is part of the Bigelow family, one of the old Guilford families. She met her husband at a Valentine Social at the Broad Brook Grange Hall No. 151 (she insists on including the number). Her mother-in-law was active in the ladies' sewing circle of the Universalist Society, which owned the historic meetinghouse that Alix and Rae can see from their porch. Vera and her husband Rodney were married in that building.

"They used to organize a Harvest Supper and feed two hundred people!" Vera exclaims. "Those ladies were a force of nature." She has been in and out of the hospital with cancer and has entered hospice. She is adamant about dying at home. She asks them if they could help host a farewell party before the doctor helps "her pass to the other side."

"Instead of a memorial service, I'd like a celebration send-off," Vera says. "How many funerals do you go to where you think, *Jeepers, don't you think the deceased would have liked this party and all those stories?* I'd like to go to my funeral."

After one of their visits to Vera, Rae and Alix stop for a swim at the Green River covered bridge.

"Vera is my role model," says Rae, wading into the gentle current in her T-shirt and underwear. "She's going to call her own shots."

"She's also a connection to the older generation in Guilford," agrees Alix, splashing water on her arms. "If we host her event, we'll have all the old-timers here. It will be a great gathering of old and new folks."

"I understand why people don't want to face death so directly. It's like looking at an eclipse. We're not supposed to." Rae prepares for a dive into a deep pool. "Only after death can we think about the scope of a life."

After swimming, they lounge on the rocks along the river, drying in the sunshine.

"Okay, I have a special present for you." Rae hands Alix a rolled-up garment with a cloth ribbon around it. Alix sits up and opens the T-shirt, one of Rae's vintage favorites. Its message reads: "Women Who Behave Rarely Make History."

"Oh yeah," nods Alix. She and Rae regularly exchange shirts, though Alix is shorter so she's unable to swap pants. "This is a classic."

Rae and Alix organize a party for Vera, what she insists on calling her "death day party." She lets everyone know her scheduled "departure date" of June 10, and her party is planned a few weeks ahead of time—"while she still has her wits about her." She tells everyone there will be no after funeral, so if they want to honor her life, this will be their chance.

Rae writes in her journal: *Vera is a local treasure and well known. She is going to show a lot of people how to go out in style. Myself, in all confidence, I can't imagine going graciously to the grave. I've always got an agenda (smile).*

•

On the day of Vera's party, over a hundred people walk up to the memorial grove. Vera arrives in an elegant green gown, carried by her two adult sons in a large, cushioned chair to the head of the meadow, where she presides over her own funeral, with help from Rae. Rae wears a white dress and colorful stole. She has made flower garlands for both herself and Vera.

Vera calls out to people, invites stories from friends, and chimes in with her own stories. She weeps openly as she talks about her life and her loved ones. She points across the field to the old Universalist Meeting House, reminding everyone that she and Rodney were married there. "One of the happiest days of my life, along with today."

There is not a dry set of eyes in the field.

Rae has put together a booklet of Vera's requested songs and hymns, and a group of Hidden River Farm singers provide a foundation to the group sing.

"I will be resting here in this grove," Vera says, pointing to the oak trees at the end of the field. "Maybe over by that willow tree. Come visit me here and talk to me."

Elliot walks around the periphery of the group with his long-lens camera, quietly snapping pictures for Vera and her family, but staying mostly invisible.

Vera weeps as her entire community and family sing "Precious Lord, Take My Hand."

"Oh dear," Vera says. "I'm blubbering away here. But I wonder if I could trouble you all to sing that one more time."

"Of course," says Rae. "It's your party!" And the chorus begins again:

Precious Lord, take my hand
Lead me on, let me stand
I am tired, I'm weak, I am worn
Through the storm, through the night
Lead me on to the light
Take my ha-and, precious Lord
Lead me home

"It's my party and I'll cry if I want to," says Vera, dabbing her eyes. "That has a whole new meaning here."

A roar of laughter and a few sobs flow from the assembled.

"I love you all," says Vera, waving a handkerchief. "Thank you for coming. Having you all here. . . I am not afraid. I am not afraid of what comes next."

A long reception line winds through the field, as people linger and bid goodbye to Vera until she whispers to her sons that she is tired and ready to go home.

Still people linger, long after Vera's chair is lifted up and paraded out of the field to a waiting van. Many remain in their seats, pleasantly stunned, taking in the experience.

"That was remarkable," says Tom Hayes, a retired farmer who's known Vera since they were children. "That's how I want to go! Where do I sign up?"

Alix's best friend, Rachel, returns to live on the farm with an idea for a complementary business to Passing Celebrations.

Raised by parents in Portland, Maine, Rachel McMullen was urged to take violin lessons at a young age, largely against her will. But now she is a talented fiddle player and grateful for her early musical training.

On a trip to Scotland with her fiddle, she met a basket weaver named Maeve who had a growing business making coffins out of woven willow branches. She spent a month apprenticing with Maeve, learning the process of soaking the willow branches and wrapping them in wool blankets to "mellow." Maeve would then weave the supple branches into different-size baskets and coffins.

Rachel was enraptured by the beauty of the woven coffins and the way that Maeve interacted with her clients, mostly older people planning ahead. Rachel wrote to Alix, Rae, and other members of their "dying with dignity" group, reporting on her experience. "I'm ready to start up a business," wrote Rachel. "I already filled a small notebook with ideas and plans."

•

Upon Rachel's return, they gather in the barn. She describes her time with Maeve. "She told one client: 'I can weave you a coffin to have on hand, but while you're waiting you can store your sweaters in it. It could be a linen trunk or even a coffee table.' Now, this woman purchasing the coffin, she seemed no closer to death's door than me. She was very intrigued by the idea of hosting her friends around her coffee-table coffin."

"Some people think that's morbid," Alix chimes in. "But it's quite the opposite. We need to be a bit more direct about the cycle of life."

"Yes, that's part of the practice." Rachel rolls her long black hair into a bun. "Maeve told me that occasionally she had to make a child's coffin. Those are typically unanticipated. But she'd drop everything to make them. Finally, she made a bunch of infant coffins and smaller versions to keep on hand."

"It's the perfect cottage industry to accompany our commemorative grove," says Rae, as they walk a section of the barn. "And I think this is the perfect space." Rae is content to be buried in her "wine-soaked tablecloth," but she believes many people would appreciate the beauty of the woven coffins.

"Vermont just reduced the depth you should be buried from six feet to three and a half," Elliot adds. "Anything deeper doesn't have the microbes we need for efficient decomposition. A willow basket will break down faster than most bodies, so it's ideal."

"What a fantastic business idea!" Rae embraces Rachel.

Alix and Rachel sit on old wooden chairs, lingering after Rae and Elliot move on.

"She's so intense," says Rachel, nodding in the direction of the seat where Rae sat moments ago.

"Welcome to my world," Alix says. "We have an intense, sibling-like relationship."

"Looks like mother and daughter."

Alix laughs and nods. "Everyone should have a mother like Rae. A fierce mama bear."

"How come she has no children?"

"I know they tried," says Alix. "At a certain point, Rae decided to parent the rest of us."

Rachel laughs at the truth in Alix's words. "That's good. Unlike me, who can't imagine bringing children into this world."

"Because of climate change?" asks Alix, touching Rachel's arm.

"Yeah, first and foremost," replies Rachel. "From my reading of the future—ecological and political—I'm not sure that would be the loving thing to do."

"Don't you think people adapt?" says Alix. "Find meaning in whatever hand they're dealt?" Alix has been thinking about this a lot, as her biological clock is ticking. She thinks of the story Rae told her about Chepa the midwife in El Salvador, how even after facing crushing loss she still delivered hundreds of babies. Rae described her as "pulling toward life."

"Sure, but at a certain point, if your life is entirely survival—trying to find food and water on a hot and toxic planet . . ." Rachel lets the thought hang in the air. She shakes her head and picks up one of willow branches. "Rae strikes me as one of those people who needs to control her environment, you know, organize everything to be a certain way."

"Yeah, I think you're on to something," says Alix. "Except there are lots of things we can't control."

"That's why I'm excited about the coffin business," says Rachel.

Soon Rachel and her apprentice, Ragan, have an organized section of the barn, including a small display area for visitors to see and touch the baskets and coffins. The weavers solicit photos of their clients to place on their work tables so they can think about these people as they weave, bringing intention and a sense of connection to their labors.

They enlist the community farmers to set aside an area of their farms to grow and coppice willow trees. Knowing that it will take several years to get willow rods that are the proper length, Rachel works to source willow from around the region. She talks to friends at Ujima, the Black women's farm collective in Newfane, about growing willow, guaranteeing them a bit of a market.

The Day of the Dead rituals that Rae organizes take on another dimension at the farm. At the approach of Halloween and the

Celtic observance of Samhain, they construct a large public altar that includes pictures and objects from all those who have passed and been honored at the grove. In the first year, the altar features a picture of Vera, in her elegant green gown, along with several childhood pictures.

A path of flower petals and small twinkle lights lead to a community *ofrenda* altar near the grove. People visit during the day and in the evening, placing pictures, flowers, and other offerings on the altar space.

On Halloween, the farm is transformed into a spook house. The driveway is flanked with playful tombstones bearing epitaphs painted on Guilford slates with names like "Barry M. Deep," "Gil O'Teen," "Ben Bedder," "Emma Gonner," and "Myra Mains." They host an outdoor fire and a movie for the older children on a large outdoor screen.

Soon their death doula enterprise is growing, and several new members join the group. Alix and Rae create a training for death doulas to complement the traditional hospice trainings.

Neighbor Tom Hayes, sometime after attending his childhood friend Vera's funeral, drives up with his two sons in a white pickup truck. They visit Rachel's small gallery of willow coffins.

"I remember when there were forty Jersey cows in this barn," Tom tells Rachel.

He speaks with Alix, who is sitting with Rachel trimming willow branches, about how they work with the dying. Tom explains that he and his wife have cemetery plots on the ridge but they both want to go out like Vera when the time comes. Alix says they would be honored to meet with him and his wife to make a plan.

Tom turns to his sons. "Okay boys, you heard it here. Willow coffins with a service led by these folks. And God willing, we'll each have a send-off party like Vera while we still have our faculties." He waves his hand and walks to the truck. His sons nod and smile at Rachel and Alix and turn to follow their father.

"That's a breakthrough," says Alix, when they are out of earshot. "I think we better book Reggie the keener for that one."

HURRICANE IRMA-MARIA

(2018)

Rae holds tight to her hat as Reggie downshifts in the little jeep, with the stenciled name, painted on the side, "Dream Lover." The open-air jeep grinds down a steep hairpin curve. She and Reggie have just arrived on Saint John, the jewel of the US Virgin Islands.

They shoot past the dirt road turnoff they are looking for, but then have to continue driving for several miles in search of a safe spot to turn around.

Earlier, on the plane to Saint Thomas, Rae dozes off, sleepily pronouncing, "My vacation has just begun." For these two, this is a first—a winter get-away holiday, flying to a sandy tropical island in February. A Unitarian congregation on the island reached out to both of them as a team, offering two weeks of lodging and the use of a jeep in exchange for two Sundays of sermons and light pastoral duties.

"Seems like an invitation we should consider," said Reggie, back the previous May when they received the request. In the months since they committed to go to Saint John—and booked the flights— two hurricanes, Irma and Maria, have slammed into the islands, bringing death and devastation. The locals refer to the double whammy as "IrMaria."

Initially, Rae assumes their trip will be canceled. Then an email arrives confirming their February visit, declaring that the congregation has survived and continues to meet. The original plan was for Reggie to talk about climate change and a just transition, but he and Rae discuss organizing some community storytelling events and they rework their presentations to be more appropriate for shell-shocked locals.

As their plane approaches the narrow runway on Saint Thomas, they see the island's devastation from the air: flattened palm trees, blue tarps covering a third of the houses, and three-story-high piles of refuse.

On Saint John, they realize that, five months after the hurricanes, people are beginning to gut and renovate houses that are not 100 percent totaled. This requires owners to disgorge the contents of their homes—trashed carpets, soaked wood panels, washers, dryers, refrigerators, moldy chairs and couches, and shattered dishes—into hills of refuse along the road. The hope is that one day a dump truck and then a barge will haul these piles away to who-knows-where.

The entire island, at least the sections inhabited by humans, is transformed into a roadside display of rotten stuff, a water-soaked American dream. Whole resorts are also completely wiped out, including the swanky Caneel Bay Plantation and several other hotel complexes, each with its own expansive dump zone.

Their small guesthouse, up a dirt road, is in fine shape. Reggie rolls the jeep to a stop on a flat gravel area next to the cottage door. They unload their luggage and provisions and survey the one-bedroom cottage with its local artwork, happy that this will be their home for the next two weeks.

"Look at the lizards," Rae says, leaning over the porch railing. "Oooh, and look—a big old iguana sitting in the road! Looks like she's been in a few scrapes." The iguana has a tattered fin on its back.

Moments later, bathing suits on, they are back in the jeep in search of a beach and a late-afternoon swim. They roll down the winding north road, passing other jeeps with a wave and a friendly *beep beep*. After skipping several beach turn-offs, they arrive at Trunk Bay and pull into the parking lot.

They've been warned that the island is denuded, but they aren't prepared to find almost every beachside shade tree toppled. Undeterred, they head toward the water, Rae with her snorkel mask already on the lookout for underwater life.

Rae starts to walk awkwardly backward into the water in her fins. Once underwater, she audibly groans through her snorkel. The once-colorful coral reef is covered with swirls of sand. Rae cannot hide her disappointment, bordering on grief. At one point she sticks her head up, pops her mask off, and mournfully yells to Reggie, "This is awful, Reggie, completely wrecked!"

Clusters of other beachgoers can be seen up and down the bay, but the celebrated beach is largely devoid of tourists. One of the justifications for Reggie and Rae to make the long journey is they could pitch in, help with the cleanup, and spend a little money in the devastated local economy.

On the return trip to the cottage from Trunk Bay, they stop at an open roadside café for conch stew and fritters. The sole operating ice cream shop in town has only one flavor, rum raisin, which seems an odd choice. But it tastes delicious, and the excursion for a rum raisin cone becomes a daily destination.

Back at the cottage, they get a visit from a congregation member named Joe, who is there to welcome them and offer a few local tips on the best places to find produce, good restaurants, and the Sunday worship routine, still several days away. He recounts his own hurricane story, riding out Irma in an empty cinder-block cistern under his house, hearing frightening spasms of wind that sounded like a freight train peeling away sections of his house. He describes the dispiriting punishment of the second hurricane, Maria, following so quickly on the heels of Irma, a double punch.

"A lot of young people have just left," says Joe, a youthful retiree who looks no older than sixty. "They were the ones who had started businesses. They were the new life of the island. A lot of them said they were not going to spend the next five years rebuilding their homes and businesses only to get walloped again in a couple years."

"But a lot of people are rebuilding," observes Rae.

"Yes, but not without a certain wariness," says Joe. "I mean, is this the new normal? Should we even be rebuilding houses here?" He points toward the hillsides dotted with houses, many covered in blue tarps. Joe recommends that they visit Coral Bay, on the eastern tip of the island, to see the impact of the hurricanes on the settlement there.

The following day, they pack a picnic and set out for a long jeep drive around the island. At the eastern end of Saint John, with a view across a deep turquoise bay to Tortola, they see that entire mangrove forests have been flattened. The trees look like hundreds—maybe thousands—of brown matchsticks, lying on the ground, many of them arrayed in the same direction.

"A mangrove forest doesn't easily come back," one local explains, a shirtless man standing by a wheelbarrow at the vista point. "There's a whole habitat there for birds, manatees, and other wildlife that is gone, maybe permanently."

The first Sunday meeting of the congregation is attended by thirty people spread out in the classroom of a small Christian academy. They pull out their stack of hymnals and a small podium with an unnecessary sound system. As part of their worship service, there is a sharing of joys and concerns, which is long on the concerns and post-hurricane updates. Congregants share news about other community members and updates about who is returning to the island soon and who is staying away.

Joe, their ambassador, uses the service to announce to others that he is planning to move off the island. "I can't take it anymore," Joe says, his voice quivering. "Having lived through five serious hurricanes in my years here, I start to get anxious and sleepless in anticipation of hurricane season. I promise to come back to visit, but I can't live here year-round anymore."

Rae studies the faces of the congregation from the front of the room. Several members begin to cry and stand to embrace Joe. He is clearly one of the anchor members of the community. And he's not the first to have announced their departure in recent months, not even counting the people who haven't returned.

Rae closes the service with, "Let Nothing Evil Cross This Door," an anthem that takes on greater meaning on their devastated island.

By faith made strong, the rafters will
withstand the battering of the storm.

Linda, one of the leaders of the congregation, invites Rae and Reggie to lunch at her hilltop home, which has been patched back together. She and her husband run a scuba diving shop and boat rental business that has slowed to a trickle.

"The first climate refugees are going to be the affluent," observes Linda. "The people with resources who have other options. But there are a lot of people on these islands who have lost everything and have nowhere to go. They are living in tarpaper shacks. They have no choice but to rebuild and prepare for the next storm."

"And this is a US territory," says Reggie. "What do you do if you're on Barbados, Haiti, Grenada, or any of these small island nations? They are caught between climate change and austerity policies imposed by the financiers. They can barely rebuild, let alone invest in resilient infrastructure."

"Yes. Oh boy, Richard and I sailed into Dominica last month," Linda offered. "They were clobbered by the same two hurricanes. But they also have billions in debt to private banks and the IMF. And the damage of climate change isn't limited to hurricanes—it's in lack of fresh water, destruction of fisheries."

Rae realizes that their pastoral work here is to help people grieve their lost futures. This island will not be their retirement paradise. Whatever vision these more-affluent island residents had of their golden years is crashing into the reality of supercharged climate change. "These folks are seeing the climate-disrupted future before most others in the US," Rae says to Reggie as they jeep home from the lunch.

Rae's vacation reading includes the next transition book club selection, *Merchants of Doubt: How a Handful of Scientists Obscured the Truth on Issues from Tobacco Smoke to Climate Change*, about the hired scientists who cast doubt on the verified facts that cigarettes cause cancer and burning fossil fuels cause climate change.

Rae has become obsessed with the emerging history of how energy companies like Exxon knew, even as early as the 1960s, that fossil fuels contribute to greenhouse-gas emissions and climate change. She has brought a pile of articles and clippings on the topic, including a report from *Inside Climate News*.

"Good reading choices to bring to a hurricane-devastated island there, Rae," Reggie teases. "That will keep you in the vacation mood." Reggie holds up his John Grisham novel and a copy of the *New Yorker*. "*This* is beach reading!"

Later, sprawled on a beach towel in a dark-blue one-piece bathing suit, Rae reads through her book, periodically looking up at Reggie and regaling him with fun facts. Reggie doesn't mind the interruptions, as he hopes to avoid reading the book club selection if Rae gives him the key points.

"Oh man listen to this," broadcasts Rae, grabbing a corn chip and pivoting to a sitting position. "In 1968 a group of scientists studying CO_2 emissions wrote a paper for the American Petroleum Institute, saying quote, 'Changes in temperature on the worldwide scale could cause major changes in the Earth's atmosphere over the next several hundred years, including change in the polar ice caps.' And that was 1968!"

"This is what most couples talk about on their beach vacations," Reggie jokes.

"It's what *this* couple talks about!" Rae laughs. "Get this: around 1978, Exxon's own internal scientists' studied climate change to analyze the risks to their business. They knew! Fifty years ago . . . they knew the dangerous impact of extracting fossil fuel and burning it. But what did they do? They funded front groups like the Global Climate Coalition to promote phony climate science in order to muddle the conversation, make it appear as if there were 'two sides,' when in reality there is a 90-plus percent consensus among scientists as to human-caused climate change."

"So, when we were in elementary school," Reggie picks up, "Exxon was conducting cutting-edge climate research. Then in the 1980s, while we were organizing around Central America, they were funding climate denial and seeding uncertainty."

Rae sits up further, an intensity in her eyes. "The maddening thing is we have wasted decades in this bogus debate about whether climate change exists. Instead, we could have spent the last three decades figuring out how to reduce emissions and transitioning away from fossil fuel. We could have kept billions of tons of carbon in the ground. Instead, the industry has intentionally run out the clock. And they're *still* proposing to extract and burn more.

"The fuckers." Rae is now standing with sand clenched in her fists. "This is the face of evil. There is a special ring in Hell for those who knowingly profit from the destruction of a habitable Earth."

Reggie can only nod. He does wonder when Rae starting using the F-word so much. When he first met her, she never swore.

Rae writes in her journal: *Being here on post-apocalypse Saint John reminds me of the William Gibson quote, "The future is here; it's just not widely distributed yet." There are corners of the world already living with climate disruption and grieving their lost future. And places like Saint John are among the richest islands when it comes to money for rebuilding. What about places we don't visit?*

Later in the cool of the late afternoon, they pitch in to help a group of local volunteers paint the elementary school, a building recently renovated after the hurricanes. The next day, they help a congregation member haul refuse out from her house to one of the roadside piles. Over the week they talk to locals who try to put a brave face on a bad situation.

The day before they depart, a furious winter storms rolls up and down the East Coast of the United States. Their original flight home is canceled, and they are rebooked onto another flight. They take the ferry to Saint Thomas for their rescheduled flight, only to learn that it has been rebooked again for the following day. They spend the night at a little beachside motel where one end of the complex has been crushed by a fallen palm tree. The next day, they are routed through San Juan, Puerto Rico, where they are stranded for yet another night.

•

Rae sits in an airport café and writes in her journal: *A six-hour return trip has become a three-day ordeal thanks to climate disruption. I guess this is the new normal. Travel is going to get harder and harder . . . everything is going be more hassle, more expensive, and more inconvenient. Ugh. I know this is a First World problem, but maybe I'll just stay put more. It's hard when loved ones are scattered across time zones. First World problems on a warming planet. The oil barons are not inconvenienced. They fly in their private jets, and if one house is underwater, they fly to their farm in New Zealand. They experience no consequences for the harm they cause the rest of the planet's inhabitants.*

With almost a day until their flight home, they exit the airport in a taxi to wander around Old San Juan and try to find a cheap motel where they can spend the night. The devastation on Puerto Rico is even more severe than on Saint John. Five months after hurricanes IrMaria, the route into the city is littered with downed trees and collapsed buildings, and blue tarps are ubiquitous. The taxi driver, speaking English, runs down some of the local statistics.

"Trump came and threw paper towels to the people, while denying the death toll," the driver grumbles. "We think three thousand people have died. And Trump and his cronies are trying to privatize our electric system. We have blackouts a couple times a day. We still don't have running water at my house. I wonder if we are really part of the United States."

Later Reggie observes to Rae, "If you ever needed to know whether the US government views Puerto Rico as a colony, come visit now."

They locate a little hotel at the edge of Old San Juan and wander the cobblestone streets of the city, now desolate for lack of tourists. They meet an old man with a cane, leaning on a wall and looking out over the bay. He asks them in English where they are from. They talk about the hurricanes and the halting recovery effort.

"That is where Roberto Clemente's plane went down in 1972," the old man says, pointing out over the water.

"Ahh," recalls Reggie. "One of the greatest ballplayers of all time."

"*The* greatest," the man gently corrects him. "He died when his overloaded plane crashed after takeoff. It was full of relief supplies bound for Nicaragua after *their* earthquake. Clemente heard that the corrupt dictatorship there was hoarding the relief donations. He was going to personally make sure they got to the people."

"Somoza killed Clemente," Reggie whispers.

"*Exactamente,*" the old man nods.

As it gets dark, they pass a cineplex where a newly released movie, *The Shape of Water*, is showing. Rae suggests that they buy two tickets so that they can escape the humid air and pass the restless hours of limbo as they attempt to get home. The movie, about a woman who falls in love with a nonhuman sea creature, is perfectly distracting.

Lying in their San Juan hotel room, Reggie immediately crashes into a deep sleep. Rae is over-exhausted and restless and can't sleep. A mosquito buzzes in her ear. Her mind loops on images from the last week: decimated mangroves, mountains of rusting appliances, tearful church members grieving the loss of their imagined future, blue tarps covering damaged buildings. With a reading headlamp, she opens her journal under the bed covers and writes: *Depleted, exhausted. Fucking oil and gas barons sitting in their comfort. Taking a toll on my usual sunny disposition.*

Their flight from San Juan gets to Charlotte, North Carolina, late. When they dash through the airport and arrive, out of breath, at the departure gate for their connecting flight back to Boston, they learn the airline has given their seats away to another party. Rae asks if there are empty seats in the first-class section of the plane, and she engages in a feverish campaign with the airline ticket agent to get those seats.

After being told no, Rae persists, her arguments becoming more intense: *This is the last flight of the day; the airline has their money; the cost to the airline is the same; do the right thing.* Finally, the supervisor relents, attempting to defuse an unseemly air-rage event. Minutes before closing the door to the plane, the ticket agent prints out two boarding passes to first-class seats. Rae, holding the two boarding passes, turns to the ticket agent and points to a very pregnant woman standing behind her who was on their flight from San Juan. "Of course, she will need a first-class seat as well."

Three days after they depart Saint John, their plane touches down at Boston Logan Airport. The entire Northeast is blanketed in fresh snow. As their flight approaches the gate, Rae looks intently at Reggie.

"This is my last flight," she says. "I'm done flying." Rae pauses, shaking her head. "I know the problem is bigger than personal consumption choices. But I think I'll stay put. I personally want to give as little money as possible to these carbon barons."

In the spring of 2020, the covid-19 pandemic sweeps the globe. The farm, with its many comings and goings, adopts its own internal pandemic rules and procedures to enable residents to function as a "pod."

A few members of the community feel vulnerable, either because of their own health issues or those of extended-family members they would like to visit. The pandemic tests their communication skills and their trust in one another to keep the virus at bay until everyone is vaccinated.

A few of the part-timers move to the farm full-time, bringing the census to fourteen residents, a great size for sharing the workload.

In May, a well-loved Guilford couple, both in their nineties, die from covid. They had been married for over sixty years. The farm hosts a large outdoor memorial service, with careful social distancing and masking practices.

"The last thing we want is for our funeral to be a super-spreader event," says Elliot.

Many neighbors cautiously attend, bringing their own folding chairs.

After the service, Alix and Rae linger at the edge of the memorial grove.

Alix leans back on one of the folding chairs. "Can you imagine being married to the same person for sixty years and having five children?"

"I can imagine it now," Rae replies. "I've been with Reggie for thirty-three years. And I've only wanted to fire him two or three times."

"Do you regret not having children?" Alix knows the story of their miscarriage, but not why they didn't keep trying.

"Yes, there are days when I wish we had children. I was built for motherhood. I wonder who will be around to come to my funeral." She looks at Alix with the unspoken thought that her own child would be Alix's age. "Of course, there's no guarantee that your own children will come to your funeral."

"I think a lot of people will come to your funeral, Rae."

Almost every week there is a memorial service for those dying either from the virus or from other illnesses. The farm becomes a destination for the grieving.

FINALE

(2022)

Rae takes Reggie's sunglasses off his face and kisses him passionately on the lips.

"Is this a reenactment?" Reggie smiles, reaching for his water bottle.

Reggie and Rae perch on a bridge, their two bicycles leaning against a masonry wall. A small waterfall tumbles down a rock-slab hillside and flows into a creek below the road. They are sitting at the exact spot where they first kissed many years earlier. "We should do this every year? What month was that?"

"It was May 24, 1986," says Rae, without pause. "A Saturday. It was a warm spring day, very much like today."

"Of course," Reggie says appreciatively. "The keeper of the cosmic anniversary calendar would remember." He holds out his hands toward Rae, inspecting them. "We are thirty-six years older. The only difference I see is that we now have gray hair and electric-assist bicycles."

"And the world has gone to hell in a gondola," adds Rae. "We didn't know anything about climate change then. And who'da thought the Supreme Court would roll back the right to choose abortion. We were trying to stop the nuke." Rae points in the general direction of where Sam Lovejoy's weather tower once stood on the Montague Plain.

Earlier in the day, Alix dropped them off in Turners Falls, lifting the bikes down from the back of her forest-green pickup truck. They would ride the loop and then cycle back to Guilford on their own steam. The three of them notice that the fish ladder at the Turners Falls dam is open for the first time in a couple of years since the pandemic. They all walk down the concrete stairs to the fish-viewing area and watch dozens of shad swimming upstream.

Alix is over-the-moon thrilled when they witness a three-foot-long eel weaving upstream among the shad. "Dang, look at that old sister. She's positively prehistoric." The docent at the fish ladder explains that the shad swim upstream to mate in the tributaries of the Connecticut. The eel, however, will eventually swim out to sea to spawn at the end of its life.

Reggie and Rae cycle down along the Turners Falls canal and across the bike bridge over the Connecticut River. They ride abreast of one another past the river valley farms, some fields recently tilled. They cross the Sunderland Bridge and head north toward the Montague Plains, terrain that Rae knows well from her pickle plant and Montague Farm days.

After a pause for a smooch break at the waterfall, they continue on past two farm stands offering late-season asparagus. They park their e-bikes on a rack at the Montague Bookmill, the funky bookstore perched over a rocky waterfall, a former mill site.

Reggie wanders the bookstacks while Rae orders a plate of cold peanut-sesame noodles and an iced tea and sits at an outdoor table. The tumbling water provides a solid-state background noise to her reading. She is on one of her relentless learning immersions, this time focused on the fossil fuel industry and its role in blocking solutions to climate change. Over the pandemic, she has had video dates with several friends of Reggie's who are investigative journalists and documentary filmmakers. She has read the lawsuit briefs filed by citizen groups against oil and gas companies and governments for failing to protect the public. They all detail the tactics of the oil and gas industry in deflecting any limits to production.

In the previous week, she and Reggie watched a three-part Frontline documentary, *The Power of Big Oil*. And now she pulls out her *Guardian Weekly*, with a special investigation on "carbon bombs," which she actively reads, pen in hand.

Reggie finally joins Rae. He sets three book purchases and a glass of hard cider on the table.

"Basically, these oil and gas companies are betting against humanity." Rae waves a fork in the air. "They are incapable of stopping themselves."

She points at what she's reading and says to Reggie, "Okay, so you have the secretary general of the United Nations saying that if we don't cut fossil fuel use, we will 'miss our chance to secure a liveable and sustainable future.' And you've got big oil and gas investing in 195 projects that will each release at least a billion tons of CO_2 emissions, what they call 'carbon bombs.'"

Reggie knows this picture, but the new data is still stunning. "Wow," he says. "Our job is to make sure those become stranded assets, that their carbon holdings remain in the ground and all that infrastructure and equipment become useless. What a waste."

Rae puts her fork down, putting her hands in her lap and leaning toward Reggie so their foreheads are almost touching. "Yeah, well these carbon barons are betting that your effort will fail, that they will succeed in buying off the global politicians long enough to extract, burn, and make a profit. I hope that pisses you off."

"Rae, that's my job. To stay pissed." Reggie doesn't say anything more in response to her provocation. He's been watching with concern as she is more impatient and righteous and sometimes even hurtful to people she loves. Recently she stood up at a local talk about beavers and criticized the analytical shortcomings of a young speaker. And she's been yelling on the phone and hanging up on Toby. And using the F-word more and more frequently.

Rae shakes her head. "The oil-igarchs are like ventriloquists, throwing their voices over there: 'Hey we're working toward net zero.' But they are spending billions of dollars to extract trillions of tons of carbon, which, if we burn it, will blow us past the 1.5 centigrade climate goal."

She looks around the peaceful café, with tourists and students sitting at tables in the spring sunshine. "I feel like its 1931 and everyone is sitting in cafés in Germany and saying, 'What's with that wackadoodle Hitler guy? Oh, he'll never go anywhere. I mean, look at everyone going along like normal.' But there's nothing normal."

Reggie focuses on Rae, watching her as well as listening. She's more agitated than passionate. He swears he sees a flicker of fear in her eyes, not her usual slow burning fire. Or is it a flavor of rage that he is unaccustomed to? *You are with someone for thirty-six years,* he thinks, *but there is still some uncharted territory in there.*

Rae notices his look. They exchange a silent glance. "You think I've gone off the deep end?"

"It just looks like your celebrated cold anger fission is hot and heading toward meltdown zone."

"Yeah, you may be right about that." Rae pauses before making a confession. "I feel something off kilter in my body, in my gut."

"I understand." Reggie looks intently at her. They both pause, and the crash of the waterfall suddenly sounds louder. "This pandemic has been hell on all of us. War in Ukraine, mass shootings at schools, Supreme Court decisions, rising fascism, climate disruption. It's taking its toll."

Rae comes home from her physical exam feeling unsettled. "They did a bunch of tests because they didn't like what they saw on my blood tests," she tells Reggie.

Later in the afternoon, when the phone rings with a call from the doctor, she answers with a pit in her stomach. Reggie watches her talk on the phone, listening to her end of the conversation. "Okay, I can come in tomorrow. Thanks, Dr. Murphy." She hangs up.

"They want to do another test, a body scan. You know, I feel fine," she says, looking at Reggie with worry in her eyes.

She can tell that Reggie is quietly alarmed. She knows that she lacks her usual invincible bravado, the confidence she carries that her own body won't let her down.

With the pandemic, they have both felt their aging and vulnerability. Rae is sixty-eight and Reggie is sixty-seven. In the last three years, extended family and friends have faced strokes, heart attacks, and cancer, sometimes fatal. And then there are many people who have died in the covid pandemic, some much younger than them. Reggie's high school friend Kevin barely survived an early bout with covid and still feels the lasting symptoms and fatigue.

The next day Reggie drives Rae to Brattleboro Memorial Hospital, where she gets additional tests. Because of the pandemic, Reggie can't come into the treatment room. But they call him to join Rae for a meeting with the doctor. They have found cancer in Rae's liver. And worse, they have found indicators that it has spread throughout her body. An advanced stage.

Rae reaches for Reggie's hand as they walk out of the hospital. She feels numb. They schedule more meetings, including one with a specialist at Dartmouth-Hitchcock Medical Center, which is a ninety-minute drive north.

Rae finds it hard to believe that, just two days before, she and Reggie took their e-bikes out for a twenty-mile ride, pumping up some steep Vermont hillsides.

At home and in waiting rooms, Rae sits quietly, her eyes closed, listening for clues within her body. She visualizes her healthy blood cells massing to vanquish the harmful cells.

They both clear their schedules. Reggie lets his colleagues at the Labor Network of Sustainability know that he'll likely be taking an extended leave. Over the next few days, they shuttle to doctor's appointments in Brattleboro and up to Dartmouth-Hitchcock in Hanover, New Hampshire. There are oncologists and other specialists who talk about various treatment options—chemotherapy, radiation, experimental treatments.

Rae slowly begins to understand her predicament—that the prognosis is not good, that there's a high likelihood that she will not live for years and years. More likely, she will die within a year, or even within months. At one point she huddles with Reggie quietly on their bed, wordlessly holding one another, shaking their heads.

At the hospital, Rae finds her inner strength and willful stubbornness surfacing, her pointed questioning of the doctors. She asks each one, "What happens if I don't do any of these treatments?"

The doctors are not used to this query or the possibility that someone might choose not to go through their beautiful treatment regime with their dice-game percentages of success. Reggie is summoned to the finance office, where he learns that so far the tests have cost $15,000 out of pocket. Would they like a tour of the new cancer treatment wing?

Among the many things they have in common, both Reggie and Rae hate hospitals and the US health care system. They pride themselves in their healthy diets, wellness, exercise, and herbal remedies outside the medical system. And they harbor a distrust of a medical establishment that largely stays silent about the role of the chemical industry and public health. Rae doesn't need to further research the connection between agricultural sprays like Roundup, with the chemical glyphosate, and damage to the human kidneys and livers.

One doctor begins his meeting with Rae and Reggie with: "We have a shot." Then he goes on a monologue about how the insurance company won't pay for immunotherapy but will pay for radiation treatment. Still, they should know that he is valiantly fighting the insurance company on Rae's behalf. Rae holds her tongue until she's in the car and then starts shrieking, "Fuck you and your fucking insurance companies. And fuck you and your shot."

Rae tells Alix, PJ, Rudy, Rachel, and Jade about the diagnosis. They enter into various states of shock, as they don't discern anything physically different about Rae. Rae spends a lot of time talking to Alix. Both of them had been death doulas for people going through advanced cancer.

After one long day of consultations at Dartmouth-Hitchcock, the doctors are ready to admit Rae. But she tells them she is going home. The doctors press her: her condition is serious and she should start treatment immediately, they tell her. But Rae now has a folder of printouts, articles, descriptions of treatments, x-rays, and other data from the innumerable tests she has consented to. She has seen this endgame before, where people are told they have only months to live and enter into aggressive treatment—and never go home.

"I'm done with them," Rae says to Reggie, as they drive down the highway. Reggie isn't surprised. "I'm not going to spend my final months getting beat up so I can live a few more months in a bed and leave you with a mountain of debt. I want to live as much as I can and die at home, if that's okay with you."

"I totally honor that," says Reggie, looking shaky himself.

Rae knows that he has been rearranging everything so he can devote his days to her for as long as she is here. He will take an indefinite leave from work. He tells Rae that his heart—the actual organ in his chest—physically aches.

"I just want to be with you and be here at the farm," she says, dabbing a tear from her eye. "I want to be outside and take walks with you and Hayduke. And I've got a few more things I'd like to do."

True to her word, Rae focuses on living her life, attending meetings of the hospice group as a worker and not as a receiver of services. She and Reggie take longer daily walks or forays to favorite river destinations and outlooks. Hayduke, the dog, gets a lot of extra attention, walks, treats, and long head-scratches. And Hayduke, sensing a change, refuses to let Rae out of his sight and wails when he is not included on a trip to town or an outing.

Rae's also going through all her personal journals and papers, milk crates full of bound sketchbooks and Moleskine journals. She pulls some pages out of journals, burning them in the woodstove. Later she arranges the journals in chronological order and puts them into boxes. One day, she drives them to the post office and sends them all to Toby at their family home in Ohio.

One night, Rae and Reggie make love after a bath and then lounge naked on top of their bed. Rae curls up into the crook of Reggie's arm and starts to weep quietly. "I'm feeling weaker," she says, her first confession that her body is changing. "And I have a plan for how I'd like to die, though I don't think you're going to like it."

Reggie turns to look in her eyes, flickering in candlelight. He wordlessly caresses her back.

Rae meets his gaze and uncharacteristically searches for words.

"I want to go out in an action," she says obliquely. "I want to make a statement about climate disruption." She has been rehearsing this conversation in her head, anticipating Reggie's concern.

Reggie squints and waits. "What are you thinking?" he finally asks, breaking the silence.

"I'm thinking of taking one of those fossil fuel CEOs with me. One of the guys who knew for decades about the harms of their business, but covered it up so they could grab more money."

Reggie keeps his gaze fixed on Rae. His mind scans her piles of books, her Bonhoeffer, her growing anger, her use of the word evil to describe people.

He has noticed that Rae has been intensely focused on a writing project, something that requires looking at her laptop computer. *Did I miss some signs?*

Over the years, he has heard Rae melodramatically talk about blowing up gas pipelines, almost as a figure of speech. He flashes back to Brian Willson and the talk about Norman Morrison, the Quaker who self-immolated himself at the Pentagon. He's noticed Rae's fascination, bordering on obsession, with dramatic actions and statements.

"Like a suicide bomber?" Reggie understands now that Rae is 100 percent serious. It's not a figure of speech.

"Well, I guess so." Rae props herself up on her elbows, her voice gaining confidence. "It's time one of these fuckers paid a price. They should all live in fear."

Reggie pauses a long time, but he can't easily censor his thoughts. And Rae wouldn't want him to.

"Hmm, well," he says, "that may be cathartic for you, but I think it's *tactically* a terrible idea."

Reggie has had these strategy discussions with some of the younger anarchists in the Brattleboro community and has weighed in with his opinions. A dog-eared copy of *How to Blow Up a Pipeline*, by Andreas Malm, has circulated around the farm.

"I've got a plan—and it won't implicate you or anyone. Or the farm. I'll keep it clean.

"You've got a plan?" Reggie feels a pang of anger and jealousy that Rae has been scheming without him. But he suspects that she knows he won't support the plan. He thinks of her bent over her computer, talking about oil companies, asking him curious questions about how to send encrypted messages.

"I'm not going to say another word." Rae kisses Reggie on the lips, ushering in a long stretch of quiet between them.

The next day, Reggie and Rae walk with Hayduke, crossing a favorite path to a lookout up on Cemetery Ridge.

"Okay Rae, I understand you don't want to talk details," says Reggie, speaking words he's been preparing for several hours. "But what about a little clearness committee to talk generally about the approach? You, me, maybe Alix, maybe someone else?"

A clearness committee is a very Quakerly idea—an intentional process to get clarity about a question. Reggie himself had been on several clearness committees, including one for a couple considering marriage. But most are centered around vocational discerning, such as "Should I quit my job?"

"Okay," Rae replies curtly. "Yes to Alix. Who else would add insight to the process?"

"Maybe someone who has thought about violence and nonviolence? But, obviously, someone we know and trust."

"Too bad Brian is on the West Coast," Rae laments, though she hasn't talked to Brian Willson in years. "Maybe Cathy? She would get it." Cathy and Rae worked hand in hand in the early days of the Pledge of Resistance.

"I'll organize it," Reggie says. "Soon as we can."

"Sounds good."

More and more, Rae keeps her own company. In her journal she writes: *My memory is sharp. I can't seem to erase some images and experiences. My mind travels to Montague Farm, the soup kitchen in Mexico, the blockade of the pipeline. I can see each scene vividly. I won't be writing much*

now. But I rediscovered this Utah Phillips quote that has new meaning for me now: "The Earth is not dying—it is being killed. And the people who are killing it have names and addresses." What action is justified in defense of my body, our one and only Mother Earth?

Rae's friend and co-trainer Cathy travels from Boston for the meeting. They all drive together in a farm truck to the top of Putney Mountain and, leaving their mobile phones locked in the glove compartment, walk a half mile to a sunny outcropping of rocks. She, Alix, Rae, and Reggie sit in camp chairs that they have carried with them. It is a cloudy, late-summer day, but they've packed extra layers and snacks in anticipation of sitting several hours outside.

"Last time I was up here was for the hawk watch," says Rae. "It was late September and there were hundreds of migrating hawks riding the thermals."

For almost half a century, a group of dedicated volunteers has monitored the southbound hawk migration from the top of Putney Mountain, counting and classifying the thousands of raptors that pass by. Rae helped with the count for a couple years, following the lead of several experienced volunteers, including a local amateur naturalist named John Anderson. She recalls him telling her, "That red-tailed hawk flying by, she nests here on the mountain all year round, so we don't count her as a migrating bird."

Everyone looks down to the valley for hawks.

"Okay, let's do a moment of silence and then hear from Rae, the question that is on her mind," says Cathy, as she crosses her legs and shifts a small, bound writing book in her hands. She assumes a lead facilitator role, in part because everyone knows that Reggie has strong opinions.

They sit in silence, a warm breeze passing by and ruffling the floppy hat on Rae's head, her hair in neat braids.

"Okay Rae, why don't you speak. But first, we must promise that everything we talk about here is absolutely confidential. Right?" Cathy looks around at everyone's nods of consent.

Rae looks at each of them. "I've spoken to each of you about my general plan. I want to hear your thinking, the pros and cons. And I want a space for Reggie and me to explore our disagreements."

She roughly outlines her idea, that she intends to consciously take her own life and bring along a highly visible executive, a "carbon oligarch," in her words, whom she holds personally responsible for blocking society's response to the climate crisis.

"As you all know, I've lived my entire life working for nonviolent social change movements, as both a personal moral code and a tactical consideration. But I've also come to the conclusion that these are extraordinary times that require extraordinary measures.

"This isn't rallying the populace to bring down a hated dictator or blocking a pipeline from being built," Rae continues, thinking of her talk with Juanita Nelson. "This is uprooting a system, an economic and energy system, that has made some people fantastically wealthy. And there are people whom I regard as evil, who fully know the harms they are causing, yet continue to do what they're doing. They are not just bystanders or accomplices, but perpetrators."

Rae leans forward, looking at each of them individually.

"They are akin to someone who leaks poison into the village well, knowing that it will cause the deaths of the entire village, including children. And yet they enjoy lives of luxury, entirely without consequences for the harms they have inflicted on others. And in our current system, they will probably live their entire lives without any consequence."

"You're right about that," Alix responds, a sort of "Amen."

Rae speaks with her eyes closed. "I have worked to live nonviolently. But I always thought that if someone was trying to kill me, I would fight back. If someone was trying to murder my baby or Reggie or Alix or my mother—or Mother Earth—I would fight to the death."

Rae sits with her eyes remaining closed. The others look at Reggie.

"We all see these guys, living lives of luxury," Reggie acknowledges. "I have feelings of hate, murderous feelings toward these guys, too. But my concern is more about the implications for the rest of us, after you've done your purging act of violence. I think it could set back the movement."

Rae takes in what Reggie is saying. "I'd like to hear more about that. But here's my view. For over twenty-five years, the movement to reverse the climate crisis has been highly disciplined and nonviolent. For a long time, we acted as if 'we are all the problem' with our lifestyle and excessive use of fossil fuels. Then the movement finally started to focus on the actual global energy companies, the fossil fuel giants, that profit from the extraction and burning of carbon. As we now know, these corporations deliberately unleashed the merchants of doubt.

"These individual carbon barons knew decades ago about the harms of greenhouse gases. And yet they did everything they could to sow uncertainty and block change—funding sham science, bankrolling climate deniers for political office. Later, when they couldn't deny the reality anymore, they agreed to meaningless symbolic actions and pronouncements about sustainability. But they never slowed down from building new power plants, laying new pipelines, and planning to extract and burn more and more. They have to be stopped."

"But it's not a few CEOs, Rae," says Cathy. "The problem is a whole system, with boards, and shareholders, and 'we the public' clamoring for cheap energy."

"Yes and no," says Rae. "There are specific men who've been working in the industry for decades. I've got my short list. They have had information about the harms *for decades*. They could have made very different decisions and they'd still be in the world's richest zero-point-1 percent. They deployed their considerable clout to block the flourishing of alternatives. They paid lobbyists to oppose higher energy-efficiency standards. They limited the choices that 'we the public' had. And they chose to expand carbon burning in the face of all the evidence. They took the money and ran. That is evil. That is willful, premeditated murder."

The group is quiet, honoring Rae's passion. The sound of crows cawing carries from down the ridge, out of sight.

"So you're saying these people had a lot of agency?" asks Alix, after a long pause. "More than the rest of us?"

"They had information and tremendous power—and they used their power to lock us onto a trajectory of self-destruction. If we had all known what they knew—when they knew it—we could have pushed faster to change our energy direction. We could have taken actions that would have given us more options today, decades later. But they didn't. They played to run out the clock. And now we've run out of time."

"Okay, let's play this out," says Reggie. "Let's say you strap on a vest and give a big hug to Tom Tillerman, who is no longer at ExxonMobil but is clearly culpable. It will be called a terrorist attack. You'll be labeled a 'suicide bomber.' The industry groups and the organized climate deniers will have a martyr. They will point to 'eco-terrorists' and lock up everyone they can. The passive and undecided elements of the population will be turned off. The climate activists of the world will be forced to denounce you and your extreme tactics. You know the drill, Rae. You've been around the block."

"What if I write a really powerful statement, explaining my actions?"

"And what if there are innocent people killed or injured?" continues Reggie. "It's going to be hard to find old Tillerman on his own. He's going to be with his bodyguards or family members."

"I happen to know he goes out alone in a boat a couple times a week," Rae says.

"Oh brother, you *have* been doing your homework." Reggie has a pained look on his face. "Are you going to appear as a lost mermaid with a waterproof hand grenade?"

Alix lets out a laugh, but no one else makes a sound. She covers her mouth, embarrassed. "Well, I'm sorry," she says, "but it is a funny image. Rae as mermaid assassin."

Reggie doesn't laugh and continues. "Think how the media and right-wing politicos go crazy about the smallest destruction of property—like when the Black Lives Matter people break a window. They labeled Brian Willson a terrorist for going on a hunger strike, and that was before 9/11. After that, they brushed aside any dissent by using the 'terrorist' label. And the environmental movement in the West had to spend decades getting past the Earth First! eco-terrorism legacy. It backfires every time."

Reggie pauses, looks around the circle, and then turns his eyes to Rae. "We have shrinking political space for dissent in this country. Your action will make it smaller. Violence against property has very little legitimacy. Violence against people will have all kinds of blowback."

"I've thought about that," said Rae. "We're at a different stage in the global movement around climate change. For twenty years we've been watching emissions rise. We've had . . . how many COP summits, with how many thousands of pledges? *And it doesn't change anything.* It doesn't change the trajectory. It doesn't stop the fuckers from planning the destruction of Mother Earth and growing their profits. As we sit here, there are men sitting in boardrooms, making decisions to invest trillions in *new* oil and gas infrastructure that will blow humanity past any sustainable temperature limits. They are planning their next carbon bomb as they set fire to our future. Directly targeting the decision-makers in the fossil fuel sector will shake things up. It will focus attention on those responsible."

Everyone in the group senses Rae's intractability. Alix cautiously watches the unblinking intensity of Rae's eyes as she speaks.

"I think it opens up another flank in the movement to keep fossil fuels in the ground. Target companies that are still extracting and their decision-makers. Let the climate movement denounce me. The rest of the movement can say, 'We're nonviolent.' We'll have the Black Liberation Army vs. SNCC. Or Earth First! vs. the Sierra Club. I hate to admit it, but a lot of social change in history has happened because of violence, or the threat of violence."

"Not so much in the USA," counters Reggie. He looks out toward Mount Monadnock in New Hampshire, rising alone on the eastern horizon. "Do you think people will follow suit? That there will be copycats?"

"Yes, I will call for others to do the same at the global level," Rae says with a steeliness in her voice. "I even intend to publish a list of targets. Yes, I want all these people to look over their shoulders until they repent."

Reggie sits back, putting his hands over his face. "Well, that's the definition of terrorism, striking terror into the heart of civilian noncombatants."

"They are not innocent bystanders," Rae said bluntly. "They *are* combatants. They are trying to murder us. We are fighting back."

"Rae, the state and these megacorporations hold all the tools, the apparatus of violence. They will use it to crush our movements. Americans won't accept revolutionary violence. It's great at getting attention and creating chaos. But it is disastrous when it comes to fostering real change. Only nonviolent mass movements have the possibility of building majority power."

"There might still be apartheid in South Africa if Nelson Mandela hadn't launched the violent wing, the Spear of the Nation. And where would abolition have been without Nat Turner and John Brown?"

"Mandela and the Spear movement didn't kill people, they blew things up," Reggie insists. "They were careful not to harm people. Vandalism. Destruction of property. Why not blow up a pipeline or a coal plant?"

Everyone is silent, aware that this is becoming an important space for Rae and Reggie to hash things out. There is a long pause.

"What about doing a Norman Morrison in the lobby of Shell or ExxonMobil? A sacrificial act, not a murder?" says Reggie.

"Who's Norman Morrison?" asks Alix.

"He was a pacifist who set himself on fire," said Cathy. "In protest of the Vietnam war. It had a big impact, including on Secretary of War Robert McNamara, apparently."

"That's the old nonviolent credo," said Rae. "Draw suffering upon one's self. Gandhi, MLK. I get that. I've lived that my entire life and I've thought about that. But I think we're past that point. We're talking about a couple dozen powerful people who have wrecked the planet because of their own greed. And they are actively doing more damage now. And they are actively blocking the efforts of the rest of humanity to avert disaster, as we sit here.

"They're betting that we won't get our act together in time to stop them. They are hoping we will go to lots of climate grief workshops and sit around crying about our lost futures. Boohoo for our grandchildren. The oil barons are building their bunkers and private jet landing strips. *Well, fuck them.* Is our society just going to stand by and let them destroy the Earth?"

The three others pause again, taking in the intensity of Rae's convictions. Rae's hands are shaking in fury.

"Bring more suffering on ourselves? I know that theory of nonviolence, and there are plenty of scenarios where I would agree with it morally and tactically. But let's say we live in a neighborhood, and every week some arsonist shows up and burns down another neighbor's house. Should we all sit around and sing dirges and pass the Kleenex? *Boohoo, there goes another house. How can we nonviolently stop the arsonist?* Appeal to their fucking humanity? The asshole is burning down our neighborhood! Are we just gonna sit there and take it? Should we set ourselves on fire? Now, what if the arsonist controls the whole fucking system? They can even turn off the fire hydrants. They even deny there are fires. And they block all our nonviolent efforts? Well, guess what: That's where we're at."

"Think about the living, Rae," Reggie says slowly. "The rest of us—the feds will be up our asses for years. They will shut down our farm."

"I've thought about that. I will do this in a way that protects you all, including you, Reggie."

For Reggie, this feels like an insult. *I don't need to be protected,* he thinks. He disagrees with Rae's course of action. This is going to be a festering disconnect in their relationship, in their final months together. He wonders silently if he will tip off law enforcement.

They agree to reconvene if Rae says the word. The meeting disbands in silence.

Rae doesn't ask to meet again.

Later, alone in their cabin, with phones and computers locked in the glove compartment of their truck, Rae and Reggie gaze at one another and lie down, not saying much.

"I love you, Rae. Let me take care of you, okay?"

"I'd like that. I just want to be with you. And when I start to lose my capacities . . ." She doesn't finish the thought. "Until then, I want to enjoy the present moment."

 •

The fall turns toward winter, and in mid-December the first snow falls. The next morning, Reggie and Rae rise early to walk in the open fields, with Hayduke bounding through the snow. They stand facing the sun, letting it warm their faces.

On the solstice, Rae and Reggie bundle up and go to a bonfire at Montague Farm, which was bought by a Buddhist group and is now a retreat center and destination for weddings. Rae is revived by the sight of the old buildings and the land itself.

"I used to love sitting in that barn," said Rae, pointing to the loft. "This was my first real home away from home. We have to come back during the daylight and walk this land," says Rae. "It holds so many happy memories for me."

"Like the smell of pickles," jokes Reggie.

"Pickles, garlic, patchouli oil, woodsmoke, and silage!" Rae agrees. "And down the road is the old site of the tower that Sam Lovejoy toppled." She leans in to whisper. "I'm still sworn to secrecy as to my role."

"Really? You held the wire cutters?"

"My lips are sealed. I'll go to my grave." Rae smiles at the memory.

"I hear he's an attorney now. Maybe I should retain him?"

"Not a bad idea," Rae looks away.

After Christmas, with many social gatherings and parties, Rae and Reggie withdraw more and more to their cabin. Rae finds it hard to stay warm even when wrapped in multiple blankets, and always with a felt hat pulled down to her eyes and Hayduke warming her feet in their down booties.

Reggie has told Rae he has a secret trip for them planned starting in late January. On the day Rae says she "can't get warm," he reveals that he has borrowed a friend's electric-powered Eurovan camper and that they are heading to the Southwest desert for as long as they'd like. They both love the Vermont winter, but Rae can't say no to going where the sun shines more warmly.

Two days later, Rae cries in delight when Reggie pulls up in the van. She climbs in the back bed and falls into a pile of pillows and down comforters. "Ah, this is the place. Drive on, good sir."

On the night before their departure, there is a small going-away party at the main common house. People bring "snowbird-"

or desert-themed presents, mostly handmade or regifted. Some gaudy sunglasses, a stick of sage, a snakebite kit, a pint of maple syrup (so they won't forget their homeland), a Hawaiian shirt for Reggie, and a Terry Tempest Williams book called *Erosion*. Alix gives Rae a dog-eared copy of Edward Abbey's *Desert Solitaire*, along with a deck of playing cards. "For the other solitaire," Alix suggests.

"Oh good, this goes perfect with my *Monkey Wrench Gang* and *Birds of the Southwest*."

Jade has cooked a batch of brownies. "No special ingredients."

Rae sits curled by the woodstove, holding court.

"Don't worry, I'm not going to die on the road," Rae jokingly reassures her group of friends. "I'll get Reggie to race home if I start to go downhill."

Rae has made a small yarn sampler that she unfolds. "This is my gift to the common house," she says, holding it up with pride. It says *"If you love them set them free to be all they can be."*

"Hmm . . ." Rudy rubs his bald head. "Sounds like a mash-up between Kahlil Gibran and the US Army."

After several hours of discussion, they decide to leave Hayduke behind with Alix, whom he loves to stay with. He'd be stuck in the van, and they will have more flexibility when staying in national parks and motels without a dog. Reggie also wants to pay 100 percent attention to Rae and not have to worry about an aging dog's needs.

The morning of their departure, Reggie loads milk crates of food, books, and duffel bags of clothes into the van.

"Do you have your Petoskey stone?" Rae asks, tapping her pocket.

"Yup," says Reggie, tapping his own pocket. He is in the habit of transferring the stone into his pants pocket every morning.

Rae spends an hour holding Hayduke and whispering in his ear.

"Hayduke, you're going to stay with Marie-Angelique," Rae says, stroking Hayduke and smiling at Alix.

"You're the only one allowed to call me by my given name," said Alix. "Hayduke and I will be just fine."

During their first day on the road, Rae plays DJ, rolling through her favorite music. The van has a CD player with great speakers, and she has brought a shoebox of her favorites. Van Morrison, the Pixies, Joni Mitchell. Smiling, she cues up a song from her Bruce Cockburn CD.

"Here's a little song going out to all the fossil fuel executives out there" Rae says in her Casey Kasum American Top 40 DJ voice. The song is "If I Had a Rocket Launcher."

If I had a Rocket Launcher
Some son of a bitch would die.

They laugh together.

Reggie watches Rae for an indication of a change of heart and plan. When he asks her a question on the topic, she silently puts her finger to her lips.

"My problem, lover boy, is I don't forget what I've seen." Rae gazes straight ahead on the highway. "I don't forget the violence I've seen inflicted on innocent people, on children. There's something wrong with me. I can't forget."

Reggie wonders, not for the first time, if he should tip off someone in law enforcement, call the FBI with an anonymous tip. But he quickly banishes the thought and the possibility that Rae might be jailed or subject to surveillance in her final year of life. *Maybe she will change her mind? Maybe we can travel for months and I can keep an eye on her.*

Rae has one requested stop on the way west, a second visit to Drake's Well in the Allegany Mountains of Western Pennsylvania. They roll the van into the parking lot at the state park about half an hour before the park closes and the sun sets.

"My dad wanted to stop here in 1973, when he was driving me to college." Rae walks up to the primitive wooden oil derrick, putting her hand against it. "Mac wanted to see where the first oil bubbled up through the ground. He was a history buff and knew how significant this discovery was. I was like, Sure thing, Pop, we can stop there. I had no idea how prescient that was for my life."

"Oil," says Reggie. "Seemed like a good idea at the time. Better than whale oil."

"If only we had acted sooner, to use it wisely and keep most of it in the ground." She raises her hand like she's offering a blessing. "Oh oil, we wish we could put the genie back in the bottle. Too bad we've been sleepwalking for seventy years, sleeping pills courtesy of Big Oil."

Rae wanders the grounds before walking silently back to the van. She perches in the passenger seat, and nods to Reggie as he climbs back into the driver's seat. "Go west, young man."

After two days they have left the snowbelt of the Northeast and are crossing the Plains states. They drive through beautiful rolling hills and along frigid rivers. But most of what they witness are strip malls, fracking wells, overgrazed pastures, crowded feedlots.

Rae takes it all in when she's not napping in the bed of the van. "On most of my 'in-search-of-America adventures,' I get depressed by how much we have degraded the land. These are almost permanent patterns of destruction."

"Not permanent," says Reggie. "But it will take a *long* time for it to rewild." Reggie has been reading Edward O. Wilson's book *Half-Earth*, about the need to preserve substantial connected wild spaces.

They've agreed that their first long stop will be at a campsite with a view in some Utah national park, and they'll stay put for as long as they like. They find a great food co-op in Moab and stock up on provisions, so they won't have to move. They are tempted to stop at Arches National Park. Rae waves her copy of *Desert Solitaire*, saying, "We have the good book." But they've both been there and resolve to go in search of new vistas.

It is dark when they decide to look for a motel. They see signs for a cluster of lodging options along a Utah highway exit. They pass several motels with "No Vacancy" signs.

"This isn't exactly prime tourism time, is it?" asks Rae.

Finally, they find a motel with a vacancy. The parking lot is full of white pickup trucks and loud young White men, hauling cases of beer.

"They're the frackers," explains the motel attendant, a young South Asian woman, sensing that Rae and Reggie are not working the rigs. "Boom and bust. Today is boom."

Rae and Reggie barricade themselves in their room, a plain space with slight essence of cigarette smoke. They play some music and Rae takes a long bath. They sleep peacefully, and early in the morning they hear the trucks pulling out.

"Off to the gas fields," Reggie quips, rolling over in the early light.

"There's a happy thought," says Rae, sliding over to spoon with Reggie. "Maybe we can go monkey-wrench their equipment?"

After a late start, a leisurely breakfast at an old-time diner, and several more hours on the road, they pull into a ranger's station at Grand Staircase-Escalante National Monument and talk to the ranger, telling her what they're looking for. She pulls out a map and suggests a few primitive campsites where a self-sufficient van can perch.

It gets dark as they drive an hour on a winding paved road, and another half hour on dusty dirt pack. Finally, they pull into the site that, the ranger said, promises some view and protection. The moonless night adds an extra cloak of darkness over the land. Reggie warms up some tomato soup and toast with melted cheddar cheese, Rae's comfort food. But Rae falls asleep before eating, drifting into a deep slumber in her nest of quilts and comforters. Reggie stays awake, looking at national park maps by lamplight and sipping a glass of Irish whiskey. He wonders if this may be the calm before the shit show and he might as well savor the clear night of stars. Then again, he hasn't heard any revenge talk from Rae since August.

In the morning, he wakes before Rae, sets up a little outdoor kitchen area, and unpacks Rae's favorite large folding anti-gravity chair with several blankets. "Good morning," he hears her warble from under her covers. "Let me know when the sun hits my chair!"

Rae finally emerges, stretching and rubbing sleep out of her eyes, and taking in the full expanse that they could only imagine when they parked after dark. Big sky, peaks, valleys, and cactus.

"This is exactly what I was hoping for," she says, pulling on her down booties and surveying Reggie's outdoor kitchen.

"You must be hungry. You missed dinner," says Reggie, realizing Rae may not have much appetite.

"I'll have some tea and granola," says Rae, rummaging through a cooler. "Maybe some of your special tea."

Reggie sits up, hearing this first acknowledgment that Rae might be feeling physical pain. He has been making a light poppy tea over the years for friends with chronic pain.

"What do you feel?"

"Just some aches," says Rae. "Hard to know what's cancer, what's postmenopause, what's a week sitting in a van." She laughs and settles into her gravity chair, which is haloed in morning sunshine.

"Don't forget growing older," adds Reggie.

A little later, she looks up from a book and calls to Reggie. "Listen to this, from Ed Abbey: 'I was sitting out back on my 33,000-acre terrace, shoeless and shirtless, scratching my toes in the sand and sipping on a tall iced drink, watching the flow of the evening over the desert.'"

As the day warms, Rae strips off her shirt and lies topless in her shorts on the chair. "I'm officially warm, after two months!" she exults.

Reggie can't imagine taking his shirt off. He's from the generation of men who were well schooled that going topless was a form of male privilege, since women could not do the same. In a testament to their generation, a topless Rae and the fully covered Reggie spend the afternoon watching the cloud formations rolling by on their thousand-acre terrace.

Rae passes her days lounging, reading, and dozing. She spends hours looking through binoculars, surveying the canyons and ridgetops or tracking birds. They take short hikes, no more than two miles. Reggie cooks and serves Rae—and brews her poppy seed tea when she asks. Occasionally Rae winces when she shifts positions.

The days stretch into a week. They decide to stay another week and drive back to town to get more food and provisions and visit the ranger station again. After two weeks in their desert paradise, Rae puts down her copy of *The Monkey Wrench Gang*.

"How far are we from Glen Canyon Dam?" she asks.

"It's a couple hours south," Reggie estimates. "Want to see?"

"Sure, if we can find another spot like this to perch." The next day, they pack up and wind their way down into Arizona. They pass several stretches of fire-scorched land and fire-blackened trees.

As they approach drought-depleted Lake Powell, they see the low water level and the marks on the steep banks of the reservoir.

"Look at the bathtub ring." Reggie points up at the tall white walls topped by red sandstone. "To think they drowned an extraordinary canyon and its Native treasures for this. And there's a shrinking amount of water."

"What folly," agrees Rae. The sight of the lake and the dam repulse her, after her initial curiosity. "Let's get out of here."

They spend another week camped along the North Rim of the Grand Canyon in another campsite with a magnificent backyard terrace. Each day gets warmer, which is welcome.

Rae climbs into bed earlier than Reggie every night, giving him hours to sit up reading, thinking, and sipping scotch. He thinks: *Rae seems content to be traveling and being in nature. She's not reading any of the books that have agitated her in the past. Maybe she has let go of her vengeance idea, turning inward as people often do at the end of life. That was more than six months ago. She seems weaker. Maybe I can run out the clock with her on the move?*

One morning Rae wakes up in considerably more pain than previous days. The poppy tea helps, but she also twists open a bottle of prescription painkillers that she has avoided until now. She spends a lot of the day in bed, moving very little and eating like a bird.

That night she spoons against Reggie as he climbs into the van. On this trip, she has insisted on sleeping closer to him than usual. "I think it's time to go home," she whispers. "I miss Hayduke and Alix. A slow southern route, maybe? A quick stop to see Toby?"

"Okay, sweet thing," Reggie replies, kissing her eyes.

Part 6
RECKONING

One must not love oneself so much as to avoid getting involved in the risks of life that history demands of us.

—OSCAR ROMERO

EASTER

(Spring 2023)

Toby is awakened in the late morning with a vivid dream. He has overslept after a late night out with friends. Icy raindrops tap on the window of his bedroom. In his dream, he and Rae are children, laying on a mossy bank in the water wonderland of their childhood. The sun is warming them and they lie quietly and peacefully listening to the sounds of the forest. Rae asks him, "Toby, where do the turtles go in the winter?"

He sits up in bed abruptly. He looks at the digital clock. It's 11:11 a.m., and he hears church bells down the road. It is Easter morning. If Mom were here they would have gone to mass. He looks over at his phone, which is dead. He plugs it in and waits for it to power up.

When did I last see Rae? Maybe three weeks ago? A month? She and Reggie were driving back from the Southwest and stopped in Ohio for a night to see him. They were glowing from their adventures in Utah and Arizona and the warmth of the winter sun in the desert. Rae was putting on a brave face, but Toby could tell she was weak and in pain.

He grilled them some chicken and burgers and Reggie ate heartily, but Rae was fussy with her food and went to bed early. After she was asleep, he and Reggie stayed up talking. Reggie told Toby that Rae would probably only live a couple more months.

His phone reboots and he dials Rae. There is no answer and it goes straight to message. Toby hangs up without leaving a message.

He calls Reggie, who answers on the second ring.

"Toby?"

"How's Rae?"

He hears Reggie clear his throat. "She's gone."

"She died?"

There is a pause and rustling sound on Reggie's end of the line. Toby is standing by the kitchen window, but then sits down.

"Yes," Reggie says without certainty. But then he adds a qualifying, "I believe."

"You believe?"

"She's not here. I suspect she went somewhere to die. I'll let you know when I know for certain."

"She's not with you?" says Toby in disbelief.

"Nope." Reggie sounds flat.

"I just had this dream, that I was just with her," says Toby. "It was so realistic. We were kids in the water wonderland. She was talking about turtles."

He hears a slight "huh" from Reggie, who then tells him, "As Rae would say, that was not a coincidence. She visited me, too. I had a dream last night that we were standing outside with Hayduke in the snowy field."

There is a long pause as neither know what to say.

"Oh Reggie, before I forget. Rae sent me a box of journals and stuff. She said to give it to you someday."

"Oh." There's another pause. "Toby, hold onto those. Put them in safe place and don't mention them to anyone."

"Okay. What's going on?"

"Toby, I'll call you back when I know more, okay." Reggie hangs up without saying goodbye.

His eyes are fixed on the Rae's personal altar that she maintains on her dresser. There is her Petoskey stone, the polished relic from her childhood that she always carries in her pocket. His taps his own pocket, reassuring himself that his sister stone is there.

Underneath the stone is a small piece of folded paper. He opens it to the words in Rae's handwriting, "I will love you forever, Reggie." His knees buckle and he falls to the floor. A loud keening wail comes from deep in his chest.

Alix turns the truck north on Interstate 91. Her heart is racing. She keeps turning the radio dial in search of news. There are only classical music programs, snatches of NPR's Weekend Edition, and a few religious Easter programs.

Her mouth has a metallic taste. She exhales a sigh as she crosses into Vermont and sees the sign, "Welcome to Vermont: The Green Mountain State." She stops at the first Vermont rest area for a pee break and grabs a cup of free coffee. She motors past Exit 1, her usual turn-off for Guilford, and continues north. *I'll keep heading north*, Alix thinks. *I'll go to Val's house.*

At about 2:00 p.m., she hears a news broadcast with the first details. A suicide bomber has killed oil executive Brian Richardson and two members of his family. The family driver and another family member survived the attack but have been hospitalized. Police have not named the perpetrator, who was killed in the bombing. The governor of New York decries the heinous crime.

Alix's hands begin to shake on the steering wheel. Rae didn't tell her why she wanted the ride, and she didn't ask. Now she feels foolish for not knowing more. *Two members of his family? What the fuck, Rae?* Her heart is racing. Feeling shaky and faint, she stops in White River Junction to fuel up the truck. Her hand trembles as she pumps the gas and pays with cash. She drives to the post office and puts the dozen pre-stamped letters that Rae gave her into the letter box. One is to Reggie; the rest are to editors at various newspapers. One is for her, unstamped. She rips it open and tries to read it as she drives, but she is dangerously distracted as she's getting back onto I-91. She stuffs it into her bag to read later.

An hour later, she turns off the highway and onto the backroads of the Northeast Kingdom region of the state. She winds her way through Sheffield, taking the back road to Glover.

She drives past the Bread and Puppet barn and museum in Glover and turns her truck down a long dirt driveway with deep ruts from mud season. She arrives at a small cabin with another pickup truck and a glowing light in the window, the home of her friends Val and AJ. They are not expecting her, but they usher her into the house when they see her distressed face.

"I'm in trouble," Alix explains. "I need to lie low."

Val looks her up and down. "I think I know why." She waves her into the house.

The next morning, Alix borrows Val's truck and ventures out to the highway at Barton to get a couple newspapers at a large Irving gas station. The story of Rae's suicide bombing is front-page news, though her name is not mentioned. In one newspaper, Alix sees a blurry picture of her pickup truck caught on a security camera. "Police are looking for the driver of this truck." Another article mentions that the suicide bomber left a note, but police have not released details.

That afternoon, Alix, with help from Val, drives her truck down several miles of dirt track road, ditching it in a mud rut next to several other rusted vehicles. Val says they are ancient trucks from prohibition rumrunners. Val shuttles her back to their cabin.

She packs up her knapsack. Val gives her a wad of fifteen hundred dollars in cash. She puts on double wool socks and sturdy hiking boots. Val drives her north to Newport, where Alix looks at the schedule for a boat tour of Lake Memphremagog, an enormous lake spanning the US–Canada border. They drive on, hydroplaning on undulating mud on a few stretches of back road. Val seems unfazed by Northeast Kingdom mud season, dropping Alix at the end of a dirt road on the west side of the lake. Alix starts walking north, with her sight set on Owl's Head Mountain on the other side of the border.

As darkness sets in, she crosses over the Canadian border, a swath cut across the woods. Val told her this is a path well known to bootleggers, smugglers, draft resisters, and wayward hikers. She leaves the trail and starts bushwhacking with a headlamp. She finds a small plateau a mile into the woods, pitches her small tent, unrolls her sleeping bag, and climbs in. She opens the letter from Rae, buried deep in her sleeping bag.

An hour before dawn, Reggie hears the SWAT team before he sees them. He has been fitfully lying awake for hours, his mind replaying conversations with Rae. *Fucking Rae. I really didn't think she would go through with it. My fucking foolish wishful thinking. She was so weak in the days before, barely climbing out from under the covers, asking to be held by me or Alix or for poppy tea and pain killers. Now what? Now people are going to want me to explain the unjustifiable. Jesus. Here comes the hammer.*

He hears the unfamiliar sound of a helicopter and several large vehicles rolling and stopping out on the main Guilford Center Road.

He looks across the field and sees a faint line of troops in battle gear crossing the field, a sort of Vietnam War–style battalion. It is three days past the full moon, so he sees their movement. Only yesterday there were sixty children in this field looking for Easter eggs. He pulls on his pants and opens his front door to meet several red rifle tracer lights fixed on parts of his body.

He raises his hands. "Go easy there, lads. I'm alone and unarmed." He hears troopers busting down doors over at the main house. "No need to break anything," he says, as he is pushed face-first into the grass, his hands handcuffed behind his back.

Reggie is placed in a van, feeling exhausted and depleted from lack of sleep and the uncertainty of what lies ahead. *Rae is gone, but instead of grieving her death I have to deal with this shit show.* Hayduke barks and howls from inside the cabin as agents scan Rae's and his belongings. Later they allow him sit in the spring sun in his Adirondack chair, holding and petting Hayduke.

Attorney Sam Lovejoy arrives to protect the residents from unlawful search and seizure. In the end, no one is arrested. Everyone agrees to stay on the premises and remain available for questioning.

The feds spend several frustrating days at the Hidden River Farm, interviewing everyone on site, disassembling Rae and Reggie's cabin, seizing computers, and basically finding nothing to connect Rae's actions to the people there. Rae's computer is gone. Adding to their frustration, their wing-tip shoes are caked in chicken shit and their cars sink into ruts in the mud. On several occasions, groups of farm residents help push out the stuck vehicles.

Agent Carl Duncan seems to be the person assigned to interviewing Reggie and getting as much information as possible. He's a bit older and more senior than the other agents. While the younger agents are like robotic cowboys, taking pleasure dumping out drawers of socks, Duncan is no zealot. He quickly figures out there's not much incriminating evidence here.

"She mentioned this idea over eight months ago," Reggie says with complete honesty. "I told her it was a terrible idea, and she never raised it again. She was depleted from cancer in the last couple weeks. She didn't have long to live."

Reggie has carried a rodent in his gut, gnawing away at him for months, knowing he was going to lose Rae. But he can't shake the shock of the last couple days. *She is gone. She did it. Goddamn you, Rae.* He thinks of his friend Tony, who took his own life. In the weeks before Tony's suicide, his depression seemed to lift. He was smiling, even laughing. Reggie and his friends stopped their careful vigils, breathing a selfish sigh of relief. *We didn't understand that Tony had made up his mind to end his life and he felt relieved. Rae had made up her mind, too. How did I not see this?*

On the third day after the bombing, a letter addressed to Reggie arrives in the mailbox with a large dinosaur postage stamp. Agent Duncan, who is intercepting all mail, brings the piece to Reggie, already in a plastic bag.

It is the same letter that Rae also sent to the press, but with a personalized scribble at the top. "Sasha, I will love you forever. Your Emma." Reggie stifles a grin, amazed at how Rae's humor is poking him from the other side.

"Who is Emma? Who is Sasha?" Agent Duncan asks Reggie.

"Oh, they're just pet names," Reggie answers, avoiding further details of Rae's historical reference. He reads the letter silently through the plastic bag and then hands it back to agent Duncan.

"As you probably already read for yourself, no one at the Hidden River Farm knew anything about this action."

"What is the significance of the dinosaur stamp?" asks Agent Duncan.

"I don't know. Fossil fuel?" Reggie guesses. "She bought a lot of those stamps when they came out. Loved putting them on birthday cards to her nieces and nephews." Reggie is stabbed again with the pain of losing Rae. He doesn't relish explaining Rae's actions to all their relatives and godchildren.

Later in the day, Agent Duncan returns to Reggie's cabin. "Where is Alix Leblanc?"

"I honestly don't know," says Reggie, unaware that Alix was involved in any way.

"Were they close?" asks agent Duncan.

"Like mother and daughter."

"Does she have a green pickup truck?"

"Yes. Amazing that thing still runs."

"And you have no idea where she may have gone?"

"Nope."

Reggie feels a sickening chill to think that Alix is involved. And he wonders if they will find his poppy plants and use that against him as well. But this crew of FBI agents don't seem interested in plants.

RAE'S LETTER

(April 9, 2023)

To all, in explanation for my Easter actions:

All my life I have been committed to respecting life and nonviolent social change.

Today, I have acted alone. There is no conspiracy. I have no accomplices. My partner, Reggie Donovan, knew no details and was opposed in principle to any violent actions. No one from my home at the Hidden River Farm had knowledge of my plan.

My action is an extension of my love for the world—for humanity, for animals, for Gaia. I have no hate in my body.

This is not a suicide. I am weeks away from dying of a terminal illness. I am offering my life, my final act, to render consequence where the powerful corporate decision-makers have been protected.

Throughout my entire life I have operated on the assumption that human beings are basically good. We may sometimes act harshly or violently because of harms that were done to us. Many of us struggle to do good while stuck inside evil systems. I have attempted to live with a profound respect for every living thing.

But in the last five years, I have seen the contemporary face of evil. This evil takes the form of greed and corruption, wrapped in an impenetrable narrative of justification. The leaders of our fossil fuel energy corporations—and their principal investors—have known for decades about the harms that their profit-making businesses are causing the planet. Yet they used their wealth, power, and political connections to muddy the science, fund climate-denial movements, bankroll politicians to block change, and obstruct alternative paths to a safe-energy future. All this was done so that they could extract profits for a few more years.

Leaders of the fossil fuel industry, like CEO Brian Richardson, knew that what they were doing was deadly and harmful. But they made a conscious choice to continue. He personally decided to invest billions to open up new oil and gas fields, to bet against humanity's survival knowing that he would not have to live with the consequences. People like Brian Richardson are personally responsible for our current ecological predicament. On one level, I believe we are all responsible for the ways that we have cooperated with an unjust system. But these evil men had all the information, the resources, and the power to shift the trajectory. Yet, for selfish reasons, they did not.

Are these men different than the perpetrators of genocide toward First Nations and African Americans forcibly brought to this country? More evil than Hitler? I believe their evil is comparable, as they are consciously destroying our one and only home, Mother Earth. Yet their actions are not the "banality of evil," as Hannah Arendt described Nazi bystanders or people directed by others to implement harmful acts. These are the people in charge, who have the clout to chart a different path. In Dante's Inferno, they will occupy the lowest ring of Hell.

I would like to think that, if I were alive in the 1940s, I would be like Dietrich Bonhoeffer and try and stop Hitler. He was executed on this day seventy-eight years ago today. But I am alive in 2023 and I am called to act in response to this contemporary manifestation of evil.

Under the current system, these men will live out their remaining lives in luxury. They will not face punishment for the consequences of their actions and inactions. And that is why I have acted—to exact Old Testament accountability. If innocents are lost with them, that is regrettable. I am deeply sorry for the loss of any life. All life is precious. But these men have caused—or will cause—the death and maiming of millions of innocents around the world, including millions of children, not to mention other living beings. I have held these innocent children in my arms. I cannot forget the harms committed against them.

I dedicate my action to those who suffer the consequences of our inaction. To the people of the island nations that are watching the sea levels rise. To the billions of people in the global South who live simple low-impact lives, who have burned the least carbon and methane, yet will suffer the most devastating conditions. I act in solidarity with those who suffered from colonialism and poverty at the hands of the extracting and overconsuming nations of the global North. They will suffer most from heat waves, droughts, fires, dust bowls, crop failures, and other forms of ecological degradation that are not their fault. They will suffer from the sun erupting on Earth.

I dedicate this to all other living creatures—the animals, the fish, the birds, the fungi, and insects that will face devastation and extinction because of human actions—and especially the actions of these Carbon Oligarchs.

My actions may unleash the violence of the state against nonviolent protesters. I urge the public, media, and politicians not to paint the actions of all dissenters with the same brush.

I urge others, like myself who are facing terminal illness, to consider taking actions similar to mine. Do not go quietly. Use this one and only wild precious life you have to make a statement. These men deserve retribution for their actions. And for this purpose, I have included a list of those who should repent for what they are doing. They should confess their crimes and atone for their actions by using their wealth and power to mitigate the harms they have caused. And they should dedicate the rest of their lives to repair the harms. Or they should live in fear and face consequences.

In conclusion, I hope and pray that love will triumph over violence. But today, I hope my decision to resort to violence will awaken humanity to act. I hope my action will focus responsibility on those who have profited from the suffering and destruction of all living things.

Rae Kelliher
Of sound mind and heart

TWO MONTHS LATER

(Summer 2023)

The blowback, as Reggie predicted, is severe. Brian Richardson is on the cover of dozens of magazines, including *Forbes*, *Time*, and *Fortune*.

The articles don't mention Rae's name in order to "avoid giving attention to terrorists." *Forbes* calls Richardson "a martyr for a demonized industry" and observes that "An unstable climate activist shortened the life of the gentle business leader and family man." The *New York Post* has the headline "Killed for Keeping the Lights On," with a photo of Richardson and his teenage daughters.

Reggie feels bitter revulsion as he watches the hammer of state repression come down on peaceful climate activists. Twenty-five participants at a nonviolent pipeline encampment in Minnesota are arrested and illegally detained for weeks. A National Guard unit in Tennessee opens fire on a group of peaceful protesters, wounding six, including a child. A right-wing militia man drives his truck into a tent encampment of Quakers planting trees. The Trump caucus in Congress calls for a declaration of martial law around critical energy infrastructure.

There is, of course, the hate mail, the threatening messages, the warped conspiratorial minds. Reggie has watched the gathering storm clouds of right-wing fascism in the country and anticipates threats against the farm community. There are days when he just wants to hide out and avoid the news, to take Hayduke for a long walk in the woods. But this is impossible with the incoming messages, mail, and visitors. He alternates between feeling numb and in shock to raw and weepy, especially when he thinks about Alix, who is missing.

What surprises him is the rapid shift in the national conversation. Within months, several media outlets publish major stories, "Are Oil CEOs Responsible for Climate Change?" and "When Did They Know? Why Didn't They Act?" Several television networks unleash investigative teams to uncover the hundreds of ways that the oil industry has used its political clout to stop investments in alternatives to fossil fuels. One magazine's cover story quotes from Rae, but without attribution: "The Carbon Industry Bets Humans Won't Get It Together to Stop Them." One divinity school hosts a symposium called "Is This a Bonhoeffer Moment for the Climate Change Movement?" Over seven hundred clergy attend in person, and tens of thousands watch the proceedings on line.

The United Nations establishes a tribunal on climate crimes, opening hearings on the role of fossil fuel executives, lobbyists, and politicians. Rae's target list, included with her letter, is excluded from most publications. But a few networks publish it on the deep web and the list circulates widely.

Every day, Reggie receives letters of support from around the world as well as spoken words of encouragement. "If I had the courage, I'd do the same." "We have a group of grandmothers . . ." "I have Rae's picture on my altar." Friends send Reggie photographs of Rae's picture on altars from island nations along the equator. A mural depicting Rae, created by the street artist Banksy, appears on a wall in India. Poster versions of the mural pop up all over the planet, pasted to lamp posts and peeking out of windows.

Reggie gets a moving condolence letter from Jim McGovern, now a member of Congress, who met with Rae many times when she was trying to shut down the School of Americas. "Dearest Reggie, I cried when I heard about Rae's death. Rae was one of the most solid activists I ever knew. I feel like our political system let her down, let us all down, in trying to avert climate disruption. . . ."

Reggie was prepared for the denunciations, even from friends and allies. The institutions of the US climate-change movement, reeling from the invasion of Ukraine and the rallying around the flag for domestic oil and gas, compete with one another in the fervor of their denunciations of Rae's action. *This is what they must do to survive*, thinks Reggie.

"God damn you, Rae," he says aloud at one point, reading an article in the *New York Times* about climate leaders distancing themselves from anyone who expresses the slightest sympathy for her action. "Sowing division and chaos with your dramatic exit."

Once again, Reggie wonders if he should have alerted authorities about Rae's impending action. In her final month, he convinced himself that she was too weak to follow through on her revenge fantasy. Now he realizes that this was his own magical thinking, his own foolish belief that Rae had lost her resolve. "In your grandiosity, Rae, did you really know what you were doing?"

It's 9:00 p.m., or "Quaker midnight," for Reggie, and there is a knock at his door. It's Rachel, wrapped in a shawl. They both assume that everything is still under surveillance. She motions for him to come outside, and they walk down the path away from the common house.

"Sorry to be mysterious," Rachel says in a hushed tone. "I just got a call from A. She wants to talk to you."

"Okay. How?" Reggie has been waiting for this call with a small measure of dread. But it's better than reading about Alix's capture in the news, he reasons. And so far she's eluded being found, which is no small feat.

"She left this number for you to call tomorrow at 5:00 p.m." Rachel hands him a scrap of paper, turns on her heels, and disappears up the path.

The next day, Reggie drives to Brattleboro and wanders around the food co-op, putting a few items in his basket. After paying, he sets out on foot to one of the few remaining pay phones he can remember. At 5:00 p.m., he dials the number, feeding a small pile of quarters into the phone.

"Hello," answers a quiet voice on the other end of the line.

"It's me," said Reggie, being purposely oblique. *Oh Alix!*

There is a momentarily pause, an inhalation. "Hi," says the voice, unmistakably Alix. "I'm so sorry to bother you. I'm so sorry about her."

"Are you okay?" Reggie asks, careful not to ask for any details.

"I want to come home," says Alix. Reggie hears Alix tearing up on the other end of the phone. "I guess that means turning myself in. I need help. Sorry to bother you. I don't know who else to call."

"Don't worry," says Reggie, his heart breaking. "I want to help. I'm so sorry you're in this position. I thought you might eventually call, so I've looked into a few options. I've got someone you should talk to, a lawyer. Ready for the name and number?"

"Yes."

Reggie gives Alix the name of a friend, a former prosecutor who can help. Over the last month he's talked to several lawyers and sought advice.

"I'll come get you," Reggie says. "When the time is right."

"Thanks. I'll write you, maybe in care of Nancy's bookstore."

"That's a good idea."

"Okay, I should go. Bye."

"Bye."

That night, Reggie again calls his two attorney friends and the former prosecutor they recommend. She will watch for Alix's call.

Several weeks pass and Reggie gets a message, through an encrypted app, to call the attorney. He learns that they are in negotiations with the feds and officials from New York State, who are being hard-asses. "Since Rae is dead, they need a living scapegoat," the attorney says. "They started with a felony murder charge against Alix, but we're getting closer on a plea bargain. It's going to mean jail time, but hopefully less than five years."

"Five years?" Reggie gulps. *Goddamn Rae.* This is the last thing Rae would have wanted. He can't think of her without bittersweet emotions.

"Well, eight years, with parole after five or six. If we can get the feds to drop some charges."

More weeks go by, and the attorney reaches out again. They've reached an agreement with the feds. Alix will plead guilty to accessory to manslaughter and will serve a concurrent federal and New York State sentence of eight years, with likely release after six years.

Would he like to pick up Alix, she asks, somewhere up north, and drive her to the surrender point in Albany, New York?

Yes, of course, he says.

The date and time of the surrender is set, and he gets another encrypted message with a time to pick up Alix the next day. He should go to a campground in the Northeast Kingdom, to a lean-to called Cedar. He is advised not to bring her to the farm or anywhere else where she might be arrested before the formal surrender in Springfield. "There are lots of law enforcement on the lookout for her."

ONE YEAR LATER – REGGIE

(Summer 2024)

Reggie sits on the porch of his cabin, using a special dog comb to pull ticks off Hayduke, who sits up alertly in a dignified pose. Rae used to do this job, sometimes sitting at the dinner table—a rather unappetizing habit. Reggie has now banned indoor tick-picking, as if Rae were still alive.

Rae appears to be everywhere—in their house, in his dreams, talking to him, him talking back to her. She visits him on what would have been her seventieth birthday to make sure he is watching out for Alix. As Rae would have done, he has a large altar on her old bedroom dresser, full of his favorite photos and some of her trinkets, including her treasured Petoskey stone. In one photo, a youthful Rae and Reggie stand naked by their cabin pond with two farm implements, Reggie with wire-frame glasses, in the classic "American Gothic" pose.

Rae's dresser is still full of her clothes, accessories, and jewelry. In the year that has passed, he has done little to sort through her belongings. Once violated by a bunch of cavalier FBI agents, Reggie carefully folded the scattered clothes and put them back as best as he could remember. The reality is that Rae was the anti-hoarder, sorting her clothes and belongings a couple times a year and gifting the surplus to others. *Maybe Alix will want these clothes someday?*

The one exception to Rae's thrift are dress-up clothes. Reggie has spent hours sorting through large boxes marked "dress-up" and "costumes." Rae had a rather extensive collection of silly hats, wigs, vintage shoes, face masks, angel wings, and theatrical costumes, a lifetime's accumulation from thrift shops and tag sales. He is motivated by wanting to liberate some space in the cabin, which is about eight hundred square feet, so every inch matters. But he believes the wider community should enjoy access to this celebratory collection.

Reggie considers Rae a sort of Emma Goldman—"If I can't dance, I don't want to be in your revolution"—but with silly hats. He recalls her reading to him aloud a passage from a book by a British ecological thinker named David Fleming called *Surviving the Future*.

Reggie was tucked in beside her on their couch. Rae was reading Fleming aloud in an animated voice: "Carnival! Celebrations of music, dance, torchlight, mime, games, feast, and folly have been central to the life of community for all times other than those when the pretensions of large-scale civilization descended like a frost on public joy."

"Sounds like life at Hidden River Farm," Reggie replied.

"More torchlight!" Rae summarized, delving back into the text.

Reggie appreciates that Rae intuitively understood this power of celebration for decades. He described her to friends as a "party in a box, just add music." She was the great fiesta planner, the celebrator of birthdays, and the enchantress of dance parties, often arriving with an outlandish costume and mask. She was the shameless adopter of all fertility, harvest, and moon rituals. Any special day was an excuse for a dance and celebration. Saint Brigid's, Imbolc, Beltaine, Lughnasadh, Samhain, Day of the Dead, Solstice, Equinox, new moon, full moon, Juneteenth, Fourth of July, Halloween, Mother's Day.

Reggie sorts the dress-up treasures into sturdier cardboard boxes and labels them for future use. "Wigs" and "Hats" get their own boxes. He hauls them to a storage room on the third floor of the common house, a well-organized space that belies the notion of "tragedy of the commons," with careful shelving systems and rules, largely followed.

Rae would say, "The only tragedy of communal life is the tragedy of the *unmanaged* commons," referring to the tendency of common spaces to be cluttered when there are no rules, or no person responsible.

Reggie is going to visit Alix shortly, taking the new fast train down the Connecticut River and along the coast to the prison, a trip of about two and a half hours. Reggie looks forward to the time on the train, a chance to read and look out the window at the passing countryside. He rarely leaves the farm. He has collected a small packet of photos and a pile of magazines and books for Alix, as she is thirsty for news about the world that is rapidly shifting outside her walls. He also packs several of her favorite farm treats (dried apples, hazelnuts), though they may be confiscated. He packs a lunch and thermos of tea for himself.

Reggie has been reading Rae's journals, the ones that she sent to Toby for safekeeping. When Reggie was ready, he told Toby to send the sealed box to Nancy's bookstore in town. They arrived neatly arranged in chronological order (after Rae had clearly removed and burned some sections). Reggie girds himself to flip through the pages periodically, finding himself rubbed raw by Rae's emotional roller coaster, her joys and bugbears alike.

One of Rae's last directives to Reggie was that he share the journals with Alix. He has already brought a few volumes to Alix in prison, and she is the only other person besides himself who has read them.

On his visits to Alix, he recalls Rae's admonitions during his final weeks with her. Rae was very insistent that he should treat Alix as their daughter, that she was indeed born at the time when their own child miscarried. This was not news to Reggie, but he heard a new intensity in Rae's insistence. He had no knowledge that Alix would be considered an accomplice and would face severe consequences.

Alix as daughter is not a leap. He loves Alix. He is always enlivened by Alix's fresh humor, playfulness, and work ethic. He is her most regular visitor in prison, though a number of the other farm aunties and friends—such as Jade, PJ and Rachel—make the trip each month. Through the chaos of the transitioning world, visiting Alix becomes his touchstone, part of what keeps him focused and alive.

ANOTHER YEAR LATER – ALIX

(2025)

Alix finishes her count. "Ninety-nine, one hundred," she whispers to herself, lowering her belly onto a purple yoga mat, turning her head to the side and breathing in. It is barely past dawn and Alix is doing her morning calisthenics, not to be confused with her afternoon exercises.

After over a year and a half at the federal women's prison, Alix finds that a number of daily practices are helping her maintain her sanity and health. These include exercise, meditation, study, and reading. Every day she writes two letters like journal entrees to her friends. She participates in a number of prison groups, including a writing class and a building trades course, while keeping abreast of outside events. *Prison as monastery*, as Rae described it, quoting Bonhoeffer.

In her first six months in prison, Alix was bitter. She felt like she was the scapegoat for public anger about Rae's action and that the stiff prison term was fundamentally unjust.

It was Reggie who helped her adjust her expectations. "It is wrong what was done to you," he counseled. "But if you hold onto that bitterness, it will poison you." She read a book of autobiographical stories about Black men wrongly convicted who had spent decades in jail and how they made sense of their lives after release.

Alix could hear this advice and understand its value intellectually. But her body could not surrender a deep feeling of being wronged. She realizes she will probably be in prison until she is forty, running out her biological clock for childbearing. This further infuriates her. Her fury is directed at Rae. Meanwhile, she sits on her twin bed mattress with the din of a television echoing from the common room, disconnected from the land she loves.

Her feelings about Rae remain complex. At the Hidden River Farm they always had a saying about their chickens and livestock: "They have rich and free-ranging lives and then have a bad final five minutes." It is hard to feel the delights of the years with Rae without focusing on the last five minutes, or five hours.

For the first four months in prison, Alix worked on the cleaning crew. Then she joined the grounds crew, which got her outside more. Finally, through her building trades class, she joined a team that spent the month sanding and staining the ancient wooden floors outside the prison library and offices. The crew of six women worked meticulously, helping one another correct mistakes and improve their skills. At the end of the month, the prison warden came and inspected the work, and then praised the craft and care that they put into the job.

"It was weird," Alix explained to Reggie on one of his visits. "I felt this pride. Like, you know, this was *my home* and I was fixing it up. After that, I felt the bitterness dissipate. I don't know how to explain it."

The news from outside the prison walls is shocking and, on some days, riveting. Alix is often the first to be standing by the prison library when the newspapers and magazines arrive. She catches some fragments of news from snatches of radio broadcasts. Access to the internet is limited and spotty. But for understanding the real undercurrents of what's going on, she depends on a few people on the outside, like Reggie, to keep her up to date and give her perspective.

By 9:00 a.m., she's sitting in the prison library scanning a pile of newspapers and magazines to prepare for his visit. She flips through the headlines and stories. "Heat Wave Continues. Death Toll Rises," reports the *New York Times*, with a map showing the red zone covering the entire central US. A massive heat wave is blasting the upper Midwest, with temperatures remaining above 100 degrees for almost two weeks without relief. For a few days, the temperature spikes to 115 degrees. California's drought continues, joined by disastrous heat waves and droughts in Plains states and the South. Alix reads about the crop failures, water shortages, the electrical brownouts, the death toll among the elderly and vulnerable.

Competing with the alarming weather is the news about the global economic implosion. Inside prison, Alix did not experience the ways that Russian cyberattacks wreaked havoc on the US financial system and the electrical grid.

From previous visits, Alix has learned from Reggie about the gridlock and breakdown of the federal political system. Reggie describes the United States as unique in its self-inflicted economic chaos. In other parts of the world, countries are shutting down coal plants, enforcing moratoriums on extracting fossil fuels, and implementing energy rationing and consumption reductions. Functional national governments in some regions invest in worker transition, steering the unemployed to socially beneficial projects such as retrofitting buildings, expanding public transit, and transitioning to renewable energy. No such efforts happen at the national level in the US, even as the economy spins into chaos. A few state governments step into the void, supporting community transition efforts.

In the United States, what is left of the federal political system remains captured by the "carbon oligarchs," who push for accelerated energy extraction. But with depression-like conditions spreading across the land, energy consumption has plummeted, creating gluts in both oil and gas. Yet nothing seems to slow the drive to extract.

Alix thinks back to what Rae always said, citing the book she read about the 1930s Dust Bowl. "There is gonna be a hardcore 30 percent of the population that is pure magical thinking." Even in the face of a human-created environmental disaster, a third of the population believes that they need to practice positive thinking or do a better job appeasing a vengeful God.

Ironically, the prison "hosting" Alix—as she would say—has its own solar array, generator, and miniature power plant for heating and cooling. And it has vast food stores, even a garden, tended by the inmates, that produces fresh fruit and vegetables. As some of the guards remind them, often with a tone of resentment as if they are privileged children, the inmates are better off than a lot of people on the outside right now.

These privileges are not lost on demagogue politicians, who thrive on fanning resentments rather than solving problems. They rail against prisoners with such amenities as air-conditioning, internet, television, three meals a day, and a recreation area that one Connecticut senator likens to a spa. At one point, the politicians, who can't agree on much of anything, vote to limit prison air-conditioning to days hotter than 100 degrees. In buildings *not* designed around the principles of open-air flow and windows, this makes for stifling conditions for inmates and guards alike. Fortunately, the correctional workers union lobbies to have the cool air turned on for the sake of their members. Turns out having an overheated prison is a bad idea, for many reasons.

Reggie arrives with a stack of magazines, pictures, and two of Rae's journals, all of which get scanned, x-rayed, and reviewed for who knows what. He wonders, Do people still put blotter acid on pieces of paper? On past visits, he has quipped to Alix, in a Dad-joke manner, that "they found the metal file I tried to sneak in, baked inside the cake." Of course, there is no cake.

Sitting in the visitor area, waiting for Alix, Reggie is bundled up in a sweatshirt and knit cap. There are two other pairs of prisoners and visitors at scattered tables. Reggie is thankful that Alix is in a minimum-security prison that has a reputation for relatively humane systems. He has visited political prisoners in other states who are not so lucky. Still, it is unsettling that she is in prison at all.

Alix saunters in, accompanied by a young female guard whom Alix appears to have some rapport with.

"Sammy, this is Papa Reggie," she says introducing them. "This is the only place in his life where he has air-conditioning, which explains his frozen lumberjack look."

"It's the only reason I come—for the cool air and the aroma of chemical cleaners."

They are allowed a quick, supervised hug. Sammy waves, smiles at Reggie, and turns to talk to another guard standing in the corner watching the other prisoners.

"Hello, my starlet," says Reggie, handing her a notecard and a book.

"No file or cake?" says Alix, beating him to the punch. "Thanks for these."

"How are you?" He scans Alix for any physical or emotional signs of imbalance. She appears positively radiant, much healthier than during his visit a couple weeks earlier.

"All right. Keeping my spirits up. Making a few new friends. Feeling less bitter about everything."

"You look thinner. Are you getting enough good calories?"

"I sort of have a rule here—which is: If it's bad for me, I don't eat it. I go hungry sometimes, but it's one of my practices. You know, they hold my body, but not my soul. They can't force me to eat toxic waste."

"Right," said Reggie. "I should try that at home."

They both laugh, knowing it isn't easy to find harmful things to eat at the Hidden River Farm. That doesn't prevent Reggie from occasionally scoring a box of chocolate doughnuts.

"Is there anything you want?" says Reggie, pointing to the vending machines in the visitor room.

"No," said Alix pausing. "Well, maybe some of those raisin packets before you leave. Everything else is . . . dreck."

Without another word, Reggie pulls some change out his pocket, walks to the vending machine, and buys three skinny packets of raisins for Alix. This little errand gives him a moment to wipe away his tears with his back turned.

Alix studies Reggie as he slowly stands and stiffly walks to the vending machine. He has aged a lot in the last two years, she thinks. Are his glasses thicker?

When he returns to the table, she asks, "Okay, what's the news I'm not hearing?" Alix will eventually get around to asking about people at the farm and other gossip. But there are certain things she can only learn from Reggie.

"Another lawsuit victory. Against Chevron." Reggie is referring to litigation where future generations and investors accuse companies of depriving them of a future. "Finger by finger, we are tying down the giant oil-and-gas Gulliver."

"Cool," said Alix. She delights in his way of speaking.

Reggie leans toward Alix and speaks softly. "The blowback continues. Oklahoma, Texas, Florida—they've all passed these draconian laws criminalizing protests against fossil fuel. Basically, the carbon-extracting areas are becoming mini–police states."

"Is maple syrup an extractive industry?" jokes Alix. She longs for the annual sugar harvest in Vermont, the all-night sap boils she would organize with friends.

"Ha!" Reggie smiles and then lowers his voice even more. "Two more copycats."

"Shit. What happened?" Alix nods, looking to the guards and around the room, which they know is monitored. Just as Alix was going to prison, six grandmothers calling themselves Good Ancestors immolated themselves in the lobby of ExxonMobil, capturing the attention of the world with their sacrificial witness. In the last year, there has been a steady stream of individual actions, mostly additional self-sacrifices.

"Private equity guy, Argyle Group, moved trillions of investment capital into exploiting new gas deposits. Out jogging. Bodyguard, too."

"Who did it?" This is the news Alix can't get in prison.

"Another terminally ill woman, with a phony flat bicycle tire."

"Oh. And?" Alix wonders how she manages to be intrigued and heartbroken at the same time. *Am I becoming jaded?*

"A self-immolation in the lobby of the American Petroleum Institute. Young guy, like your age. Great statement. Totally shaking things up."

"Wow. The big boys must be freaking out."

"Oh yeah, they are hunted men. Protecting the carbon oligarchs is one of the few growth sectors in the unraveling economy. Home security, surveillance systems, bodyguards, and bulletproof SUVs—that's big business. Some of these companies are forming private armies to defend their assets and people, even though their economic fortunes are plummeting. And some have formed their own mercenary hit squads. Oh, and a there are a lot of early retirements, fossil fuel executives with public statements of apology and renunciation. They all suddenly want to spend more time with their families."

Alix leans toward Reggie to hear his softening voice.

"This one retired CEO from ConocoPhillips, his name is Walker," Reggie continues. "He releases this statement that is confessional. He's like, 'I'm sorry for my actions that prevented our company from leading the fight against climate change. We were wrong and I personally apologize for my role in delaying our country's response.' Unbelievable, eh?"

"Interesting," says Alix. "Are they donating their stock to climate mitigation?"

"Their stock ain't worth much anymore," says Reggie.

They both laugh.

"Much publicity?" she asks.

"Oh yeah. The industry groups try and keep this stuff out of the news. But they can't plug all the holes. And the actions have a lot of public support, believe it or not. These carbon barons have no legitimacy as things start to unravel—the heat waves, fires, the economic meltdown. There are huge support vigils around these actions."

"I read about Line Three," says Alix, referring to a major gas pipeline project in Minnesota that was sabotaged a week earlier.

"Yeah, and there are more organized operations moving into the space." They say nothing more about this, in part because they don't know the source of these actions, what some call "black ops."

The visitors at the table next to Reggie and Alix are arguing loudly about something, so they lean in to hear one another better.

"The Trumpers have a big appeal to people upset about change. They will subscribe to every conspiracy theory about what's broken. The only explanation that is off-limits is: 'Maybe we consume too much.'"

Alix takes this in. "Yeah, the national religion is being tested here." From her conversations in prison, she's come to believe that the national story is loneliness.

Alix has read about how some red states are doubling down on voter suppression, punitive social welfare policies, corporate tax breaks, and support for fossil fuel extraction. Reggie adds another dimension: these states are becoming more authoritarian police states, cracking down on protest and criminalizing women's reproductive choice.

On the other hand, blue states are making it easier to vote, establishing universal basic incomes, expanding social housing, encouraging regenerative agriculture, and investing in renewable energy while going fossil-fuel-free. Vermont is the bluest of these states, rekindling the periodic discussions in the Green Mountain State of secession.

"Yup," Reggie concludes, "it keeps the demagogues very busy concocting new enemies to blame for our changing way of life."

"But I get the sense, from my prison cell window here, that the rest of the world isn't buying it," says Alix, shaking her head. "They're focused on making real changes, not purposely stalling."

"That's right. And here's the good news you won't read in most media," says Reggie, tapping the small stack of magazines on the table. "Huge segments of the US population aren't buying it either. The carbon authoritarians may win political office in some places, but there's a significant powering-down happening, and all the stuff we've been working on for twenty years—local food, energy conservation, local business trumping global suppliers, eating in season—these things are flourishing. And not just in the Northeastern states, but in pockets all over the country."

"So, is there a quickening of the culture shift?" Alix asks with hope. She wants so much to be part of making the change. But she knows to pace herself emotionally, given her years ahead in prison.

"I think it's exposing that there is a huge segment of the population who never bought the whole package to start with. They want decent lives and basic security, but they never took the excess bait. Grannie the food canner is a rock star now. Everyone wants to borrow Rae's back issues of *Mother Earth News*."

"Cool," says Alix, leaning forward to better hear Reggie's voice.

"Fun fact," says Reggie. "An expansion in 4-H clubs and local soil associations, young people getting involved in farming, basic animal husbandry, soil fertility. A whole generation learning skills and getting country strong."

"Country strong," says Alix, flexing her arm muscles, which are rather impressive. "What's the farm news?"

"Well, as you know, we have a lot of new people showing up at our door," says Reggie. "You could call them climate refugees. They're the second wave of friends and family who are escaping from climate disruption and political repression in other parts of the country. We've had a lot of long meetings about our membership policies and how to absorb new people."

"Ooh, long meetings," jokes Alix. "I bet you love that."

Reggie shakes his head, acknowledging this personal flaw. "I'm actually on the replication committee, helping all these new groups get access to land and create new ecovillages. And there are landback and reparations funds being established. We can still absorb more people at Hidden River Farm, but a lot of people want to start their own communities, too, with extended families, or without White people, to create what they call 'decolonized space.' We now have about a dozen communities in our mutual aid federation, sharing tools and knowledge and trading for basics. Some city dwellers show up who don't know which end of the shovel to hold."

"It sounds like cities are getting harder to live in." Alix thinks about the letters she gets from friends leaving Boston and New York for northern New England.

"Yeah, a bunch of coastal cities are seeing the writing on the wall, especially after last year's hurricane season. And there are frequent food shortages, not to mention the lack of potable water, and electrical outages."

"Where will everyone go?" asked Alix.

"Well, the future is rural. We know that. And the reality is that our communities have a lot of land, water, and pretty good soil. We can sustain a lot more people if we don't get slammed with a prolonged drought. Same around the Great Lakes and up north, around the Saint Lawrence River in Quebec.

"We're trying to welcome a lot of new people. It's what Rae called 'the work of the open heart,' moving away from a place of scarcity and fear." Reggie pauses, then nods. "It's great to see your spirits up, Alix."

They both pause for a moment and their eyes meet. Reggie smiles and Alix feels a pang of loss from not being at the farm and being able to talk with him every day.

"It's because I'm so happy to see you." Alix grins and pops the rest of the raisins in her mouth.

Reggie takes this in, and then continues. "Another undercurrent: We have a new local currency, backed by cordwood and maple syrup—the *heat and sweet* economy! Everyone knows the value of those two things, and they are widely traded commodities."

"I love it!" Alix exclaims. "How's our maple syrup supply?" This was one of Alix's chosen jobs, harvesting and boiling down the annual sap collection.

"We miss your sugaring skills!" Reggie laughs. "Now that it's a form of currency, more people are into it. And Jade and I and a few of the recent arrivals from Afghanistan, Honduras, and Ukraine fixed up the sugar shack to double the capacity. We got a new evaporator, retrofitted from an old one. The international refugees are super into harvesting and processing sap."

Sammy the guard pops her head into the room. "Five more minutes, you two."

"Whaa!" shouts Alix, looking at the clock. "I think they're messing with the clocks."

She looks gratefully at Reggie. "Thanks for coming. It means the world to me."

"Of course. It's the highlight of my week," Reggie says, smiling. "And you would like the train ride."

"I'll enjoy a one-way train ride home," Alix says, with a hint of sadness. "Hey, did you bring me those pictures I asked for?"

"Oh yeah," Reggie says, tapping an envelope on top of his care package bundle. "A few pictures of Rae."

She opens the envelopes and spreads five photos out on the table. One is Alix's favorite of Rae and her together, standing by a cookout grill.

"I love *YES!* magazine," says Alix, flipping through the pile of magazine offerings.

"And here's the latest installment of the Rae journals." Reggie hands Alix the two black volumes. "There's great stuff from her travels in Central America, sort of a lonely time. A lot of her impressions about the people she met."

"Fantastic," said Alix, who has been inspired to start her own journaling practice after reading Rae's reflections.

After saying farewell to Reggie, Alix returns glumly to her cell. She pulls the pictures from the envelope that Reggie brought her, looking at them over again. She adds them to her small altar, built on a shelf next to her bed.

FIVE YEARS LATER –
RAE'S BIRTHDAY CELEBRATION

(May 5, 2030)

Alix leans against Rachel as they sit on the ground, surrounded by others in the memorial grove. Reggie steps forward to the tree-stump podium.

Reggie looks at her. "Alix is back." There is a joyous cheer throughout the group. "Seven years later, this is a good time to think about Rae's life."

Rachel gives her a gentle bump and puts her arm around her.

Reggie waves to Toby, inviting him forward. "We are thankful that Rae's brother, Toby, is here. He drove out from Ohio to be with us. More than anyone, Rae would say, Toby shaped her early life—teaching her about animals, nature, mushrooms. Toby, thanks so much for honoring Rae and all of us with your presence today."

Alix cranes her neck to see, as she has never met Toby in person. He stands up, steps forward, gives Reggie a bear hug. Reggie told Alix that Toby looked thinner and more robust than the last time he saw him. He arrived with a woman named Noreen who looks to be his age and height and has stayed resolutely by his side.

Toby turns to face the gathered, most of whom he has never met. He thinks about the dream he had a week earlier when Rae visited him. She is about eight years old and is wearing a flowing green embroidered dress that falls to her ankles and almost covers her fabric booties. They walk in the woods to the water wonderland of their childhood. Rae is singing and skipping. Toby is pointing to hidden mushrooms. As they lie on the green peninsula, they become adults and Rae looks into Toby's eyes, unblinking and with affection. "I had a baby," she tells Toby. "I lost her. To the suffering of the world. Alix. Take care of her. Treat her as my daughter."

Toby awoke blinking from the vividness of the dream, almost believing it to be true. *Alex? Who is Alex?* Then he remembers the young woman who drove Rae to New York who served time in jail. *Is that Alex?*

This dream clinched his decision to enlist Noreen to drive with him to Vermont and join the celebration.

Now he scans the attentive faces of these strangers who intimately knew Rae, and he begins to speak. "It is safe to say I was the only person here that was present on the day Rae was born. For the first ten years of our lives we were inseparable."

He tells everyone the story of how Rae got her name, which gets a friendly laugh. He pauses and takes a drink of water. He feels Rae's presence, her love flowing into him.

"Thank you all for gathering in celebration of my sister's life. I've had seven years to think about Rae, our family, our relationship, and her final day.

"Rae was loyal to me, even when I was critical and hard to be around. I was a pill, but she just hung in there with me. I now understand, many years later, that I was angry when she left home, that I felt she was rejecting me personally and our family's life in Ohio. Like a lot of men, I had a radio that only played two channels—hot anger and simmering resentment. I didn't have a lot of tools to feel loss and fear and woundedness. I now understand that Rae wasn't rejecting me or our family, or our town, but that she was called to something else, something different.

"Rae and I had a vast woods and pond that we loved. I stayed and watched those woods get bulldozed by development. I know my experience is not unique. Like many of you, we have witnessed our special places get destroyed. The developers didn't just mow down the trees and bulldoze the ground, but they sprayed who-knows-what defoliant to kill the undergrowth. We played and hunted mushrooms in those woods. I sometimes think that if Rae had stayed in our little town of Rosemont, we could have stopped that development . . . together. Rae would have figured out how.

"Rae taught us all about altars, right?"

There is a ripple of laughter and nods of assent.

"She encouraged all of us to establish an altar tradition. On my altar, in Rae's old bedroom, are pictures of loved ones whose lives have been cut short by cancer and covid. My friend Rob passed away and two other neighbors—all from some cancer that undermined their kidneys, liver, and immune systems. We don't really know what killed Mac, our father, or what contributed to Rae getting cancer. Was it the defoliant in our woods? Who knows?

"What I now understand, and it's something that Rae always understood, is that there are corporations in this country that will always put their profits ahead of people and the health of our communities. And there are men in charge of these companies who make decisions that harm us every day, out of their allegiance to short-term profiteering. They don't give a shit about you and me and our children."

Toby pauses, looking toward Reggie and Alix, who nod to him in encouragement.

"We have to stop them. We have to organize to protect our communities, to protect our bodies. And we need to build alternatives—like this farm—to live our best lives.

"I wish I could look Rae in the eyes today and apologize for how I acted. And I wish I could thank her for never giving up on me. Of course, you and I know what Rae would say, right? 'I'm right here. I'm listening. I forgive you. I love you.'

"So, Rae, thank you for being the best big little sister a brother could have. And give us all the internal strength to stop the harms and fix the future. Guide us to a vision to live in harmony with the earth, with one another, to build a new way of being."

Toby sits down to warm applause.

Reggie stands slowly and approaches the stump podium. He reaches into his pocket and pulls out the two polished Petoskey stones, the stones that he and Rae exchanged as part of their City Hall wedding. He places them on the podium. "Thank you, Toby. You are right. Rae always loved you. One of her biggest regrets is that she didn't invite you to come our wedding at Boston City Hall. She regretted that all her life."

Reggie invites Alix to come forward and stand beside him. "We are thrilled to have Alix back among us," Reggie says, followed by applause and shouts and cheers. "The process of grieving the loss of Rae has been complicated, to say the least. Many of us who loved Rae didn't get to grieve they way most people do when a loved one passes. Rae's decision to end her life the way she did had dramatic consequences for all of us, especially Alix. She served her time. She protected this community from outside attack and pressure. Welcome home, Alix."

Alix stands at the stump podium and looks at the faces, most of whom she hasn't seen in more than six years. There is Yearwood, an old friend who she thought was living in Oregon. And there are several teenagers who were children when she last saw them.

"You can imagine how special it is to be back with you," Alix begins, swallowing back her emotion.

"I thought about you all every day. I thought of this spot. I imagined this moment when we would be together again, and that sustained me. So here we are. Today. Now. Wow. Phew."

People laugh. There is a scattering of applause.

"Dreams really do sometimes come true. As Rae taught me early on, visualize it and it will come."

Alix shifts her body and closes her eyes. "Accompanying Rae on her last day was a great honor. I have no regrets. I would do nothing different.

"I have not told many of you the story that at my final parole hearing I sat face to face with the extended family of the deceased. A bunch of them held pictures of the three people Rae killed. They were testifying against my release. They were full of animus and hatred toward me. They saw me as a murderer. My lawyer advised me not to speak. There was nothing I could say that would change their minds or heal their hearts. So back I went to prison for another year.

"If I had spoken, this is what I would have said: When I was driving Rae to New York, I was serving as a friend and as a hospice worker. I did not know that Rae was going to commit a murder. I was accompanying a dear friend to the end of her journey. We worked together doing hospice, and this was her final wish. And she asked me for a ride."

"I never condoned Rae's action or celebrated it. I think it was wrong. And there were many days when I was furious at her and felt betrayed by her. I still believe in the transformative power of nonviolence and loving witness. I believe that humans can change, transform, evolve, and make different choices. I don't believe that people are evil.

"I could not kill someone. But I recognize now that Rae had a long life journey, full of formative experiences that were very different than mine. I know this from reading her journals from when she was my age and before. I now understand how she thought that Brian Richardson, through his actions and inactions, was responsible for the suffering and deaths of thousands, if not millions, as the future unfolds. It was personal and visceral for her. She saw in 2022 that Richardson was betting against humanity, that he was going to reap billions of dollars in profits from extracting millions of tons more carbon and methane in reckless disregard for the consequences. She saw him attacking *her* body and our one and only biosphere. Rae's question to us would be: *If you don't like what I did, if you consider me a murderer, then what will you do to stop the Brian Richardsons of the world from their direct assault on Mother Earth? What will you do that is more effective?* For Rae, the intimately personal question became: How do you stop the maniac determined to poison the village well?"

Alix pauses and looks around. "That is still a relevant question for us all."

After letting this sink in, Alix continues: "Rae's life started on this day, seventy-six years ago. And it ended on Easter 2023. I was blessed with her motherly love and friendship right up until the end. Happy birthday, Rae. I love you and I miss you."

Alix sits down next to Rachel, clasping her hand and accepting Rachel's arm around her shoulder. The quartet sings another song, the gospel standard "Precious Lord." She remembers Vera's memorial service and her request to sing it twice.

After the song, Jade stands and invites everyone to stay after the celebration to add to the altar or build a mandala out of items from the forest. Then she turns and nods to Reggie.

Alix trembles for a second in Rachel's embrace. She watches as Reggie stands at the stump with a single sheet of paper and looks at her. "We are blessed to have Alix back. It brings the circle to a close. Without Alix here, this memorial birthday observance has had a missing chair. I know I speak for everyone here, Alix, from the bottom of our hearts: Thank you."

Alix feels many eyes on her back, but she keeps her focus on Reggie, who looks down at his notes and begins to talk about Rae's life. Alix knows most of the story, but she is eager to hear any new twists or insights that Reggie has assembled.

"Let me tell you the story of Rae, as best as I understand it today. Not every biographical detail, but the parts that may have influenced her final hours. I have a few quotes from her journals. While this may not justify her action, it helps explain her state of mind. What she did was wrong. But one thing Rae would want me to say is: Don't psychologize her motivations as some form of childhood rebellion. Don't dismiss it as a response to bullying or abuse or anger at her father, who she loved. She acted with, in her words, "as an adult with sound mind and heart.""

For Alix, the question remains a mystery: *How did someone shaped by nonviolence—who had the extraordinary elders she had—commit such a violent act?*

"I've spent the last seven years reading a lot of the books that shaped Rae," Reggie continues, "looking for clues, looking at the quotes she underlined, getting a window into her consciousness and the impact of these thinkers. I'll be sharing the Rae Kelliher booklist for anyone who is interested."

Reggie speaks for almost an hour. It appears to Alix that no one moves an inch.

Alix loves the stories that Reggie recounts of her six months in Mexico and Central America. "It made a deep imprint on her. Her memory of these months was vivid. And she retained this global mindset, especially when it came to consumption and energy use as a form of imperial conquest. Oh, and she also cut about three thousand onions in three weeks as part of a post-earthquake soup kitchen."

Reggie describes the people, teachers, and mentors that shaped her early days, her housemates at Montague Farm, her connection to Brian Willson, Sam Lovejoy, and Wally and Juanita Nelson.

"Rae made a point of learning the history of colonial conquest and, later, how climate disruption would disproportionately hurt those who had burned the least amount of carbon. She wanted her life to be friction on the machine, as Thoreau said. She wanted to drive a spoke into the wheel of injustice, quoting Bonhoeffer."

Reggie tells a few stories Alix didn't know from their days living together in Jamaica Plain, the struggle against the pipeline, and the evolution that led them to the Hidden River Farm. "She was a bookish girl," Reggie says. "She never finished college, but she was one of the most studious people I knew.

"She believed ideas mattered. She loved a good story. She learned a lot through books and doing things. And when she felt blue, she would curl up with a book like *The Mists of Avalon* or *The Lord of the Rings*. Her life was informed by people and ideas, and some of them came to her through books. People she read about were as diverse as Dorothy Day, Franz Fanon, Emma Goldman, Starhawk, Nelson Mandela, Dietrich Bonhoeffer, Rachel Carson, Winona LaDuke.

"She was, of course, an activist, a doer, a change agent. But her actions were based on ideas. She organized our 'transition book club' that informed our move to Vermont and the creation of this farm community.

"As many of you know, Rae cherished life." Reggie seems to choke up, just a little. "Not just humans but all life forms, from animals to plants to the forest spirits that are, she would observe, gathered around us today."

Alix is aware of his choices of words, how much of his vocabulary—and hers—is shaped by Rae's turns of phrase. *All life forms. Forest spirits.*

"Rae also was witness to the darkest aspects of human evil. She understood how systems of violence work—and how good people get caught in bad systems. But she also believed that we are each responsible for our choices. She would say that you cannot ignore the consequences of your actions *and inactions*. She had an unusual sense of agency and, as you may have experienced, some impatience with other people's inability to act."

There is a trickle of laughter. Alix looks around at the shaking and nodding heads. As she suspects, each person is probably thinking back to their interactions with Rae, both the soulful and the judgmental.

"Rae had a quality I would describe as 'sometimes wrong, never in doubt.' She could be pig-headed, but she would say that was unfair to the pigs."

Even more laughter.

"She was moved by a sense of being called to something greater. She understood the power of witness. In the words of Oscar Romero, she 'let her life speak.'"

Reggie looks up and finds Alix's eyes. "A couple years into our relationship, Rae and I got pregnant. She was thrilled to be an expectant mother. But we had a miscarriage in the first trimester. It was on the same day in 1989 that we learned the Jesuit priests in El Salvador had been assassinated. From reading her journals, I learned that Rae believed this was a sign. She decided she would not be a mother, but would act on behalf of all children. She channeled her mothering energy into social transformation." Reggie recounts Rae's immersion into the work of shutting down the School of the Americas. "She directly understood the connection between the US-trained military and the suffering of children. She had some religious friends who told her things like "Suffering is the human condition, blah blah. You have to sit with the suffering." She didn't buy it. This was suffering caused by the US government acting to defend our selfish economic interests. Projects like shutting down the School of the Americas were her children.

"People would ask me, was Rae a Christian? Was she religious?"

Alix smiles at Reggie's comment, knowing she was one of those who asked Reggie these questions.

"Like me," Reggie goes on, "she was raised in the Catholic Church, steeped in those traditions and the teachings of Jesus. But let me be clear, and I mean no offense by this, Rae was more Christian than the Christians. She lived a life that followed the teachings of Jesus better than almost anyone I knew who was affiliated with the institutional church, including priests and bishops. Respect for life. Radical simplicity. Preferential option for the poor. Radical hospitality. Love across borders. Queer liberation. Noncooperation with injustice.

"She viewed the church as captured by patriarchs and people who built a comfortable protected class. When she interacted with these people, she would say, 'I try to live by the teachings of Jesus as much as possible. It's not easy. It's no cakewalk. If you still won't invite me to your clubhouse, that's your loss.'"

People laugh. Alix isn't the only one leaning forward to hear every word from Reggie.

"Let me say something about the word *comfortable*. Rae had an ambivalent struggle with the concept of 'comfort.' As a practitioner of radical hospitality, Rae wanted you to be comfortable when you visited—to have a comfortable bed, pillow, food that was comforting to you. She wanted you, the visitor, to be emotionally comfortable, to have a feeling of safety, a place to rest, to feel free from attack and trauma. She thought about this a lot—whether you were visiting for the night or a migrant coming far from your home to live here at the farm. And I think everyone here would agree, she excelled in this practice.

"Yet she also believed that most of us are excessively *comfortable*. That we reside in emotionally comfortable places that don't challenge our ways of thinking and keep us numb to reality. And she thought the physical and lifestyle comfort demands of those of us living the middle-class life in the USA were destroying the world. She believed the US affluent classes were consuming the planet. She questioned our need to always have luxurious levels of physical comfort, to have everything be the right temperature. Okay, here's a trivia question: Did you ever hear Rae complain about the weather being too hot or too cold?"

He let the question hang in the air. No one responded. Alix scanned her own memory of Rae. Almost everyone smiled.

"No. You didn't. Part of her spiritual practice was being comfortable with uncomfortable conditions. It was part of her aspiration to 'nonattachment,' of not having the need to always have things be a certain way, a certain physical or emotional state. Nonattachment— to roll with whatever. At the end of her life, Rae had a hard time feeling warm, even with her long underwear and wool knit cap and a hundred layers of this and that. She longed to just lie in the sun like a lizard on a rock. But she never complained. Only once do I remember her saying, 'I can't get warm.'

"If she could improve an environment—make a room more beautiful or fix something broken—she would do it. But if it was something she couldn't control—like the weather—she aspired to be emotionally nonattached.

"Societies need people like Rae. They are unique. And they are willing to go beyond. They step out of their comfort zone all the time."

Reggie pauses and allows a moment of silence.

Alix notices there is only the slightest shifting among the participants. One parent carries a fussy child farther into the woods.

"In another age," Reggie resumes, "Rae might have been a nun, part of a women's religious order. Fortunately for me, she also celebrated intimate love and partnerships."

Alix thinks, *And fortunately for me, she treated me like a daughter.*

"She believed that the Hidden River Farm is what *discipleship* would look like today. She thought modern religious orders would be like this community with a vow of simplicity and a commitment to hospitality, of welcoming the stranger. These were religious tenets: the intention to live in harmony with the Earth, humble and in alignment with Gaia, listening for her messages, observing her wisdom ways. Love and care for one another, and all living creatures, and building a beloved community. Celebrate, dance, laugh, fiesta. A commitment to bread labor of growing and preparing food—each according to their needs and abilities. This is the modern religious order, in her view.

"She acted out of a reverence for life, not from a place of hatred. She stood out there on Guilford Center Road with a reflective vest and flashlight to ensure that the wood frogs and salamanders would make it across the road alive.

"And in the end, Rae was a Bonhoeffer Christian. Killing to stop greater evil becomes the righteous thing to do. You may be offended by the killing, by the loss of innocent family members. Or you may have supported Rae's actions. But in the end, Rae didn't care what you or I thought. This was her best understanding of what it meant to 'let your life speak through you.'

"I believe what Rae did was horrific and wrong. At the end, her body wracked by illness, something flipped for Rae. Her impulse to strike out, for revenge, overrode her lifelong sensibility. Alix paid the price for this. I know Rae would have been mortified that she caused Alix to suffer for her actions."

Rachel squeezes Alix shoulder. Alix exhales silently, her eyes filling with salty tears.

"Rae, who kept the birthday calendar and observed anniversaries, knew that Easter, April 9, 2023, was the seventy-eighth anniversary of Dietrich Bonhoeffer's execution. She monitored these things. Rae's Passamaquoddy elder friend, Ralph, would say, 'That's what you White people call coincidence.'"

People laugh and smile. Alix is relieved to see Reggie laugh himself.

"For me," Reggie goes on, "and for all of you who got to be close with Rae, I think we can all agree: Life is better with Rae. Life is more alive, more connected, more meaningful, more fun, with Rae. I cannot speak of her in the past tense. She is here with us.

"Be yourself. Don't be attached to comfort. Be like Rae. Don't do what Rae did. But do something audacious and bold to save the Earth. Let your life speak.

"I'll close with this poem by Nicaraguan poet Giocanda Belli, 'Tell Me.' We read it at our own simple marriage ritual." He slowly reads the poem, concluding: "For in the world we will always find shelter somewhere, and a piece of land to nourish us."

There is a long silent pause and a breeze of exhalation ripples through the trees.

Rachel rises from beside Alix and steps forward with her fiddle, lifting it to her chin. She plays an anthem, a Scottish tune called "Lament for King George V," a piece Rae always asked her to play.

At the end, Jade invites everyone to linger and add to the altar to Rae. "Please stay for refreshments and food, to gather under the tent or in the afternoon sun."

Sitting by the stump podium, Alix greets many old friends. After half an hour, she stands and surveys the entire group, scanning for Toby. He and Reggie are standing side by side in an informal receiving line, Noreen standing attentively at his elbow. They both shake hands and embrace people, accepting their condolences and wishes. Seven years after Rae's death, Reggie and Toby stand like family together. She could join them but waits for the line to shrink.

People migrate toward the altar or to the tent for refreshments. Others wander into the sacred grove.

Alix approaches Toby. Noreen thoughtfully steps away to give Toby and Alix the space for a private connection.

"I've always wanted to meet you," Alix says, looking at the familial resemblance in Toby's green eyes. "I'm so glad you came."

"Likewise," says Toby. "You were very important to my sister."

Alix is surprised. "Did she mention me?"

"Oh yes," says Toby, without revealing that it was in a dream. "She said you were an amazing cornhole player." He must have spied her playing early in the afternoon, while wandering around the farm before anyone recognized him. "You have a unique way of tossing."

Alix laughs. "I've had a lot of practice over the last few years."

"She asked me to give you something," Toby says, reaching deep into the front pocket of his blue jeans and pulling out an unusual stone. "She called this the Eye of the Goddess stone. She kept it on her windowsill in the house where we grew up." He places the stone in Alix's hand and she holds it up to the light.

"She had it since childhood?"

"Yes, she found it in this special place, a secret pond we called the water wonderland."

"Wow, thanks," said Alix turning it over in her hands. "It is very special. I remember Rae's stories about water wonderland."

"I figured it was time this stone made the trip to Vermont and to you." Toby watches Alix closely, as she puzzles over the gift. "It's what she wanted."

Alix knows how important rocks were to Rae. She recalls the story of Reggie and Rae's Petoskey stones. And to have a significant stone from Rae's childhood is a true talisman.

"I will treasure this," says Alix. "Can I give you a hug?"

"I would like that," said Toby. "Come visit us sometime. In southern Ohio. Things are progressing there, but not as quickly as here. But maybe you could come speak in our community about Rae. People would like to understand."

"I'd like that," says Alix.

She walks toward Rae's memorial rock, putting the Eye of the Goddess in her pocket. It feels warm to the touch and Alix feels a tingling sensation, a protective light surrounding her.

ACKNOWLEDGMENTS

On the Altar. This story is very personal altar. It is an altar to those living and dead who have made life more joyful and have shouldered the work to build a more just and ecologically sustainable world.

This story is in part about *formation*, how one person is shaped and influenced by the people, ideas, and movements around them. Like the main character of this story, Rae Kelliher, I was fortunate in sharing some of her elders and influences. Among those who have passed to the other side are Wally and Juanita Nelson, Chuck Matthei, Karen Brandow, Howard Zinn, Rev. Terry Burke, Bill Moyer, Dorothy Day, Msgr. Oscar Romero, Janet Axelrod, and Duncan Murphy. As Terry would say: *May the light perpetual shine upon them*—and may this novel be one of those candles on the altar.

Fortunately for us, many of these movers and shakers are still alive. I'm grateful to Sam Lovejoy, Brian Willson, George Lakey, Tom Lesser, Roy Bourgeois, Verandah Porche, Temka Rosenbaum, Rev. John Gibbons, Rev. Anne Bancroft, Rev. Martha Neibank, Peter Kellman, and Nathan Phillips, who were trusting enough to allow me to use their names and take fictional liberties with their stories. When I approached Sam Lovejoy for permission, he replied, "If it adds magic, wonder, or just plain fun, use my name." Magic indeed!

Readers might recognize similarities to many other real people in this work of fiction. My apologies in advance for anyone who takes offense or objects to any of the portrayals within. I accept responsibility for any shortcomings. My hope is that readers will be intrigued by their stories and want to learn more. Toward this end, I've included Rae's reading list and a few additional resources. And much more at my web site: www.chuckcollinswrites.org.

Gratitudes. I've had a lot of help with this work of fiction. Joni Praded was kind enough to do a thoughtful early read and made substantive suggestions. Kimberly French provided feedback on an earlier version of some of these chapters. Thanks to my many readers who marked up early versions of this story and shared their ideas and reactions. They include: Andy Davis, Nora Collins, Georgette Verdin, Andrea Zaleska, Anne Ellsworth, Bert Picard, Nancy Braus, Nina Schlegel, Tim Crellin, Jodi Solomon, Carrie Kline, Chris McCorkindale, Persis Levy, Kay Cafasso, Jenny Ladd, Anna Gyorgy, Gigi Collins, Mary Wallace Collins, and John Cavanagh.

Many thanks to these writers, readers, thinkers, and activists who kindly encouraged this effort and provided inspiration: Kim Stanley Robinson, Vicki Robin, Richard Heinberg, Winona LaDuke, Rae Abileh, Frances Moore Lappe, May Bove, Katherine Power, Dedrick Asante-Muhammad, Tim DeChristopher, Adam Hochschild, Tope Folarin, Kimi Eisele, Ruairi McKiernan, Frida Berrigan, Bill McKibben, Gus Speth, Rivera Sun, Harriet Barlow, Danny Faber, Asher Miller, Rob Dietz, Nate Hagens, David Korten, Fran Korten, Sherri Mitchell, Starhawk, Marla Marcum, Jom Michel, Ellen Dorsey, Cathy Hoffman, and Astrid Montuclard.

Blessed be the booksellers: Nancy Braus, Ann Zimmerman, and Clea B. at Everyone's Books; Reinee Reiner at Phoenix Books; Kate Layte; Papercuts JP; Roy Karp and collective at Rozzie Bound.

Several people helped with specific aspects. Thanks to Day Schildkret for the stunning cover art. Thanks to Casey Williams for her delightful maps and Nate Smith for help with events. Thanks to Julie Ristau for insights about death, dying, and earth mandalas. Katherine Power about prison experience and living underground. Anna Gyorgy about violence and nonviolence. John Cavanagh in sorting through the history and reaching out to endorsers. All my colleagues at the Institute for Policy Studies are a daily inspiration to the work of social movements in making history, including Tope Folarin, our novelist in chief and fearless leader. Gratitude to the original "transition book club," including Dakota Butterfield, Sarah Byrnes, Alexa Bradley, Greg Buckland, Orion Kriegman, and Andree Zaleska.

The team at Green Writers Press has been encouraging and artful in aiding this nonfiction narrative writer along the path to fiction. A thousand thanks to Dede Cummings for your beaming positivity and creating the Press and bringing a wide variety of talents, including design, storytelling, bookmaking, and marketing. The ever affirming Rose Alexandre-Leach lovingly engaged with the characters and provided fantastic coaching and suggestions. Mike Fleming brought his own sage insights and editing extraordinaire. If I didn't follow their advice, it was at my peril. All three of them are terrific writers and poets in their own right and I'm most grateful for the help they provided to this first time novelist. Thanks to Liv Cohen for help with permissions and other tasks.

The village of friends and neighbors who inspired and advised me along the way include Peter Gould, Melany Kahn, Starr Latronica, Robin MacArthur, Andrew Boyd, Lois Canright, Tim Plenk, and Lissa Weinmann. And thanks to the Springs Farm crew, including Mellissa Morgan, Oliver Bolz, and Mary Wallace Collins, and also to our three cats, Samhain, Lilith, and Moxie, who did their part to jam the printer at critical times.

Mary Wallace Collins was a great sounding board and is my "party in a box, just add Guinness," as well as the love of my life.

You are all on my altar of gratitude.

RAE'S READING LIST

*Additions to Rae's Reading List, a book group Discussion Guide,
a Q &A with the author, and more can be found at the website
www.chuckcollinswrites.com*

Fiction
Edward Abbey, *The Monkey Wrench Gang*
Octavia Butler, *Parable of the Sower*
Octavia Butler, *Parable of the Talents*
Denise Giardina, *Saints and Villains*
Barbara Kingsolver, *Flight Behavior*
Ursula K. Le Guin, *The Dispossessed*
Emily St. John Mandel, *Station Eleven*
Jenny Offill, *Weather*
Richard Powers, *The Overstory*
Kim Stanley Robinson, *The Ministry for the Future*
Starhawk, *The Fifth Sacred Thing*

Nonfiction
Sharon Astyk, *Making Home: Adapting Our Homes and Our Lives to
    Settle in Place*
Matthieu Auzanneau, *Oil, Power, and War: A Dark History*
Adrienne Maree Brown, *Emergent Strategy*
Tim Egan, *The Worst Hard Time: The Untold Story of Those Who Survived
    the Great American Dust Bowl*
Charles Eisenstein, *The More Beautiful World Our Hearts Know Is
    Possible*

Franz Fanon, *The Wretched of the Earth*

David Fleming, *Surviving the Future: Culture, Carnival and Capital in the Aftermath of the Market Economy*

Amitav Ghosh, *The Nutmeg's Curse: Parables for a Planet in Crisis*

John Michael Greer, *The Long Descent: The User's Guide to the End of the Industrial Age*

Paul Hawken, *Drawdown: The Most Comprehensive Plan Ever Proposed to Reverse Global Warming*

Richard Heinberg, *Power: Limits and Prospects for Human Survival*

Rob Hopkins, *From What Is to What If: Unleashing the Power of Imagination to Create the Future We Want*

Robin Wall Kimmerer, *Braiding Sweetgrass: Indigenous Wisdom, Scientific Knowledge, and the Teachings of Plants*

Naomi Klein, *This Changes Everything: Capitalism vs. the Climate*

Elizabeth Kolbert, *The Sixth Extinction: An Unnatural History*

Elizabeth Kolbert, *Under a White Sky: The Nature of the Future*

Aldo Leopold, *A Sand County Almanac*

Johanna Macy, *Coming Back to Life: Practices to Reconnect Our Lives, Our World*

Andreas Malm, *How to Blow Up a Pipeline*

Bill McKibben, *Falter: Has the Human Game Begun to Play Itself Out?*

George Monbiot, *Feral: Rewilding the Land, the Sea, and Human Life*

Esther Perel, *Mating in Captivity: Unlocking Erotic Intelligence*

Didi Pershouse, *Ecology of Care: Medicine, Agriculture, Money, and the Quiet Power of Human and Microbial Communities*

Vicki Robin and Joe Dominquez, *Your Money or Your Life: 9 Steps to Transforming Your Relationship with Money and Achieving Financial Independence*

Juliet B. Schor, *Plenitude: The New Economics of True Wealth*

Stephanie Seneff, *Toxic Legacy: How the Weedkiller Glyphosate Is Destroying Our Health and the Environment*

Merlin Sheldrake, *Entangled Life: How Fungi Make Our Worlds, Change Our Minds & Shape Our Future*

Rebecca Solnit, *A Paradise Built in Hell: The Extraordinary Communities That Arise in Disaster*

David Wallace-Wells, *The Uninhabitable Earth: Life After Warming*

PERMISSIONS

ABOUT THE AUTHOR

CHUCK COLLINS is a campaigner and storyteller who has worked for decades on environmental and economic justice campaigns. He is the Director of the Program on Inequality and the Common Good at the Institute for Policy Studies where he co-edits Inequality.org. He is co-founder of DivestInvest.org, a global movement to divest from fossil fuels and invest in climate solutions; and trustee of the Post-Carbon Institute and Resilience.org.

His 2021 book, *The Wealth Hoarders: How Billionaires Pay Millions to Hide Trillions*, is about the wealth-hiding industry (Polity). He is the author of the popular book, *Born on Third Base: A One Percenter Makes the Case for Tackling Inequality, Bringing Wealth Home, and Committing to the Common Good* (Chelsea Green) and, with Bill Gates Sr., *Wealth and Our Commonwealth* (Beacon Press), a case for taxing inherited fortunes.

He lives with his family in Southern Vermont. *Altar to an Erupting Sun* is his debut novel. See more about his books and writing at www.chuckcollinswrites.com.